Margaret GRAHAM

Annie's Promise

arrow books

Margare.. and

This .... es
ar............

First published in Great Britain in 1993 by
William Heinemann Ltd

Arrow Books
Random House, 20 Vauxhall Bridge Road,
London SW1V 2SA

www.randomhouse.co.uk

Addresses for companies within The Random House Group Limited can
be found at: www.randomhouse.co.uk/offices.htm

The Random House Group Limited Reg. No. 954009

A CIP catalogue record for this book
is available from the British Library

ISBN 9780099585800

The Random House Group Limited supports the Forest Stewardship
Council® (FSC®), the leading international forest-certification organisation.
Our books carrying the FSC label are printed on FSC®-certified paper.
FSC is the only forest-certification scheme supported by the
leading environmental organisations, including Greenpeace.
Our paper procurement policy can be found at:
www.randomhouse.co.uk/environment

Printed and bound by CPI Group (UK) Ltd, Croydon, CR0 4YY

For Sue

Acknowledgements

My then eleven-year-old daughter, Annie, whose birth spurred me to write my first novel *Only the Wind is Free* (reissued as *After the Storm*), had long been trying to persuade me to write a sequel – so that at last she could know the fate of her namesake Annie Manon when she returns to Britain after the Second World War. *Annie's Promise* is due entirely to her nagging! But I'm immensely grateful to her because it was a great pleasure to become involved with Annie Manon again, a character imbued with the essence of my mother – another Annie.

My thanks to my Aunt Doris who spent twenty years in India and was so generous with her memories and memoirs and – as always – Sue Bramble and her staff at Martock Library. Also, my thanks to Chatterley Whitfield Mining Museum, Stoke-on-Trent and their splendid guides – all retired miners – and to Beamish, The North of England Open Air Museum.

I especially want to thank certain friends (who wish to remain anonymous) for their help with drug experiences in the 1960s.

Annie's Promise

CHAPTER 1

Young Sarah Armstrong felt the sun on her face. The heat had caused the lettuces in the allotment to look limp and parched. She hugged her knees, resting her chin on them, laughing as her cousin Rob Ryan flicked grass at his brother Davy, and groaning when her other cousin, Teresa Manon, tightened her mouth and said, 'When Davy smiles like that his face creases and it looks as though his freckles meet. You die when that happens.'

Sarah looked at her and wanted to punch her nose. 'Still a bundle of laughs then, Terry.'

'My mother doesn't like you to call me Terry, especially now I'm ten, but then you wouldn't care about that. My mum said you'd lower the tone when you came home.'

'That's why Davy's smiling, because I'm back and I'm lowering the tone, but then we're only nine – we've got another year to improve.' Sarah pulled a face at Davy. 'It's a grand smile, look, it's made the sun come out, or has it come out because I'm here?' She gave a regal wave and ducked as the boys bombed her with grass darts, then chased her round the raspberry canes, netted against the birds. Davy caught her and pulled her to the ground, tickling her until she screamed. Then Rob stuffed grass down his shirt. Teresa had not joined in, but she never did. She just pursed her lips together like a prune and sniffed.

Sarah lay on the ground, laughter still in her throat, closing her eyes against the sun. She was so glad to be back here in the north east, in Wassingham with its slag heaps and back to backs, and Grandma Betsy, Uncle Tom, Aunt Gracie and the boys. It was July 1956, her father Georgie was out of the Army, and her mother Annie was starting her textile business. They had come home and would live in her mother's house in Gosforn an hour's drive away. Unfortunately Teresa's family lived in that town too, but you couldn't win them all.

'Give us a swig of water, Rob,' Davy called.

Sarah rolled on to her side and watched as he flapped his shirt and the grass scattered to the ground. She loved Davy, he was three months younger than her and they'd always fitted somehow.

'Give us a minute.' Rob was dragging the bottle from the bag.

Davy sprawled on the ground beside her, and she watched him flick back his auburn hair. 'Your mum said we could go for picnics, now I'm back,' Sarah said.

Rob tossed them the water bottle and Davy drank from it, throwing his head back. His throat moved and suddenly Sarah felt as parched as the lettuces, and hungry. When would lunch be ready? She looked towards the entrance to the allotment but there was still no sign of her mother.

She sat up to take the bottle from Davy, and put it to her lips. The water was warm. Then she passed it to Teresa who wiped the neck carefully with her handkerchief before sipping once, twice. She patted her mouth and replaced her handkerchief. Only then did she hand it back to Rob who looked as though he could kill for a drink.

No, Teresa, you haven't changed a bit, have you, Sarah thought, hugging her knees again, looking down at the cracks in the ground which her mother, as a child, had thought went all the way to Australia. Sarah liked the idea of sitting where her mother had once sat. She looked up again at the old shed which smelt of creosote and the nettles which her dad said attracted butterflies. He had sat here too, when he was her age.

She closed her eyes and saw the shape of the shed against

2

her lids. Would it be roast beef for dinner? Her mum said no one cooked Yorkshire pudding like Grandma Betsy and she was right. She looked towards the lane again. No one was coming. A growing girl could die of hunger. It was all right for the grown ups, they'd all be there, sitting round Betsy's table drinking beer or tea and dipping crusts into the fat before Betsy made the gravy. 'You'll want to play,' her mum had said as she clattered them out of Betsy's kitchen, 'and the grown ups will want to chat.' Davy had said, 'No, we want to eat.'

Rob was standing up now, looking towards the lane too. 'I'm so hungry I could eat a horse. Where's your mam then, Sarah?'

Davy aimed a grass dart at him. 'Sit down, it's only been half an hour, it'll be a while yet. Let's have a gang, what d'you think? A gang for the summer now that Sarah's back.'

Teresa said, 'Gangs are common, they're for council school children. We're not allowed them at the convent.'

Sarah remembered her mum's words as they'd driven over that morning. 'Be nice to Teresa, we're back with the family and she might feel put out, you know, jealous. She's been the only girl for so long and if we're coming back to the north for good we don't want to spoil it. I'm being serious, Sarah. I know you don't get on with her very well but you've got to try. Families must stick together.'

Sarah dug her chin down hard on to her knees, swallowing the words 'toffee nose' and saying instead, 'But this would be a gang of cousins.'

'Teresa's got a point, but it's not common, it's just child-ish,' Rob said, looking bored and playing jacks with the pebbles he carried everywhere.

Davy held his nose and pulled an imaginary chain. 'You're only eleven and it'd be real good so stop that click-clicking.'

Sarah smiled. 'There you are, Terry, it'd be a way of getting together . . .'

Teresa was standing up, dusting off her dress. 'Anyway, they're not really family. My father says their dad's not really his brother, he's Grandma Betsy's bastard.'

Sarah watched Teresa's face screw up against the sun, she saw the redness on her forearms where the sun had caught her skin, the green stains on her bum from the dock leaves which her cousin had so carefully placed between her and the ground.

She didn't watch Davy's face, or Rob's, she just felt the silence all around and the anger which was choking her. She moved towards that smug cruel face, but then Rob sprang to his feet, hauling up Davy, grabbing Sarah's arm.

'Davy's right. It's a canny idea to have a gang and if Teresa doesn't want to join us she can go and get stuffed. Who needs a convent snob anyway?'

'That's right,' Davy shouted at Teresa. 'And we know our dad's a bastard, everyone does, thank you very much, and it doesn't matter to anyone except you. And anyway, Barney Ryan was brave, he was killed in the trenches and he loved our grandma, Da told us and he would have married her, he would, so there.'

Sarah stood with them, watching Teresa, hating her, but then she saw the uncertainty in the other girl's face, the flush in her cheeks, the shame. Perhaps her mother was right and Teresa was jealous? Perhaps she was just hitting out because she was frightened of being pushed out. Sarah had felt like that sometimes when her da had been posted to another area and she had had to leave her friends behind. She had hated the letters they'd written talking of new friends, it made her feel alone, angry, frightened. Sarah touched the other girl's arm.

'Look Teresa, be part of this, we're family, we really are and anyway Betsy's really kind to be our grandma too. She needn't be. She really only belongs to the boys but she treats us all the same. You know she does. Come on. Our parents wouldn't like it if we weren't friends.'

Sarah saw Davy shake his head at her, his eyes still angry but she said again, 'Come on, Teresa, they sent us here to play.' She looked towards Davy again and now he nodded and so did Rob.

'Yes, come on, Teresa, Sarah's right,' Rob's voice was tight.

Davy was looking towards the shed, the fence with its spare tyres, its old doors, then at the bar at the entrance to the allotment. 'OK, we'll all be in it, but first we'll have to pass a test to prove we're good enough. That's fair, isn't it?'

Sarah nodded, looking at Teresa, who paused, then said, 'I suppose so.'

'Right,' Davy said, pointing to the allotment entrance. 'We all need to swing three times over the bar without putting our feet to the ground.'

Sarah grinned. Her da had taught her when they'd been back on one of their holidays. It'd be easy.

Teresa was looking down at her dress.

Sarah pitied the girl. Uncle Don would never swing over a bar let alone teach anyone how.

'I'll help you. I'll keep your feet off the ground.' Sarah volunteered, touching Teresa's shoulder.

Teresa looked at her, her eyes travelling over the dungarees that Sarah wore. 'It's all right for you. It's always all right for you, you're wearing those stupid dungarees your mother makes.'

'Come on, let's get on with it,' Rob called, ambling over towards the bar. Sarah watched as Davy followed and saw Teresa look at them with a tremble to her lips.

'I'll get you some sacking from the shed,' she offered. 'You go on. I'll catch you up.'

The shed was dark and dusty and smelt good. She could see the runner beans through the window and as she picked up the frayed hessian she wondered how long her mother would be. She was hungry and fed up and she wanted to punch Terry on the nose again.

5

Annie and Betsy walked through the narrow streets, black grimed from the coal. The doors were closed on the ritual of Sunday lunch. Annie smiled. 'You didn't have to come, Betsy, those kids won't need any dragging you know, my Sarah especially.'

Betsy laughed quietly, her arm tucked in Annie's. 'That they won't but I just wanted to be with you, bonny lass. I can hardly believe you're back, see. It seems just yesterday to me that you were getting scruffy round the runner beans yourself.' She became serious again. 'Sometimes I wondered if you'd ever want to come back again after all you've been through.'

Annie felt the cobbles uneven beneath her feet as they crossed over, away from the shadows. Oh yes, she'd always wanted to come home again. But Betsy, she thought, squeezing the other woman's arm, it doesn't seem like yesterday to me. She dug her other hand deep into her pocket, smelling the coal which pervaded every inch of this small town as it had always done.

Annie had been fifteen when Sarah Beeston, her godmother, had taken her away from here driving over these same cobbles to middle-class Gosforn and a different life. Georgie had left Wassingham too then, feeling the loss of Annie as much as she had felt the loss of him, leaving the darkness of the pit for the hardships of the Army. But soon everyone had felt some hardship as war had erupted.

What was it Sarah Beeston had said as she had driven her from Wassingham? Ah yes. 'I'll educate you, so that you can make choices about your future, it's the least I can do now your father is dead.' Annie had chosen nursing. She smiled wryly, looking up at the cloudless sky. 'You can travel with nursing my dear,' Sarah had said. 'You can expand your horizons – decide whether you do still truly want to marry Georgie.' Well, her horizons had expanded all right, right up to the wire of a Japanese prisoner of war camp. Thank God her beloved Sarah Beeston had died by then.

6

They were approaching the allotment now and Annie could hear the children's whoops of laughter. They stopped, listening, smiling, relishing the moment.

'You're giving your Sarah what you didn't have, my dear,' Betsy said. 'A steady homelife and a good mother.'

'I won't have that talk, Betsy,' Annie's voice was fierce. 'I mean, look how you stuck it out with Da in that Godforsaken shop, hauling those barrels of booze around. You were as good a mother as anyone could have been, living like that. You never treated Don and me differently to your Tom, and I don't know how you did it.

'We love you, all of us and we're back now, for good. Georgie's out of bomb disposal, I'm up to my ears in plans for the new business, the *family* business, and it's all going to be great.' Annie kissed Betsy's soft warm cheek and together they walked down the lane, both of them comforted, seeing the children now, swinging over the bar.

Betsy laughed. 'Well, wonders will never cease, it looks as though they're all getting on. I thought Teresa might be a bit prickly.'

Annie nodded. 'Yes, it was more than a possibility. She's just so like her father. Why's *he* so tense today.' They paused again and Annie brushed her hair back from her face. 'I mean, he's my brother but I feel as though I'm more part of Tom, not him.'

Betsy nodded. 'It's his nature. He's always been the same. You have your da's depth, he has your Uncle Albert's – oh, what's the word I'm looking for?'

'Tight arse, I think,' Annie whispered, looking at her stepmother and now they laughed.

'I should clip your ear for using language like that but maybe you're right, lass,' Betsy said at last, wiping her eyes with her handkerchief. 'No wonder the old skinflint left him his pawn business – and lord knows what else. But I reckon it's the fact that you're back that's bothering Don today. He's liked being the only Manon around and of course, you're taking back Sarah Beeston's house. He won't think you've been right kind to let him have it free all these years, he'll just be sour because he can't go on having it.'

Annie nodded then looked up as she heard Sarah calling to her, beckoning her forward. 'We've made a gang, all of us and we could eat a horse.'

Annie heard Betsy's chuckle and felt a surge of relief at the laughter of the four children. At least there was no tension here.

'Come on then,' she called to them. 'The Yorkshire pud will be just right by the time we get back.' Annie turned to Betsy. 'Don'll be all right after Tom and I tell him about our business ideas. I haven't explained anything properly to him yet. I thought I'd leave it until after lunch. We wanted to ask him face to face to be the financial director, then it'll be all of us in it, just like I've always planned. Everything will be all right, Bet. I know it will.'

Betsy was laughing as the children came running up to them, their faces eager, pulling at them to hurry. 'Nothing can go wrong now that you're back, Annie. It's all going to be just wonderful,' Betsy said.

The Yorkshire pudding *was* wonderful, the gravy rich and smooth, the beef tender and there had been little conversation from the children, from any of them as they ate. There had just been the sound of knife against plate, laughter as Sarah's carrot had skidded from beneath her fork and landed on the table. Don's wife Maud had tutted, but then she'd tutted when she'd seen Teresa's dusty dress.

There had been banana custard for pudding and Annie had wanted to kiss Betsy when she'd sprinkled a sheen of sugar on Sarah's to prevent the formation of skin.

They drank tea when the meal was finished and nodded when the children begged to go and play in the allotment again, though Maud would not allow Teresa to swing on the bar. 'Let her wear a pair of Sarah's dungarees,' Annie had suggested and had thought Maud would faint at the mere thought.

8

Annie stood at the sink now, her arms covered in suds as she waited for Tom to bring the last of the dirty dishes from the table. She looked out across the yard where geraniums lolled in cut down rain-butts. The stable was empty now, Black Beauty was long gone.

'Do you remember Beauty, darling?' she called to Georgie who was putting the bowls in the dresser over against the wall. She heard him laugh, heard Tom and Grace laugh too.

'Remember?' Tom called. 'Bye, she kept us in sweet money with her plops. "Does wonders for your rhubarb," you'd say to people. "Better than custard." Your da would have died if he'd known.'

'She was a bonny pony,' Betsy said, leaning across Annie, refilling the kettle. 'Just one more cup, eh, lass?' She smiled at Annie, who kissed her cheek.

'I told you then and I'll tell you now, that was a bloody silly name for a gelding. God knows what Da was thinking of, giving it to you. He should have sold it and put the cash into the shop. But then he didn't know what he was thinking of most of the time – bloody dead loss he turned out to be.' Don's voice was loud, terse and Annie felt her shoulders tighten.

'Don't let them get you down, Don lad,' Georgie laughed. 'They've got an idea they can change the world, so what's a pony's sex? And they will change it, you know, or Wassingham anyway, just you wait and see. This business is really going to take off.'

Annie felt her shoulders relax. Only she and Tom would have recognised the anger in Georgie's voice, but he had saved her from exploding. She looked out into the yard again. God damn you, Don Manon, you always were a miserable little tyke, never comfortable, never understanding, always pinching my wintergreen when we were kids, always spoiling things, always belly-aching. You're still belly-aching, misunderstanding. But then she hadn't understood either for a long while, had she? She watched a sparrow perch on the gutter of the stable.

Poor Da, how had he felt, coming back from the trenches, having to start all over again with his off-licence business destroyed, his fine house gone, the mother of his kids dead? He'd felt hopeless, that's what he'd felt but she hadn't understood that then. None of them had – or his suicide. She had realised though, after her own war. In fact she had very nearly followed him.

She looked back, round the kitchen they'd grown up in, smelling boiled tea towels, imagining the round shine-splashed boiler. Thank God they were all wiser now, tested somehow, more able to make the future work.

'Where are those plates then, Tom Ryan?' she called, turning round, seeing Maud still sitting at the table, polishing her long red nails, and she remembered that Don had been easier for a while but it hadn't lasted. Perhaps Maud was the reason why. You'd never think she'd come from a back to back in Wassingham too.

'Hang on, Gracie needs another tea towel and then I'll be there. Work, work, work, but worth it. That was a canny lunch, Mam.' Tom threw a tea cloth to his wife and then brought the plates to Annie who called to Maud. 'We'll bring gloves next time shall we, then you can help?'

Tom grinned at Annie and muttered, 'You'll be lucky, can't be breaking a nail, can we?'

'I'll break something of hers soon and it won't be a nail, bonny lad,' she murmured back.

Betsy called from the stove. 'Tea's brewed, Annie. Leave those to drip, you as well, Gracie. Come and sit down and have a last cup. Those bairns will be glad of a bit more time.'

Betsy smoothed her apron with hands that were still gnarled from shifting Da's kegs, but they were not as swollen as they had been.

'Are you happy Bet?' Annie asked quietly, sitting down beside her.

'Aye lass, I was before, you know with my bairn living in the top of the house and his bairns rushing through my kitchen to get to the yard but now it's even better – there's your Sarah with them too, and you.'

Annie touched the elderly woman's hand. 'I know what you mean. There's a continuity, isn't there?' She watched Georgie bring the teapot to the table, then looked round, seeing her brothers, their wives, Betsy pouring the tea, pushing the mugs out to each of them. Where had the years gone – did she really have as many lines as Gracie? She knew she had.

'Could have given us more notice of course.' Don's voice was cold. 'Had to get out of the house in a bit of a hurry didn't we?'

Annie looked at him. Here it comes – wind him up, let him go. Not many lines on your visage my lad are there, but then you weren't down the mine like Tom, in the jungles like Georgie, in the camps like me. Oh no, you were in the Supply Depot, building up your contacts, lining your pockets, not your face. She clamped her mind shut against these thoughts, put down her mug and answered calmly.

'You've had my house for nine years, without charge Don. Please remember that I wrote to you telling you of Georgie's discharge months ago. I think I made it clear that we would want to come home.'

Maud put down her tea which she had been drinking left-handed. Annie knew it was because their lips had used the other side. She caught Tom's eye and grinned – they were back, what did all this matter?

'That's all very well, Annie,' Maud said. 'But we've put a lot of work into Sarah Beeston's house. We've hung a chandelier and redecorated you know, got rid of all that dreadful bamboo.'

Annie breathed deeply as tension clenched every muscle of her face. She forced herself to look steadily at Betsy's patchwork cushions.

Think of the stitches, the thread. Please God, let me be

angry and not afraid – let the past be over. She felt Georgie's hand on her thigh, she felt its warmth, his nearness and she waited and could now hardly breathe because she feared so much that she would smell the stench of the camp hospital, the pleading of the patients, the helplessness of the nurses. She feared she would see Lorna's execution, feel the pain of the guard's boot thudding into her own body, or the rope around her wrist which had tethered poor mindless Prue.

She waited, barely breathing, feeling the silence, the grip of Georgie's hand but there was no pain, no darkness, there was just irritation, just the words 'Stupid bitch' in her mind, just a normal reaction to a silly woman. At last she relaxed, even as Tom leaned forward, slopping his tea, banging his mug down.

'You did what, after all Annie went through with those bloody nips. For Christ's sake, the thought of decorating Sarah's house kept her going, you bloody knew that. It helped her to actually do it when she returned.'

Annie reached out to him, shaking her head, relishing her own response but not his. 'Maud's right you know, think about it. That design wouldn't appeal to others, it was personal, it grew out of me, it was therapeutic. Business people have got to produce the goods the market wants, not just what we like, or what comes from our past.'

She looked from Tom to Georgie but their faces were set. She spoke again. 'Look, please, all of you stop worrying about me. I'm much better – I keep telling you. Yes, the bamboos might have been a trigger – I was unprepared but I'm fine, Maud's done us a favour. It's proved to you that it's all behind me, just as I've been saying all these months.'

Annie took her husband's hand in hers and kissed it but though he smiled when she looked into his eyes she saw only anxiety.

She said softly, 'I promise you, my darling, it's over. This just helps to prove it. Please listen.'

She looked from one to another. Oh God, would they never understand that the past was gone, finished? Yes, she'd had a breakdown in India, where Georgie had taken her after the war. Yes, she'd tried to kill herself there too, but they had come home and slowly she had recovered, couldn't they accept this? What more proof did they need?

'So, you're still going ahead with this business idea then?' Don asked.

Annie smiled, grateful for once that her brother had no heart. There was no concern in his eyes, or those of his wife. There was only a flicker of interest at the thought of the business they were embarking upon and she replied calmly, holding Georgie's hand tightly as she did so, willing him to believe.

'Absolutely, Don. It's the textile business we've always talked about, even when we were kids. Tom's designs, my practical knowledge, Georgie's management expertise . . .'

'Cosy, just the three of you, again.' His voice was hard.

'You didn't let me finish. You're a businessman, doing well from your property development, we'll need a financial director. You could fit it in with your other work.' She was glad to be back in the present, glad to be talking of the future and she wanted to grab the others out of the past too.

She looked at them all, smiling, listening as Don grunted then pulled out a cigar. Betsy rose, walked to the window and opened it, then pulled the door right back. Don knew Bet hated the smell soaking into her patchwork cushions, her curtains, her rag-rugs so why did he do it?

Annie watched her brother, and wanted to rip the cigar from his mouth and stub it out in Maud's mug. That really would be something for her to turn her nose up at.

'Tell me more about it,' Don said, blowing smoke across the table, leaning back, putting his finger in his waistcoat pocket.

'We'll operate it, as Tom and I have always said, in

Wassingham with facilities for those who are mothers. There'll be a nursery, childbirth leave and so on. There will be a bonus twice a year, a sharing of the profits.'

'That's it then,' Don said, his finger still hitched in his pocket, the smoke from his cigar spiralling up into the air.

He'll blow a smoke ring in a minute Annie thought and then I'll slap him and ruin all my good intentions.

'What do you mean, that's it?' she asked, trying to keep her voice level as he blew a smoke ring and Tom caught her eye.

'Crazy. It's your old half-baked nonsense, isn't it? It's the "life must be fair" rubbish again,' Don said, stabbing the air with his cigar. 'It's like Albert and I always said, the bottom line is profit – you need to drive your workers, not nursemaid them. What about your union work, Tom, are you coming out of the mine?'

Tom shook his head. 'Not right away, we've got to get it up and running first. Gracie and Annie are getting the garments made up working from home, then Annie's got some outlets set up to see which lines go best. Betsy's helping with the sewing, just so long as her hands cope, isn't that right, Mam?'

Betsy nodded. 'I wasn't much good to you in the early days pet, it was all so difficult with the shop and everything,' she said quietly. 'I want to be useful now.'

'I've told you, you were wonderful to us, and yes, we couldn't do without you but only for as long as it suits you.' Annie turned back to Don. 'Just listen. It's founded on sound sense. Workers will respond to fair treatment. You see, Don, you don't have to deal with workers in your line of business but because of Tom's pit work, Georgie's time with his men, and mine in the wards, we think we know how to treat people.'

'Meaning I don't.' Don blew another smoke ring.

'No, not meaning that at all, meaning that in property development you are not producing a product and so haven't

14

had that kind of experience but you do have financial know-how.'

'Sounds like amateur night to me,' Don said.

Annie saw Maud produce a nail file. Good God, how do you improve on perfection?

Georgie said, 'Tell him how experienced you are, Annie.'

'Yes, Annie,' Gracie called. 'Tell him about Mr Isaacs in Camberley and the shocked wives.'

Annie laughed as Maud looked up, her nails forgotten.

'Relax, Maudie, no scandal.'

'Better not be either,' Georgie grinned.

Don was scowling, looking at his watch, the gold plate glinting in the sunlight streaming through the open window.

'Sorry, Don, I'll get on with it. Right, I worked for Mr Isaacs in his rag trade business while Georgie was at Staff College at Sandhurst. The other wives were shocked, not the thing at all, though I probably made the bras they bought.'

'Bras,' Maud was shocked.

'Oh yes, Maud, they are made, they do not just arrive under gooseberry bushes.' Annie fingered her cigarettes but knew better than to smoke in Betsy's kitchen. She'd probably have her ear clipped. 'I learned to calculate how many rolls of cloth would be needed, how to use rotary cutters and sewing machines, how to pack and invoice. I learned business management really. Then I set up my market stall.'

'Market stall,' Maud murmured faintly. 'Not with an apron and things, not shouting out.'

'Oh yes, d'you want to hear me.' Annie stood up while Tom and Georgie began to laugh.

'No, I do not.' Maud was tapping her nail file on the table.

'So, how did it go, did you sell much?' Don asked, stubbing his cigar out on one of the clean sideplates, ignoring the ashtray.

Annie emptied the cigar in the bin, washed the plate and called back, 'Oh yes, we used the money to buy a machine and supplied other stall holders, but it's best to keep the middleman out really.'

'What did you make?'

'Knickers.'

'How common,' Maud said as Annie came back to the table. 'I mean, Annie, you won't be making those round here. Surely you could go into something, less, well less . . .'

'Essential?' Georgie asked, leaning forward, his hand on Annie's thigh again, squeezing gently.

'Or don't you wear them?' Tom leaned forward, his eyebrows raised.

Maud blushed, the nail file tapping even faster. 'Don't be absurd.'

Annie said quickly now, before the laughter got out of control and alienated these two completely, 'We will make knickers Maud, because they are essential but also because I can make them out of offcuts. It's much cheaper and while we're trying to get a toe hold in the market we don't want to invest too much capital in stock. We need to see which lines work well, then once we've realised our assets we can set up premises. Do it step by step.'

Don asked them about the forward planning of the business and Annie explained that to begin with they would produce only garments but as soon as possible they would go on to designing and printing their own fabrics, extending into home furnishings and wallpaper in due course.

'We'll need premises of at least two thousand square feet to begin with, and once we're into the textile side we'll need more space and must be near a sewage works.'

'I beg your pardon?' Maud said.

'Effluent,' Annie explained. 'You know the chemicals, the pongs.'

16

'Oh dear.'

'Quite,' Annie said.

'All of this to take place in Wassingham?' Don asked.

'Oh yes, it must be for the women of this town. It must,' Annie said, because it was a promise she had made to herself many years ago before she had left Wassingham. She reached across and grasped Don's hand. It was thin and cold. 'Join us, it would be the old gang again.'

Don looked at her. 'No, it's not my kind of business. It doesn't stand a cat in hell's chance. Just think about it all of you, it's daft, the whole damn thing.'

Annie sat back and looked at him and wanted to pummel him, make him see that he was wrong, make him see that he was standing aside from the family, as he had always done.

'We must go. Get your coat on Maud. We've cocktails at six and we'll be late. We'll pick up Teresa on the way.'

Georgie stood up. 'Hang on, Don. We need to talk to you about the money Sarah Beeston left Annie. Have you converted the investments you've been handling for her? We thought you'd have the figures for us today. Even if you don't want to be involved you should realise we need to get the show on the road.' Georgie's voice was loud, angry and Annie pulled him down beside her.

Don shrugged himself into his jacket as he answered. 'I'll see you about it tonight. I'll drop round to the Gosforn house. No time now.' He waved to them and followed Maud out into the yard, calling back, 'About nine tonight then, Annie.'

Annie didn't reply, just looked at the others. 'I thought he was going to join us after he showed so much interest in the premises and our plans. I just don't understand the man.'

'You tried,' Georgie said. 'He's just so difficult. You've done all you can, more than you should.'

Tom said, 'He's just different to us. He always was.'

Sarah stayed at Gracie's that night and Annie made scrambled eggs on toast back at the Gosforn house, which she and Georgie ate with champagne, toasting one another, toasting their future and Wassingham Textiles. They handed a glass to Don when he arrived, then sat at the dining table beneath the plastic chandelier which Maud had left. Don drew out a cigar. What the hell Annie thought, it's a celebration.

She reached behind her for an ashtray from the sideboard, placing it in front of her elder brother, and held her hands tightly together, hardly able to sit still.

'Come on then Don, stop shuffling through those papers, I can't stand this waiting.' She looked from Don to Georgie and winked. 'He's enjoying his moment of glory. He's dying to show off about how much he's increased Sarah's legacy.' She felt the pressure of Georgie's feet as they squeezed hers, the love in the look he gave her, the pleasure he too was feeling.

Don cleared his throat, tapping his cigar gently on the side of the ashtray, put it to his mouth again, blew a smoke ring and then picked up the top piece of paper. He looked at it again and replaced it.

He looked at her now. 'I didn't tell you this this afternoon because I was still hoping against hope that I could sort something out but I couldn't. There's no easy way of saying this.' Don looked at Georgie, then back to Annie. 'There is no money, Annie, none at all.'

Annie tried to laugh. She hadn't known him to have a sense of humour before. Perhaps he was learning after today's fiasco, but it wasn't amusing.

'Come on, Don, get on with it,' she said, prodding his arm.

He looked at her again, and then at Georgie before looking back at her. 'Don't be stupid, Annie. This is hard enough for me as it is. I'm not joking. I have to tell you that there is no money. I invested it but the stocks have crashed. You have nothing, nothing at all. I'm so sorry.'

Annie felt first the cold shock of his words, and then a searing panic.

CHAPTER 2

Breakfast was a silent affair. Annie's lids were heavy as she watched Georgie put one, two, three, four, sugars in his tea.

'Too many my love,' she said.

'Ichi, ni, san, yong,' he replied, stirring, stirring again and again.

Her hand tightened on her cup. Yes, all right, she'd dreamed of the camps, of roll call, of the terror, the camp hospital, but for heaven's sake their future had gone, in a few short words, it had gone and it was her own fault. She felt despair rise in her as it had done again and again throughout the night, but there was no time for it, she must keep telling herself that.

'I know I dreamt, it does me good. It's not serious, Georgie.'

'I'd call it a nightmare not a dream and when I hear my wife scream and chant in her sleep I call it serious.' He wouldn't look at her, couldn't look at her because she had been hurt in Singapore and he hadn't been able to stop it, she had been hurt again in India and he had allowed that to happen. She had been hurt last night, they had all been hurt and he could murder that bloody brother of hers.

Annie sipped her tea. She didn't want it, how could she want it after Don had told them his news? She sipped again, then looked at Georgie, how could so much have changed in such a short time?

'I could have smashed his face in, Annie, sitting there

20

with his cigar, apologising, simpering. God, he almost bloody wept.'

'We all nearly wept didn't we, and it wasn't his fault, it was mine. I signed the form he sent me, didn't I?' The cup slipped and fell, chipping the saucer, spilling tea. She ignored it. 'It was me. He was trying to please me by investing in a local firm, putting all my eggs in one basket because I'd prattled on about supporting the community. He knew it was what I'd want.'

The tea was dripping on to the floor, she watched it, heard it, counting one two three, ichi, ni, san – no, not that, there was no time for that. She turned from it. 'It was me. He wanted to be sure it was what I meant, which is why he sent me the letter explaining it all, and the form to sign. He knew there was a risk, he told us this last night, for God's sake. I read it, signed it, sent it back and was so damn busy sewing knickers I didn't think about it, and now I can't even remember doing it.'

She picked up the spoon and saucer, cutting her hand. Georgie came towards her and she pushed him aside, grabbing the cloth from the sink, wiping the table, throwing the saucer into the bin. 'I'm just so damn stupid, so stupid – I mean, just look at this mess. We're having a crisis so I spill the tea.' Her voice was rising, tears were near and she stopped.

'He shouldn't have done it. He should have had more sense. Tom Mallet for God's sake. He's one of his black market friends. I'm sure it sounded good, rebuilding the bomb sites, but he should have known he'd scarper and his mates with him.' Georgie wrung the dishcloth tighter and tighter. 'He should have known.'

Annie sat down. What was the point of talking about it any more, they'd gone round and round it last night and at midnight and at two, and at four in the morning until at last they'd slept, if you could call it sleep. She leaned back in the chair, stretching her neck, her eyes throbbing. No, there was no point in talking about it any more, it was gone, finished, or their original plans were but she was damned if she'd let it all go, not after all the years of waiting, and in the long hours of the night she'd thought, planned, made decisions.

'Georgie, I want you to listen to me carefully, hear me out.' Her mouth was still, her hand hurting, she wrapped her handkerchief round it.

'Whatever way you look at it I agreed, sanctioned the investment. I was stupid, clumsy, careless.'

'Don't say that. You're not careless. So you muffed a paper, what's that? It doesn't do any good to keep on blaming yourself.'

'Then stop blaming Don,' she flared at him.

Georgie leaned back now against the window, his jaw set, his eyes cold, then he looked away from her out into the garden where the house martins were swooping and Annie wanted to take back the anger, take back last night, the form, Tom Mallet, but all she could say was, 'I'm sorry, but you see I'm not a leader, I get muddled, confused, I allow myself to shout and scream, I allow myself to make mistakes.'

Georgie started to speak but she shook her head. 'Please let me finish. I decided last night that I want you to run the business. You're trained for it. You can organise, you're methodical. You weren't born to fiddle about in Gosforn doing any piddling little job, you were trained as an officer, you know how to manage.'

He turned now, leaning back against the sill. 'Don't be so daft, darling.' His voice was gentle now, all coldness gone. 'I can't sew, or cut, or talk design with Tom and aren't you forgetting something rather crucial? A small matter of capital? We're broke.'

'Please – just listen.' Annie sat quite still. She could hear the ticking of the clock they had brought back from Cyprus. 'OK, so we haven't any capital, or very little anyway. We will sell the house – as we decided last night. We'll buy a smaller one.'

Georgie scratched his chin and took a packet of Kensitas from his pocket. He looked across at Annie then brought the packet over, lit hers, lit his own, and returned to his seat drawing in the nicotine, blowing smoke up above his head.

The first of the day always tasted good she thought as she spun the ashtray in front of her, even on a day like this.

'You see, my love, we can still start the business, but in a different way that won't depend on capital. We'll work from home, extend our list of customers, then set up homeworkers as the business expands, always ploughing profits back in, taking just enough to live on and making sure we build up a capital reserve as we go along. That way we can set up premises eventually.' He was listening to her, nodding, and she drew on her cigarette then continued. 'It will take longer but there's a market for our stuff – we know that. It can be done, should be done, for the sake of us all, for Wassingham. They need our sort of industry. We mustn't let this hiccup crush us.'

'Sounds good in theory, my love,' he said, flicking his ash out of the window, catching her eye as he did so. 'Good for the roses, they like a bit of potash.'

She laughed and was surprised – she'd thought that today she would not hear that sound.

'But there's no way we can both do it. I'll keep on looking for work, you do all this,' Georgie said.

'No, that's the point. I can't, not any more.' Annie stubbed her cigarette, squashing and grinding it until there were only shreds. 'You wouldn't have made that mistake. You wouldn't have signed. You've got to take it over. The army trained you to take control.'

Georgie was laughing now. 'Oh yes, I'll cut out, shall I, or sew on flowers? Give me a break, Annie, you're being daft. Of course you can do it.'

Annie shook her head, she knew she couldn't, she knew she'd been ridiculous to think she could. Oh yes, she could cut out, sew, come up with ideas, but manage – forget it, Don had shown her that.

'I rang Don first thing, he's buying the house.'

Annie paused, rubbed the table, it was still damp. 'I also

23

rang the local hospital. I worked there in the holidays while I was at school. They're taking me – I'm going back to nursing, Georgie.'

He said nothing, then straightened, moved and came towards her, his body tense, his shoulders set, his mouth hard. 'You're bloody not. You're not going back. It'll kill you. It'll all start . . .'

He was at her side now, gripping her arms, pulling her up, 'It'll all start, it'll kill you. This time it'll kill you.' His face was contorted, he shook her. 'This was why you had that dream, you'd got nursing in your mind and it all came back. For God's sake, if the thought of it does that to you, what about the reality? It'll be the end.'

'Of course it won't, I keep telling you it's over, this will show you that it is. I'll do the cutting out when I'm off shift, I'll help, I've worked it all out. Look, you were born to *lead*, for goodness sake, it makes sense, you've got to see that it makes sense. You're hurting, Georgie.' His fingers were too tight, he was shaking her harder. His face was too close, too angry.

'Georgie, listen to me.' She wrenched free, shoving the chair out of her way, backing from him, putting the table between them. 'Listen. I'm going back to nursing. I'm going to prove to you that I'm all right, I'm going to earn the money while you get the business going. It's the only sensible thing.'

He was walking away, out into the hall, his feet clicking against the tiles. 'Don't turn your back on me,' she shouted. 'Come back here. You've got to let me do this, it's the only way.'

He stopped, turned. 'You were nursing when the Japs came to Singapore. You were nursing when they cut off Lorna Briggs' head, and smashed your finger, when you buried – how many of your friends, breaking their bodies so that they'd fit into the boxes? What do you think it will do to you, to go back. It'll flip you over again.' He wasn't

24

shouting, he was speaking so softly she had to move into the hall to hear him.

'I'm nursing. You are setting up the business because I can't – I'm no good at that. You're so much better suited.' She put her hand out to him but he had turned from her, was walking away again.

'Georgie, come back,' she called as he opened the front door.

'I'm going to Tom's to tell him we've lost the money.'

Annie ran after him. '*I* lost the money. I lost the bloody money, not we, Georgie. That's the point. It was me.'

He was opening the car door. 'Are you coming?' His face was cold.

'Of course I'm coming.'

'I thought it was the market this morning.'

'Damn the market.'

They drove in silence, through villages and ironworks that belched foul smoke. She could see the chimneys of Newcastle in the distance. There were sweeps of fields too, darkening and lightening as clouds scudded between the earth and the sun. The barley waved as the wind caught it and all the time Annie's stomach was taut and her head ached with the tension of their row, with the strain of the silence which hung between them and she wanted to reach out and touch his hand which was tanned and powerful on the gear stick, but she must not give in. Once and for all, she must show him that she was strong, that the shadows of the past had gone, and that, since yesterday, she realised that the future was best in his hands.

Georgie pulled in for petrol, not looking at her. He stood with the attendant, chatting about the weather, about the north east.

'Born round here, were you?' the man asked.

'Aye, born a *pitman*,' Georgie said, and she knew that that was for her ears too and the row was not over yet.

They drove on, through a pit village with mean dark streets where children played or lounged. George drove carefully, meticulously for mile after mile until at last he was changing gear for the long climb up the hill which overlooked Wassingham. At the top he pulled in, stopped, opened his window, and rested his arm on it but said nothing.

Annie looked out across their birthplace, seeing the bombed site which had been Garrods Used Goods, the gap where Gracie's library had once stood, seeing the school where they had all sat at desks and where Davy, Rob and Paul now sat. She could see the football pitch where Da had led out his team of unemployed miners, and way over in the distance she could see the lightening of the sky where the sea washed the shore.

They sat and out of the silence came the voices of the past, the images, the laughter and tears and now she remembered the warmth of Aunt Sophie's arms as she held her in that small warm house in Wassingham Terrace, consoling her after her mother's death, putting aside her own grief at the death of her sister, taking her into her home to live, Don too – baking scones and making toast, rubbing wintergreen on her toes, loving her with every breath she took.

She remembered leaving Aunt Sophie and Uncle Eric to live with her father and Bet, but at the shop there had been Tom and love and laughter again to soothe the darker days. There had been the heat of the sun in the allotment, the smell of leeks, the sound of metal coins being banged out for the fair, the sound of the bees in the nettles, Georgie's daisy chains around her neck at the beck, the gangs, Georgie's kisses as they grew, and such love had grown between them.

Then there were the tears when Sarah Beeston came and Annie had run to Tom in the morning as he stood outside school, her misery jagged in her chest. She had held him, told him she was leaving but he wouldn't listen, instead he had pulled at her undone bootlace, shouting at her that she'd get blisters. The tears ran down their cheeks and all the time the cables were grinding up the slag heap, clanging and tipping. 'It's like a big black gaping hole in me belly,' he had said, 'to think of you gone from here.'

There had been agony when Georgie had come to the yard to say goodbye. He had leant against the wall, taken out his cigarette paper, rolled it round the tobacco teased along its centre while she had stood close enough to touch the length of her body against his as he licked and lit the cigarette. She had breathed in the scent of sulphur as he sucked in the smoke. She had opened her lips as he slipped it from his mouth to hers and she felt his moisture. They stood and remembered without words those months, weeks and every minute they had spent together.

He hadn't kissed her, he had cupped his hand about her cheek and laid his face against hers. 'I've still to teach you to swing on that bar,' he had said, and she had replied, 'I'll love you all my life, my love.' He had smiled and made it easy for her to go, and she had driven away with Sarah up the hill that she and Georgie now looked down from but how her heart had been breaking, and his too.

She felt Georgie's hand now on hers. It was warm, he was always warm and now she couldn't see Wassingham for the tears which hadn't yet spilled from her eyes.

Georgie lifted her hand to his lips, she felt his kiss, and his tongue running between her fingers, and then his arms which drew her to him. He kissed her eyes. She heard his voice. 'We need some fish 'n' chips to go with all that salt, bonny lass.'

Then his mouth was on hers, his scent was close. 'I'd like to come back here, lass. I want to come home,' he said against her mouth.

'Yes,' she said. 'It's been so obvious, how could we not see it?' Now her daughter could tread the same paths, the same fields, the same streets. She could hear the same sounds, smell the coal, feel the kindness of Wassingham's people.

'So we're going for it are we, darling?' she said softly, her hand stroking his head, his neck, his lips, kissing lashes which she had thought were as thick as hedgerows when she had first seen him, and still thought so. 'You'll do it then — Wassingham Textiles is on the way?'

'Yes, it's really on the way, this time.' He kissed her cheeks, her eyes, her nose, her mouth. 'I love you for what you've offered me today. I love you for your courage.'

There was a light in his eyes, a zest in his voice which had been missing since the Army and she was at peace because now they both had challenges to face and that was as it should be.

Georgie started the engine. 'We'll go home, shall we, bonny lass?'

She nodded, and they started down the hill to Wassingham.

Tom shouted, swore, banged Bet's table with his fist in his rage at Don. He fell silent when Annie said she was going to nurse, that Georgie was going to run the business. He stared at her, then began to speak but Sarah and Davy ran through the yard from the back alley, hurling themselves amongst the adults, Sarah hugging Georgie and then Annie.

'We're going fishing for minnows, Bet's tied us up some jam jars. Are you coming?' She looked from one to the other.

'Not now, darling. Not just yet, this afternoon perhaps,' Annie said, twisting Sarah's plaits round one another. 'Off you go now, see you soon.'

Sarah grabbed Davy's arm. 'Come on, Bet left them in the stable.' They ran out again.

'I could kill that bloody sod, he's just cocked everything up. And stop being so daft, Annie, it's not your fault. You're crazy to even think it is, crazy to think of going back.' Tom was speaking quietly now, slumping down into the carver chair that Bet used as her own. 'Don Manon's as much a crook as that crony of his. By God, I remember Tom Mallet all right, Don's got air between his ears, must have to trust that bugger.'

Annie went round to Tom, gripping his shoulders, telling him Don had only tried to help, that it would be better with Georgie and he in charge.

She felt his hand on hers now, gripping it, then holding it

more gently as he rubbed his cheek against her broken finger. 'You can't nurse, bonny lass. You can't, not after the camps.'

Sarah called through the door, 'What camps?'

Georgie, Tom and Annie looked round.

Davy peered over her shoulder into the kitchen, at his father, his uncle and aunt. 'When're Bet and Mum back, Dad? Can we go now? We'll be back for tea.'

'Aye, lad, hop it, and leave a few in the stream.' Tom was smiling, his shoulders relaxing slowly beneath Annie's hand.

Sarah still stood there. 'What camps though?'

Davy jerked her round. 'Don't be daft, camps are the things Scouts have.'

Sarah looked back into the kitchen. 'Scouts with toggles you mean, wobbling about? Did you have a toggle, Mum?'

Rob came up behind Davy now. 'No, only boys have toggles, don't you know anything?'

Annie laughed but the men were quiet. 'Now that's enough from you, Rob Ryan. Get yourselves off to the beck and no falling in.'

She watched them as they left. Tom's hand was still on hers. She clasped it, then went towards the door. 'We didn't tell them we would be living here.'

'Keep that until later. Don't think there'll be any complaints from anyone, do you?' Tom was smiling now, but then he dropped his head, picking at the grain of the deal table. 'Talk her out of it, Georgie, for God's sake, man.'

Annie stood with her back to the room, looking out at Black Beauty's stable, remembering the snuffles which used to greet her when she opened the door. There was only the sound of the back alley now, the clanking of tubs, then the sound of Georgie's voice.

'We've discussed it as much as we're going to, Tom lad. But I've a few things to do. Come on, she's said we're partners so let's get on with it.'

She heard him move towards her, sensed him stop and then felt his lips on the back of her neck. 'We'll be back soon,' he murmured, slipping past her with Tom, taking his cap from his jacket pocket.

'Have a beer for me then,' she called and Tom grimaced.

'You're a bloody mindreader, woman. Bad as Ma Gillow and her tea leaves, but Ma was prettier.' He ducked as she grabbed a tea towel and threw it at them. Georgie caught it, flicked it up on to Bet's washing line and walked out with that crispness to his walk again.

When Bet arrived ten minutes later she argued and so did Grace when they heard of her plans but Bet, in the end, rang Matron, a friend of hers from the WI.

'You can go straight there,' she said to Annie, coming back into the room. 'But I wish you wouldn't, bonny lass, and I can't believe your Georgie agreed.'

Annie brushed her hair, smoothed her skirt, kissed Bet and pretended she hadn't seen the look her stepmother exchanged with Gracie. 'He did you know.'

The walk through Wassingham was hot and the climb up the hill to the posh end was hotter still. Her hands were sweaty but not slimy as they had been in India when the darkness in her head had gathered. She touched the palm with her finger. Yes, definitely only sweaty.

She could see the small hospital in the distance. She looked to the right, at the grand stone houses which lined the streets in this part of Wassingham. This is where she had spent the first three years of her life, before her mother's death.

Annie stopped now, drew a deep breath, then another. The hospital was closer. It was where her mother had died. She ran her hand along the picket fence where once there had been wrought-iron railings.

'Gone for the war,' she murmured, running her hand along the newly painted wood. Poor Mam. Poor Da.

Matron's house was built of stone too, but much smaller than her da's had been. She stopped to smell the Peace roses which lined the garden. They had greenfly, she began to wipe them off but then the door opened.

'Annie Manon, or I should say Armstrong.' A small

stooped elderly woman came out on to the grass holding out her hand.

Annie looked at the greenfly smeared on her own, wiped her hand quickly, and looked down into piercing blue eyes which held laughter and smiled herself as she shook the proffered hand.

'Well my dear, that's one way of dealing with pests. I often feel I would like to do that with some of my patients.' Mrs Antrop took her arm, walked her into the cool of her sitting room and served her barley water.

'Thought it more appropriate than coffee, just too hot m'dear.'

Annie sat stiffly. She was nervous, tense, frightened that the camps might come back. She might be wrong. She might not be offered the job. She might be offered it. But then Mrs Antrop began to speak.

'Betsy tells me you wish to work nights at this hospital. I placed a call to the Newcastle Infirmary.' She lifted her hand as Annie started with surprise. 'Oh yes, I know all about you, my dear. Betsy and I often talk and I do have tentacles in lots of pies – mixed metaphor but who cares. Newcastle think very highly of you, but much has happened since those days as we both know and it is of this that we must speak because obviously it might have affected your aptitude for the work.'

They talked first though of Annie's mother who had taken her own life, drinking poison from an unlocked cupboard whilst in the care of the hospital.

'There are no unlocked cupboards in my hospital. There is no unrecognised despair,' Mrs Antrop said.

They talked then of the war, of the camps, and of Annie's despair. Mrs Antrop nodded as Annie told of the nightmares, of the depression which had slowly eased, of the concern of her relatives that she might regress and attempt again to take her own life as her mother and father had done before her.

'I won't though,' Annie said, clenching her hands. 'I won't

and I have to prove to them that I won't. I need the job for that reason, but I also need it so that the business can begin.'

Mrs Antrop reached over, touched her hands. 'Relax, I'm not an ogre, believe it or not. We have to talk of these things because I have patients to consider and I must satisfy myself that you are capable also of considering them.'

Annie reached forward, drank her lemon barley. It was cool, fresh.

Mrs Antrop went on. 'I assume you need the night shifts because of your daughter.'

Annie smiled up at Mrs Antrop, then replaced her glass carefully on the lace coaster. Her hand smeared the polished rosewood table.

'Yes, I must have as much time as possible with her. There are always Bet and Grace, but I love her, I want to be with her as much as I can and I want to be able to help my husband by doing the . . .' She had been going to say sewing, but Matron might feel an extra work load would be to the detriment of her patients so instead she said. 'By being there as a sounding board.'

'So, we have discussed your well-being and your family's but what about my patients?' Mrs Antrop was sitting back, resting her head on an antimacassar, her arms resting quietly on her lap.

'If, when I start, I do not feel for them what I have always felt I will resign, immediately. If, when I start I feel that I am sliding, I will also resign, immediately.'

Mrs Antrop nodded, tapped her thin fingers but said nothing. Finally, peaking her fingers in front of her chin she said, 'My sister was in China as a missionary. She was beheaded by the Japanese. Even though I was not there I also dream and rage and I feel it saves my reason. I think what you are about to do is extremely sensible. I have a husband. Sometimes they get in the way of a full recovery, do they not, though we are fortunate their claustrophobic care is informed by love, and not by jealousy.' She put her hands on her lap again and leant forward. 'Yes, Annie, I think you would be an asset to the hospital. You will begin when you move here?'

Annie walked back down the hill and felt a smile on her face, a lightness in her step. One problem to cross off the list, now she just had to make sure it did not unearth a bigger one.

She passed the church without a tower, the space where Garrods Used Goods shop had been. She had bought her shoes there for the party at which Georgie had first danced with her when she was what? Fourteen, so many years ago. Was she really forty-two?

She moved on, walking from light to shade, crossing the cobbles, smiling to the women who were sweeping the pavements or washing coal dust from their sills. Yes, they were coming home, it was working out, they were moving forward again and not before time, Annie Armstrong, she thought. Good grief, you're almost an old boiler, and suddenly she was impatient to move, to watch Georgie's eyes brighten even more as he brought the business into being and saw that she needed no more protection.

She was crossing the road alongside the railway line when she heard the sound of running feet behind her and Tom's laughter, Georgie's shout of 'What's a pretty girl like you doing in a place like this?'

Then she felt them each grab an arm, march her between them, panting, laughing. They were too fast, the women in the streets gaped and laughed, leaning on their brooms whilst she struggled and told them to pull themselves together, asking how many pints they'd downed, laughing with them as Georgie kissed her mouth – but there was no smell of beer.

They walked down street after street and they wouldn't even stop when she called out to them that she had news for them, they could really get on now. Georgie just turned and kissed her again, saying that he knew they could. They were turning a corner into a street with compact terraces either side. She heard the sound of a train, close by, behind the terraces on the left. She strained to see the name, but they were past. It was all so familiar.

'Slow down,' she pleaded, panting.

'No time,' Tom said, clamping his hand across her eyes. 'No looking either.'

'Then slow down or I'll break my damn neck, you idiots.' Annie was giggling, laughing just as they were.

They slowed but their grip was so firm, her trust in them so complete she knew that even if they ran with her she would never fall and in the darkness she revelled in the firm touch of the two adults she loved most.

Georgie stopped, she felt him pulling her to the right, she felt the cobbles beneath her shoes. He turned her round, stopped. Tom took his hands from her eyes and in front of her was a terraced house with a For Sale sign screwed to its front wall. She looked to the right and left, then back at the house. Now she knew where they were. She searched down the street again looking for the name – Wassingham Terrace.

She moved towards the front door. It was Aunt Sophie's house and inside would be a sitting room which had once had a neat parlour, a kitchen where wintergreen had been kept on the mantel and, in the yard, a pigeon loft. She shut her eyes and could hear the soft coo and flutter of Eric's birds, she could smell the lavender water which Sophie used, she could feel arms lifting her tight and close.

She opened them, looked from one to the other. 'How did you know it was for sale?'

Georgie put his arm round her telling her that everyone had known but no one had mentioned it because they had been going to live in Gosforn.

'Do we want it?' he asked.

Annie looked at Sophie's and Eric's house again. 'Do we want it? Don't be daft.' Her voice was restrained, quiet or else she would weep her pleasure. She peered in through the front room window. Where were Sophie and Eric now? They had left for Australia immediately Da had taken the children from them, unable to bear the loss of Annie in particular,

34

Bet had said. There had been Christmas cards from Australia then nothing. But Annie knew that had been her fault. She had never replied, wounded at their leaving, jealous at the news of a daughter they had named after her. She had felt that they had replaced her. How cruel children could be.

She turned to Tom but he was backing off, shrugging at Georgie. He saw her looking at him, grinned, then looked again at Georgie. 'Well, it's up to you now, man. I'm not going to be here when the bomb goes off. Be gentle with him, Annie.' Tom was smiling at her. He looked pleased but nervous, as he used to when he'd pinched one of Bet's scones and knew he'd get a walloping.

'What's going on?' she asked, looking from one to the other, then calling after Tom. 'What's going on?'

'I'll tell you in a minute – have another look,' Georgie said.

She smiled, shook her head, tugged at his arm and drew him back to the window, peering in, telling him how wonderful he was, how clever, telling him it looked so clean, but would need painting, wondering if the old oven was still in the back room, deciding where they would put the walnut table, their pictures, hearing his voice as he told her that he hadn't known how much he'd missed Wassingham until he'd talked to the bloke at the garage. And now she looked at his reflection in the window, his eyes, his face, his happiness – but there was something else too – there was nervousness and she felt his hand steer her round now to face the street.

She listened to his voice, now so quiet as he cupped her cheek with his hand. 'Look at this, Annie, hear it, smell it.' He paused, then continued. 'It's me roots see. All this, even though Mam's taken the boys to the pits at Nottingham, all this is still me home, me roots, your home, your roots.'

She listened closely now, hearing the Geordie back in his voice as though the years away had not existed, hearing something else as well and now fear took hold.

'Tell me what you've done, Georgie. Just tell me.' She was no longer looking at the street, no longer listening to its sounds. She could see Tom, standing by the corner of the street, just standing, waiting.

'Just tell me what you've done,' she repeated.

'You heard me say I was born a pitman, Annie. You were going to marry one, remember, you were going to scrub me back for me as me mam did for me da. Well, I'm going back down the pit, you're running the business, that's what we've been fixing up this morning.'

Annie watched Tom, still standing, waiting. She looked at the woman who was polishing her letter box, a boy who was riding his bike over the cobbles, his cheeks juddering, just as her heart was doing, and her mind. Where were the words she needed, and the breath to speak them?

'Are you mad?' she asked quietly at last. 'Or just stupid?' She stopped, the boy was turning the corner, the sun was shining on the slag, the filthy dirty slag. 'Don't you remember Gracie's da, and Tom's marrer?' She was no longer quiet, she was shouting, gripping his arm, pointing to the winding gear, the steam house, the slag heap. 'It kills, it takes arms, legs. You're joking or irresponsible, I said I'd nurse didn't I, what are you talking about?'

'Yes, you said you'd nurse. I didn't say I agreed. Neither did Tom.'

Annie couldn't speak, what could she say to this man who had given her Sophie's house and then taken her nursing and perhaps his life from her? There were no words of her own in her brain, or in her mouth. She could only roll his around and around, trying to absorb them, trying to grasp them as more came and now he was holding her hand and telling her that he'd been to Bigham Colliery with Tom, smelt it, seen it, heard the shift going down, the other coming up.

'It's a club. They need one another to survive. They're a team, like the Army. I know the life, it's in me bones. It's what I want, I know that now. I knew it when I stopped the car but I think I've always felt it.'

Annie found words at last, pointing to the slag, asking why anyone should want to go down some bloody great hole, asking what was the matter with him, telling him he would go down the mine over her dead body and didn't anybody care what she wanted?

She felt his kisses on her face, his breath as he said, 'But you see, I do want to go down that bloody great hole, bonny lass, so you don't need to nurse.'

She pushed herself from him. 'Don't you call me bonny lass, Georgie Armstrong. You're just messing up our lives so don't you dare call me that.' The words were quiet, strained, they hurt her throat, she was gasping for breath and she ran from him then, wanting to catch Tom, wanting to drag him back, make him talk to Georgie, down street after street, it felt like miles. The breath was catching in her throat as she pounded up the back alley, into the yard, into the kitchen. 'Bet, Tom, Gracie,' she shouted, leaning on the table, panting hard. She heard Georgie coming in behind her.

She turned, there were so many words now, tumbling out, hurling themselves at him, 'How could you. I thought you'd accepted the change. How can you be so stupid, how can you do this to us and what about my plans, how dare you just push them aside when they make so much more sense?'

Georgie was leaning against the doorpost grinning, breathing easily and she couldn't bear the thought of the dust and the grime, the weight of the coal above his body. She couldn't bear it and so she went to him then, leant into him pleaded with him, wanting him to be safe, wanting him to be as far from the pit as possible.

He pulled her back out into the sunshine, the smell of geraniums strong as the early afternoon sun beat against the brick wall, and told her that she was to start off the business and forget the letter. Everyone was allowed a mistake.

'Not in the pit, Georgie. Mistakes kill you – they are not allowed, for God's sake.' She was shouting so loud that her throat ached.

He asked her to remember that they had promised one another a future and now they were there, in that future and he needed to earn his place back here in Wassingham, he

37

needed to prove that he hadn't run away from the pit, only from life without her. He'd had the ears and eyes of a pitman, he wanted to know he still had and that he could still read the old sow like a book. He wanted their neighbours to know that they were the same as them, that they weren't just piling back into the area on the side of the bosses.

He was stroking her hair and the words made sense, in some ways they made so much sense but what about the danger for him, what about the days and nights of worry she and Sarah thought they'd left behind? What about her nursing?

She looked into his face, his eyes and there was so much love, always there was love, but there was need too, now, just as there was in her own.

She leant back on the wall, closing her eyes, feeling the heat on her face.

'It's got the edge I had in bomb disposal. I miss that, I know now that I need it,' Georgie said quietly. He said nothing more as Annie heard the humming of the bees, the distant sound of children and the pigeons fluttering in the loft in the next yard. He had let her go when Sarah Beeston came, it had broken his heart but he had let her go, just as he had let her leave India, so what could she do? She could only agree and pretend that she was not afraid.

CHAPTER 3

The next month passed quickly. Annie sold most of the Gosforn furniture to Don because there was so little room in Wassingham Terrace.

'Don't let him have it,' Georgie said on their last night but she shook her head.

'No, he's so sorry, you can see he can't even look us in the eye. If we don't let him have it we're being petty and vindictive and it will only lead to a real breach between us all.'

As well as the walnut hall table she kept the small tables, the pictures, all the things that were Sarah Beeston. She arranged to keep on the Gosforn stall, and took on two others on the route to Wassingham, talking another stallholder into trying her goods, sale or return. Soon there would be more, there must be more.

'It's too much,' Georgie murmured into her neck as the moonlight played on his body, on his scars.

'No, not enough,' she whispered, holding him close, touching his skin, wondering how much more torn it would become when he started in the pit on Monday. He had passed his medical which she had prayed he would fail. He did not need to retrain because of the apprenticeship he had already served. She must see to it that the business thrived because he must get out of that pit and stop playing these stupid games.

In the morning Annie did not look back at the Jaguar which was pulling in behind them. She did not look back at the home which she had shared with Sarah and Val but reached across and held Sarah's hand.

'We're going home then, bonny lass.' She felt her daughter's hand tighten on hers.

'It's going to be so good, Mum.'

When they were scrubbing the kitchen floor the next morning Annie looked across at Sarah, hearing Georgie's hammering, his curse, a crash.

'Bet you didn't think it was going to be as good as this, did you?' she laughed, settling back on her heels, dragging the hair from her eyes.

Sarah's hands were red from the water, her dungarees were splashed and dirty. 'This isn't good, this is awful. Davy's out playing, Mum, it isn't fair. They're going up to the farm after lunch, said we could go too.' Sarah dropped the brush back into the water. 'I bet you didn't have to do this when you lived here.'

Annie nodded. 'It's as well we didn't have money on that, my girl. I scrubbed, brushed, washed dishes, fed the pigeons . . .'

There was another crash from upstairs. Annie raised her eyebrows. 'You'd better go up and see if you can hold something. He's trying to put up a shelf in your room. You can put my father's paper knife on it.' She smiled as Sarah leapt to her feet, throwing the brush back into the pail, dodging the spray. 'I hope you thanked Betsy for it too.'

'I did, Mum. She's going to the farm too, please can we go, please?' Sarah was hanging on the door, her face flushed and then there was another crash. 'Goddamn this bloody thing,' they heard again.

'Perhaps we'd better if the house is going to survive. Go and tell him he has only another half an hour.'

Annie finished the floor, carried the pail into the yard, tipped the water down the drain, sat on the step feeling the sun on her face as she looked at the pigeon loft, remembering Uncle Eric banging, crashing, cursing as he repaired it one year, remembering the cooing of the birds, the gentleness of his hands, his leg which had been irreparably damaged in the trenches.

'That dreadful war,' Aunt Sophie had said. 'It ruined so much.'

Annie leaned forward now and touched the lavender plant she had dug up and brought with her from Gosforn. So, Sophie, has Eric got a smithy at some mine or in an outback town, or are you in Melbourne, or Sydney? Oh God, I wish I'd kept in touch, I wish I'd written back.

She remembered the old railway prints on the wall, the best white table cloth, and then the tears Sophie had cried as Annie left to go to the shop with Da.

Annie's shoulders tightened at the memory. She had never seen an adult cry before and it was as though the ground had lurched beneath her feet, as though there was no safety, no certainty left in the world, and she shook off the memory, watered the lavender, swept the step, polished the mantelpiece and the fireguard which was still as it had been when Sophie had hung her tea towels on it to dry.

When she and Betsy were walking together past the oaks later that day, she asked her if she had heard anything of Sophie, but Bet had not.

'You could try and find her though, lass. Not all that many people in Australia you know. Mind, she'd be getting on a bit, in her seventies, and Eric too. Lovely they were, kind to me, kind to you.'

The sheep grazed around them as they walked up the hill and the wind took their breath as they breasted the rise. The sky was light in the distance, over the sea, the rocks cut through the scant soil, the gorse-bushes, yellow spiked, jigged in the breeze. Yes, she would try when she had more time but this week there were garments to make up, deliver, sell, there were the days to get through while Georgie was down beneath the ground they were standing on.

'Varies each time you know,' Tom said in her ear, his arm creeping round her waist, his finger pointing to the broken-down cart in the farm-yard beneath the hill, the tractor splashing its colour on the scene, the slipped tiles on the farmhouse showing up dark.

'You should know, you've painted it often enough.' Annie's voice was cold.

His grip tightened. 'Don't be cross, bonny lass. He wanted it.'

'You needn't have talked them into taking him, you needn't have vouched for him, wriggled him in.' Annie shrugged herself away from him and stood, watching the children playing tag on the hill, hearing Tom coming up behind her again.

'No, I didn't have to, but it's what he wants. Stop sulking, if the wind changes you'll stay looking like that and it's not a pretty sight, Annie Manon.'

Annie turned now, gripping Tom's arms. 'I remember you being smashed up beneath coal, I remember the lads in the hospital. You're a bunch of kids, all of you, just a bunch of stupid kids but without the sense of that lot down there.'

They both turned and looked at their children and again Tom put his arm around her and this time she leant into him. 'Remember us, Annie, at their age, always together, always up to something, always just managing to rescue the situation. If you don't, I do. I remember how you always looked after me so d'you think I'd not make it as safe as I can for him if he's set on it – and he is you know. I've put Frank on with him and he'll have the good seams, the easy seams. I took him into the lamp room, down the shaft to try and put him off but he just breathed in the air and said "Ambrosia". Trust me, and for God's sake put a smile on your face.'

Annie watched Sarah being chased by Davy, was she going to get back to the stump, was she? Yes, she'd made it and Annie kissed her brother's cheek. 'You're a good boy, Tom Ryan, and my daughter can run faster than your son, just like her mother.'

She grinned at Tom because he was right, she must smile, she must rise at five, pack Georgie's bait tin, watch him leave, wait for his return, and smile, just like every other woman in Wassingham had always done and always would do. But more than that, she must work.

Sarah and Davy sat panting on the stump while Rob blew on blades of grass, his cheeks straining with the effort, the sheep nearby moving away as he did so.

'Just look at your mam run,' Davy said, coughing and pointing.

Sarah shaded her eyes, holding her throat as her breath rasped in and out, in and out, she nodded but couldn't speak, not yet. She had beaten Davy but she'd thought her lungs would burst out of her while she did so.

'She's faster than you, Sarah,' Rob said, then blew the grass again.

'Not as fast as Da though, look at him go,' Davy was standing now, laughing. 'Look he's almost caught her. Your dad's chasing them now, and Mam.'

'Blimey, it'll be Bet next,' Rob said, standing too, no longer whistling, just shaking his head. 'Parents are embarrassing. I mean, they're too old.' He looked around. 'No one can see them anyway or you lot would never hear the end of it. Doesn't matter to me. They wouldn't hear about it at the grammar.'

Sarah laughed now, her breathing easier. 'Unless we told them.'

Rob turned on her. 'Don't you dare. Don't you bloody dare, it's going to be bad enough without that.'

'You worried then?' Davy was sitting on the ground now, flicking grass at a stone.

'Course not, it's just new, that's all.'

Rob walked off, up to the crest of the hill, his hands in his pockets, his head down.

'Spect your da feels the same too,' Davy said watching his brother, then the adults still chasing one another.

Sarah squatted at his side, rubbing the dry soil with her fingers, forcing it into the cracks. 'Don't know why he's going into the pit, Terry said Mum should have nursed, said no

43

one would really want to go down the pit. It's dirty and smelly. She says there are no lavs, that's horrid.'

Davy looked at her, then up at their parents. 'He wants to though, he said that.'

'Terry said her mum said he would say that. I don't want him to go down. How could anyone want to go down under this.' She pushed more soil into a crack. An ant ran over her finger. She cupped it in her hands, letting it run, but not escape. 'She says Mum should have nursed.'

'Since when have you listened to Terry or her mum. I told you, he wants to go down and it's daft, but then, grown ups are daft, look at them.'

Sarah watched her mother trip and fall, watched Tom and Georgie stop, pick her up, one by the shoulders, one by the feet and give her the bumps.

They both looked round now to see that there was no one from town to see it. Yes, they are daft, she thought, stupid and daft and she put her hands on the ground, letting the ant run on to the ground.

'People die though, don't they Davy? It's like Dad's bombs. You never know which one it will be that's going to get you.' She squashed the ant, rubbing her finger over and over it until there was nothing left.

'Well, my da was in the pit for ages and he looks all right and Frank, his marrer, still goes down. All the Wassingham men do, seems right somehow. They do get cut and the scars go blue, but I don't think it's like the bombs. No, not the bombs.'

'But people do die?' Sarah was looking at him now, holding his arm.

Davy was quiet, then he nodded. 'Yes, they die.'

There was a silence between them and then Sarah felt his hand holding her arm, his fingers tight, his skin warm, his eyes troubled but only for a moment because then they heard the shouts, the laughter, felt the pounding feet and her father scooped her up as Tom grabbed Davy, and swirled them around until they gasped, set them on their feet, held their hands and ran them down to the bottom. It felt as though she was flying, as though she would never stop and at the bottom she hugged her father.

'I love you Da, I love you,' she shouted.

Annie was up before Georgie, stoking the range, cooking him bacon, eggs, sausage, not thinking, just doing. She checked the clock. Five a.m. She heard him in the hall, padding through in his socks. She held out his boots as he came through the doorway.

'There's no need to get up, Annie, you've a busy day.' He took the boots, sat down, shoved his feet into them and ate his breakfast, pulling a face at the milk she gave him.

'Drink it, it'll line your stomach against the dust.'

She packed his bait tin, filled his water bottle, his cold tea flask. She stood behind him as he drank, wanting to hold him, press his strong body against hers, wanting to run her hands down his chest, his thighs, wanting to make him forget all this and stay here. But she did nothing except hand him his tin, his old clothes stuffed into a holdall and his flask. She kissed his mouth, touched his face and smiled, opening the door into the yard at Frank's whistle, walking with them to the gate, watching as they walked together towards the pit, joining others as they came from their yards. Georgie did not walk as they walked, he did not hold himself as they did. Couldn't he see he wasn't one of them any more?

Their boots were loud on the cobbles as they walked to the pit-yard, the buildings crowded in on them and Georgie and Frank nodded to each man as they joined the group. There was no talk, it was too early, too grey, these were not men on a ramble, they were workers facing a full day, heavy with sleep. There was no surprise in their faces at his presence, word spun round quickly in a pit town. There was wariness though as he had known there would be and he was glad that he was here, proving himself to them, proving that his

45

family had the right to come back into their midst but more importantly, proving something to himself.

Once inside the entrance they passed the canteen, then clattered into the locker rooms and Frank pointed out the one that would be his from now on. He changed into old clothes, locked up, then walked with the others to the supply room, collecting his helmet, kneepads, steel-capped boots, gloves, belts. It was like the Army again, it was like coming back into the team.

'Come on man, let's get your lamp.' Frank shouldered past the other men, leading the way into the lamp room. Tom had shown him this last week but he still felt the same surge, the same sense of being a boy again. He handed in his metal tag to old Jock who exchanged it for a lamp.

'Good to see you, lad. You keep your bleeding head and back down, and your feet up and your wits about you. I don't want to be left with a spare tag at the end of the shift, your Annie'll have me guts for garters.'

Georgie grinned. 'No she won't, bra straps perhaps. You've not aged at all, you old devil.'

'You have, you were a boy last time, just you remember that, Georgie Armstrong. Reckon you need your head examined, what d'you think, Frank?'

Georgie was moving along now, being pushed from behind.

'Too right, Jock, but I reckon he thinks it's good for the soul, or maybe he thinks he can talk us into buying Annie's bras for ourselves.'

The men were laughing and Georgie stood at the cage while he was frisked for matches, lighters, cigarettes. He'd left his Kensitas in his trousers and the checker flung them in the bin and growled. Georgie flushed and Frank dug him in the ribs. 'Nice one, lad. Don't happen to have a bomb in the other one, do you?'

There was more laughter but it was good humoured and Georgie relaxed. Bloody fool, don't do that again, he told himself, knowing he'd have had more to say if it had been one of his bomb team.

He waited with Frank whilst the miners queued for the cage. There was the low hum of the dynamos running the air pumps, he'd forgotten that, but not the feeling in his stomach as he waited to plunge into the darkness.

'You OK, lad?' Frank murmured, shifting his weight from one foot to the other waiting for the banksman to get the men in, the wire guard shut. Georgie nodded, his arms hanging loose, emptying his head as he had taught his men to do. They were all in now, the gates were closed, the cage dropped. Jesus Christ, he'd forgotten how your heart lifted, how silence fell, how the faint surface light faded, how quickly you travelled, how the light from the helmet lamps flickered on the surface of the shaft, the cables, the pipes, how your mind persuaded you the earth was closing over you, how the ground bounced beneath you as the cage stopped, how you breathed out as the cage door opened. Jesus Christ, he'd forgotten and now he was grinning, stepping out with the others, their bait tins clanking against one another, their batteries too.

He breathed in the air, sensing its motion, its warm lifelessness. Yes, it was the same. He blinked, then narrowed his eyes in the brightness of the light. He'd forgotten how like a tube station it was.

'Need a few advertisements, Frank lad,' he said quietly as they headed for the paddy train.

'None of this comfort when you were down last, eh Georgie? Shanks's pony then,' Frank grinned, squashing himself into a seat, pulling Georgie in.

'Shove over, let a tiddler in,' Bernie Walters grunted, sinking back as the train started. 'Bloody Ritz for you, isn't it, Georgie?' He stuck out his hand, shook Georgie's. 'Worked in the old seam with your brothers. Like Nottingham, do they? Good thing you came back down, lad, they'll open up to you now, would've been difficult otherwise.'

Georgie nodded, smiled. He knew he'd been right. He looked to the sides, electricity still lit their way, they passed stores of fire-fighting equipment and first-aid stations. He moved with the motion of the train knowing that any minute they would be plunged into darkness and now they were and their lamps picked out steel pit girders and unpainted brickwork.

'You'll be working with wood props at the pit face,' Frank said.

Gorgie nodded. Tom had told him. He saw traces of coal on the walls, the roof. There was already stone dust on his lips, in his throat. Thank God for that, flash fires were less likely. The train stopped, they eased themselves out, their feet kicking up the dust, tasting it in their mouths.

He moved along the roadway, his lamp picking out Frank's back, the roof, the walls. 'Pick your feet up, man,' Bernie hissed behind him, 'it's like a sandstorm back here, and keep up.'

He moved more quickly now, remembering to feel with his feet, bending as the roof lowered to four foot, remembering the pain that dug into his back and legs. His lamp was picking up the roof and the floor and the sides, but in front there was nothing but a wall of blackness because Frank had left him behind. Bernie turned off down another roadway. God, he was alone. He moved more quickly, carelessly, caught his back on the roof, felt the jagged slash, the sharpness, the dampness of blood, black blood. He moved even faster, straining his back as he kept low, straining his thighs. Come on, come on, keep moving until his lamp at last picked up Frank and now the roof was higher, they were upright, but it was so hot.

'We'll strip off here, gets too bloody hot, d'you remember?' Frank asked.

'Aye.' He could do do more than grunt in the heat and tiredness and he hadn't even lifted a shovel yet.

He felt the blood on his shirt, sweat in his eyes, the taste of it in his mouth. He wanted a drink but not before Frank took one.

They walked on inbye until there it was, the old sow's black face, scarred and blasted by the night shift who'd cut it and now, together with others, they shovelled the coal on to the clanking rasping conveyor but it wasn't until ten o'clock that Georgie at last managed to maintain the ceaseless steady rhythm of the others. His throat was dry and his head splitting with the noise of the conveyor but he knew that the cutter would be much worse.

The broken coal came away quickly, leaving the jagged roof exposed. He and Frank propped it, sawing, heaving, banging and it was easier than Sarah's shelf. It really was, and he laughed and Frank shook his head, then called 'snap' which was picked up by Bernie further down, who called it too, and so it was echoed down the line and at last they sat in amongst the coal dust, listening to the creaking roof, checking it with their lamps while they ate and drank and pee-ed.

Georgie's right hand was sore, blistered through the gloves. Both his hands were so stiff he wondered how he'd ever get them round the shovel shaft again, his back was so stiff he wondered how he'd ever bend again, his legs were shaking so much that Frank laughed and told him the only time he'd shaken like that was when he'd brought Tom back from the beating the fascists gave him at Olympia and delivered him to Annie at the hospital.

'Thought she'd damn near kill me I did,' he laughed, squatting on his hunkers.

'Did she?' Georgie asked, working his hands, rolling his shoulders.

'No, but I expect she damn near killed you when you said you were coming back down.' He tossed Georgie a piece of gum to chew.

'I guess you could say that but what about you, are you still in politics?' Georgie didn't want to think of Annie's attempt to nurse, her courage, her self-sacrifice, her nightmares, her rage and worry at his plans, he just wanted to be here, in spite of the pain and the tiredness.

Frank shook his head, his jaw moving in the same ceaseless rhythm that he had used when wielding his shovel. 'Kids' stuff, you get too old to stand there mouthing off at demonstrations somehow, and with Tom scratching away at the business idea he's had no time for anything but that and the union. You'll go into the business, will you?'

Georgie nodded. 'Aye, this'll keep us until it's off the ground.'

'Canny move too, the blokes'll get their wives to look out for your stuff, there's some who're good with sewing too. Get Tom on to that, then you'll not get any bad workers to be a bloody nuisance.'

Frank stirred, packed his tin away, looked at his watch but waved Georgie back down. 'Few minutes yet.' He leant back against the wall, and Georgie's lamp picked out the sweat which ran in rivulets down Frank's black chest and belly, just as it would be running down his. His back was too sore to lean against anything.

'So what d'you do with yourself now then, Frank?'

'Pigeons, that's what I do. Got a real good 'un.' Frank took his gum out of his mouth and stuck it on the sole of his shoe. 'Looks what he is, a belter. Got a good eye, make a good racer. You should get that old loft of Eric's fixed up, he raced a few good ones you know.' Frank checked his watch again and nodded. 'Best be getting at it.'

Frank came across and heaved Georgie up and for a moment he thought his legs wouldn't take his weight but they did and he could straighten his back, just.

After another two hours his blisters burst and Frank took gauze and cream out of his underpants and bound them. 'Full of surprises, my old lady says. Always happens first day back and you'll need to use them tomorrow lad, that's if you're going to make a real pitman.' He slapped Georgie's shoulder. 'You're doing well, Georgie, real well.'

He talked above the noise of the conveyor as they worked now and Georgie knew it was to ease the last hour for him. He learned about squeakers and then about ringing, training, and the race which had been spoiled by gale-force winds.

'You should get yourself a squeaker. Have one of mine if you like.'

Georgie laughed, heaving another shovel load on and then another, then breaking off to help Frank heave in another prop. 'Fat chance of that, any free hands around our house and you get a pair of pants stuffed into them, or a bra, or if you're really lucky, an apron.' They both laughed as the prop went in and picked up the shovels again, though Georgie had to use his to force himself upright and then lean against the prop as a wave of giddiness brought the nausea to his throat.

'Your Annie's got it right though you know, got to work hard at the beginning. She deserves success, she's a right bonny lass, Georgie.'

Georgie knew that she was, knew that she'd say nothing about his hands, his back but her eyes would flare until anxiety overtook the anger. He'd be all right though, and today had shown him that he could listen for the old sow's mumblings just as well as he'd always been able to, except for the noise of the conveyor.

Annie and Sarah stood at the yard gate waiting and watching for Georgie, Frank and the others and for a moment they couldn't pick him out because his walk now was that of a miner, measured, feeling the ground.

As he reached them he nodded to Frank, put his cap in his pocket, kissed Annie and stroked Sarah's hair with his bandaged hand.

'No need to scrub me back, little Annie, they've got pit showers now.' His smile was tired.

'Well, you can't win them all, then,' Annie said, her smile broad because that was how it must always be, though the anger had flared at his hand before anxiety had taken its place.

'Never mind, lad, nothing wrong with your fingers, you can still pick out the faulty stitching on the knicks.'

She heard Frank laugh further down the lane and then Georgie and Sarah too and now her smile reached her eyes, and her love was in her lips as she kissed his ear. 'I love you,' she whispered and left her relief at his return unspoken.

CHAPTER 4

Annie lay in bed and watched another rocket soar, then explode. Would that mean a stick in their yard in the morning? It was supposed to be good luck wasn't it? Maybe she'd get that big order they desperately needed.

'Four months gone and where is it?' she said softly to herself. 'Four months of slog and still I can't get my foot in the door, what on earth am I going to do?'

She ran her hands through her hair and could still smell the sulphur from their own fireworks, hear Sarah's shrieks as the Catherine Wheel had spun off its stand by the bonfire on the wasteground. Georgie had stepped forward, then stopped as Annie held him back. 'You're not defusing that, bonny lad,' she'd said and handed him a charred baked potato instead.

She turned away from the window, stretching her hands across the emptiness next to her. At least he and Frank had had time to come to the bonfire and at least on night shift they'd be turning over the conveyor rather than working behind the cutter but she still worried and she still missed him.

Annie turned again, then again and heard yet another rocket. Who was still up? Kids probably. She looked at the clock, two a.m. Oh God, she was tired. She must get some sleep or she'd be going to the market traders with bags under her eyes big enough to hold their week's takings.

She sat up now, resting her head on her knees. She'd try the traders to the west and north of Wassingham in early autumn. They'd taken the pants in the summer – now she would try them with the aprons with Christmas looming.

There were fifteen regular orders from stalls to the south and east but no money up front, that was the problem, and they were still asking for sale or return plus thirty days' credit and she had to go with that for now. At least though she'd hooked into two new shops in Newcastle. They were keen on the pants and bras which was good but they paid on thirty-day invoices too and even then they had to be chased. At least the markets paid up promptly.

She lay down again, watching the clouds scudding across the moon, pulling the bedclothes up around her neck, feeling the cold on her face. Would Georgie be cold? No, it was never cold deep down he said, and it might not be, but it was hard and she could see the tiredness more deeply etched on his face with each passing day and feel new cuts and ridges on his back. If they weren't getting enough garments into the retail outlets how could they sell? She must try harder, cut their profit margins if necessary, create a need and she just had to crack the big stores.

'I'll try offering the department stores a much bigger discount, even extended credit, but not too much, we can't carry it.' She could see her breath in the moonlight. Did everyone talk to themselves? But why worry, she wasn't growing hairs on the palms of her hands yet, Sarah had checked today and had said she might sound mad but so far wasn't.

She turned again and again but sleep would not come and so she went down to the dining room. There was no point in wasting time if they had to get more garments out. She walked over the thread-strewn floor. She must hoover in the morning – what was it Isaacs had said? 'A clean workroom is a happy room, Mrs Armstrong,' and then he'd handed her the Hoover. She touched the boxes of pants Gracie had brought in at the end of the day. She must put them into packs of twelve but that could wait until the morning. There were Bet's pants on the table, she'd re-do those now.

Her neck ached and her fingers were sore as she began

and she wondered how to tell Bet that her hands and eyes could not do the work, but even as she thought it she knew that she could never say the words and so she unpicked, re-sewed, stacked, unpicked, re-sewed, stacked as she always did for Bet, and then checked Gracie's and her own. The quality must be good right from the start. She stopped and wrote a reminder to ask Gracie to stack her garments into dozens, it would mean one less job for her.

Now she cut out the work for tomorrow and shrugged aside the ache in hands swollen from using the scissors too much. What did banana fingers matter just so long as the work was done – pain was nothing, it would pass but there were tears in her eyes after half an hour.

For a further hour she sewed samples of their bras, of the new pants because she had decided she must tour the Madam shops again. She wouldn't ring in advance this time, she'd just go. She sewed more aprons and gloves because she'd noticed two new kitchen and craft shops setting up on her way back from Gosforn market last week and she'd call in on them too. She'd do Durham, Newcastle, all the towns.

She needed to sound out Brenda Watson down Edmore Street again, make sure she'd really be available to help her train up the homeworkers if they got the big ones. No, not if, *once* they got the orders.

Tom and Georgie had talked to the men, they'd got four reliable wives picked out as homeworkers but how long would they wait, they might go and get other jobs.

'No, there *are* no other jobs, you idiot woman, that's why we're here.' Annie leant her head forward on her throbbing hands. Her back was stiff, her feet were cold, her lids were heavy.

She packed up the samples, checked through her list of calls, checked off the quantities against the orders – still needed twenty-four more vests and . . . she checked through the orders again, yes, there was an order for four dozen pants. It was for Fairway Market – how had she missed that? Gracie

54

and she could have done them on Sunday. She gripped the chair. They were to be delivered tomorrow.

'For God's sake, we can't afford to be so careless,' she groaned and looked at the clock again, it was so late, she was too cold, too tired but then she shook herself. 'Get on with it.'

She went through to the kitchen, stoked the range, brewed tea, smoked a cigarette, stood in the open door looking out into the yard, there were no spent rockets and so she flicked her cigarette across the yard, watching it arc in the cold November air, watching it smoulder and die – 'Good as a rocket any day, Annie Armstrong, now sort it out.'

She drank her tea, curling her hands around the mug, ignoring the throbbing, wondering how many pants would be returned from the other stalls? Could she bank on twenty perhaps as part of the four dozen, but no, what if they'd sold the lot? She rinsed her mug, then cut and sewed the full forty-eight, checked and packed them, and the twenty-four vests.

If she had any returns she'd have to put them back into stock and sell those on at the next trader. She checked her route. Yes, she could do Fairway and still be back for Sarah because she stayed for piano until four.

Annie checked the clock again, her mind a blank, her eyelids heavy, she rubbed her eyes. Georgie would be in at half past six, she'd give him breakfast and finish packing before Sarah got up, but then she saw the invoices. She had to do those so that Georgie could look at them before she left. She insisted that all paperwork was checked because she was unable to trust herself. Maybe all orders should be too, but no, everyone had enough to do, she'd just make sure she checked through each evening.

Her hands were shaking as she wrote but then they were all exhausted. Tomorrow she must tell Gracie that they had to produce more than they were doing so that they could build up a reserve to call on, rather than going from hand to mouth like this. Could Gracie produce more? She'd have to, even though she had the two children. Could they work harder without telling Betsy otherwise she'd insist on doing more, which would only mean more unpicking? Annie slept for an hour.

The bacon was crisping and the sausages spitting as Georgie came through the door – safe, thank God, yet again. 'Sausages are almost ready, the bacon's crisp, the invoices are there.' She nodded to the table, then laughed as his arms came round her, as his hands stroked her breasts and he said, 'Since you don't have to scrub my back take me straight to bed, Mrs Armstrong. The sausages can wait, the bacon can burn, the invoices don't need checking.'

He pushed the frying pan off the hotplate and pulled her through the door, undoing her dressing-gown, leading her up the stairs, closing their door with his heel, stripping off his clothes, removing hers. He held her, stroked her, kissed her mouth, her breasts, her thighs and she could still smell the pits on him.

'I love you bonny lass, little, little Annie,' he said as he lay on her, moving with her, kissing her eyes now, her hair. 'I love you, I love you.'

Though she was tired she held him, kissed him and then felt her own passion rise as it always did for this man, for his strength, his kindness, his love. Later, they lay in one another's arms but only for a moment because Sarah must not be late for school, Annie must not be late for the rounds, so she eased herself from the bed, dressed and crept towards the door. She turned as he spoke.

'Forgot to tell you, love. An order was phoned through from Fairway on Saturday, I stuck it in at the bottom of the pile – it should have been on the top, shouldn't it?'

'Next time, Georgie, I shall murder you!' Annie blew him a kiss because this time the mistake had not been hers and so perhaps the days of carelessness were over.

Sarah ate Georgie's breakfast while Annie cooked another for him and packed up sandwiches and an apple for her daughter's lunch. She pricked the sausages, turned the bacon.

'D'you need another slice, Sarah?'

'No thanks, Mum, but I'll have his rind.'

'No you won't, your da likes it, you've got your own.'

'You're as bad as Miss Simpson. She's mean too.' Sarah was buttering her toast, putting on too much marmalade. Annie smiled.

'Surely not like Miss Simpson, she breathes fire, doesn't she?'

'Almost. She's been going on about the eleven plus but I don't want to go to the Grammar, it'll mean breaking up with Davy and . . .' Sarah waved her toast at her mother, 'and, it'll mean all girls, I'll get like Terry.'

Annie put Sarah's lunchbox into her satchel. 'I don't think we'd let that happen somehow.' She checked her watch, ten more minutes before they needed to leave. She turned the sausages, grilled more bread and looked across at Sarah. 'If you did pass, it would give you more opportunity you know, both of you. I mean Davy might want to go and if you're spouting about not splitting up he'd maybe hold back. You'd get the bus in together and meet up afterwards.'

Sarah was quiet as she finished her toast. Then she took Georgie's tray from Annie and ran upstairs with it while Annie hurried with the boxes out to the car, balancing too many, but Sarah rushed out and caught them as they fell.

'Well done – but go in and brush your hair, Sarah,' she laughed, 'and give Miss Simpson a chance and more importantly, don't influence Davy. Let him make up his own mind.'

She followed her daughter through to the kitchen and wiped the drainer. Then she shrugged herself into her coat, put on some lipstick and smoothed her hair. She straightened her daughter's collar.

'Are my seams straight?' She turned her back to Sarah.

'Yes, and Davy's made up his mind anyway. He wants to go to Art College so I'm going too.'

Annie picked up her handbag and looked carefully at Sarah, smiling gently. 'But you might not want to do art, darling.'

'I don't, not like he does, he wants to paint designs like Uncle Tom. I want to be like you, have ideas, make them work, learn how to move a strap and make something better but I want to stay here with you for the rest of my life. I don't ever want to leave Wassingham, or this house.' Sarah was moving towards the door as Annie reached out and pulled her close.

'I felt just like you when I lived here. I never wanted to leave but I did, and then I came back. You do that when you're grown up you know but the love never dies between families, it's always there. And I think it's a very good idea to go to Art College, if that's what you want to do but there's plenty of time to change your ideas. Listen to Miss Simpson though, she's maybe a wise old dragon. Now scoot, you'll be late.'

She watched Sarah walk through the yard and out into the alley, knowing she would pick up Davy outside Tom's, and was moved not only at the thought of the children's friendship but at the memory of Sarah's words. That night she wrote to the Australian newspapers in Sydney, Melbourne and Adelaide explaining that she was trying to trace Sophie and Eric Shaw and asking them to print her letter. Later she worked into the small hours because it might not just be the adults' future she was building up, but the children's too.

As November became December there seemed almost no time to eat, let alone sleep. She picked up orders for a further two Madam shops, and five market stalls, and still ran the Gosforn stall, though she never saw Maud or Teresa there. She spent her evenings with Sarah, her nights working.

She called on the kitchen and craft shops. The manager of one was rude and turned her away, the other took a dozen aprons and gloves, then rang for more. Tom suggested that they sewed holly on to the knickers with Christmas approaching and they did so, though Annie felt they would surely not sell, because there was no way she would wear a pair, or Gracie. But sell they did and once again she made a note

58

not to allow her personal taste to influence her view of the market place.

She rang shops and stores offering larger discounts but only a few buyers from the smaller shops saw her and only one placed an order. In desperation she took Davy and Sarah to Newcastle for tea in the restaurant of the main department store.

They ate meringues with forks and watched the mannequins parade while she told them of the pantomime she had seen as a child and how she had clapped with all the other children when Tinkerbell was fading, and was convinced that it was only because of her longing that the fairy had lived.

She told how, long before that, she and Don had played jacks on the thick white cloth while they waited for Sophie and their father to finish talking in the front room, how she had wanted to turn herself into gossamer and float beneath the door so that she could listen to all that they were saying.

'I've not heard back from Australia,' she said. 'Sophie can't have seen my letter.'

'Mum, you're just putting it off. Go on, you wanted to talk to the buyer,' Sarah said, drinking her tea.

'Plenty of time for that,' said Annie, playing with her meringue. She still had a problem with rich food after the deprivations of the war. So did poor old Prue from the sound of her last letter from India in which she'd told Annie not to send out a Christmas pudding as usual. Just can't cope, darling. So unfair, she'd said.

'Oh damn,' Annie said, 'I haven't sent off Prue's biscuits.' She sat back in the chair, there had been no time, too much to do. 'I'd better nip off and get a tin and we'll send it on Monday.'

Sarah looked at her. 'Mum, just go and talk to the buyer, she won't eat you, she's not like Miss Simpson.'

'So, how is your work going both of you?' Annie asked, leaning forward.

'Auntie Annie, go and talk, we'll stay here and we won't

59

pinch the sugar lumps and we won't spill our tea.' Davy was picking up her handbag and scarf.

'Yes, go on, Mum, just put on some lipstick, that's right, you look great.'

Annie stood up, her legs were trembling. She hadn't rung to make an appointment, there was no point.

'Be good,' she muttered.

'You be good, sell it to them, that's what Da said.'

Annie nodded, well, he would, wouldn't he, tucked safely down a thousand feet under the bloody ground. She checked her samples, pulled her skirt, and had a word with the head waitress who nodded and smiled. 'Yes, I'll keep an eye on them, no bother.'

The lift to lingerie was crowded, carols were playing in the store as she weaved between the stands, checking the stock, the pants, the bras. There were none like hers.

'Can I help you, madam?' the salesgirl asked, her face fixed in a smile which disappeared when Annie said, 'May I speak to the buyer please? It's Mrs Armstrong from Wassingham Textiles.'

The girl ran her finger along her eyebrow, her nails were red.

'Have you an appointment?'

'No, I just happen to be in the area.' Annie pulled out the pants. 'We make pants and bras to any specification.'

The girl didn't even look but said in a flat, bored voice, 'Mrs Wilvercombe doesn't see anyone without an appointment.'

'Then how do I get an appointment?' Annie asked as first one woman came to the till and then another.

'You phone or write,' the girl replied. 'Now if you'll excuse me I have customers waiting.'

Annie stood for a moment, wanting to take the girl by the collar and march her to Mrs Wilvercombe – wherever that old battle-axe might be.

'I am in a hurry you know,' the woman behind her said and Annie moved to one side, her face flushed. She rammed the pants back into the box, then the box into the bag and walked towards the lift. She passed a phone by the stairwell and stopped, looking back at the girl. Damn it, cheeky little monkey. She fed in coins, rang the store, asked to speak to Mrs Wilvercombe.

'I'm actually in your store, at the stairwell, I have improved discounts to offer and an excellent range of under-wear,' Annie began.

'I'm far too busy, it's pre-Christmas you know. Perhaps you could try again in February.' Mrs Wilvercombe's voice was brittle, hurried.

'But we're offering extended credit to big stores,' Annie said.

'Thank you no, try again in February.'

'Thank you so much,' Annie said, wanting to ask what she had to do to get a foot in the door – beg? Probably she told herself as she replaced the receiver. She walked up the stairs to the restaurant, paid the bill and shook her head at the children. They grimaced, took her bags, held her hands and came with her while she bought biscuits for Prue. All the time the carols played until she could have screamed.

In February she rang Mrs Wilvercombe again who said that she was too busy. She rang all the other stores and was told that there were no more appointments available, they had all been reserved for the wholesalers who would be touring with their samples in two weeks' time – didn't she know? No, she hadn't known, God damn it, and she sat that day and did nothing but think and use the telephone. That evening she called a meeting and discussed mail order with Georgie, Tom and Gracie.

'It's direct selling, the money comes in first then the orders are filled, none of this chasing for payment, none of this long slow build, this tortuous begging.' She had cleared the dining-table and lit the fire and she watched as the flames darted and curved around the coal. Her head was aching, she was tired. It was all so slow. Georgie was still in the pit,

61

the lines on his face more deeply etched with each week that passed. 'We're just not breaking in.'

Georgie tapped with his pencil. For God's sake don't do that, she wanted to shout. What was the matter with her?

'We knew it would take time, Annie, and we can't afford to gamble on mail order. What d'you think, Tom?'

Annie looked across at Tom who nodded. 'Too much outlay. We'd have to set up the advertisement, place it, order up the cloth, probably retain homeworkers to make sure we had them for the push and what if we guessed wrong and the design didn't appeal? We don't know enough yet.'

Annie tried not to hear the tapping of the pencil and looked at Gracie. 'What do you think?'

'Too much of a gamble and we are building, Annie, don't be too impatient.'

'But for heaven's sake, we're way behind the schedule we set ourselves.' She pushed the minutes in front of them. 'Look at Georgie, he's worn out.'

The pencil tapping stopped and Georgie looked at her, his eyes angry. 'Don't tell me how tired I am, bonny lass, you're panicking – we just need the big order, that's all. It'll come.'

'When though, Georgie, when? I'm your wife for Christ's sake, I know when you're tired, when Gracie's tired, we're all tired.' She was trembling. Was her face as tense as Georgie's? Tom's expression told her that it was and she sat down and hung her head, gripped her arms, took a deep breath. 'I think mail order is worth a shot, we can keep on the regulars as our cushion and we'll end up with direct and indirect sales. Please think about it, we're getting nowhere fast the way we're going.'

They did think and talk and argue and she told them how she'd rung and sounded out suppliers of second-hand rotary cutters and sewing machines during the afternoon, how she'd contacted the estate agents and yes, the warehouse was still vacant so they'd have premises to move into once the mail-shot got them off the ground.

She ignored Georgie's raised eyebrows and continued. 'I've

62

talked to the homeworkers, they've agreed to a retainer of two pounds a week once the advertisement has gone out but there'll be some capital outlay on training them up to the required standard. Brenda will help while Gracie keeps up with the regulars.'

'We'd need too much capital to fund it,' Georgie said.

'We've got it in the bank, we've built up that much of a reserve,' Annie countered.

'But if it fails, we're back to square one,' Tom said, drinking his beer.

'You've got a moustache,' Annie snapped. 'It won't fail.'

'I think we should respond to definite orders or we're working blind. Look how far on we are, after all, we only had two accounts in June,' Gracie said.

'But it's not fast enough, can't you see that? We had December blocked in for a big order, and it's February now. For heaven's sake, we're working flat out and the money's trickling in. We've got to make that leap so that we can employ others, push the goods out. At the moment we're working all hours of the day and night to virtually stand still – it's just not cost-effective.' She paused. 'Look, we need a shop window to show our wares, to tempt people in. Mail order would do that for us, and once the big stores see we've something good to offer they'll want us too.'

Georgie was writing, working out figures, he shoved the pad over to Tom who nodded, passed them to Gracie and then to Annie.

'Look at those, darling. It would run us right down. If we guessed wrong we'd jeopardise the house and we can't do that, not again. We'll just have to respond to orders, keep to the plan.'

Annie sat back, looked at her hands, at the carpet covered in threads, at the fire which had died down, at the ash which had spilt on to the hearth, the word 'again' ringing in her ears. Suddenly she wasn't as sure as she had been.

'I insist on a vote,' she said, but the crispness had gone from her voice.

It was three to one against and it was then that the frustration exploded and she banged her fist on the table and shouted, 'So what the bloody hell do we do now, I can't get through to the buyers, I can't get through to you, so what exactly do we do?'

There was silence and then Georgie said, 'For a start you can come out into the kitchen and help me make another cup of tea.' While they made the tea he told her that she was working too hard, that there was nothing to worry about, that she was over reacting, the business was fine and she said nothing but wanted to shout at him, at them all, Isn't it enough that you won't let me nurse, now you won't let me lead the business, don't you understand anything?

The next day she worked in the morning, and then sat and thought until Sarah came in. That evening she phoned Mr Isaacs and then called another meeting. Tom and Gracie came at nine p.m. and she barely gave them time to remove their coats before calling the meeting to order. 'OK, no mail order but we need to get professional. We need to get on the wholesalers' tour. I've rung Isaacs, he's told me the route, explained the wherewithal. One of us needs to take the samples to Edinburgh, Glasgow and all towns en route, then down to Liverpool and across to York. We need to phone ahead and make appointments with buyers at the time that other wholesalers are doing the same thing so we become part of the circus. I've got the timetable.' She pushed it towards Tom. 'We need to book into hotels, a cheap bedroom but a good room for the presentation and order up coffee by room service for each buyer and we mustn't try and sell the same stuff to competitors. I think I know those.' She passed round the list she'd written up earlier. 'We need to display the wares and discuss terms, they'll try and hem us in but as long as it's a reasonable margin we can deal with it, but we can't go any longer than thirty days' credit. We must have the cash flow. While Tom's doing that, we can do the same in Newcastle, Durham, and so on . . .'

'Hang on a minute,' Tom interrupted. 'I'm not going, this

is your patch. You have the expertise, the knowledge, you're the right sex for God's sake. Otherwise it's a damned good idea.'

'Not as good as mail order. I'm not going, I've got Sarah. You can use your holiday.' Annie insisted.

They argued long into the night again but Tom wouldn't go despite Annie's best efforts to persuade him. Georgie agreed with Tom, Annie was the one with the knowledge, and after all, for Tom is sell pants and bras personally to women alone in a hotel room wasn't right.

The next morning Annie was on the phone, ringing up buyers, talking her way into appointments, using Mr Isaacs' name as he had said she could – his only proviso that she should leave London, the South East and the West Country alone. That afternoon though, she left the phone and the samples and walked round to Betsy. She drank tea with her, talking of her plans, then took Betsy's stiff swollen hands in hers and asked her if she would mother Sarah and Georgie in her absence.

'They need someone they love, someone who will have a meal ready for them and ears to listen to them.'

'I'd love that, I'd really love it, pet, but what about the sewing? I'd not have time for much.'

Annie spoke carefully, gently. 'Listen, if all this goes well then we'll have made the jump, we can set on a homeworker so don't do anything while I'm away.' She still held Betsy's hands. 'The thing is, Bet, I'll need someone to mother me too, when I get back. I can't cope any more with the dinner, the ironing. I need to be out or in the dining-room for more hours in the day but how can I with Sarah?'

She looked at her stepmother and Betsy nodded, then said, 'Can I come and cook for you, lass? Can I be there for Sarah and for you? I don't like to think of you working when most folks are asleep and I'd like to have another go at looking after you.' She took her hands from Annie and reached for her cup. 'But I feel bad about letting you down with the sewing.'

'Anyone can sew, not many can keep the three of us in order,' Annie said, smiling gently.

A week later Annie took the train to the north to show the bras and pants 'in the hand', not on models. She and Gracie had worked into the night all week, cutting, sewing, checking the garments, listing them for insurance purposes, packing them in reams of tissue paper which Sarah and Davy pinched, wrapped round combs and blew until Annie shouted and their lips were numb. She arrived in Dundee, lugged her skips to the taxi, fell into bed and saw the first of the buyers at ten o'clock the next morning. She called for coffee but the buyer drank tea, then said that the the jute trade was in a bad way, had been since '53 and there wasn't a lot of money around. He couldn't take anything.

The last buyer said her budget was already committed but yes, she'd like coffee and perhaps a cake. At Stirling, Perth and the Lowlands they liked the samples and said they'd take a few 'to help her out', but they'd want extended credit. She refused but offered them another five per cent discount. One refused, the others accepted but when she took the train for Edinburgh she knew that so far their costs had not nearly been covered.

In Edinburgh a central buyer told her she should get her stationery and advice notes and invoices printed up properly. 'Can't expect anyone to take you seriously unless you put on a good front,' the woman said. 'Come round again in the autumn, let's see how you're doing then. May I have your card?' Annie did not have one, had never had one.

The buyer bought nothing, and Annie toured the Madam shops and sold six dozen bra and pant sets. A buyer in Glasgow liked the samples but had committed his budget almost before the tour began. 'Might be an idea to put out a catalogue,' he said as she left.

With what? Annie longed to ask.

She took the train to Liverpool, Manchester, Birmingham, Sheffield, Nottingham and York and sold a total of thirty dozen pants and bras, fifteen dozen aprons and gloves. It would perhaps pay for printed stationery but not for the train fares, the hotel charges or the taxi fares, she thought as she caught the train from Newcastle to Wassingham and wondered how she could tell the others.

Georgie was waiting for her at the station, running towards her, lifting her in his arms, kissing her, then hauling along the skips. She told him the total sales and then, when he seemed not to care, she set those against their expenses, but he just shrugged, heaved the skips into the boot and opened the door for her.

'We need proper stationery, proper advance planning, collapsible boxes for neat presentation, we must dip further into our resources, Georgie, it's not that much to ask.'

He smiled at her, touching he shoulder. 'Come on, we've got to get back, I'm nursing the phone.' He climbed into the driver's seat and started the car. 'I've had a call from a wholesaler, Nigel Manners, who supplies hundreds of small shops. Apparently his wife was in Newby's while I was trying to flog some to the buyer. She liked them, or so he says. I've sent him a sample and he's ringing back tonight at half past eight. Says if the terms are right he'll want thousands, so I've sorted it all out for you, darling, there's no more need for you to worry.'

Annie looked at her watch. It was eight o'clock. She looked ahead and made herself smile because all the months she'd worked, all the miles she'd travelled had been a waste of time – she'd been right in the first place, it was Georgie who should have run the business – and the knowledge churned deep inside her.

CHAPTER 5

There was no call at half past eight but at nine o'clock Nigel Manners rang and ordered eight thousand bra and pant sets as per the sample but with a few modifications.

Georgie mouthed to Annie, 'We're on, we're actually on,' his eyes alight. He turned back to the phone. 'My wife will drive across tomorrow.'

'Sorry, no, never deal with women. You've another director, surely?'

Georgie shook his head at Annie, raised his eyebrows. 'Fine, Tom Ryan will be with you at . . . shall we say eleven?'

Annie lit another cigarette as Georgie wrote down instructions and now she wanted to leap in the air, wave flags from the rooftops. What did it matter who had brought in the deal, the fact was it was here and her husband would soon be out of the pit and working in the firm alongside her and Tom and all regrets were gone. She stubbed out her cigarette, moved nearer to him, held him, kissed his cheek and mouth as he spoke to Mr Manners, feeling his arm coming around her, holding her close, squeezing her until she could hardly breathe, lifting her off the ground in a bear hug when he had finally put down the receiver.

'I love you, Annie, you little belter, and your ruddy knickers – we've done it, we're on our way.' His mouth and body were against hers and she could feel the heat of him through her dress. She had been too many nights away from him, and he from her.

The next day Annie ordered the rotary cutter and some new cloth. They needed more than end rolls for this though she would confirm in a few days, she told the supplier. Tom drove to Newcastle, arriving back at tea-time with a list of specification changes.

'Bloody nit-picker, wants the bra strap moved half an inch, the flowers in blue and the thigh line higher on the pants.' Tom handed her the sheets. 'I'll work on the new designs tonight, put them in the post tomorrow.'

She nodded. 'If you could, Gracie and I have to finish and deliver the regular orders. If he approves the new designs – which he must since they're his ideas – I'll run up samples for him. I've sorted out a printer for cards and stationery. We'll need a professional invoice, don't you think?'

Tom put the kettle on, nodding, turning, leaning on the guard, his face alive with excitement and pleasure. 'It's happening, isn't it, bonny lass? It's happening at last. We've just been talking and hoping for so long and now we're here. Give us one.' He nodded to the cigarettes.

Annie shook he head, tapping the packet. 'No, you've given up.'

'Oh come on,' he said, grabbing for the packet. 'It's a celebration and I need one after that Nigel Manners.'

Annie shook her head again, snatching the packet back, putting it down her cleavage. 'Just try and get them out of there and it'll be clipped ear time. We're celebrating tomorrow anyway, it's Saturday and we're off to the beach.'

Tom turned as the kettle boiled, pouring the water into the pot, bringing it back to the table, pushing aside the invoices Annie had been writing up. 'Brass monkey weather for the beach, isn't it?'

Annie smiled wryly. 'Bracing, the bomb man called it, the one who likes the edge.'

Tom grinned at her. 'He's coming out of the pit though, at last. We haven't heard much about his famous edge recently, have we? I think he's just about realising he's put on a few years since he was sixteen.' Tom held the pot over her cup and she nodded. 'Still, you were sensible to let him do it, Annie, he needed it.'

She reached for the milk, poured it, stirred it, heard the spoon click against the side, watched the spiral, thought of the three men who had been killed on Georgie's shift a month ago, and the countless others who were the walking wounded. 'I had no choice, Tom, you know that, no choice at all.'

The beach had been as cold as Tom had said it would be and now the children huddled in Annie's kitchen, pressing against the guard as their parents sipped hot soup.

'Come on, Rob, don't take all day,' Sarah said, rubbing her feet, brushing away sand. 'You're not the only one with chilblains, I've got some whoppers and Davy's are blinking away at me.'

She watched Rob take his time, stroking in the ointment until she wanted to slap him. 'You're such a little snot,' she said, hugging her knees, feeling her toes throbbing, smelling the salt on her skin, pinching it, making a bum out of her knee.

Rob grinned and threw her over the wintergreen. 'Your turn, and don't be vulgar.'

Sarah passed it to Davy. 'You have it first.'

Davy's chilblain's were belters and she winced as she saw him rub the wintergreen in harder, knowing how they were itching, because hers were too, but bye it had been worth it. She looked over her shoulder at her da. He'd run like the wind to catch her mum, waving seaweed until she screamed and then he'd come for her and she'd run and run as though she'd never stop, until there'd been no breath left, aching with joy and terror as she heard him coming closer and closer.

'That was a good tackle you did on me, Da,' she said to Davy, taking the wintergreen, stroking it on at last.

'Too good,' Georgie called over, 'I'll have a bruise for the next three weeks and just where did you put the seaweed you tried to shove down me neck?' He was laughing as he passed back Tom's new season designs.

'Outside the door, it'll tell the weather for us,' Sarah called back but he wasn't listening now, he was talking to Tom about the business and she was glad he was. She looked at her da's blue ridged hands, his coal-stained skin. Yes, she was glad he was because soon he would be out of the pit and then she'd sleep at night.

She looked at his shoulders, his arms, his legs. Norma's da had been a fast runner too, he'd won the fathers' race. He'd died a month ago in the pit, with his two brothers. Norma sat next to her in class and had forgotten how to laugh.

She rubbed the wintergreen in deeper, digging her nails into the chilblain, wanting pain, not itching. She screwed on the top, tossed it back to Rob.

'You're bigger,' she said, nodding to the shelf.

'Anything more, your worship?' he grunted, stretching, tucking it behind the clock.

'A few jelly babies would be nice,' said Sarah, her mouth rounded into posh, her little finger raised. 'But only the red and green ones, so sort them out first. I like to save the head till last, so cut those off too.'

She ducked as he flicked a paper pellet at her. 'Not nice,' she minced. 'Really, not very nice – common one might say.' They were all giggling now.

Annie smiled as she listened to Sarah.

'Did you hear me, Annie?' Georgie's voice was sharp.

'Sorry, I was miles away.'

'Well, get back here. We're trying to sort out the plans for the year. Now, are we all agreed that we need to send out a letter requesting an appointment and then a follow up phone call? Did you catch that, Annie, d'you agree?'

Annie looked at Georgie, sitting there with his pencil poised, and said gently, 'Of course I caught it, Georgie, I wrote it, remember?'

But he was already on the next point and didn't hear and

as she watched this man's confidence, his eagerness she knew it didn't matter that he'd take her place as chairman – the sharpness in his voice was only excitement, it would pass and soon he'd be safe.

'When's Manners coming back on the amended designs?' Georgie asked Tom.

'Monday,' he said. 'Strange man though, thought not dealing with a woman went out with the ark.'

Annie lit a cigarette, playing with her lighter, wondering where she'd heard that name before, pushing it around her mind as she'd done the first time Nigel Manners had been mentioned.

'Did you hear that, Annie?'

Annie looked at Georgie, 'Sorry, miles away again.'

'Who's going to train up Meg and Irene?' Georgie asked again, and Annie pointed to the notes she had written down for him. 'Brenda and I are, there you are, point six.'

Her voice was gentle and now Georgie looked at her, his face reddening and he touched her cheek. 'I'm sorry, I'm being an idiot, I just feel so impatient, I want it underway.'

She nodded at him, feeling the touch of his finger on her skin, seeing the softness of his eyes. 'I know, we all feel the same.'

They drank beer then and discussed the new designs properly and Gracie said, 'You've done dungarees here, Tom? I thought elastic wouldn't work?'

Annie nodded. 'By the autumn, we'll have premises and enough cash to buy a button holer, but we can hold buying it until we see if there's enough take-up on the design. Brenda said she'd do the button holes on the samples.'

They discussed the extra homeworkers they would need once the orders built up, and they would, once their stock came pouring out into Manners' outlets and their name became known nationally.

They discussed Briggs' warehouse. Bill the estate agent had told Annie they could relax, take their time because there was no interest at all, but soon they must think of planning permission so that they were ready to convert when they centralised the business.

It was then that Tom lifted his glass, looked over the top at them all. 'I reckon that day's not far away so I think there's a toast in order, to Georgie, who brought this whole thing off, and to Wassingham Textiles. We've finally made it.'

Annie drank, sitting back in the chair, looking at the children, the range where Sophie had baked, where she now baked. She ran her hand along the scrubbed wooden table and felt complete.

On Monday Manners required yet more changes but Isaacs had often had the same problem and so Annie and Tom worked late into the night adjusting the designs yet again, interrupted only by a phone call from Don, asking them all to the convent's Open Day in three weeks' time. 'Teresa's playing the piano at two. Perhaps you could be there in good time, Annie. Hats will be required, and gloves.'

'You will, of course, be wearing chiffon?' she asked, then wished she hadn't. 'I'm sorry Don, just a little tired.'

'Yes, I'd heard you'd landed a big one. Tell me more when I see you. Bye.'

Tom looked up as she put the receiver down. 'My what big ears he has,' Annie said. 'And my, how word gets around.'

'What did he want?'

'To tell us to be on parade in three weeks' time for the Convent Open Day.'

'Not bloody likely.'

'Oh come on, Tom, we should go. Terry's playing the piano and he's trying to make amends. They gave us nice presents at Christmas and now this. He wants his family there, in hats and gloves.' She was laughing now but Tom just groaned, then shook his head.

'God in heaven, he's such a pompous idiot. Come on, let's get on with these.'

Annie spent the next week training up Meg and Irene with

73

Brenda who had to be paid a full salary, she explained to Georgie, because she was already doing a job, not just sitting waiting for Manners' go ahead.

'But what's the hold-up?' Georgie said, shovelling down his breakfast, throwing on his coat and stepping out into the cold morning air.

'This is what's called business, my love.'

'Christ, it's worse than waiting for the coal to creak and the roof to come down.'

'Just call it the edge then, Georgie.' She pulled him back, kissed him. 'It will be all right, my darling. He's just fussy, he wants exactly the right thing, we'll have to go with it, it's no problem.'

She watched him leave, then hurried into the dining-room. She still had the regular orders to pack, the first of Tom's samples to make up, the invoices to draw up, Gracie's work to check, her own to complete and still a ruddy hat to buy.

In the middle of March Manners finally approved the samples and increased his order to sixteen thousand. It would take up all their capital, plus a loan to increase the order with the supplier, Annie told Georgie, who nodded. 'Just have to. I'll fix it.'

Annie alerted the suppliers, the homeworkers, Brenda.

'We'll be starting any moment,' she said. 'Just waiting delivery of the machines, the cloth and the trimmings.'

But Tom phoned from his pit office at eleven a.m. as she was sewing the last of the aprons for Gosforn Market.

'Annie, he wants exclusive use of the designs. He's just called. What the hell do we do?'

Annie said nothing, just held the phone. Exclusive use? Exclusive use, for God's sake. 'How dare he,' she finally said. 'How bloody dare he? He's messed us around and now this. Tom, we've used those designs for all the new market stock, the Madam shops, but put on different trim. He said that was fine. What's he playing at? Go back to him. Tell him they're out on the stalls but with different trim, just as he agreed. Just tell him.' She was shouting.

She hung up, leaning her head on the banister, then paced the hall, running her fingers along the wallpaper, twisting the door knob, dusting the mirror with her handkerchief, running her fingers through her hair. This was outrageous, dangerous, they mustn't agree. She pounced on the phone when it rang. 'Manners says the copies are to be off the stalls by tomorrow at the latest or the order's off,' Tom said.

Annie breathed deeply, who the hell did Manners think he was? The man was nothing more than a bully and she'd had enough of them to last a lifetime. Good God, it meant ruining their existing markets, it made the business too vulnerable, there'd be no fall-back if anything went wrong. And these traders were her friends, they were loyal, they'd been with her from the start.

Her knuckles were white on the phone, her arm was trembling, her head was aching. What the hell was going on? Did he really expect them to go along with this?

'No Tom, you'll have to tell him no. If I pull back the traders' stock it leaves them with nothing. We're their sole suppliers. We can't do that to them. Just tell him no. Call his bluff, we can't just be restricted to him, it's bad business, it's dangerous – we're out on a limb with debts to pay.' Her hands were shaking, her legs too. He'd gone too far.

There was a silence. 'I'll tell him we'll ring him back tonight, let's think about it – it's the big one, Annie. I know, see how many you can run up of the old stuff for the stalls.' Tom's voice was taut. 'I'll say I can't get a decision, catch Georgie as he comes off shift, discuss it with him. He'll know what to do, we don't want to blow it.'

There was a click as he put the phone down and Annie held the empty receiver. I know what to do, her mind shouted. I know what to do too – we wait until the new tour, do it sensibly. It was all she could think as she sewed up the oven gloves, one after another until her fingers were sore. Then she dragged out all the boxes she could find and counted through the stock. There was very little left. She checked through next season's designs, perhaps she could bring those forward but she'd never get enough done in time for tomorrow's delivery and the traders hadn't approved them anyway.

She threw the sketches across the table. Why the hell should the stall holders suffer because of that man?

She stoked up the range, dragged on an apron, mixed flour and margarine, slammed the oven door, not caring that there was flour on the floor, waiting, because she knew that Georgie and Tom would come.

She watched them open the door, stand and look at her. 'We've rung Manners and agreed,' Georgie said.

She checked the scones, took them out, tipped them on to the rack. She had known they would, but they were wrong, they were being panicked, they hadn't thought it through, not properly, couldn't they see that? She washed the baking tray, trying to contain her anger as she spoke. 'If we agree to Manners we'll be putting all our eggs in one basket. We did it with Sarah's money, we'll be doing it again. We must just wait for the new tour.' Her voice was quite calm, quite quiet.

Georgie dragged out a chair, threw his lunch-box on the table, slumped into the chair. 'It's not the same thing at all, Annie, that was a stupid mistake, this is business. It's a good order, you can see that – you're the one who's been going on about it, pet. About needing it now and we might net nothing from the tour. At least we know we've got this.'

Annie rolled the words around in her mind. Stupid mistake, yes it had been, and hers too, but this would be as much of a mistake and she couldn't let it happen. Tom leant back against the draining board, looking at the clock.

'How did you get off work?' she asked, drying the tray, putting it way. She sat down again and tested the hot scones with the tip of her finger.

'They can dock me pay, this is important.' His face was drawn, his eyes anxious.

A headache was beginning to pound down one side of her head and neck. Georgie was pushing his bait tin round and round.

'Look both of you,' Annie said, still calm, still quiet. 'I've taken months to build up the traders. They've always been loyal, always paid, we're their sole suppliers. If we withdraw their stock they'll have nothing to sell, they could go broke, our name'll go down the Swanee. Manners will have us in the palm of his hand. If something goes wrong we're finished, we'll have nowhere to go, we'll have ditched everyone else. We must say no – we must wait. I don't want to any more than you but it's just too dangerous.' She turned the scones over, there was flour on her fingers and the smell of baking filled the kitchen.

Georgie rubbed his hand over his eyes, his movements quick, irritable. 'Don't be daft, Annie, what could go wrong? We'll have a contract for God's sake, we'll be covered.'

'Isaacs had a contract too. They rejected the order, said it was of insufficient quality.'

'Ours won't be,' Tom chipped in.

' "Said" being the operative word. There was nothing wrong with the stock, it's all just part of the game.'

'It's not like you not to gamble, not to go for the big one. It won't happen anyway, I've checked him out, he's bona fide,' Georgie said, his voice louder now. Annie swung round on him.

'It's more than a gamble, it's letting down the small men, it's exposing us and we can't do it. Manners can just go and bully some other idiots. Anyway, he's probably bluffing.'

Georgie pushed the tin round, faster and faster. 'Manners doesn't bully, and he doesn't bully idiots, or am I one, is that what you're trying to say?'

Annie flushed, shaking her head, wanting to pound the table. 'Of course I'm not, I'm just – '

'We need this,' Georgie broke in, his voice cold. 'We hooked in – I hooked in. So I'm saying we're going for it, we've got to.' His jaw was set, his eyes narrowed. 'I'm telling you, Annie, we're going for it, it's too important to bugger up. We'll just have to risk losing the traders, it won't matter when we're in the shops, we won't need them. It's not dangerous, it's foolproof, we'll have a contract. The stall holders are businessmen, they'll understand. Who did they dump to take you on? What d'you think, Tom?'

Tom was looking from one to the other. 'I don't know that I like the idea of the traders copping it. Annie's got a point, Georgie.'

He was looking at Annie now.

She felt the scones again. There were currants in six of them, which would Sarah prefer? But the anger was boiling up.

'As a matter of fact, Georgie, they didn't dump anyone to take us on, the old man died and we won the orders on merit, on my workmanship.'

'How's the old stock?' Tom broke in. 'Can we take that out to replace the exclusives so we don't let them down?'

Annie shook her head, waiting until she was calmer. 'I've thought of that but there's not nearly enough though there are the new season's designs. I was just wondering if we could pick one, make those up, take them out cold, no samples, do a straight exchange but I'd need to set the homeworkers on. We'd need to pay them over the odds to work round the clock so I could get them to the stalls before Manners' deadline.'

Georgie nodded, easing his back. 'Fine, get some of those out but we can't afford homeworkers, we're already down for enough of a loan, we can't afford to extend it. If you get a few out to them it'll be enough. If they're loyal like you say they'll wear it. We'll get some more to them by the end of the week. If they make a fuss, kiss them goodbye, they're not worth the hassle.'

Annie stood up, banging the table, shouting at her husband. 'But why the hell should they *wear* it? Manners is being totally unreasonable, the whole thing stinks, and it's we who will be damaged too, not just the traders. What's the matter with you, Georgie. Look, I'm telling you, watch my lips – without them we're just too vulnerable, we'll not just lose today's order but future ones. We need to supply them properly, we need to put money out or maybe you're going to sit up throughout the night sewing?' She gripped his arm.

Georgie shook free and now he was shouting too, his lips drawn tight. 'No, I'm not because I'll be down the bloody pit earning the money that's kept this afloat until someone like Manners came along and I'd like to remind you that I was the one who went out and got that, without a load of money being wasted on trains, taxis and bloody coffees. So no, I won't be sewing, I'll be down there with that bloody cutter screeching and the conveyor clattering until I can't speak, let alone think, that's where I'll be.'

He slammed back into his chair and there was silence until Annie said, 'I'll ring the traders at home tonight, explain, promise delivery of the new season's stock by the end of tomorrow, or at least enough to keep them going.' Because what else could she say? She knew from his face that the edge had finally gone, that it was the thought of more time in the pit that was pushing him and it should be pushing her – what the hell was she thinking of? This man had had enough.

She and Gracie worked throughout the night even though Annie thought her head would explode with pain and in the morning she set on Brenda, telling Georgie she would hock the walnut table to pay for her if necessary and so he said nothing.

In the afternoon she drove round, collecting back the Manners exclusives, restocking as far as she could, but there were not enough, not nearly enough and that evening she told Tom and Georgie that they were no longer the sole suppliers of most of the traders, in fact they had been dropped by half of them. She kept her voice neutral and didn't tell them of the comments that had been made to her, the disgust which had been voiced, because she agreed with every word. That night she didn't sleep and there was space in the bed between them because she couldn't bear the thought of him touching her. In the morning the rage was still there and she wanted to shake him for putting them in this position, for going down the pit in the first place.

Tom phoned to say that Manners wanted to change the delivery date from 1st July to 1st June and Annie clenched the receiver and said that she'd only begin work when she had a contract, until then nothing was going to happen. 'Nothing, do you hear?' she shouted.

On Wednesday the written order arrived and it was only now that Annie asked for delivery of the machines and the cloth and their terraced house shook as the lorries pulled up at Wassingham Textiles and off loaded. She called to the neighbours. 'Sorry about the noise.'

'That's all right, Annie, d'you need a hand, lass?' Mrs Warren called from across the street.

'If I do, you'll be the first I call on, Pat, bless you.'

The children took the machines round on their carts after school and Annie set up the rotary cutter in the dining-room. She cut out all evening and delivered to Brenda, Meg and Irene before breakfast. If they had to supply this man, then they'd do it perfectly.

She cut out and sewed the stock for the remaining market traders and the small shops throughout the day, and so did Gracie and they checked them as carefully as Manners' stock because they also deserved perfection.

She sewed for her own stall.

'But you won't be going in now,' Georgie said on Thursday evening. 'There's no need.'

'There's every need,' she replied.

'That's crazy,' he said, pulling off his boots, warming himself by the range.

'I need to be seen there, I need to recover the situation as much as I can.'

'It's not necessary any more, you'll get too tired. You won't be able to do the job you need to do.'

'We're all too tired and we're all doing the jobs we need to do, you more than anyone.' Annie left him in the kitchen, not wanting to discuss the markets, not wanting to think of the hours he was down there, for her. But for himself too, God damn it.

She sat at the sewing machine, working, her head bent low, nodding as Sarah and Davy brought in the completes from Brenda and Meg.

'Rob's gone for Irene's,' Sarah said and Annie nodded.

'There're some scones in the tin – and thank you, you've been wonderful.'

'Shall we sew some roses on, Mam? You look so tired.' Sarah's hand was on her shoulder and for a moment Annie leant her head against her daughter's and felt warm arms round her neck.

'You've done enough, my love, now go and have a scone.'

'Dad can sew them then, I'll send him in,' Sarah was following Davy from the room.

'No, your da's tired, I'll do it. He can pop you into bed through and I'll come up later.'

She watched as they shut the door. No, she didn't want Georgie in with her. She stretched her arms, rolled her shoulders, eased her neck then sorted through Brenda's, they were almost perfect, just seven rejects. She'd re-do them later. But Meg's smelt of cigarettes and there were ash marks on twenty-four of them. Dear God, as though things weren't difficult enough.

Annie threw her coat on, walked through the kitchen smiling at them, closing the door gently behind her.

Georgie took the scone that Sarah offered him, breathing in the scent that Annie had left behind, knowing that her anger would leave her when Manners paid up, knowing that they could hook back the traders when they had more time. He'd just go and talk to them as he'd talked to Manners – it'd be easy and then she'd see that all they'd been doing was prioritise. She just hadn't grasped how to kick-start a business. He tasted the scone and pulled a face – he didn't like currants.

Annie walked round to Sindon Terrace, walked past the

pigeons cooing in the loft. Frank had said that Geoff kept pigeons but they never won races, they were overfed.

Meg opened the door, her face surprised. 'It's nine o'clock, Annie, I'm just making Geoff's supper.'

Annie nodded. 'Yes, I'm sorry but, Meg, I've a bit of a problem. You see, I can't have you smoking when you're sewing. It's a fire hazard and when we move into the new premises it will be forbidden. But it's not just that, it makes the clothes smell and there are ash marks on two dozen of them.'

She was speaking quietly, not wanting the neighbours to hear, feeling her embarrassment making her blunt. 'I'm sorry, it's my fault, I should have told you, you weren't to know.'

Meg's face flushed. 'Keeps me weight down you see, smoking does. But I won't, not while I'm sewing.'

The next night there were no ash marks but there was still the smell of smoke and Annie had to walk to Sindon Terrace again. This time Meg told her that she hadn't smoked at all, though her husband had, and he wouldn't stop. Annie nodded, pressed the woman's arm, said, 'Not to worry, I'll just air them then.' There were tears in Meg's eyes.

She called in on Tom. 'Why did you suggest Meg?'

'Because her old man's a bugger. She needs the money, the sense of doing something for herself but if there's a problem we'll drop her, this is too important.'

Annie shook her head. 'There's been too much dropping and no, there's no problem, this is why we started this business, remember? I think she'll do very nicely, Tom.'

Each evening she aired Meg's garments and told Georgie that it was common practice to hang things up when they'd just come in.

The next morning she called in at the estate agents as Georgie had asked, checking that the rent was the same. Then she called in at the planning office on her way to the stalls, checking on their requirements, noting them down, referring them to Tom so that plans could be drawn up and presented as soon as possible. Once they were in premises there would be so much less rushing around and besides Meg could work in peace.

She worked eighteen hours a day, and so did Gracie. Tom redesigned the autumn collection and Annie ran up samples. The stationery was ordered, collapsible cardboard boxes for the presentations were costed. She checked and rechecked the homeworkers' garments and had to have one of the sewing machines repaired which held them up, but by the day of the Convent Open Day they were still on schedule with six weeks to go. At the eleventh hour she realised that she had forgotten to buy a hat and asked Pat Warren if she could borrow hers. It was pink, with flowers, and Sarah laughed.

'Well, I think you look lovely, Auntie Annie,' Davy said, 'Like a spring garden.'

'You're a smooth talker, Davy Ryan, just like your dad.' Annie smiled as Davy flushed. 'You are, you know, just like your dad.' She made a note to speak to Tom about Davy, he must include him more, Rob took too much of his time.

They were driving up and out of Wassingham, Sarah and Davy in the back, Tom, Gracie, and Rob following. Betsy wouldn't come, she had too much cooking and washing and ironing to do, she had said, but give the lass my love, and Don and Maud of course.

'Bet just didn't want to come,' she said quietly to Georgie.

'Did any of us?' he replied and Annie didn't answer, just felt the tension coil around them. She watched the country-side as they travelled the road she felt she could now navigate blindfold.

They arrived in good time and as Georgie drove in through the school gates Annie looked at the sloping gardens she had not seen since she had left the school so long ago. The rhododendrons were still there.

'They grow wild in the foothills of the Himalayas,' she said over her shoulder to the children. 'Your dad's seen them, haven't you, Georgie?'

He nodded, smiling now. 'Saw them but missed your mam

too much to notice them.' Annie sat silently, watching his hands on the wheel.

'Will this do?' He swung the car into the car park and they all walked across the gravel to the front of the school where the yew hedges were still set in squares. 'I love you, I'm sorry I shouted, I can't bear it when you're angry.' He took her hand.

They stood close together seeing the spring flower beds within the hedges and Annie remembered her sense of loss when she had begun here, her sense of only being half a person because Georgie was not here. She looked at his face, the pit's deep lines, the love in his eyes, the weariness, and knew that nothing could really hurt their love, nothing. They were together, that's all that mattered. 'I love you too,' she said.

They strolled amongst the other parents, their hands tightly gripped, his thumb playing on her skin and she knew that he felt the same, that he always would, and now her smile came from deep within her.

They walked down the paths, and she showed them the runner beans the nuns had always grown, the cloakrooms where she had had her peg, the chapel which was still painted white with brown beams.

'There was a lot of spectacles, testicles, collar and cuffs, was there?' Sarah asked.

Georgie and Annie just stood and stared. 'What did you say?' Annie managed to say eventually.

'Norma told me they did a lot of that at convents, you know, made the sign of the cross. That's how they remember, she said.' Sarah was looking at the lectern. Tom and Georgie were grinning, Gracie and Annie caught at Sarah's coat and hurried the children out, hoping that no one had been close enough to hear.

'Oh no, there they are,' Sarah groaned in front of her and Annie poked her with her finger.

'Smile,' she hissed, walking towards her brother, kissing

Don, clashing hats with Maud, asking Terry when she was playing.

'Time for a quick look round then,' she said, looking at Don and he smiled, his starched white shirt digging into his neck.

'Are you going to show us then, Terry?'

'Teresa,' said Maud.

'Or course,' Annie murmured not looking at Sarah, Davy, or any of the others.

They toured the hall where there had always been chrysanthemums in the late summer. That had been the smell she had remembered when the Japanese had come to the cathedral in Singapore to herd them to the camps. Annie shook her head free of the memory.

Terry led the way to the cloakroom again and Annie shook her head at Sarah. 'Be quiet,' she mouthed. 'Just look interested, again.' They passed the form rooms this time and Annie peered through the glass. Was 'Sandy loves Sister Nicole' still carved on the desk? Where was Sandy?

'Is the conservatory still cold?' she asked Teresa. 'Detentions were such a misery there.'

'Teresa has never had a detention,' Maud said, her heels clipping on the wooden floor.

'Of course,' Annie replied.

There was tea set up in the hall and Annie sat at one of the tables, gesturing to the other chairs. 'Time for a cuppa.'

Maud glanced around quickly.

'Sorry, time for a cup of tea I think,' Annie said, drawing out her cigarettes.

'It's no smoking in here, Annie,' Don said.

'Of course it is,' Annie replied, trying not to smile, looking across at the children, ignoring the grins of Tom and Georgie, suggesting to Teresa that she took her cousins to see the gym, and perhaps the music room.

'Miss Harding used to poke my hands with a pencil when I made a wrong note. She was a dreadful old witch.'

85

'I won the Miss Harding Prize, this year, that's why I'm playing.' Teresa's mouth was as prim as Maud's and Don's.

'Of course you did,' Annie said faintly. 'Well done, Teresa.'

'We're not going to learn the piano,' Sarah said, frowning at Annie who saw she had no intention of being shown anything by Teresa, who equally, had no intention of being the guide. 'We're going to play skiffle, aren't we, Davy, then we're getting guitars.'

Annie turned and looked at them, then at Georgie. 'Well, we learn something new every day, don't we? I thought the old washboard had disappeared.' She raised her eyebrows and accepted the tea that the senior girls brought round. Georgie caught her eye and grimaced, he'd have killed for a beer, and she was so glad they'd come to Gosforn and left the anger behind.

They sat in the hall for the performance, it still smelt of chalk and polish and while Teresa played Annie thought of the languid days, Georgie's first letters from the Army and she touched his hand, felt him hold hers, lift it to his lips and it didn't matter that Maud tutted, that Don frowned.

Teresa was very good and only stumbled once and Annie felt for the child as Don's lips tightened and he tapped his programme on his lap. She clapped all the harder because of this, and congratulated Don and Maud on Teresa's playing. 'It's so clever to be able to recover, says a great deal for her skill.' She was having to shout over the noise of scraping chairs as people rose and filtered out of the building. Georgie took her arm as they followed, calling to Don who led the way. 'Really must go, we've got a lot to do but it's been a great afternoon, Don.' She squeezed his arm because he was trying to be pleasant and she knew it was for her sake.

Don walked on, keeping up with the flow but stopping on the drive in front of the school, brushing at dust on his sleeve, smiling at them as he shook Georgie's hand. 'By the way, how's it going?' he asked. 'I heard about the Manners order on the grapevine, this is the breakthrough for you, isn't it, it'll give you the credibility you need – word gets round quickly, whether it's good or bad.'

Annie nodded, watching Sarah and Davy walking up to Teresa, pleased to see them smiling, knowing that Sarah had seen Don's irritation at his daughter's mistake.

She heard Georgie's voice harden as he said, 'Not likely to be bad at this stage so yes, it's what we've been needing. It'll set us up and we're already drawing up plans for Briggs' place.'

His shoulders were tense again but then Don said, 'I've heard that Manners is straight, shouldn't have any trouble. I should go for it.'

She felt Georgie relax, felt herself relax too at those words. Please God, let it be true. Don took out a cigar. 'Mm, taken out the lease have you?' He was rolling it under his nose.

'No smoking, dear,' Maud said and Annie was glad that she'd bitten back the very same words.

'Good luck to you both anyway. Thanks for coming. Hope it goes well – business is a tricky game.'

He was putting the cigar back into his pocket, shaking their hands, kissing Annie and she hugged him because it was the first time her brother had done that for more years than she cared to remember.

They worked day and night until the end of May but there were no more headaches because Georgie held her when she did finally fall into bed and touched her when she passed him. He sewed on the roses sitting next to her, and kissed her when the final set of underwear was completed, then handed them to Sarah and Davy to box.

'Brilliant, wonderful, you've been so good,' Annie told the children and Sarah said, 'Now he'll come out of the pit, won't he?'

'Yes, he'll come out, my love.'

'That's all that matters then.'

This time they didn't go to the beach, they bought

champagne and drank it in Bet's kitchen with the homeworkers and Brenda while the kids played their washboards in the yard and sang *Hound Dog* though Georgie called for *Mona Lisa*, or *Red Sails in the Sunset*.

'You're so square,' Sarah groaned. 'And we really need guitars for rock, not washboards.'

Annie looked at Tom. 'Maybe when the cheque comes in?'

He grinned. 'Maybe, after all, they could end up making us a fortune.'

They drank a toast to Manners and Annie downed hers in one because even Don had vouched for Manners and both he and Georgie could not be wrong.

During the next week they continued to provide stock for the stalls but there was no longer the need to work into the small hours and Annie put Brenda, Meg and Irene back on to the retainer but there were no complaints because they all knew it was temporary.

They submitted the plans to the planning office and Annie went over their figures and offered discounts to all traders to try to make amends and draw back those who had left them. But it was too late, they would not reconsider, and they were no more friendly than they had been last time.

Georgie shrugged. 'Who cares,' he said but Annie cared very much, and worried about it, but she wouldn't allow it to come between them again.

She looked at second-hand guitars but they seemed so large and she decided that there would be time enough for guitars when the children were older. But a gramophone at Christmas would soften the blow and maybe the adults' ears.

In the second week she hoovered the house free of threads, wielded the rotary cutter and sewed in the afternoon, helping Betsy with the supper, helping Sarah write up her project comparing the yearly pattern of an oak and a horse chestnut.

She slept eight hours again that night as she had done for the last ten days. 'I'd forgotten what it was like to be lazy,' she murmured to Georgie who was on late shift and could sleep in for much longer.

She packed Sarah's lunch, and checked her project, her collar and her nails. 'Good, sparkling clean, though I'm surprised you've any left after all that washboard work.'

'If I had a guitar I wouldn't have to suffer like this.' Sarah put her hand to her forehead.

'Out,' laughed Annie. 'Wait and see what Father Christmas pops into your little stocking, and no, it won't be Elvis Presley, so you can wipe that smile off your face.'

Sarah slung her satchel over her shoulder. 'Don't want Elvis, only his guitar.'

'Out.'

She washed the dishes, wiped the floor, heard the post. Picked up the letter. It had a Newcastle postmark and was addressed to Wassingham Textiles. She opened it. It was from Mr Manners telling them that their goods were of inadequate quality, that they had therefore defaulted on the contract and he would be returning the whole order later today. There would be no payment of course.

CHAPTER 6

Georgie passed the canteen walking in the midst of the other men, though not with them, Jesus, not with them. He took his lamp, handed in his tag. He stood still for frisking. No cigarettes, no matches – no bloody nothing – not any more. He'd lost them the lot. It was his order, he was the big I am who'd thought he'd cracked it for them all, thought he'd pushed them up when all he'd done was shove them down.

'Get on with it, man,' Frank said, pushing him forward into the cage. 'Left your brains back home, have you?'

Georgie nodded. 'Something like that,' but his throat hurt to speak, it felt swollen with rage, with anger, with hopelessness. The gates crashed into place, the surface disappeared, the cage dropped, dropped, thumped and they were out on to the paddy train.

'We're down the old workings today, setting the props.' Frank was squashed against him and Georgie wanted to break free, to smash his fist into the brickwork they were churning past. It was he who had pushed his way into the chair, taken over the meetings, insisted on the exclusives. God, if only he'd listened.

They walked inbye, crouching down, beneath the roof, the bloody creaking roof which could come down at any minute, which had come down on Wassingham Textiles. They stripped, ducked under the roadhead, their lights playing against the side, their faces in darkness, thank God, because he could feel the tears on his cheeks, dropping down on to his chest. She'd just held the letter out to him – 'it's part of the game' she'd said. 'Just part of the game. We'll get back on our feet,' and she'd smiled, held him. 'He's a bugger, we nearly made it, we very nearly made it, we couldn't have known, just think of that, nothing else.'

Georgie crouched lower, lifting his feet above the dust, feeling for uneven surfaces. There were broken props here, the roof had been working overnight.

'The old cow's splintered the buggers,' Frank said stopping, his lamp playing on the weakened props. 'There's another.'

Georgie turned away, wiped his face. No, she was wrong, she had feared it, had wanted to wait, had wanted to keep the markets but he'd pushed them – for Christ's sake he'd pushed them because he'd given her no choice, he'd shown her how he felt about this hot, dirty great hole which *he* had insisted he worked in. They'd never get back now, their name was gone – how long would he be down here now? A lifetime is what he bloody well deserved.

'Don't just stand there, man, let's get on with it.' Frank was heaving at the prop which had been left by the early shift. Georgie nodded. Yes, let's get on with it, there was nothing else to do.

He measured a prop, sawed it, erected it, tightening it into place, hammering it into position, feeling the judder up his arm, glad of it. He hit harder – harder – harder, feeling the coal dust falling on his face, in his mouth. Again and again . . .

'For Christ's sake, man.' Frank grabbed his arm. 'D'you want to bring the old sow down?' Frank's face was coal black, streaked with sweat, angry. Georgie dropped the hammer, heard it clang, coughing now, his mouth claggy with dust, his eyes sore, sweat and grime filled.

'You do the bloody thing then,' he snarled, snatching his arm away, wanting to smash his fist into the face of this pigeon man who held him, wanting to kick and pound the prop into nothingness.

Frank stood silently, watching him, then reached down for

91

the hammer, handing it back. 'For Christ's sake, Georgie, leave your rows with the missus at home and remember you're in a bloody pit. It's not just yourself you'll kill, it's your marrers.' Frank turned his back, tightened in his own prop, stopping, listening to the roof, watching for the fall of dust, and Georgie felt the hammer cold in his hand, felt the sweat running down his forehead, his chest, back, legs and arms.

He swung the hammer again, more carefully now, tightening the prop into place, hammering in a wedge of wood at the top, making sure it was straight, making sure that the pressure came down true and he felt the heat not just of the mine, but of his shame because he was part of a team, or at least while he was down here. Up there . . . but what was the point of thinking about up there any more?

They propped until all was secure, then drank in deep gulps of cold tea because the heat and the dust were thick. Frank went under the head with his pick, turning back what he'd loosened, cursing, swearing, toiling while Georgie shovelled the coal into tubs because there was no conveyor at this old, small face. And for once he longed for the noise of the conveyor's rumbling, or the harshness of the cutter because they filled his mind and his body, killing thought and feeling. 'Down the bloody drain,' he murmured, 'Down the bloody drain.' But he mustn't think of it, not now, not down here. Annie had said that. 'Don't think of it, we'll sort it out. Concentrate, Georgie, no need to worry, just concentrate.'

She hadn't wanted to show him the letter until the end of the shift, but he'd seen her face when he came down, and before that he'd heard Tom's voice, but by the time he reached the kitchen Annie was alone with the door open and a draught blowing at the ashes on the hearth. Her eyes had been guarded, her kiss intense, her hug too tight, her laugh too loud as she called him a lazy toad who probably wanted a three-course breakfast now.

Frank was easing out from beneath the head. 'Your turn now, let's see what you've remembered.' He was panting, his elbow had been rubbed raw, his side grazed. Georgie was glad to be handed the pick, glad to crawl beneath the coal, to lie on his side, dig the pick in, heave it out again, burrowing into the seam, panting in the heat, feeling his breath sore in his throat through thirst, not tears, straining his back, grazing his side because it kept him from thinking of her face smiling, her arms comforting him, her eyes shadowed and desperate, but not as desperate as his.

It kept him from thinking of her voice telling him it wasn't as bad as it looked, they could start again, work on the traders, repair the damage, go further afield where their name wasn't damaged – her voice telling him to concentrate, for God's sake concentrate. Calling him back as he crossed the yard, begging him not to go in, stay at home, get over the shock.

They stopped for snap but he couldn't eat. He sat back on his haunches and listened to Frank, hearing his words but thinking only of the future, which was this, nothing else. Christ, oh Christ. He thought of her eyes, her smile. What if she couldn't cope, what if she broke down again? Why hadn't he listened to her?

They moved on after snap.

'Roof's bad down at number six,' said Frank.

'No, it's fine now,' called a passing deputy.

It wasn't fine, the floor was dirty which meant the roof was a bugger. They crouched lower ducking under the jagged outcrops, by-passing the props bent out like crooked elbows.

'Jesus, that'd twist out soon as look,' Frank swore. 'Careful there, Georgie.'

Georgie didn't reply, just nodded; looking, feeling, listening, just as Frank was doing, then calling out. 'There's a bad one to your left, Frank.'

It was six feet to the face conveyor but the roof was so low they had to squeeze between the motors of the two conveyors.

'Timber up, the man said, so timber up it'll be but we've drawn the short straw today, Georgie.'

Georgie nodded. He knew that already. His lamp played

on the props in the new track, all pushed out of the vertical by fifteen degrees, even the new ones. They eased along the track under four yards of unsupported roof.

'Four broken.'

'I can see that,' Georgie snapped, then shook his head. 'Sorry man, bad day.'

Frank just nodded. 'I'd never have known it, but never mind, we all have 'em. Sometimes me birds don't win, sometimes the squeakers die – yes, we all have 'em.'

Georgie laughed. God, if only it was a question of a couple of bloody squeakers and he felt fury rise again at Manners, at Frank, at everyone, but most of all himself – then shook his head. Concentrate, the lass had said. Concentrate – and don't blame yourself. It's no one's fault, only Manners.

There were two middle sets broken too and they sawed, hammered, wedged, tightened. Georgie dug down to the solid floor to stand in the last prop, putting it side by side with the old broken one. He had to use his hands because there was no room between the props and the conveyor; he cut the prop with the tadge, set it, listening, always listening for the roof, watching for dust trickles, concentrating, always concentrating like the lady had said.

'Got to move on down to the undercut,' Frank grunted. 'Bloody long shift this is, with all this bitty work.'

Georgie nodded. He didn't want to go up now, he wanted to stay here, wedge, tighten, listen, look, hide because he didn't know what to do any more up in the open air, in the world of high finance he'd thought he'd conquered.

They cleared the gum beneath the undercut, shovelled it on to the conveyors and the noise was kind to him, filled his head, made it ache. His hands were kind to him because they were cut and sore. They worked in the heat and the dust and the noise, stopping, drinking warm water, wiping sweat from their eyes, easing their backs, stretching their arms. Frank looked across at him and grinned, his teeth white in his black face. Georgie realised that the anger was oozing out of him along with the sweat and he smiled now

94

when Frank joked, nodded as he panted and talked of his squeaker.

It wouldn't be so bad Georgie thought, spending years down here. It wouldn't really be so bad, especially working with Frank, and he could go on the training schemes, work his way up. They could pay back the debts, they could supply distant traders, he could apologise to the local ones. Yes, perhaps after all, they could manage.

Just before the end of the shift was called they picked up their bait tins and started to walk to the paddy train, then stopped, they had no clothes. They were still in a pile down by the old face and they laughed as they trudged back down the jagged roofed roadway, crouching, wheezing, grinning in the light of their lamps, slapping one another's arms as they finally dressed, then eased their way back for the tadge which they had also forgotten.

'Let's take the tub road, catch up with the paddy train further on,' Georgie said, the laughter still in him, and hope too, because he still had his body hadn't he, he was still a pitman wasn't he – one who could read this old sow like a book.

They stepped over the tub rails, walking close into the walls, passing the manholes, easing back into one as a run of tubs trundled by, feeling the wind and Georgie remembered when he'd been a lad and they'd had a runner and he'd thrown himself hard back into the recess, almost cowering and had been ashamed until his father had told him that anyone who didn't do that was a bloody idiot. 'Bits of coal are a damn sight easier to pick up than bits of Georgie Armstrong.'

They were scrunching down an incline now, Frank ahead, his head down, his shoulders rounded. They were tired, and Georgie thought of the shower he would have and longed instead for a bath in front of the fire with Annie scrubbing his back. He would hold her when he clumped home, he would tell her how sorry he was, how he wished he'd listened. He didn't mind the pit any more, now that he knew it was for good, now that he'd stopped playing games with 'the edge', with the business.

He thought of the letter, felt the anger again, deep inside, churning, twisting, and he didn't hear the tubs behind him, way behind him, thundering and clanging, but suddenly he felt the ground, looked up, heard Frank yelling, 'Runner! runner!' There was nothing but darkness ahead though, he'd lagged too far behind Frank. Where was the bloody manhole? Georgie ran, stumbling, dropping the tadge, dropping his bait-bag, looking for the manhole.

The tubs were closer, louder, his lamp beam was jogging up and down, seeking safety, trying to hear Frank's voice above the noise, sucking all thought from his head except the need to hide because there was a bend in the track, he knew there was. How close was it? The tubs would come off – they'd come off over him.

He was running, running but they were close, so close and then there was the manhole, Frank was standing there, his light guiding him. He'd make it, thank God he'd make it.

But the leading tub leapt the track, the others smashed and spilled and there was only dust and debris and silence and Georgie thought that at last a bomb had got him, at last he'd been clumsy, that the CO would curse, Annie would cry and he wouldn't be able to tell her that there was no pain, just a growing lapping darkness.

Annie knelt on the floor, checking through the returned underwear box by box, the tissue paper piling high around her, but there were no faults and the workmanship was excellent as she had known it would be. She also knew that there was nothing that could be done. She sat back on her heels, then leaned forward, smoothing out the tissue paper, flattening it. It could be used again. She laid piece after piece on the pile, flattening, smoothing, not thinking, just for a moment.

She heard Tom enter the kitchen, heard him come through to the hall, heard the heaviness of his tread and called out

96

quietly, 'Don't worry, lad, I'll think of something. We'll sort it out, but not today. Today, when Georgie and Sarah come in let's all go to the sea, blow the cobwebs off, paddle, let the kids drop seaweed down our backs. We'll leave the thinking until tomorrow – what d'you say?'

She turned. He stood so still, so white and there was no need for him to speak – she knew. The moment she saw him she knew.

There were no words either as he drove to the hospital, just agony at the slowness of the car, the length of the journey, the thought of the tubs, the coal, on top of Georgie, on top of the man she loved more than life itself.

She picked at the threads on her skirt, rolling them into balls, dropping them on the floor. Clenching her hands into fists, gritting her teeth, urging the car faster, faster. 'They don't know,' Tom had said. 'They don't know if he'll live.'

How could he live after tubs and coal had fallen on him? How could he live with that filth deep in his cuts? How could he live? But he must. He had to. How could he not? What did they know with all that dirt? They couldn't know.

'Gracie will bring Sarah, won't she?' Annie said, turning to Tom. 'He'll want to see her, he'll want to talk to her.'

Because of course he would live. He had to live. He'd have just caught a bit of the coal. Yes, that was it. He'd just have caught a bit.

'Course she'll bring her straight away. The coach was due back at three.'

Annie nodded. 'She'll have had a good day. She likes school trips. She can tell him about it. Take him when he's out.'

She felt Tom's hand on her knee and gripped it, the tears coming in great gulping sobs. 'We've come so far, Tom, through so much, he doesn't deserve this. He'll be all right, won't he? He's got to be all right, it's only fair that he's all right.'

Tom held her hand, nodding, but how could anyone be all right after they'd taken the full force of smashed runners

97

for God's sake and who said there was anything fair about this bitch of a life?

Gulls were wheeling over the hospital, the light was brighter as it always was by the sea. Yes, they'd go to the sea, but not today, they'd go when he was better, when his cuts were stitched, his bruises gone. Yes, that's when they'd go. They passed the statue of Queen Victoria looking down her nose at the lobelia – they'd laugh about it, she and Georgie.

Tom stopped the car and they ran now, shoving at the doors, leaving them to slam closed, rushing through into Emergency. A nurse directed them down a corridor, towards a bench. 'Sit down, someone will be with you, I'll bring you a cup of tea.' Her apron rustled, her eyes were kind.

'I don't want tea. Where is he?' Annie said, putting her hand out to the woman. 'Please, where is he?'

'With the doctor, Mrs Armstrong. They've taken him upstairs. He needs surgery but he's in shock.'

Tom pulled her to the bench, went after the nurse, spoke to her, nodded towards Annie. The nurse smiled, spoke quietly and Tom came and sat down with her. 'They know you nursed here now. It'll help.'

Nothing will help, she thought. They've taken him straight up, he needs surgery but he's in shock. They can't operate until he's out of it and so he'll die. He's dead. But no, don't think those words. Don't you dare think those words.

They sat and waited, and she breathed in the smell of disinfectant, of cleanliness, of her past, and then Frank came through from the far end and on him was the dirt of the pit, the sweat-streaked dust and in his eyes was the same look that had been in them all those years ago when he had brought Tom to her here, after he had been beaten by the Blackshirts at Olympia.

He stood in front of her and she smiled, held his hand, drew herself to her feet, smelling the pit on him, 'You've seen him?' she asked.

'I travelled with him, Annie.' He looked at her, then at Tom. 'He thought a bomb had blown up. He didn't know where he was. "Tell her it doesn't hurt,"he said in the ambulance.' He was still looking at Tom.

'How bad, Frank?' She was standing close to him, wanting to hold his face, make him turn to her so that she could see his eyes. It was always there that you saw the truth.

'Very bad, Annie,' He turned now and there it was, in his eyes, and she sat down on the bench again, her hands in her lap, watching the nurses in the distance, watching the clock leap and jump the minutes, seeing the glare of the white tiles, the shine of the floor – all so clean, so very clean.

Staff Nurse called her then, holding open the swing door. 'Sister Manon, come on through.'

'Annie Armstrong now, Staff,' Annie said gently as she left Tom and Frank. 'Annie Armstrong.' She walked with Staff past stretchers, screened examination-beds, then into the lift, up and up, then along another corridor. They stopped outside a door.

'The doctor is with him,' Staff said. 'He remembers you, that's why you're here but also it will help your husband. He needs to hang on, somehow he needs to hang on. Talk to him, Annie. Whatever the doctors say, just keep talking to him for as long as it takes.'

Staff's face was lined, her hair was grey at the temples. 'I don't know you but several do. They know what happened after Singapore too. Will you be all right?'

Annie nodded. The screen was cold in her hand, she breathed deeply, eased herself through, saw the doctor, walked to Georgie who was so clean, so very small somehow, and there was no colour in his face or in his skin.

She laid her hand on his cold fingers which were unhurt though nowhere else seemed to be except his face, his beautiful face. His legs were in splints, there were hot water bottles around his body, a cage to keep the weight of the blankets off. She could smell the shock on him.

'John Smythe, you won't remember me, I was a Junior when you were here.' The doctor's voice was warm, gentle,

99

his eyes were almost the same colour as Tom's. He looked so young.

'Tell me,' she said. 'Just tell me what you've done and what needs doing.'

She listened as he explained how Frank had saved George's life by leaning on the femoral artery the moment he reached him. 'He'd have died then, without his mate,' the doctor said, standing the other side of Georgie, feeling the pulse in his neck. Annie did too. It was so faint.

'Look, how honest do you want me to be?' Dr Smythe said quietly. 'How much can you take?'

'As much as I have to.'

'OK then. I tied the artery, cleaned up the legs, the abdomen. The bones have torn through on both legs. The right is badly splintered, the left not so bad. Lots of dust and debris deep in. I've given him a heart stimulant. His chest is bruised but seems OK. His abdomen likewise. It's his legs. If he lives I'll try to save his legs. If being a very big word Annie. He's very poorly, lost too much blood, very damaged and is too shocked to operate yet.' He paused. 'Now, if we don't operate he's no chance. If I do, he has some chance so we just have to wait and hope that he comes out of shock soon enough to get him into theatre.'

Sarah was in the back seat, sitting with Betsy, not talking, no one was, not even Davy, not even Rob who sat in the front and read the map. Reading made her sick, made her throw up and she wanted to be sick now. Why, when she wasn't reading? She felt the cold sweat come again.

Sarah looked at the lunch-box in her hand. Why did she still have that? She shoved it from her lap and heard the clink of the stones they had collected from the river, heard the clatter of the spoon she had used to eat her strawberries. She'd probably been eating them and laughing while her da was . . . She felt the cold sweat again, the bile and now she was sick all over her lap, all over Bet, who mopped up and poured water from the flask Gracie handed over the seat saying, 'It's the shock.'

Davy gave her his handkerchief and she leaned back against Bet, feeling tired but she mustn't feel tired, not while her da was hurt because he was only hurt, nobody had said he was dead. No, not like Norma's dad. But on the hill Davy had said people died and Terry had said . . .

'Nearly there, we're nearly there.' Aunt Gracie said.

They were shown to the bench where Tom stood, where Frank sat and the grown ups talked of the river, of the wild flowers they had seen, drawn, of the diaries she and Davy would make for the teacher. They didn't talk of Da, why didn't they talk of Da? She sat and didn't listen to them any more. She sat and watched the nurses in their uniforms carrying charts, bringing them tea.

'No thank you,' she said. 'I want to see me da. Where's me mam?'

Gracie pulled her on to her lap but she was too old for that, stupid woman. Stupid, stupid, woman. 'Your mam's with your da.'

I want to be with me da, she wanted to shout and struggled to push herself from Gracie's lap but she was held firmly, soothed, when all she wanted was to be with her da.

A sister came and talked to Tom and he nodded, speaking quietly so that Sarah couldn't hear. Stupid man, stupid, stupid man. He turned. 'Come on, Sarah, let's go and find your mam.'

He took her hand and it felt good. They walked together, following the sister through the swing doors while he told her that her da was very ill. They wanted to operate but he was just too ill at the moment, she must be brave and help her mother.

They went up in the lift and she left her stomach behind. She'd done that when they went to the department store in Newcastle, trying to sell those knickers, those stupid, stupid knickers.

'You'll see your mother in a moment. She'll be able to talk

to you, to tell you more. Your mother is well known here, she was a wonderful nurse,' the sister said, putting her hand on her shoulder and now Sarah wanted to cry, wanted to stop the lift and run out anywhere, run and run and not hear what her mother had to say.

The lift stopped, the doors opened and there was another long corridor but it was lighter. They walked and the sister's shoes slurped on the lino. They waited outside the door. Tom sat down, his face looked so old. Gracie's had looked old too. Sarah walked up the corridor, her shoes were slurping too. Where was her mam? How was her da? She felt the cold sweat again, saw Norma again, heard Davy's voice telling her that people died, heard Terry telling her that her mam should have nursed.

She waited and waited and then her mother came out, her eyes red. She looked at Sarah and held out her arms. 'He's alive, my love, your da's alive, so far.'

Sarah ran at her then, reached her, hit her, slapped her, screamed at her as her mother reeled back. 'It's your fault. You should have been a nurse, shouldn't you? If you were so wonderful you should have been a nurse.'

Tom was up now, holding her arms down, lifting her off the ground as Annie was pushed against the wall. 'For God's sake, Sarah,' he said but Annie came to Sarah, held her, hugged her, and now Sarah wept, clung to her mother, sobbing and Annie looked up at Tom. 'It's all right, bonny lad. It's just too much for her, it's all too much and isn't she only doing what we all want to do – kick and scream and weep?'

Sarah and Annie drank tea that the sister brought. There was sugar in it. 'For shock,' the sister said.

Annie pulled a face when she had gone and Sarah laughed and leant against her mother, listening as Annie told her that they would stay because the doctor wanted to operate. 'If Da is well enough.'

'If he isn't?' Sarah asked.

'We'll have to see.'

102

Annie took Sarah back into the room with her and they sat one side, with a nurse the other, and talked to him, though he never moved and they could scarcely see, or hear him breathing. Sarah listened as Annie talked of the fright Tom and Frank had given her when they had staggered in from Olympia, how Tom had fought and become well, how the hospital had fought with him, how they would fight with Georgie too.

Sarah told him of her day at the river. The nets the teachers had bought out of the money from the jumble sale they had held last term, how they paddled, how he must get better soon, then they could all go paddling. She looked at Annie, who nodded at her to go on, and Sarah saw that her eyes were full of tears. She turned quickly, not wanting to see this because her mother mustn't cry – mothers didn't cry because if they did, there was nothing safe in the world.

Annie listened, dabbing her eyes as Sarah turned away. The anger had left the child, just as she had known it would.

Annie talked of the letters Georgie had written to her of the plains of Lahore, the corporal's stripe he'd got out of the fighting between the Muslims and the Sikhs – of the Himalayas; the clouds which gathered and dispersed, the geese and ducks that flew overhead, the bullock carts plodding by the stations, the musk-roses.

'Can you smell them, my love?' she murmured, nodding as Tom beckoned for Sarah to go and eat, shaking her head, feeling the pulse in his neck. Was it stronger now?

The nurse checked again too. She thought so too, the doctor also when he was called. Annie helped to refill and replace the hot water bottles, then talked on and on as the hours passed – of the whitebeams with their huge leaves and fruit which changed to colours of the English autumn and which he'd loved. Of the rhododendrons which were purple, not red as those at the convent were – and now she remembered that she had not told Don of his accident.

The doctor checked again, talked quietly to the nurse, left, brought back an older man who examined Georgie, then smiled at Annie.

'I'm Mr Adcock, the Consultant. I examined your husband when he first arrived. We're going to try and operate now. We'll take him into X-ray first but he's too shaky for thorough surgery.'

Annie nodded. 'Please let me fetch my daughter. She must see him – just in case.' Because otherwise she knew that anger could erupt again, and a resentment would be born that would never die.

Mr Adcock turned to the nurse. 'Bring Mrs Armstrong and her daughter down to X-ray, they can catch up with us there. Hurry though.'

They did catch up, they kissed him, touched his hand, though he never moved. Then they sat with Tom, though not the others because Gracie had taken them home, to sleep or to try. Georgie was brought out of theatre and he was still alive, Mr Adcock said in his white gown and cap.

'He has four broken ribs, lacerations of the abdomen, arms, back. I've patched, cleaned and set the right leg, cleaned and sealed the left, and injected a saline solution.' He nodded to the nurse who called Sarah over to hold the door for her as she carried things in and out.

Annie stood now, Tom with her, his arm around her shoulders as Mr Adcock lowered his voice.

'I couldn't do more. He was sinking. We've just got to hope that he keeps holding on. I've asked nurse to make up a bed for you and the child. You too, Mr Ryan?'

Tom shook his head and Annie too. 'No, we'll wait, but Sarah must sleep.'

They sat for the next two days as Georgie sank and rallied and sank. Don came, sat with them, said how sorry he was, brought fruit. They didn't talk. It was too much effort. Don left. They waited, waited, and Annie held Sarah who had slept the first night, but then not again. She stayed with them. Georgie rallied and Adcock said that if he lasted another night he would have a chance and he smiled, for the first time, and the hours crept by until the dawn broke and Georgie was still alive and now Annie dared to hope.

CHAPTER 7

Georgie opened his eyes to the sunlight streaming into the room and saw shapes to the right and left – what were they? He looked up – what was that? He lay and could feel nothing beneath him or above him. He could hear nothing, he just saw. He looked up again and slowly he knew it was a ceiling. He looked to the left and saw a jug, to the right, a person. It moved. It smiled. It was a woman, a nurse.

He could feel the sheet beneath his back. He moved his fingers and touched the sheet which lay on the frame. He spoke and his voice seemed too loud in the silence and the light.

'Where am I? Where's Annie?' and then darkness came again, floating him away to a warmth which nursed him.

Annie came in when the nurse beckoned and sat with him, pulling Sarah to her, holding her child against her because they must share each moment as it happened.

She spoke softly to Georgie, Sarah too and then paused, knowing that to listen, even sub-consciously, was tiring now that he was back with them.

That night she slept in the bed next to Sarah because Georgie's colour was better, his breathing, his pulse too and there was no pain. So far there was no pain.

Georgie woke before dawn and all he could hear was a clicking noise. The light was on above his bed, the nurse sat quietly, knitting. His mother used to knit, Annie too before she had to cut and sew and now he was remembering the past, Manners, the business. He stirred.

'I must be up tomorrow. I must be back at work. I need to work.' His voice was a croak, his throat was sore. Why was that? 'What's wrong with my voice?'

'You've had an operation,' the nurse said, putting her knitting to one side, feeling his pulse, putting her hand on his forehead. 'Any pain?'

Georgie shook his head. 'No, so I must be better, I need to work.'

The nurse said, 'Sh, no need to worry about work. There's plenty of time for that.'

'There's no time, no time.' But he was drifting again, sinking in the comfortable warmth and darkness.

Annie ate breakfast in the staff canteen, a breakfast which she had not been hungry for, but which she must eat for then Sarah would eat. The bacon was as she remembered, the tinned tomatoes too. She let Sarah pick up the rind and eat it with her fingers.

'I wish it was crisp,' Sarah said, chewing it, pulling a face.

'It never was,' Annie smiled, nodding to the Staff Nurse who had taken her up to Georgie on his first day.

'Mum, why didn't you nurse?' Sarah said quietly, laying the rind on the side of her plate, wiping her fingers on her napkin.

'Because it seemed better at the time for your father to go into the mine. It was just one of those things and perhaps it was a mistake but we must just try and put it behind us, try and live each day as it comes, help your father to recover. Perhaps you should try to finish that diary of the school trip, then you could show it to Da.' Annie drank her tea and longed for a cigarette to calm the ache in her chest because she knew it had been a mistake, of course it had been a mistake, but how do you tell a child her father wanted the edge above all else? You couldn't, especially now, because Sarah had said her father can't have really wanted to go back down if he loved her. Bet had said that it would all fade in time and so it would, it had to.

They sat with him while he slept and talked gently to him and Sarah promised him her finished diary. He opened his eyes and smiled at them, returning the pressure of their fingers and they talked gently, watching his eyes become heavy lidded, his mouth become slack as he drifted, then came back.

'I've got to get back to work.'

'Plenty of time for that,' Annie said, knowing that it would be months, if ever, though she had promised Sarah that he would never go into the pit again.

That evening Tom took Sarah back to Wassingham to sleep in Annie's old room next to Davy. 'It's school for you, young lady,' Annie insisted, 'and yes, don't worry, you'll be here tomorrow evening and I'll ring if I need you. I promise.'

She watched them go, feeling Tom's kiss on her cheek, Bet's too then sat with Georgie, sitting opposite the nurse, smiling when Dr Smythe came in, nodding as he said, 'So far, so good. Out of danger as I said this morning but we'll need to look at those legs again soon.' He checked the chart, smiled at Annie. 'Will you be all right here? I know you're competent. I must talk to nurse for a moment.'

Staff Williams blushed and Annie smiled.

'I think perhaps I can manage, I do hope you like the sweater she's knitting you.'

Dr Smythe laughed. 'The patients seem to like the click of the needles, that's all.'

Oh no it isn't, my fine lad, Annie thought, feeling old as she watched them brush hands on their way to the door. But yes, I expect the patients do like the timeless sound of knitting needles, I always did.

She looked at the chart now, straightened Georgie's sheets, checked the corners. Oh yes, very good, Staff Nurse, she thought, then sat again watching him, glad too be alone with him at last, glad to be able to lean over and kiss his eyes, his lips, his fingers one by one. The smell of his skin was coming back, the shock was almost gone and soon the pain would begin.

'I must get back to work, Annie,' he murmured and she bent over him, holding his face lightly in hers, brushing his lips with her kisses, feeling the response in his.

'No, there's no need.'

'There's no money, Annie. We've debts.'

'I said there was no need. I shall nurse, my love.'

He jerked his head. His fingers gripped hers, saliva ran from his mouth – she released his hand, wiped his lips with gauze. 'I shall nurse as I'm doing now – see, there's nothing wrong with me.'

His eyes were flickering, his mouth working. 'You mustn't, you mustn't.' His voice was rising, his breathing erratic, his head was turning from side to side. 'Get me up out of here. Get me back to work.'

The nurse came in, saw, called the doctor, asked Annie to leave. She sat on the bench, looking out across the city, out at the lightness of the sky above the sea and didn't think, didn't feel, just clenched her hands until they came and said he was asleep again, though he had been very disturbed and that was dangerous now. Very dangerous.

She cursed herself, knowing that she had nearly killed him.

The next morning he told her again that he must return to work and this time she said there was no need to rush, now that they had the mail order up and running. They had used Manners' pants – there was nothing to worry about, nothing, and his face cleared, his fingers touched hers and Staff Nurse smiled at her before she went off duty.

That evening Sarah sat with Georgie while Annie bought Tom tea in the canteen and told him about the lie she had told Georgie.

'But it needn't be a lie,' she continued. 'I'm going to put up the house as security, get a loan, set up a mail shot – it's all I can do.'

Her spoon was stirring, clinking, why did she do that when she was tense? Why did anyone do anything? Tom was holding his cup between two hands, bending his head to it – he always did that when he was thinking.

'We should have done that in the first place, we should have listened to you, bonny lass.'

'No, you can't say that. Manners' order might have worked.'

'Then why didn't it, Annie? What went wrong?' Tom slurped his tea, his shoulders hunched.

'I don't know. It could have been that the outlets weren't as willing to take them as Manners thought or maybe he was over-extended, just couldn't pay us, or he found someone cheaper. We'll never know, but it's happened before and it'll happen again. Come on, let's go for a walk, I could do with some air.'

Tom grinned at her, putting his cup in the saucer, pushing back his chair. 'You could do with a fag, you mean.'

'How well you know me.'

The evening air was cool, the days were so long. Was it really still only the first week of June? It seemed as though it should be December. Annie smelt the roses, touched them. 'Has anyone watered my lavender?

'Bet's been in each day, don't worry.'

'So, what d'you feel about the mail shot, shall we go for it?' Annie asked, drawing deeply on her cigarette, blowing the smoke high into the air, looking back at the hospital. Which was his room?

Tom was breathing in her smoke. 'I'd kill for one of those.'

She shook her head. 'Shall we go for it?'

'It's all we can do, especially as we have Manners' sets.'

Annie stopped, dropped her cigarette on to the ground, stood on it, picked it up, tossed it into the waste bin. 'That's the problem, Tom, we can't use those.' She put her hand up as he turned to her. 'We can't. If Manners saw the advertisement he might just cause trouble, write in explaining that they had been rejected once. We can't risk it for the first one. We've got to make our name and we'll run those out for the next shot, just change the trim.'

Tom nodded. 'Yes, I can see your point.'

'So, I'll have to get a loan against the house, get supplies in not just for the first mail shot but for more of Manners' pants. We must get the same roll runs that we had for those while the suppliers still have them, put it 'under the counter' until we need it. But Georgie mustn't know about the loan or the new designs. Can you get some drawn up?'

They were walking out of the gates now, their heels clicking on the pavement. Were Staff Nurse's needles clicking in Georgie's room? Annie looked at her watch. 'I must get back, be within earshot, just in case.'

Tom linked his arm in hers, turning her, squeezing her. 'What about his legs?'

'I don't know, all I know is that he's alive and that's the first problem over.'

They walked in silence up the drive, into the hospital. 'We'll share the loan,' Tom said. 'I'll sort it out with the bank. I'll bring in the designs, I'll speak to Gracie and Brenda, get them alerted. You just relax, stay with him, get him better.'

'We'll need to set up the advertisement too, book the space, provide the copy and a sketch. Let's make it twenty-eight-day delivery; that will give us three weeks to clear the cheque, package, and a week for delivery.'

Tom smiled, 'Fine. Don't worry.'

The next day she sat with Georgie as he drifted in and out of consciousness and each time his eyes opened he said, 'Why are you here, why aren't you working?'

'Tom is doing it.'

'He can't be, he has work to do. I should be up. I shouldn't be here.'

His breathing was irregular again, his pulse weaker, and the doctor said that she should go, if only for the morning because it was hindering his recovery.

When he came to again he said once more, 'Why are you here, why aren't you working?' and she told him that she was waiting for Tom, that she would go home with him this evening and return tomorrow in the afternoon and then Georgie rested, his breathing calmed, his pulse too.

Sarah wouldn't speak to her in the car, she sat stiff and straight until Tom stopped at the verge and turned. 'The doctors told your mam to come home, get the business going. They told her to do that because your da is worrying, it's making him worse. Now stop being such a claggy little beggar and smile – look, you've made the sun go down.' He pointed to the darkness ahead and around them and Sarah glared, then smiled, then laughed. 'It's gone down because it's ten at night, Uncle Tom, and if that's what the doctors said then that's all right.'

Annie and Tom raised their eyebrows at her.

'So all I have to do to get you to tidy your room next time is to give Dr Smythe a call, is it?' Annie asked, and laughed when Sarah sighed, and said, 'Bet and Aunt Gracie haven't made me do anything while you've been away.'

'Tough, I'm home now, so it'll be the hardship of Armstrong life again my girl, I just don't know how you'll survive.'

They rang the hospital when Tom dropped them off and all was well, then Annie cooked Sarah's favourite macaroni cheese, and they sat together for half an hour, just talking, thinking, stoking the fire. 'He'll be home soon will he, Mum?'

'Very soon I hope, but he needs another operation, just to check his legs.'

That night Annie sat up in bed drawing up plans for the mail shot, confirming twenty-eight-day delivery, deciding on just three sizes and a choice of two colours.

In the morning she rang the wholesalers, reserving more of the Manners cloth, white and cream cotton for the first mail shot. She spoke to the bank manager and they arranged that Tom would liaise for them both, then she drove back to the hospital for the afternoon, holding Georgie's hand and telling him of the advertisement Tom was drawing up. She pushed down the thought that it could all go wrong. It mustn't, it wouldn't.

She stayed at the hospital all night, driving back early the next day, calling in on Brenda and Meg, putting them on stand-by. She gave up her stall in Wassingham Market but arranged to supply the new trader. She ran up samples of Tom's designs. Yes, they were good, the trim was broderie anglaise, quite expensive but would look good on the advertisement. Could they get free publicity, a feature? She would write to the newspaper in which they set the advert. Tom had decided on *The Mail*.

She drove back to the hospital, taking Bet with her and now there were two pairs of needles clicking and Georgie smiled then and laughed and the doctor had a glint in his eye and the Staff Nurse a ring on her finger. Annie wished them well when the doctor called her out of the room, telling her that they were operating on Georgie the next day, they were concerned for his legs, especially the left.

She told Georgie quietly as Bet drank tea in the canteen with Sarah who had arrived with Tom and Gracie. He nodded, his eyes sunken now with pain, though he said nothing, and she wanted to hold him, take him far from here, but all he said was, 'But the business is all right? The mail shot is going through?'

When Tom took the others home, Georgie told her to go too. 'You must have work to do, or it'll not go well, you know.'

She drove home with Sarah and there was no stiffness between them now, there was just fear at the thought of tomorrow. They ate without appetite sitting either side of the range, their plates on their laps, and Bet stayed with them, taking Annie's plate from her as the phone rang and she ran to pick up the receiver. Was it the hospital?

No, it was a market trader from South Warnsted, one of those who had dropped her. 'We heard about your man at a meeting last night,' he said. 'Deliver what you can, we'll take the lot.'

Five more rang that night and two in the morning. She told Georgie as she sat with him and his smile brightened eyes that were clouded with pain and a face deeply lined.

He was wheeled to the theatre at two and Tom brought Sarah as Annie had asked. Together they sat in the corridor for the two hours it took, waiting for Mr Adcock to come out and tell them that he was fine, he had come through, his right leg and been tidied up nicely though his left was still giving cause for concern.

The Staff Nurse took Sarah for a cup of tea and Mr Adcock told Annie that he might have saved the left leg, he wouldn't know for a while and she nodded because what else could she do.

Tom held her though, when Adcock had gone, gripping her tightly, not speaking. How could he speak without his voice breaking because Annie was so tired, so thin, so brave, and so was Georgie and none of this was fair.

That night Georgie was in post-operative shock but rallied in the morning, then sank, then rallied, and sank again. His cheeks were hollow, his eyes too and Annie signed the forms that Tom brought in from the bank, reading them line by line because there were to be no mistakes this time. Georgie would need a firm to run. Yes he would, he bloody well would she said inside her head, pushing aside the look of him, pushing aside the smell of him, the weakness of his pulse, the quietness of his breathing. She wouldn't let him die.

She took Sarah in to see him when she arrived, telling her it was much worse than it looked, much much worse. He stabilised in the afternoon and the pain tore at him, and his eyes sank deeper into their sockets until they gave him pain killers and he drifted again.

Annie used Staff Nurse's phone to ring Brenda and Meg, setting them on to work on the traders' stock, telling them to give the completes to Tom and he would bring them in for checking. She couldn't get home tonight.

'How is he?' Brenda asked.

'Holding his own.' And he was, just.

She sent Sarah to bed in the hospital room at eight p.m. and checked through the stock. All but ten were perfect. Meg's smelt of smoke again and she told Tom to hang them on her airer overnight. Brenda could re-do the rejects. Could Gracie deliver to the traders tomorrow?

Tom nodded, showing her the figures for the week. Thanks to the traders there would be enough to pay the household bills. He also brought her a letter for Georgie from Don, asking when he could come and visit.

'Not yet,' Annie said, looking towards Georgie's room. 'Best not yet.'

The next day Adcock told her that the antibiotics had lost the battle, the leg was gangrenous and must be removed if he was to be saved, and Annie nodded. Somehow she had always known it, and her heart broke for Georgie and for Sarah when she told her because the child looked old and crushed and in pain – just as she felt.

In the theatre Adcock worked fast, severing the left leg well above the knee, sewing the flap of skin over the bone but Georgie was weakening, his pulse was becoming faint. He tidied, finished. 'The heart's stopped,' the anaesthetist called.

There was a stillness, a silence, then Adcock jabbed with a needle, took Georgie's wrist, and felt nothing. He waited and then there was a thread, a flutter. 'He's there.'

Adcock finished, and George was wheeled to intensive care.

Adcock spoke to Annie. 'He's in shock again but he should recover, he's very strong, though there's always a risk, my dear.'

Annie nodded. She knew that, oh yes, she knew that. She and Sarah waited. It seemed to be all that they'd ever done.

Georgie woke fourteen hours later and Staff Nurse was there, but no knitting – how strange – then the darkness came.

He woke again to streaming sunlight, to searing pain, to parched thirst, to a nurse who was holding his wrist.

'Please, it hurts.'

'It'll ease,' she soothed, wetting his lips which were cracked and dry.

It didn't ease, even when Annie came it didn't ease and he couldn't bear the touch of anyone's hand, even hers. He couldn't bear the pain.

They gave him more pain killers and for a moment he slept. When he woke the pain was there, digging deeper, deeper, and Annie was gone. He called but she didn't come. He was alone with it and he couldn't bear that, it was coming again and he needed her.

Then she was there, thank God she was there, but don't touch me. Don't touch me he screamed, but his lips didn't move. She hadn't touched him. She knew, she could see inside his head because she was part of him but why wasn't she stopping the pain?

Annie made Tom take Sarah away. She mustn't see this, she mustn't see her father's glistening, grey, waxy face, the eyes which knew no one, which sank deeper with each hour into the darkening hollows.

Georgie called again, Why? The pain was fading, then it was here again and there was sunlight. It hurt his eyes. The pain was sweeping through him, clawing at him and he groaned and groaned again and then darkness came, and there was nothing.

Annie let Sarah into the room now. 'He's in shock, he's unconscious, now you must go back to the children's ward, help there until I call you.' Her voice was quite calm, she was too tired for it to be anything else.

She helped the nurses to roll him, to avoid lung congestion. She checked the garments that Tom brought over, checked the advertisement. It would go in in two weeks' time.

'Three,' Tom said, coming again the next evening. 'One of your Glasgow buyers rang. He wants me to take up some samples. He's decided he underspent his budget after all and wants a presentation but is it OK if I leave you?' He nodded towards Georgie's room. 'I'll be away two nights.'

116

'Yes, go. You can't do anything and by then it'll be decided one way or another.'

Georgie came to in the afternoon of the next day and Annie gave him a drink, putting the spout to his lips, letting the water trickle into his mouth. There was a stubble on his chin and his face was less waxy. The pain killers were given again and took the edge off the pain more efficiently now.

They changed the dressings as they had done each day and Staff Nurse peeled off the last of the lint from the raw wound as Annie leaned across, hiding the stump from Georgie, talking to him gently. She saw the naked agony in his face even though they had soaked the dressing in warm water and was glad that when he was unconscious at least he was spared this.

She sat and talked with him in the afternoon, telling him of the Glasgow buyer, of the diary Sarah had at last finished.

'Why aren't you working?' he murmured, too filled with pain to speak properly.

'I am, I have it here.' She held up the traders' pants.

'Those aren't Manners' pants.'

'No, these are for the traders. The mail shot goes out in three weeks.'

The pain came through the pain killer, it roared and raged and took him away from Annie, took him down dark tunnels, twisting and turning with him until day became night and now he woke again and there was a rim of light, a nurse but no knitting, thank God, for the click, click would have jarred on the pain.

He looked for Annie. She was there, watching him, smiling.

'I wish they'd cut the bloody thing off,' he groaned, wanting to touch her, but not being able to bear the pressure.

'They have, my darling,' she said.

'No they haven't, I can feel my toes. Why don't they cut it off?'

The morning came and he woke again and there was Tom with Annie and he was holding her hand. Georgie was glad someone was.

117

'It hurts,' he said to Tom. 'If they took it off the pain would go.'

Tom looked at Annie. 'They have bonny lad, they've taken it off.'

'That's what Annie said, but they haven't because it still hurts.'

The nurse told Annie she must get some sleep that night and Tom insisted too, and she fell on to the bed and slept though she dreamt of the camps, of Prue, of Lorna, of the parade ground.

Again Georgie woke and there was the nurse, and the light, but no sun. It was night then. His mind was clearer, the pain was less, wasn't it? Yes, a bit less, he felt different, stronger. He turned his head. Annie wasn't there.

'Is she sleeping?' he asked the nurse. She nodded.

He lay still, thinking of Annie's face, her eyes, her laugh, her voice. What had she said? Tom had been here too, holding her hand, talking. He'd been talking. What had he said? Georgie looked up at the ceiling, floating, drifting in and out of pain. Oh God, why didn't they take it off?

Then he remembered what Annie had said and Tom too, so it must be true, but what did it matter – there was still the pain, which was swelling, growing, taking him back into the darkness.

CHAPTER 8

Georgie improved a little that night, more the next day, the
greyness went from his face and the pain eased though they
still injected pain killers to calm his tortured nerve endings.
He didn't ask again about his leg, so Annie just waited.

At the end of the week he told her that she shouldn't be
sitting here while Tom and Gracie did all the work and he
smiled at her. 'Get on, or there'll be nothing for me to do
when I get back on my feet.'

Annie felt despair. He still didn't know. She looked at the
nurse, who shook her head. So she grinned. 'OK slave driver,
I'll be back at four.'

'Make it six,' Georgie said, 'Then I can have me tea in
peace.'

He watched her go, seeing the looseness of her clothes, the
tiredness in her shoulders. It would give her time to eat hers
in peace too. He lay back on the pillows and now, with just
the nurse there, he lifted the sheets. Yes, they had taken his
leg off. He really was a cripple. They had been telling him
the truth and he wept the tears he had not wanted any of
his family to see, knowing that they must be hidden again
by this evening.

Annie sewed most of the day, then checked the Glasgow
garments which Brenda and the homeworkers had been
sewing. Oh God, there was still the smell of smoke on Meg's
and they needed to be packed tonight. Annie walked round
to Meg, standing on the step, asking her if she'd work in
Annie's house because if there was no time to air the clothes

now, what would it be like when the mail shot began next week – if it worked that is, and it had to.

That afternoon she talked to Tom, checking that last month he had put in for planning permission for Briggs' warehouse. He had. 'We should know if it's been granted this week, then we'll be set up for when we need to take on the premises.'

'Thank heavens for that. Well done, Tom, we'll have to take it the moment we can. It's going to be chaos next week, absolute chaos.'

'We hope,' Tom said.

'It's just got to be. It's going to sink in soon about his leg and he'll need something to get hold of, to work at.'

Georgie listened to Mr Adcock telling him that losing a leg was a great inconvenience but not fatal. 'Mobility can be obtained with a false leg and of course, wheelchairs. We'll be getting you along to physio soon, and then to the special unit where we'll fit your leg.'

Georgie nodded. He smiled until Adcock left, then sank back on to the pillows, slept again and dreamt that he was running across the sand with Sarah, chasing Annie, catching her, pushing seaweed down her neck.

He smiled again when Annie came, kissing her, smelling the summer on her hair, her skin. He'd forgotten about seasons, it was just dark or light in here. He listened as she talked of the last minute preparations for the mail shot and Meg's sewing machine which they had installed on the kitchen table.

'Geoff smokes, that's why I used to hang them on the airer, I just didn't want to tell you but of course you'd have understood.'

'Of course,' he said as she bathed him, washing his arms, his chest, his leg.

'I know about my leg,' he said then, quite quietly, casually, and he was proud of himself. 'I know and it doesn't matter, I can learn to walk again, it's just an inconvenience.' He looked at the ceiling, at the wall, and then at her. 'It's all right, Annie, tell everyone it's all right.'

She touched his face, kissed his lips gently. 'Inside you must be destroyed but I shall tell them because it will be. I promise you it will be.'

He wouldn't talk about it any more and so Annie told him of the greenfly which were annoying Bet, of the kids' gang and the carts they were making out of old prams, of the world which seemed a million miles away to him and he was glad he was here, hidden behind the nurses and these walls, out of sight of that world which hadn't yet seen him as he was now and into which he must one day stumble.

Annie came in over the weekend with Sarah, dressing his stump and she didn't speak then, just concentrated, as he should have done, he thought.

'Where did you get the capital for the advertisement?' he asked when she had finished, when he could trust his voice not to shake from the pain.

'Don't worry about that,' Annie said, taking the bowl from the room. But couldn't she see that he did worry? But then he felt tired again, so tired and the agony that was his stump took all his energy.

'Where did you get it?' he asked Annie again when she returned.

'The profit from the Glasgow deal,' she replied because she had had time to think in the sluice.

But he didn't hear, he was asleep.

'He's just not thriving at the moment,' Staff Nurse told Annie. 'It often happens when they discover the facts. Just keep on as you're doing, it's fine.'

The advertisement appeared on Tuesday and the first orders came through that morning.

'They must be from the newspaper staff,' Gracie said, opening the envelopes, stamping the coupons, passing them to Annie who entered them into the book, packing up their orders, stacking them under the window, going out to bank the cheques, to wait for them to clear before sending the orders off.

On Wednesday there was a deluge of mail, and they opened the envelopes, stamped coupons, filled the orders from stock, and told the homeworkers to keep on with the traders until their orders were filled and only then moving on to the mail shot, since they had enough in stock.

That evening Annie delivered the traders' stock on her way to Georgie, grateful that they didn't ask for sale or return any more – smiling when they asked how Georgie was.

'Coming on, he'll be riding a bicycle soon,' she laughed. That night she told Georgie of the two hundred orders already received, that she needed him alongside them, longing to be able to lift the darkness which hung behind his eyes.

He was even quieter tonight, feverish and he wouldn't eat. 'Ring me,' she told the staff. 'I must know if he's any worse.'

'It's because he knows, he's trying to adjust, he's depressed, but you're doing fine.'

She sewed all night, without rest, she had to re-order from Glasgow, she had to write up the schedule for the homeworkers. She rang the hospital at dawn. His fever was down and his spirits too. Is it any wonder, she thought. 'Shall I come?'

'No, he'll only start fretting because your nose isn't actually on the grindstone. He needs some time to himself to accept things.'

At eight-thirty the postman knocked, emptied his sack on to the floor. 'Mrs Norris is right glad you warned her of this,' he said, pushing back his cap. 'Me wife sews you know.'

'No, I didn't, get her to bring round a sample, Joe, today if possible.' One of the homeworkers that Tom had picked out had moved with her husband to Nottingham last week.

Annie packed, stacked, then cut and sewed until lunch, then checked through the girls' work, approving Joe's wife's sample, keeping her in reserve. She drove with Sarah to see Georgie in the evening, her head aching, her eyes and fingers sore, but her smile was warm though he looked no better – and so quiet.

They sat and she knitted because he liked it, but her hands were sore as the wool rasped and rubbed. She dressed his stump again, soaking the old dressing, easing it, feeling his pain as though it were her own. Her hands were trembling, the air was heavy, the smell of healing flesh strong. She tried not to breathe, then to take shallow gasps. Don't rush, you'll hurt him. Don't rush, whatever you do don't rush. There, it was done.

She took the soiled dressings to the sluice, putting them in the waste, the dishes in the sluice, leaning against the wall, then putting water on her face, more and more. She was tired, that was all.

She sat with him, knitting, always knitting, until eight-thirty.

'Sarah must get to bed, she has school, my love,' she told him, though he was sleeping again.

'He'll be all right, you're doing fine,' Dr Smythe told her and she wanted to scream because if she was doing fine, why wasn't he improving?

She worked when Sarah was in bed, and the same again the next day, but only after her visit, and the next, and still the orders were pouring in and she should have felt excited, pleased, but she didn't because still he was not thriving and exhaustion was clawing at her. Now she couldn't get the smell of the dressings out of her head, and when she grabbed at an hour's sleep she dreamt and woke herself up chanting ichi, ni, san, yong.

On Saturday there were more orders, many more orders, and they opened, stamped, entered, banked, then Tom sent her to the hospital because they could sew, package and check between them, he said.

'Now scoot.'

As she drove she talked to Sarah about the fields of ripening wheat they passed, of the villages they drove through, of Bill Haley's new song which Sarah loved, of the need for a catalogue that they could send out with the orders to save on advertising costs.

'I must get Tom to design some more sets. We could extend our range.'

'I wonder how Dad is?'

'Better, much better I think. Do you think we should have a catalogue?' Annie asked because she didn't want to think of Georgie's despair which she couldn't touch, or the dressings she must do yet again.

'Oh I don't know, Mum, I just want to see Dad.'

There was silence in the car. Yes, I want to see him too. I'm just tired, she thought and her hands felt slippery on the wheel. She wiped her left one on her skirt.

It was as though the car drove itself now, down the drive, parking near Adcock's reserved space. It was as though her feet knew their own way to his room, it was as though her smile flicked on independently as her eyes took in the darkness in his, the flatness of his voice. Her hands became busy and they were nothing to do with her, soaking the dressings, peeling them, redressing. They washed themselves in the sluice, again and again, then dried themselves, again and again.

She walked back to the room, but they were still not dry. She rubbed them down her skirt, putting on her smile, walking into the room where Sarah was sitting, where the nurse was taking his temperature.

'Fever again today, Annie,' Staff Nurse said, 'and he won't eat you know. Can you try him with some ice cream?' She handed the bowl to Annie who sat down by the bed.

'I'm not a child,' Georgie said faintly. 'Just not hungry.'

Annie held the spoon in her hand, then dug it into the ice cream, lifting it, carrying it to his mouth. 'Into the hole then,' she said, 'the rabbit wants to go into the hole,' and the room was so hot, her hands so slippery and it was Prue that she saw there, the light of madness in her eyes. It was the sound of the guards, shouting and screaming that she heard and she couldn't breathe, couldn't move and then she turned, looked at Sarah.

'Feed him,' she said thrusting the bowl at her, walking from the room, down the corridor, down the stairs, not the lift, out into the air, breathing in deep gulps, clearing her head of images, of sounds, gripping her own arms, holding herself tight.

She sat on the bench, feeling its cool hardness and then she heard the gulls, saw the dark brick of the hospital, felt the cotton of her dress, looked at her hands. They were quite dry. She looked at them again, they were scored with needle marks, they were sore from opening envelopes, from entering, from stamping. They were sore from knitting, God damn it.

She rose then, walking back to the entrance, taking the lift, going back into the room, taking the bowl from Sarah.

'He won't have it, Mum.'

'Oh yes he damn well will.' Annie said because there was no time for either of them to sink, they had a future to get on with. 'Oh yes you will, my bonny lad. Open up.'

Georgie looked at her. 'I don't want any.'

'Well I want you to have some, because until you start really getting better, my love, we can't have you home. We need you there, for us, and for the business. We can't manage without you, so come on, eat up.'

Staff Nurse came back into the room but Annie didn't care.

'Come on, Georgie, you're not doing justice to yourself. Get this down you, get yourself sorted out and come home.'

Annie held the spoon, looking into his face, into eyes which were still dark and dead.

'Mum,' Sarah shouted. 'Stop it, how can you, he's ill!'

Staff Nurse said, 'He's not ill, he's better now, or he could be, your mother's quite right – just you remember that my girl. It doesn't do anybody any good to spoil them. We've been waiting for this to happen.'

She stood behind Annie and neither of them looked up as Sarah ran from the room.

'Come on, Georgie,' Annie said again. 'I can't do it all on my own. I need you to get better, to come home.'

He opened his mouth then and his eyes were brighter, she fed him once, then gave him the spoon. 'Come on then, you know you like strawberry.'

'I like you better, Annie Armstrong,' his voice was still faint but now there was a smile and it lit up both their eyes.

They managed to keep their supply level-pegging with demand and Annie pinned up a series of coloured stock control boards giving an instant picture of availability. These she updated as the garments came in and went out. They needed to set on another homeworker, to set up another design, plan for the next mail shot, sort out that catalogue.

'We need some coverage too, I'll chat to the newspaper, tell them of our success, try and swing it this time, they weren't interested for the first one. Talk to the nationals as well can you, Tom? See if the fashion page will mention it in *The Mail* since we're placing the advertisement with them. We'll set Joe's wife on, isn't her name Jean?'

They received requests for outsize and filled them – it was surprising how little sleep a person really needed, Annie thought, brushing aside her headaches, her trembling hands.

She asked Mr Adcock to move Georgie into the general ward and Staff Nurse concurred. 'He needs company, he needs to be eased into other people,' Annie said.

Adcock agreed and asked her if she'd like a job. She thought he was joking but he wasn't, or only half.

'Sorry, I've got to get this lot on the road,' she answered because she didn't need to prove anything any more did she, she had pushed back the shadows, hadn't she?

'We'll send out a catalogue with the next one or two, shall we?' Annie asked Georgie the next day as he sat up in bed, squeezing his hand round rubber balls, trying to build up his strength.

'Yes, let's sort that out, it's a good idea. By the way Don's been in, talked quite a lot. I told him about you, and the business. He was surprised, I was proud.'

'Did Maud come?'

'Towards the end. Still flashing her nails. Thought I'd be in a room on me own, she was quite put out – all these beds, all these people and no one quite knowing where they'd been.'

'Nice of them to come. Did they eat your fruit?' Annie looked at the spidery grapeless stalks. Georgie nodded and they laughed.

'Left me some chocs though, take them home, pig yourself, you've got too thin, bonny lass.'

Annie left them in the cupboard, 'Share them with this lot,' she said, looking round the ward, grinning at the other patients, and visitors.

Georgie nodded. 'I'll lick all the nut ones first though. What about the tour, are you going?'

He didn't look at her as he said it. Annie looked out across the ward.

'Couldn't, I'll need to be home when you get back. I shall expect to be snatched up and tangoed down the street, just to shock the neighbours.'

He laughed. 'Maybe a waltz.'

'I'll settle for that and we shall picture Tom presenting his knicks and bras to all the female buyers. They'll love it.'

Two days later they received another large order from Glasgow and they were tripping over one another in the dining-room, trying to check, trying to pack, snapping at each other, making errors, and in the kitchen there was nowhere for Annie and Sarah to eat because Meg's sewing machine was on the table and her garments had to be moved from there each evening or they smelt of the food they cooked.

The mail-shot coupons were still arriving in sacks. Annie ordered a further roll from the supplier. He was pleased, surprised.

'Really taking off then?'

'It's wonderful, and we've a buyer's re-order from Glasgow too, so stand by your phone in the autumn after the tour, we'll need more, if your prices are still competitive, Jack.' Annie laughed, knowing that word would travel fast via Jack, or Big mouth as he was known in the trade.

'So eat your heart out Manners,' she said to herself as she poured the tea.

Tom came in that afternoon, leaving the door, open, propping himself up on the drainer.

'Planning Permission's come through for the conversion of Briggs' place, so come and go over these with me, Gracie's just coming.' He waved the balance sheets at her, hauled her into the yard, pushing an upturned tub towards her with his foot, shutting the door.

Annie sat there, relishing the peace of a sewing machineless world. 'This is where I need to set up my office, on an upturned tub next to a downbeat pigeon loft. What more could I want, and if it rains, I shall just roost *in* the loft – perfect. I can even smoke.' She pulled out her cigarettes, tapped one out, lit it, inhaled. God, she was tired. God, it was noisy in there. God, it was a mess and this evening she must take time to clear up, then just sit and talk to Sarah, and most of all listen to her day – there had been no time last night, or the night before.

'Well, while you're sitting there, puffing, have a read of these.' Tom handed her the balanced sheets, smiling at Gracie as she came through into the yard. 'Look at the profit so far.'

Annie looked. She couldn't believe it. She'd been working so hard she hadn't even thought of profit and loss, of money. She had just paid the bills that had to be paid, worked, visited the hospital, and slept when she could.

'Tom this is wonderful, we're in profit. It's that Glasgow one that's done it. It's tipped us over, well over.'

'Right, and we've already paid up for the next mail shot because we're using Manners' stock aren't we?'

Annie smiled. 'Yes, we'll get away with that now. We'll

128

change the trim, it wouldn't be worth his while to start rumours, the success of this will stifle anything like that. We can just get on and set up the next range, and the wholesale range. The traders are really picking up now and I've had three more Madam shops this afternoon. Big-mouth has done us proud.'

She passed the sheets to Gracie, drawing in on her cigarette, arcing it out over the garden.

'You are so disgusting. That'll have to stop.' Tom groaned.

'It's for luck, bonny lad. It brings us luck, don't you know anything?' Annie said softly, leaning back, looking at him. 'Because you're thinking what I'm thinking, aren't you?'

Gracie looked up at Annie, then at Tom who was nodding, grinning. 'What are you two up to?'

Tom raised an eyebrow. 'Briggs' place.'

'We can afford it.' Annie leaned forward, her arms on her knees. 'We could move in over a weekend. We'd need lights, shelving, tables immediately, heating by the end of the month and we've just about enough money for it. We'll get everyone under one roof, Gracie and I wouldn't have to deliver cutouts, or pick up completes, or liaise between the two houses. We wouldn't have to eat on our knees, our kids would have their homes to themselves – and we've got to get set up and out of here before Georgie comes home anyway.' She stood up. 'Let's do it now – move in when the lease is finalised. Shouldn't take long. Bill's been in the picture about it and he'll know about the planning permission being granted – or he will when we get round there.'

Tom stood up, walked to the cigarette butt, picked it up, dropped it in the dustbin. 'The only thing is . . .'

'I know. There'll have to be a no smoking rule. It's going to bleeding well kill me, lad.'

Annie and Tom called in on Bill the next morning and she had been right, he had heard that the planning permission had come through. He had also been informed late last night by his area manager that Briggs' Warehouse was part of a parcel of properties taken over by a London-based consortium. The lease was still available but the price had tripled.

Annie looked at Bill, his face reddening, his eyes flicking from her to Tom. 'I'm so sorry. There's been no interest for months. I can't understand it but it's all part of a bigger deal that's been handled in Newcastle. It's been on offer there as well and they didn't let me know this was going on. I'm sorry Annie, Tom.'

She looked at Tom who had gone pale and clenched her hands to keep them steady, hardly able to believe what she had heard, knowing that all their profits would be wiped out. They needed heaters by the end of the month, phones installed, electricians paid, carpenters for the work benches, the shelving, and there was the material Jack was keeping under the counter for the next mail shot. She looked at Tom.

'It's the only place here and we've got to stay in Wassingham, we promised ourselves that. Talk to them, Bill, talk to them.' Annie was standing now, turning to leave. 'Ring me at home when you have. Come on Tom.'

She cut out, checked, packed, talked to Sarah as they drove to Georgie, asking how long she could bear to eat on her knee, laughing when she said, 'I like it, Mam, you don't nag about me keeping me elbows in, or putting me elbows on the table, or clattering the plate.'

They walked down the ward, nodding, waving, chatting to the men. She told Georgie of the packing, Big-mouth, the three Madam shops. She showed him the preliminary sketches Tom had done for the autumn tour and asked for his go-ahead.

'There'll be more for the next mail shot.'

She didn't tell him that they would be using Manners' stock because he had thought they were using that first. She would merely bring in the designs they had used on the first shot, the samples too. Neither did she tell him of the premises because he would ask to see the figures and would veto it because Annie knew that another loan would be needed and she knew that Georgie would not go into debt, not after

Manners. And she knew that they must move, because Sister had told her that on Monday they would be trying him in a wheelchair, that soon he would be transferred to the special unit where he would learn to walk again, and soon he would be home.

Bill had spoken to his area manager who had asked for a revised price for the lease. It was refused. The bank agreed a loan, shared by Annie and Tom again because they had no choice but to accept the consortium's terms – Georgie was coming home, there were no other suitable premises, there never would be in Wassingham. Their solicitor forced through the paperwork. The consortium co-operated because otherwise Annie threatened to withdraw and open up in the next village. 'Eager to have their bloody money,' Tom cursed.

'Afraid that they'll be left with a pup,' said Annie.

It was agreed that they would move in over the weekend.

'It's as though some bugger is second guessing us, Tom,' Annie said. 'It's as though every time we have enough to make it just that little bit easier the rug is pulled from under us.'

They moved in at nine a.m. Saturday morning, brushing, washing paintwork, until their hair was thick with dust and the air too. The children painted the woodwork when Annie had finished the whitewash.

She cleaned the lavatories, remembering Uncle Albert's and how she had hoped that he had chilblains from the cold and an inky bum from the newspaper he used because he was too stingy to replace it with proper stuff. 'Horrid old man,' she murmured, then raised her voice and asked Tom to start the tables out in the yard. 'We'll cover them with tarpaulin if it looks like rain and no sawing and hammering when I've just painted or you'll know what its like to be glossed from head to toe.'

They ate bread and cheese at lunchtime. The men drank beer but not too much for there was still the wiring to be done, the shelves to be erected, the tables to be finished.

Annie and Gracie pretended not to hear the curses as drills

were broken or hammers dropped though Davy and Sarah kept a notebook and wrote all the new words down.

They ate fish and chips on the floor by the light of hurricane lamps and laughed at the sight of Tom's back which was white from the gloss paint he had leaned against.

They laughed the next day too, as the tables were put together and Rob asked where the union man was to have his office.

'Union woman you mean,' Sarah said. 'Or hasn't Uncle Tom told you all about the birds and the bees.'

'No unions necessary here yet, lad,' Tom said wagging his finger at Sarah.

'No unions necessary at all,' Annie said. 'We've only got six workers and that includes Gracie and me.'

'We're all in it together – like a big family. There'll be a bonus scheme with the profits. Some will be ploughed back, the rest shared,' Tom added.

Sarah looked at Annie. 'Well, we kids deserve a share too, look how hard we've worked.'

Annie looked at Tom and Gracie, then at Betsy. 'We'll see, when the weekend's over.'

The electrics were finished at three, the tables too. Brenda's husband had helped Tom without charge.

They moved in the machines, stacked the cloth, the trimmings, everything. Annie put up her stock-control charts and asked Tom about printing up some two shilling discount vouchers 'off the next purchase' to be put into each packaged order.

'Good idea. They'll come back to us. We can build it into the price to some extent.'

They moved in her rotary cutter, Tom's design board. The carpenter erected a partition for Annie's office. The phone would be installed on Monday. 'I'll ring round and tell everyone our new number then send a circular to all potential customers.'

They erected a partition for Tom's design department. He

placed his board beneath the skylight, and asked for just one more shelf.

Betsy brought them flasks of tea at nine o'clock. 'Bloody ambrosia,' Tom said, drinking his in great gulps.

'I've brought in a kettle, and put in a box of provisions,' Bet said. 'We'll not be able to run a business without a good cuppa.'

Annie sat back on a table, took out her cigarettes, put one in her mouth, then looked up as a silence grew. Bet, Gracie, Tom, Rob, the carpenter, Sarah and Davy, even Brenda's husband were all shaking their heads and she took it from her mouth, put it back into the packet and joined in the laughter and the conversation which swelled and continued until late into the night.

In the morning Annie told the staff that they were forbidden to eat or drink and especially to smoke at their tables. They could make tea in the restroom and smoke there in their breaks.

She told them of the revised Glasgow order which she had taken this morning when she rang the store. She pointed to the coupons which Joe had brought to the premises.

'We're still inundated but it's getting better so there'll be a new mail shot soon. Don't worry, we can cope with the existing Manners' stock, we'll just be altering the trim to fill the first orders, and only then making up new ones. We are paying a basic wage – I don't believe in piecework, as you know. And there will be a bonus as and when we are operating at a profit. Sadly the leasehold has tripled. It has swallowed our profit and we now have debts to repay but the direct and indirect orders are pouring in and growing all the time. Things will improve,'

She worked throughout the day, walking to the restroom frequently to light up, sucking the smoke in deeply, wishing the trembling in her hands would stop, and the headaches too. Brenda said, 'It's not fair you know, Annie, Jean smokes and she can't keep leaving her machine.'

Annie nodded, 'You're right,' she said and walked back to

her office, then to the cutting machine. She must keep her hands busy and her mouth shut. How had Tom stopped and not screamed at them all every minute of the day? Didn't Brenda know what it was like to starve yourself?

Gracie took over in the afternoon and Annie visited Georgie with Sarah. As they walked up the stairs to the ward Sarah said, 'When we were laughing yesterday I forgot Da, forgot he was in here.'

Annie nodded. 'I did too, but that's what he'd want. It means things are getting better. We're not so worried. Soon he'll be home.'

They walked down the ward, waving to the men, saying hello, waving to Georgie who was sitting up in his bed at the end of the row.

'Cor, been riding up and down the ward in his throne today he has,' Old Jed said.

Annie smiled, not understanding, then Andy called from the left. 'Proper little Hitler. Telling staff to turn left, right and then fast forward. Come and have an apple, Annie, lovely they are, the Missus brought them.'

Annie moved across as Sarah ran down to Georgie. 'Hello Mrs Ganby, how do you put up with this husband of yours?' Annie took the apple, feeling Andy grip her fingers, pull her closer.

'He's been in the wheelchair today. He was faint, frightened. He's not himself,' Andy said quietly.

'Thanks, Andy.' Annie touched his hand, smiled at Mrs Ganby, took the apple across to Georgie, watched his empty smile as they talked, his shoulders which were straight and tense. She told him of the move, of the help that Sarah had been.

'You can see from her hair,' she laughed.

His laugh was strained.

'The girls are busy. Everything's set up, there's a new order from Glasgow and there's talk of another from Edinburgh.'

Georgie nodded, she waited, listening as Sarah told him of her new cart, the latest Elvis Presley, Bill Haley's *Rock around the Clock*, of Annie's quick temper now that she wasn't smoking, then there was silence.

'So, how are you, darling?' Annie said.

'Fine, just fine.'

Staff Nurse took his temperature, his pulse, straightened his sheets, caught Annie's eye and gestured towards her office. Annie nodded, she would stop and talk when visiting ended.

'You look better, you've some colour.'

'So I should, I've been having my exercise. I've been having my constitutional. I've been pushing myself up the ward in a wheelchair, practising to be a cripple.'

Sarah's face went blank with shock, she turned to Annie as the bell rang and the wives bent to kiss their husbands, squeeze their hands, tuck in their blankets. Annie did all these, then took Sarah's hand and his, saying to both of them. 'There will be days like these but it will improve. You'll be frightened now, it'll seem strange to be upright, to have to be helped. You'll feel faint but just remember, you'll come home and pick up your life again and that's what we want more than anything else because we love you, we admire you.'

She held Sarah's hand as they walked down the ward, turning to wave at Georgie, feeling her own tears but knowing he must never see them fall at the thought of him in a wheelchair.

Georgie watched them go. God, she looked so tired and Sarah so small – he must be crazy. 'Annie, Annie,' he called but she was gone and he hadn't told her that he'd wanted to cling to the bed, stay where it was safe, that he hadn't wanted to look down once he was in the chair and see the gap where his leg should have been. He hadn't wanted to be pushed down the ward so that everyone could see it too. He couldn't tell her that he loved her, wanted her to hold him, make him better, bring back his leg, take him to a time before any of this had happened.

He couldn't tell her that they would be moving him to the special unit now that his stump had healed sufficiently for a leg to be fitted. He would practise walking again and then he could come home and pick up his life. He couldn't tell her that that thought frightened him more than death, because what sort of a life would it be? They had all moved on without him.

CHAPTER 9

Georgie wheeled himself down the ramps on to the grass of the special unit. It was his first morning and the scent of roses hung in the August air. All around were other patients in chairs, wheelchairs and on crutches. It made him feel at home.

He sat and watched the breeze ripple the lake.

'You'll be able to walk down there soon,' a passing nurse called. 'I'm telling you, just you wait and see.'

He looked after her, watching her stride across the lawn towards the building. Could she also tell him how to join a firm which had not existed before this had happened, a firm which he had had no hand in, which had only thrived once he had gone?

Could she tell him how to show his body to his wife, make love to her? Could she tell him how to break free of this great black bird of depression which hovered over him, day and night?

The next morning he wheeled himself down corridors which did not shine as they had in the hospital. 'Don't want you all slipping and sliding about do we?' the nurse said, walking behind him.

He eased himself up on to the bed, hitched up his dressing gown and watched as a man in a white coat smiled at him and then slipped a thin sock over his stump.

'Taking a cast for the pylon,' he said. 'I'm Bill by the way.' Bill whistled through yellowed teeth as he slapped plaster on.

137

He needed his white coat Georgie thought, as the plaster splashed him, we all need a bloody white coat, as some landed on his own lapel.

In five minutes it had set.

'OK. I've got a pair of your shoes, haven't I? Come back in a week, same time, same place, I'll be waiting.' Bill grinned. 'I'm not as tempting as Marilyn Monroe but who cares.'

It took a week to build up his strength – a week of physiotherapy and exercise, a week without Annie and he was glad because then there was nothing to remind him of the world outside.

On Sunday she came with Sarah and they walked across the lawn towards him, Annie so thin, so tired, Sarah so eager and it was at Sarah he looked, at Sarah he smiled because she wouldn't see that behind the smile there was only uncertainty and fear.

They drank tea and watched the ripples on the lake and the glitter of the pale afternoon sun and talked of the following week, when he would begin to walk.

'At last, darling,' she said, 'you'll be up on your feet, and soon we'll have you back terrorising the neighbourhood. Remember that waltz you promised me?'

They could only stay for one hour because the drive back was long and besides, Sister Barnes had said that he was tired, depressed, and needed his peace.

She watched Sarah and Davy crouching on the grass making daisy chains and Annie remembered how Georgie had made one for her at the beck when they were children, his strong brown fingers sewing the stems through the eyes, his fingers lifting her hair as he settled it round her neck, and the smell of his skin had hung between them.

'She's growing so much,' Georgie said.

'I know, the time just seems to rush by somehow, one minute they're babies, the next they're singing rock 'n' roll.'

'I don't want to talk about time,' he said quietly, his voice flat and empty.

Annie put her hand on his, wanting his firm grasp but

there was nothing and so she talked of Brenda because that at least was safe.

'You see, Georgie, she feels one girl should just sew seams, another the gusset and so on. Apparently it's how it was done in her old workshop. I don't agree, I think there's a pride to a finished garment. What do you think? You've such a steady head on you. I wish you were back – we need you.'

Georgie looked at the trees. The leaves had already begun to change and soon there would be a chill in the air. Sarah and Davy were down by the lake now, running round it, counting how many times they could do it before they had to give up, out of breath.

He looked at Annie. What did he know about gussets and seams? It was a world away. He shrugged. 'You'll sort it out.'

Annie drove away from the white building with its columns, its sloping lawns, its roses. The gravel crunched beneath the wheels, the children chatted in the back. She looked in her rear-view mirror hoping to see him waving but he had turned and was pushing his way back to the lake. He hadn't been interested in her, or in the business, but it was only uncertainty, she knew that, she was a nurse, goddammit, and she knew that his battle was not nearly over, that he was in danger of drowning and that she could do nothing to help.

Georgie wore trousers down to Bill's. The sister had pinned his empty leg up. 'Tidier,' she'd said.

We must be tidy, he thought, remembering how he'd told his men this. For God's sake be tidy or the bomb could blow. Isaacs had told Annie that. What was it – be tidy or Georgie Armstrong will mess it up?

Sister held the swing doors open and he wheeled himself through and there was his leg standing against the wall, shiny, new, tidy, covered in rivets, nuts and screws, wearing his sock, his shoe.

'Shapely, don't you think?' Bill said, lifting the leg, point-

139

ing towards another set of swing doors. 'Come into the Palais then, just don't jive the first day.'

Georgie's hands were damp as he pushed himself through into a whitewashed room with a large rubber mat on the floor and a huge mirror hanging at the end of low parallel bars.

Bill steadied him as he heaved himself from the chair on to a stool. He wriggled his trousers down as Bill asked, feeling unsafe, glad of Bill's help as he lifted first one buttock then the next, easing his trousers from beneath him, removing his shirt. 'Good, Sister said she'd told you to wear a vest. Leave it on, you'll need it. The harness is a bit like a new pair of shoes which rub your heels – have to wear them in a bit.'

'I knew there was a good reason to lose a leg,' Georgie smiled, nodding at his false leg. 'No blisters to worry your heel any more.'

Bill laughed. 'That's the spirit. Gets some people down, this does.' Bill pulled on a short woolly sock over the stump then eased the deep socket of the pylon over the leg, buckling the leather belt which was attached to it round Georgie's lower abdomen, then buckling his leather braces to the body-belt. Georgie felt helpless, uncomfortable, ugly. 'It's like harnessing up a bloody horse,' he said.

'Not a bad comparison – you're going to be working like one in a minute and if you're good you can have a carrot,' Bill said rechecking the harness. 'Now listen to me, there's a hinge in the knee and the instep to "give" when you walk. It'll all feel very strange and you'll have no strength in that stump. Upsadaisy now, time to take your partners for a glide across the floor – you've drawn the short straw – two blokes.'

A younger man had come through the door and they each helped him up, steadied him and let him sink his weight on to the pylon. Christ, he had no strength at all. He was going to fall, he felt faint, so high up. Christ. Georgie took deep breaths, his body trembling, the pylon was pinching, his stump squeezing it, hurting. For God's sake he couldn't bear

140

any more pain. The harness was digging into him and cutting. Don't let go. For God's sake don't let go!

'I can't, sit me down. Sit me down,' he was shouting.

Bill said, 'That's what they all say so don't worry, we're here. I might look small but I'm tough, or that's what I tell the girls. So's John. Put your arm round me – I promise not to kiss you.'

Georgie leant on them both.

'Look up, Georgie, pretend that chap in the mirror isn't you but our Marilyn walking over a vent. Go on get your head up.'

Georgie couldn't move. He'd fall if he moved even his bloody head just a fraction, couldn't they see that?

'Go on, look in the mirror, see that man standing looking at you?'

Georgie lifted his head now, slowly, very slowly and saw a man, thin-faced, pale with hair which hung over his forehead and a metal leg. It was the man who had once run on to the beach with his family, the man who had fought in the jungles, who had struggled over passes and down through valleys. It was the man who had once been Georgie Armstrong.

'Try a step,' Bill suggested.

Georgie looked at him then, turning his head slowly, slapping the smile back on to his face. 'Just one, I thought we were going to have a jive Bill?'

Bill's face was gentle now. 'Just one and we'll trip the light fantastic tomorrow, eh, make your wife jealous.'

Georgie looked back but not at the mirror, as he tried to swing his leg forward but nothing moved. 'Hold me, hold me,' he panicked, feeling his right leg trembling, feeling nothing but pain from his stump. Bill's arm tightened around his waist.

'Try flicking the stump forward, the knee will bend automatically. Then when it's forward, kick the stump down and it'll straighten out on the heel. Imagine you're at home and the wife's cracking the whip.'

He did, the knee straightening as the heel hit the rubber mat. He jerked, lost balance, felt Bill tighten his grasp, felt his own arms bearing down on their shoulders. 'Don't drop me.'

'OK, you've got that far, now finish it,' Bill said.

Georgie couldn't move, the leg was stopping him, it was just stuck there in front, obstructing him. It was lifeless, dead. 'I can't move.'

'I know, no one can because that leg isn't part of you, it's not listening to your brain. It's got no spring because there are no muscles. It's an obstruction you have to push yourself over, using the momentum of your body.'

'I haven't got any bloody momentum,' Georgie ground out, the sweat of the effort running into his eyes, down his chest, staining his vest and the leather of the harness.

'Imagine it's Marilyn over there and the draught from the vent's becoming a bloody hurricane.' Bill was laughing and Georgie joined in, though there was no mirth in him.

'Pull me,' he ground out, ashamed of his failure.

'They all say that too,' Bill said. 'You're doing fine.'

They pulled him forward until he was balancing on his stump, frightened that he would fall. Oh God, if he was like this with two men holding him what would he be like alone? It was all too difficult, too damn difficult.

'Move your good leg then,' Bill urged, gripping his arm. 'We've got you.'

He didn't dare. He'd never thought about lifting a leg to walk but you did. You lifted it off the ground, and that would leave him balancing on a bit of metal. He couldn't – he'd fall, he'd never be able to do it.

'Hold me,' he begged.

'It's all right we've got you. You're doing fine.'

They held him, he balanced, lifted his leg, moved it forward so slowly, very slowly, don't jog, don't fall. There, it was in front.

'Now the other one.'

He flicked his left stump forward and they pulled him up

and over it. He moved his good leg but not quite so slowly this time. He was closer to the mirror but he couldn't see himself because of the sweat in his eyes. Now the left again. He flicked it, it stuck. God, it was going to push him backwards. It didn't but there was sweat all over his body now.

'Keep going, we've to reach the stool by the mirror and then we can all go and have a nice cup of tea.'

He kept going, jerking, flicking, balancing. So much to remember, so difficult. Too difficult. Try, just try. Keep on trying. He looked up, almost there. Once more, flick, stop. 'Pull me, please.' Over and down. Thank God. He felt Bill and John take his weight as he sank on to the stool, glad that the sweat was rolling down his face, his chest and his body because he feared that there might be tears there too.

'It's always the same the first time. We'll try you on shorter steps this afternoon.'

They did and it was slightly easier, but that was all.

He dreamt that night of the beach, of Annie when she was fifteen, of their bodies lying together, of his hands on her, his lips on hers and she was calling him a beautiful bonny lad, and stroking his legs, both his legs. When he woke he was bathed in sweat and he longed for her to be here, to be with him but that was before he remembered.

The next day and the next he worked and still it was hard, frightening, and so bloody difficult and by Thursday his stump was chafed and raw and Sister Martins said he must rest it but only for two days. He wished Sister Barnes had been on duty because she would have said a week.

He pushed his wheelchair into the garden and watched the lake, it didn't matter because at least for this moment he wasn't in that room streaming sweat, struggling, despairing. He breathed in the freshness of the morning savouring his solitude, glad that he was here, alone, where the hours blended and life moved on without him and there was only dark nothingness for company.

The weeks passed and by the third he was flicking, balancing, pulling himself over without help. By September he was

143

turning himself round, lurching in a tight semi-circle. In September too, Sarah told him of her first week in her new class, showed him her satchel and he nodded and smiled but it seemed too far away.

Annie told him that Mrs Norris was talking of retiring but that she wouldn't until he was home for the farewell party.

'I've dried the lavender, made pot pourri for the bathroom. You'll think you're back at Gosforn. Oh Georgie, I can't wait until you're home. You look better, my darling. I love you so much, miss you so much. The house is all ready for you. I hope you like the wallpaper in the bedroom.'

She talked of the town, of the independence of Malaya, Frank's pigeons and he nodded, but what had any of this to do with him?

'I had to insist that Brenda go back to the girls sewing complete garments because production's fallen off, they need the satisfaction of seeing the finished article, is that all right?' Annie said, wishing he would say he loved her.

He nodded.

She told him that the children helped them with packaging the garments each evening because they were saving towards a gramophone, that the new mail shot was up and running, that they all missed him, loved him.

'We need to replace two of the machines though. They have no interlockers and just one wrench will pull apart the seams so Meg and Jean have to hand-finish, it's ridiculous. I've some on order – do you agree?' She wanted him to feel part of it, to feel necessary.

He listened, though what was it to do with him? Here it was the lake that was important and the roses which were past their best, and his leg. Her world was too far away. It was too dark, too difficult.

As Annie walked back through the building towards her car Sister Barnes called her into her office, telling her that Georgie would be ready to leave before the end of September. 'He's very much better physically and should be independent by then and confident in his mobility,' she said. 'But there's always a psychological adjustment to be made, Mrs Armstrong, and it can take some time.'

Annie nodded, looking out at the lake, at Georgie sitting there, his hands resting on his stick.

Sister Barnes continued. 'Georgie's depressed, uncertain. Can you manage?'

Annie didn't like Sister Barnes, she was blonde and silly, she giggled. She wished that it was Sister Martins sitting there. 'He'll need great care, these men have suffered a great deal, they turn inward and need kindness, forbearance, patience.'

Annie nodded. She wanted a cigarette and she did not want to listen to his silly woman telling her how much her husband had suffered. Did she think she was blind, or deaf, or just plain stupid and had noticed nothing over the days and weeks? All she wanted was to have him home and then she would make him come alive.

'Now, do you have a downstairs room? I suggest you set up a bedroom for him there. He says the stairs are narrow. It would be a problem for him, especially at first. He's asked us especially to mention this to you.'

Annie looked at the clock on the wall, then back at the lake. Yes, the stairs were narrow, yes she would set up a bed but it would be their bed and she tried not to feel pain at the thought that he could not make that request himself and wanted to go and drag him to the car, back to Wassingham because it was more than time that he came home.

The hospital rang Annie at the end of the third week in September to ask her to collect Georgie at ten o'clock the next morning, Sunday. Tom came round and helped her to dismantle her double bed and lug it down the stairs into the front room. Sarah and Davy brought down the bedside cupboards and the dressing table when they came home from school.

Annie bought food from the market. Plaice because it was his favourite and strawberry ice cream.

Sarah said, 'Oh, Mum, it's going to be so good to have him home, have him here eating with us, talking to us.'

'He'll be rather changed, he'll need time to adjust. He'll be depressed, my darling.'

'No he won't, he'll be glad to be home.'

He was quiet on the journey, sitting with the seat pushed as far back as possible, his false knee bent, and Annie let him just absorb the countryside, which must seem strange and threatening after the restrictions of the world he had lived in for nearly four months.

They approached Wassingham from the north, coming in below the slag heaps. 'Nothing changes,' she said, knowing that everything had.

He gripped his stick.

She turned into Wassingham Terrace and there were Tom and Sarah, Davy and Rob, Gracie and Bet and the neighbours, so many of them, waving, smiling.

'Oh God,' said Georgie.

'They're so pleased to see you, so thrilled you're home.' She touched his knee and he jerked away from her, staring through the windscreen.

Annie pulled up, and came round as Tom opened Georgie's door. She saw him lever himself erect, smile at the neighbours, at Tom, Sarah and the others, saw him walk towards the door, flicking his leg out, kicking, moving over, his jaw set in concentration, his smile rigid. She hardly breathed until he reached the doorway and then she relaxed until she remembered the step.

She moved forward to steady him, but it was too late. His foot caught, he toppled, grabbed at the door, at her, fell out and into the street and there was silence.

She bent down, put her hands beneath his shoulder, saw Tom doing the same. 'I'm so sorry, Annie,' Georgie said and the smile was still fixed on his face, and there was nothing in his eyes and her heart broke for this man she loved so much.

'Bloody step,' Annie said, heaving him up, looking across at Tom. 'Daft bloody step, it's tripped me up more times than I can count. We'll go in and have lunch.'

Sarah moved ahead of them, the others behind, but Georgie stopped at the door to the front room.

'I'm tired. I'd like to sleep.' Annie saw Sarah's face and Davy's too but said, 'Fine, we'll eat later.'

He wouldn't let her help him change and whilst he slept they talked in the kitchen about anything but how dark Georgie's eyes were, how lonely, how cold he looked. He wouldn't eat all that day, he just lay in the front room until everyone had gone, until Sarah was in bed and when Annie came to him at last, he said, 'I toss and turn. I don't want to keep you awake.'

She lay upstairs in the camp bed in what had been their room thinking of the shape of just one leg beneath the blankets and she didn't sleep, and so she worked because the tour was coming up in two weeks and the catalogue needed to be proof-read, the samples finished off, their forward planning rechecked because it stopped her thinking of the bleakness in his eyes and her helplessness.

Georgie didn't get up the next morning. He ate breakfast in bed. Annie worked all morning and though she knew that Bet was in the house she still rushed home at lunchtime to give him salad and tea. Bet and Sarah gave him scones at four, tucked him in tightly, talked to him, soothed him and when Annie came in she helped him to the bathroom, pinning up his pyjama leg before she did so.

'Can you pass me my crutches?' he asked.

'Why not put your leg on?'

'I'm too tired.'

She handed him the crutches Sister Barnes had put in the boot saying that they might be useful and she liked her boys to have them. If she had been here now Annie would have slapped her.

He wouldn't allow her to stay. He locked the door and she wanted to shout, I'm your wife, let me in and throw those crutches away but she didn't know what harm that would do.

She didn't sleep that night either. How could you sleep when your husband was in the depths of despair and you didn't know what you should be doing? But anyway, she had only slept for a few hours at night for so long, what did lack of sleep matter? It didn't make the headache any worse, or the trembling in her hands.

All week she soothed him, talked to him, told him she loved him, kissed his lips but there was no warmth in his. Did he blame her? She asked him and he said no.

'Does it hurt?'

He said, 'No.'

'Are you very tired?' He said yes and there were dark circles beneath his eyes and that night she wanted to come down to his room, hold him, comfort him but he had said he wanted to be alone.

She sat and talked to him over the weekend, Sarah brought him tea, books, biscuits, love, and by Sunday Annie knew that in spite of what that stupid blonde Sister Barnes said there was too much love around him, too much care. Her husband was drowning and none of this was helping and so that evening she sat on his bed.

'Darling, it's time you got up. It's time you helped me, became a father, a husband again. Please come into work with me in the morning. Eat with us this evening.'

'I'm tired, Annie, can't you see that? I'm bloody tired.'

He lay down, closed his eyes and she left him, closing the door quietly and he wanted to call to her. Annie, I need you, stay with me, hold me, love me, stroke me, but how could he ask that of anyone when he was as he was?

How could he go into work when all he had ever done was

misjudge Manners? How could he go out into the street and fall again and see the pity in everyone's eyes?

On Monday morning Annie looked into his room before she left for work.

'I won't be back for lunch, Georgie. You'll have to make you own because Bet won't be in today.' She didn't tell him she had instructed Bet not to come in and neither did she wait for a reply but sat in the office all morning, working, but not properly, wanting to smoke, but not doing so, wanting to run home but sitting, just sitting.

She returned at half past five. Sarah was not yet in, Georgie had gone without lunch. She stood in his bedroom looking at this man she loved and knew that she had fifteen minutes before Sarah arrived and that she must use those minutes to try and break through to Georgie and to do that she must speak words that must only ever be heard by the two of them.

'Help me with the tea, please, Georgie.'

'I can't, I'm too tired.'

'Yes, you bloody can, George Armstrong, you just won't. There's nothing wrong with you, you're not ill, you've just lost a leg – now just get your bum out of that bed, perch it up on that leg and get going. I need help. I'm the one who's tired, I'm the one who's busting a gut trying to keep this business going. You're the one who wanted an edge, you insisted on it. Well, you've got one for the rest of your life, so face it and get on with it.'

He looked at her now. 'Yes, that's right, you're the one who's keeping the business going and I'm the one who nearly ran us on to the rocks so I'm best out of the bloody way. Get off my back, woman.' He was leaning forward, his lips thin, his eyes hopeless. There was no anger in his voice, no resentment, nothing and Annie turned away, not knowing what to say or do now only knowing that a great despair was pouring over her.

'Mum!' Sarah was standing in the doorway, her face white

149

and there was enough anger there to make up for any lack in Georgie.

Annie stood still, Oh God, Sarah had heard. She grabbed her daughter's arm, shut the door, and pulled her to the kitchen as the words spilled out of Sarah's mouth, white hot, wounding as she had known they would be. 'You bitch, you cruel bitch. You're just mean. He's me da, you can't say anything like that to him. You don't love him, you just want him working. He's not well, he's hurt, he needs . . .'

'A bloody good kick up the pants,' Annie shouted back, then said more quietly, 'Listen to me, do you remember the nurse in hospital who said I was right not to spoil him, not to make it easy? She was right, Sister Barnes is wrong. I should have had more sense because if we don't get him up off that bed I don't know what'll happen. You've just got to try and understand and if you can't, then be quiet, because I can't cope with any more.'

Annie sat down as Sarah spun away from her, rushing out of the room, running up stairs, screaming down, 'I hate you, I hate you. You went off and left him today, all alone and then you shout at him. You don't care about anything but that bloody business. I hate you and if you'd nursed none of this would have happened.'

Annie sat at the table, running her trembling fingers up and down the grain, feeling the headache worsen. How could that be when it was already such agony all the time? She held up her hands, trying to hold them steady. They were clammy. She ran them over her face. God, she was hot and she didn't know what to do any more.

She went into the yard. It was dark, her hands were wet and she leant back on the wall, looked up at the sky, closed her eyes and heard the sound of screaming, of shouting, of counting getting louder and louder. It was even louder than the pounding in her head and it was taking her away from this. Thank God it was all coming back and taking her with it, into the darkness again.

There were the smells, Dr Jones, her face smeared, kind,

her hands coming out towards her, waving her on. Where was Prue? There at the end of the rope. 'I'm coming,' Annie called. 'I'm coming back.'

But then she heard the small sound of crying. A tiny sound and it was coming between her and Prue, between Dr Jones, between the smells and the noises and the counting, between the pounding in her head and they were fading, growing weaker and she couldn't hear the counting, she could only hear the crying.

Annie felt the wall behind her. It was cold, rough, she opened her eyes, the sky was dark, cool. There was a wind, the crispness of autumn all around her and from Sarah's room there was the sound of crying.

She walked over to the pigeon loft, feeling the rotten wood at the ends, remembering the fluttering of Eric's birds, the soft cooing and now her head was not even pounding any more, there was nothing but cool, clear thought and she knew that she would never again be visited by the past – it was over, her family had pushed it away, consigned it to its proper place.

She went to Sarah's bedroom, kissed her damp hair, and held her while her daughter cried and then Annie told her that tomorrow her da would be up, but that she must help. She also told her that from now on she would be home from work earlier, that life was too short to be working when there were children to enjoy.

That night she slept and there were no dreams and no head-ache in the morning, there was only the same clear freshness. The next morning she phoned Gracie asking her to open the factory.

'Sarah and I have a few things to do.'

She rang Tom at work and found that Frank was on the afternoon shift.

'God, you're not getting him sewing knickers too, are you?' Tom asked. Then his voice became serious. 'How's Georgie, have you got anywhere?'

'Let's just say, we're about to.'

Frank came round just after she called him. Sarah played the radio in the kitchen. It was *Worker's Playtime* and she sang along loudly to it while Annie and Frank hammered in the yard, then piled their tools and the wood near the back door.

'You can stop now, Sarah,' Annie called.

They cycled round to Frank's and came back with one of his wicker boxes which they carried into Georgie's room.

'Since you won't feed yourself, perhaps you'll make sure you feed this,' Annie said nodding to Sarah.

Sarah lifted the squeaker out, then looked up at Annie.

'Yes, please darling, put it on the bed.'

Sarah hesitated and Annie smiled gently. 'Shall I do it?'

Sarah shook her head and put the squeaker on Georgie's bed.

'Now, we're going. We shall be back at the end of the day. Frank says they're like kids – only two things on their mind – food and a place to roost. He's left food but you need to mix it. There are small pots out in the yard. It's a late bred bird, too late for this year's races but it'll need exercise and training. There's a note explaining everything.'

Georgie said nothing, just looked at the bird and then at Annie.

'It'll do plops if you leave it there, Da,' Sarah said.

They left. Annie dropped Sarah into school with a note which said she had needed to be at home on a medical matter and then sat in the office, looking through the mail-order catalogue proof. They would enclose one with each order and get spin-off sales. She looked at the clock. It was midday.

She checked the invoices, then walked to the restroom, needing a cigarette, asking Brenda for one of hers. She refused.

'Oh go on, I need one. It's a special day.'

'Georgie?'

'Yes, I can't go home for lunch. I have to stay until five

and then I hope he'll be in tomorrow. Go on, let me have one.'

Brenda shook her head. 'No, you've done so well, I'd get fired if I let you.'

'But I'm the boss.'

'I know and you'd fire me tomorrow.'

Annie laughed, walked from the room, as Brenda said, 'I'll keep my fingers crossed for him. You look so much better today, different somehow.'

Annie knew she did.

She checked the design table and approved the smock Tom had sketched. He had one more week to do at the mine and then he was coming in full-time. Their turnover was high enough now to support the two families, and there would be a bonus at Christmas for the girls.

She looked at the clock. One o'clock. Was he up? Would he ring?

By two there had been no call. She walked round the machine room, checking the garments. She had two girls on mail order and two on wholesalers and traders. It worked well but was too much work for her – she desperately needed Georgie to carry the mail order. More could be done if they could spread the workload.

She rang the hotels, confirming the bookings for Tom's tour next week, they were going later than they should be, but the buyers had said they would see him anyway.

It was three o'clock.

What would she do if Georgie didn't make it – if her husband, and Sarah's father, gave up?

She rang the reporter that she'd met at Terry's sports day and talked him into doing a feature on Wassingham Textiles using the angle of a local employer employing only local people and growing fast. Maud would be annoyed that she had dared approach a fellow parent but then Maud was always annoyed.

It was four o'clock.

The phone rang at five past four and it wasn't Georgie,

but the Central Buyer of T. Jones and Son, the Midlands department store chain and he was interested in the look of the mail order shot and wanted to discuss a pants, bra and slip set.

'It must be exclusive and our own label.'

So what's new, she thought. 'I think we can help, Mr Harborne. Can we arrange a meeting between you and our Chief Designer. He's tied up for the next two weeks but will be in your area on . . . let me see,' Annie reached for her diary, flipping through until she found Tom's tour dates. 'How about lunch in the week of tenth October? I'll get him to call you tomorrow to finalise.'

She put down the phone. Twenty past four. She beckoned to Brenda and told her the news. It was what they'd longed for and an exclusive to a Central Buyer was safe as long as the quality was good. This wouldn't be another Manners.

It was twenty-five past four, and he still hadn't rung so even this good news meant nothing.

She couldn't stand it any longer. She picked up her coat. 'I'm going . . .'

'Yes, I think you're right, I can't stand the waiting either. I'll lock up.'

Annie kissed Brenda, then ran out to the car, throwing her briefcase into the back, starting the engine, roaring into the street, rattling over the cobbles, pulling up at the kerb, turning the key in the lock, passing his door. It was open, the bed was gone, the cupboards too and the table was back.

The kettle was on the range, steaming quietly. The back door was open and there was the sound of hammering and then a curse. 'Bloody woman, bloody finger.'

She walked to the door and stood there watching him. He had wedged himself for balance between three tubs. His leg was on, his stick was leaning against the loft, the squeaker was fluttering in the basket.

'That's a grand loft, bonny lad. Eric would be proud of you. I'm proud of you.' Annie was surprised that she could speak through the tightness of her throat.

He turned and put his arms out to her and she went to him, holding him gently, feeling him find his balance, kissing her.

'No point in having any plops on the bed. Our Sarah couldn't sell them for rhubarb, could she?' he said.

Annie felt his lips on hers, so soft, so gentle, so full of love. 'Frank and Bernie moved everything back upstairs – it's where I belong.' He kissed her again. 'I lost my way for a moment, Annie.'

Annie stroked his hair, his cheek. 'Tonight I'll race you up the stairs,' she said and now she cried because at last there was time.

CHAPTER 10

After a week it was as though Georgie had never been away but it was so much better – the worst had happened and they had survived, he told her when he first made love to her again, tentatively, differently, but completely.

He said it again at the end of the week, as they lay in the moonlight.

'Now all I have to worry about is you getting jammed in an interlocker,' Annie said.

Georgie laughed. 'Never mind the interlocker, it's the pigeon loft we need to worry about.'

Annie shook her head. 'Tell you what, let's not worry about either now.' She turned, kissed his eyes, cheeks, lips. 'More physio I think, my darling?' She was laughing and so was he and then the laughter faded as passion came, and Annie relaxed into his arms knowing that there would still be adjustments, tears, and for him there would always be bouts of pain, but that they were now going forward.

By the end of October they had taken on another worker because Tom had brought back two large orders from the tour, and several smaller ones. 'We were as professional as the next man,' he told them as they sat on the beach in the mildness of the Indian summer. 'I was flashing me cards about all over the place.'

'As long at that's all you were flashing,' Gracie snapped, then shrugged and laughed. 'Daft really, but I don't like the idea of you sitting there having lunch with all these smart women, then holding up knickers and bras for them.'

Annie nodded, hearing the shrieks of the children as they ran in and out of the foam, seeing Gracie's face and the hurt in her eyes.

'You go with him in February,' she said firmly, squeezing Gracie's shoulder. 'We should have thought of that, I'd have been upset if it had been Georgie. It needs two anyway. We can manage.'

'Does it matter that Jones wants exclusives?' Georgie asked and Annie felt Tom's eyes on her, because they had wondered when Georgie would say this.

Annie chose her words carefully. 'Jones is dealing with an established company. If he messes us up, it will do him more harm that it will us. From the business point of view, you know, it was a blessing that Manners happened when it did. It shook us up, it made us very careful with our quality, taught us a few lessons.'

She looked at Georgie, then at Tom.

Georgie said, 'Set you up with the mail order anyway, didn't it?'

The children were running up the beach now, trailing wet seaweed behind them.

'Not exactly,' Tom said and Annie looked at Georgie, at Gracie who was sitting quite still, as she was now, because she knew Tom was going to tell Georgie the truth about the loan. 'We've been trying to find the right time to tell you about this but you see, we had to put the houses against a loan to get mail order underway and we saved the exclusives for the second shot. We couldn't risk Manners putting the word about that we were selling rejects. It all worked out, Georgie, and we paid off the loan, but had to put up the houses again for the premises.'

They told him then about the consortium, about the need to keep their salaries right down in order to repay their debts and build up their capital reserves again in order to update the machines, increase bonuses, and then go on into textiles.

Georgie's face was set. The children were close now, Sarah was panting, laughing and then suddenly Georgie was too.

'I thought, way back in hospital, that you'd both lost your touch when you said you'd used the rejects for the first shot. Seemed crazy to me but I was too busy trying to live at the time and then I forgot. Sounds about right, all of it. Sounds pretty bloody wonderful. Now let's have this picnic.'

They ate chicken with sand in it, bread and butter with sand in it and laughed as it grated between their teeth because there were no lies between them any more, the last hurdle had gone. 'Ambrosia,' said Tom. 'Bloody ambrosia. Now all we need is Jones' order.'

'Come into the sea now, Uncle Georgie,' Davy said, throwing his crusts to the gulls.

Sarah looked at her father, at the trousers he wore, at the other children on the beach, some from Wassingham.

Georgie watched the gulls calling, swooping, soaring, then the fathers wading into the surf with their children, jumping the waves. He felt Annie's hand on his, the softness of her grasp, her love. 'No, not this year, lad. Me leg would go rusty.' He smiled but cutting through the laughter of the afternoon came the pain as they had both known it would, on some days.

Sarah looked away, at the men who were lifting their children and dipping them into the sea and felt anger so sharp that it took her breath away and when her mother brought strawberry ice cream out from the bag, unwrapped sheet after sheet of newspaper, and passed one to her, she pushed it back.

'I hate strawberries. I hate them,' she shouted and ran down to the sea, away from them all, away from the memory of her mother feeding her father strawberry ice cream and shouting at him in the hospital. Glad that he hadn't paddled, glad that her friends hadn't seen him hopping with his stick because you couldn't go into the sea with a false leg, didn't Davy know anything? And she wondered where all the anger had come from.

The Central Buyer of T. Jones and Son confirmed his order

158

in early November and Brenda insisted that the machines needed updating immediately.

'You're absolutely right,' Annie said and rang the supplier, ordering them for immediate delivery, explaining to Tom and Georgie, vetoing another worker at this stage in favour of better machinery, showing them the outgoings against the incomings. 'It'll be cheaper and the girls are coping. They're interested, busy, and the new machines will be a better investment right now. Brenda is doing a training session when they arrive to get maximum efficiency, though it might be an idea to do that on a regular basis anyway, just to keep them up to the mark. I'll talk to her, but not tonight, it's five-thirty, time we were home.'

She drove them, taking the accounts and designs with her. She and Georgie would discuss these later, but only when Sarah was in bed. The beach had shown them that Sarah needed to make her own adjustments and that they must be there for her.

'Sarah's been very good and done half Miss Simpson's work,' Bet said as she put supper on the table. 'But only half mind.'

Sarah pulled a face. 'I don't have to get it in until Friday and it's only for this eleven plus and I might not want to pass, even if I do.'

'I think perhaps you need to finish that work, judging from the muddle you got yourself into there,' Annie said, easing herself on to the chair next to Bet.

'Frank brought round those three youngsters for you Georgie,' Bet said, shaking pepper on to her stew.

'Sit down,' Annie laughed as he started to get up again, nodding as Sarah pleaded to be able to see them before the next round of homework.

They ate, talked, laughed and then later they held the birds in their hands, pulling out their wings, fanning their tails, listening to Georgie's plans for his Red Chequers, feeling the silkiness of their feathers as he told them that they would fly dry even in the wettest weather. 'They'll win, I know that, but they'll not beat Tiger. He's just a beaut.'

'When are you going to teach them to trap, Da?' Sarah said, holding the bird against her chest, stroking it gently.

'Pretty soon.'

'Can I help?'

'Course, and Davy too, and your mam.' Georgie put the youngsters back in the loft. 'But finish Miss Simpson's work first. It's good of her to give it to you, she doesn't have to, you know.'

'Oh, can't I stay? Go on, Mum.'

Annie smiled at her, 'Homework, or you can clean the loft if you'd really rather.'

It was no contest and Sarah was in the kitchen faster than she'd ever been whilst Annie laughed softly, cleaning the loft with the scraper, hearing the fluttering, the cooing, the soft sound of Georgie's voice. 'Ambrosia,' Annie said quietly, blessing Frank for all the months he had talked pigeons to Georgie in the darkness of the pit, because it had bred the same love in him for them and in Sarah too. It was holding them all together, it was pulling them forward because Georgie's disability made no difference in this sport.

All through the early winter they gained new orders, working themselves hard, their staff hard, and in the early evening and weekends they trained the pigeons lightly. 'But never when my washing's out,' Annie insisted.

They trained them to trap – taking them from the loft, keeping them in their basket overnight across the other side of the yard. Annie barely slept that night, glad that their neighbours had moved and taken their damn great cat with them and hoping that whoever bought the house kept goldfish instead.

Before work they released them, watching them flap and flutter. Would they go to the landing board or soar away, into the freedom of the skies? Sarah clung to her hand and they watched as they lifted.

'Oh no,' Sarah wailed.

'Sh,' Georgie said.

The pigeons were straining up, up, then they came back down, on to the landing board, then through the trap, heads deep into the food hoppers.

'Greedy little pigs,' Annie murmured.

The next week, before feeding time, they allowed them out of the loft on their own, having cut their morning feed in half. Again they stood and watched and Annie whispered between clenched teeth.

'Your bloody pigeons are going to give me a nervous breakdown one day. It's worse than Manners' orders, all this. What if they fly away and cats get them? What about the hawks?'

Georgie laughed softly. 'That's why I've got Red Chequers. Hawks like white ones, they're always picked off first.'

'I'm glad I'm a brunette,' Sarah said, holding her da's hand, feeling his warmth, her eyes on her own bird, Buttons, as he flew higher and higher.

'OK,' Georgie said. 'Call them, Sarah. Use the feeding tin, rattle it and call as well.'

Sarah looked at him. She didn't want to, what if they didn't come? What if she wasn't loud enough?

'You do it, Da.'

Georgie didn't want to. What if they ignored him, what if they kept on flying?

'Go on, Sarah, pretend it's Terry running off with your drum sticks.' Annie's voice was gentle. 'They'll come back, kids always do when they're hungry, just think of yourself.'

Sarah called them, again and again, until they circled lower and lower and trapped.

'Greedy little pigs,' Annie murmured again, feeling her muscles relax.

On the weekend before Christmas they put them in their basket, hearing their scratching, their fluttering, driving out past the slag heaps towards the north. Only one mile, Frank had said, then turn left, down the track. They bumped and

161

rocked and Sarah and Davy said the birds must wish they were flying already.

They stood in the whipping wind and Annie's hands were numb as she fumbled with the leather straps because Georgie still found it difficult to reach to the ground.

'God, worse than your harness, Georgie,' she grimaced, smiling as he laughed, noticing that Sarah laughed too and she felt relief wash over her.

'I hope they're ready for this, Uncle Georgie,' Davy said, squatting next to Annie.

'So do I lad, but they had no supper last night and they've been flying round in a flock for a week or so now, so they should be fine. They'll race against one another, just like you kids. If they're on their own, they'll mess about.'

'Just like you kids,' Annie laughed, looking up at Georgie. 'Shall I let them go?'

He nodded, checked his watch and she lifted the lid, letting it drop back, standing up as the birds left, watching them soar, dip, rise again, keeping together. Just like Sarah's gang. She looked at her daughter, at Davy. Yes, they'd all keep together but would they if some got through to the grammar? She still wished that Don had not pulled apart as he had.

The birds were at home, waiting for them and Frank's grin was all they needed when they told him the exact time that they had been tossed.

'They're good, aren't they?' Georgie said.

'They'll do,' Frank replied.

By Christmas, Jones had re-ordered because their exclusives had sold so well.

'The wholesale division,' Tom called out over the remains of the Christmas lunch at Bet's, waving his cigarless hand, blowing imaginary smoke rings. 'The wholesale division is thriving.'

'Mail order could still do better,' Georgie said patting his stomach.

'Your stomach's really fat, Da,' Sarah said. 'You're gross.'

162

Georgie grinned and patted it. 'There, sounds better than your drums.'

'Urgh. It's because you've only got one leg for all the food to go down. You'll have to eat less, Da.' Sarah was laughing, they were all laughing because there had only been humour in Sarah's voice, and acceptance again.

Annie caught Georgie's eye and they both knew what the other was feeling and, if they could, they'd have tangoed round the kitchen. She grinned, watched Tom lean forward, hand Georgie the wishbone, saw their little fingers pull, leaving Tom with the wish. It didn't matter, they had all they wanted.

She looked round the kitchen at the red and green decorations, there was tinsel on the tree that they'd helped to hang last night and the smell of turkey all around. No cigars this year.

'Don looked well, and Maud.'

'They should have come today instead of last night, then they'd have seen the gramophone,' Sarah said.

'We could have taken Terry down to the club, let her have a go on the drums.'

'Does she go to a Youth Club?' Bet asked.

Sarah shook her head. 'No, she says her mother wouldn't like it, she might meet the wrong people. People like us, she meant.' She and Davy were laughing, Rob too, but Annie, Tom and the others looked at one another, seeing the same anger until the children pulled them to their feet, dragging them out through the yard, down to the football field where Georgie refereed as they kicked a ball around on the frost stiffened grass until the breath jogged in their bodies.

Tom looked at his watch. 'Time you kids were at the club,' he called and Annie sank on to the cold ground, grateful that there was a halt, moving her toes inside her shoes, walking back slowly with Georgie, taking his arm in case he slipped on the frost.

'It's OK for you,' she murmured against his sleeve. 'You only get chilblains on one foot, we get them on both.'

Georgie laughed, 'But I've got a fat stomach, your daughter said.'

'She's always my daughter when she's in trouble.'

Georgie squeezed her arm, then called to Tom. 'You know mail order needs perking up – what about an outsize department? I know we wouldn't get enough response to make it worth a special mail shot but what about a special catalogue mailed out to all those who've ordered outsize before, plus including it in all the orders sent out.' He turned to Annie. 'What d'you think?'

'Good idea and we could extend the ordinary offers to include outsizes, not just respond to specific queries.' They were nearing Bet's, walking through the yard, into the house, stripping off their coats, drinking the tea Bet brought over, working out figures on the paper she brought to them when she heard their conversation. They decided on a thirty per cent ratio to hold ready. Tom would run up catalogues. Not glossy, they decided. Keep that expense for the tour. Just run off some copies.

'And what about a special kitchen mail shot next year, using red and green fabric and special Christmas motif. I haven't seen any but maybe we could find some?'

'Or maybe we'll be able to set up the printing sooner than we thought, make our own?' Georgie said, grinning at Tom.

They drank more tea, smiling, talking, feeling the same excitement, loving it.

Outsize went well. By the end of January 1958 the turnover was higher but Brenda said that the girls were bored with underwear and aprons. What about fashions – would that be a good idea?

Annie put it to them all at one of the monthly meetings which had been held since the firm began but explaining that there was no falling off in underwear demand, no reason to take a risk just at the moment. They needed to consolidate, because their profit margins were still tight. 'Remember how small the bonuses have been?'

The workers nodded.

'Have a look at the balance sheets, but we won't forget fashions. Tom has a smock he's playing around with.'

'He hasn't got the legs for it,' Jean called out.

'Couldn't agree more,' Annie said, passing round the balance sheets. 'We'll go into fashions one day, girls, don't worry, but we must be patient, think how far we've come and very quickly. We must just be careful.'

Georgie felt his birds were not just bored with their loft, but cold because the wood was so rotten it was crumbling, letting in draughts. Annie told him that he must be patient because there was no way she was going out and building a loft when they were in the middle of a mail shot.

At the end of February, once another mail shot was up and running and the tour over, he said he'd have to start rubbing wintergreen on Tiger's legs if this went on. So Annie spent her evenings with him, mapping out a new loft tight against the left-hand fence, its front facing the house, leaving space at the side for later extensions.

Annie groaned. 'Why don't we just move in there and let Tiger and his mates have the run of the house?'

They sawed, screwed, hammered, banged their thumbs and cursed but not seriously because there was the same excitement inside them for the pigeons too. It was all part of their lives, which were going forward.

It was fifteen feet long and seven feet deep, divided into three compartments. They made it seven feet high, covered the roof with corrugated asbestos and Annie said they needed to make their underwear out of it to keep out the wind.

'Must keep the air moving,' Georgie said, covering the window frame with fine-mesh wire netting.

'Rather them than me,' Annie said, pulling her woollen hat down over her ears.

They could only work a few hours each night and then only by the light from the kitchen and it wasn't until the middle of March that it was finished, just as they were starting to send out summer samples to the traders who had promised that their orders would be up on last year.

'We'll be increasing too,' Georgie said as they transferred the birds into the new loft. 'Should be some eggs in a couple of weeks but Frank says we've got to breed lightly as they're late-breds. Says not to start their yearling training until July. They're OK on the youngsters' schedule.'

They made nesting bowls in the evening and Annie laughed as she wrote to Prue, saying that she wondered quite what she'd done with her life until pigeons came into it.

'Sat back and eaten peeled grapes,' Prue wrote back a few weeks later. 'I'm glad Sarah liked the sari and the ring. Did she know that all saris should be able to go through a ring, or did she think I'd gone bonkers and sent her a large napkin?'

By the end of March the pigeons were settled and had laid eggs and an overseas buyer had written, saying that he would be arriving in Britain in the near future and would like to see them with a view to placing an order.

They drank a bottle of beer on the yard step to celebrate. Sarah and Davy had lemonade and told Annie that the Youth Club Committee were trying to win the table tennis league, but that they all really wanted a tennis court.

'Raise funds and build it yourself,' she said watching Georgie checking the birds, knowing that he wanted to lift them off their nests. 'Leave them alone, poor little things. You've already taken one egg away and now you're poking about.'

The yard gate opened and Don came in. 'What's he poking?'

Annie stopped with the glass midway to her lips. 'Good heavens, where did you drop from?'

'Just passing and thought I'd see how you were, didn't know you'd built a new one. Bit grand, isn't it?'

'Only the best for his pigeons,' Sarah said, getting up, sidling out, grabbing Davy, taking him with her. 'See you later, Mum.'

Annie poured Don beer, sat with him in the weak sun and listened to tales of Teresa's success at school, of Maud's ambitions for her, her piano, her ballet, and it felt strange to be here, standing in a Wassingham yard, just talking with her brother. It felt good.

'What does Teresa want to do?' Annie asked gently, watching as Georgie weighed out the food for the birds.

'I don't know. What her mother wants of course.' Don sipped his beer, took out a cigar. 'May I?'

Annie was surprised, he didn't usually ask. 'Of course.' She wanted one herself. She would have smoked old socks, anything because she still missed her cigarettes, still dreamt about them.

They sat and she breathed in his smoke, laughing at Georgie's face as he saw her do it. They talked about his business, about cigarettes and how difficult it was to stop.

'Try cigars,' Don joked and Annie smiled, wanting to hug him, to keep him as he was at this moment because she hadn't seen this Don for a very long time.

They talked about Wassingham Textiles and the Central Buyer's order, the success of the tour, the overseas buyer.

'He'll be coming here, will he?' Don asked, blowing smoke rings as she had known he would.

Annie shook her head. 'No, we'll have to go to him. I'll get Tom to meet him wherever he is. Take our samples. It'll be so good if we break into that market without having to plod round the European Trade Fairs – it just saves so much money. We hadn't even thought of expanding abroad just yet, though we can handle it.'

She offered tea as the beer was finished but he had to go, he had people to see, cocktails to drink. Of course, Annie thought, as they waved him away, glad that he'd been, warmed by his interest, eased by his chatter – perhaps Georgie's accident had done what nothing else could.

'Come again,' she called as his Jaguar purred away. 'He was nicer than he's been for ages,' she called to Georgie.

'Makes you wonder what he's up to.'

'For goodness sake, can't he be nice without that sort of remark?' Annie stood with her hands on her hips. 'It's her, she gets him on edge. He was perfectly pleasant then, so maybe he's trying to reach out again.'

'Are you going to give us a hand?' Georgie asked, cleaning the loft. 'And I hope you're right, pet.'

'I'm sure I am. He's not a bad lad, not really. He was nice once and no way am I helping with that loft, I'm making the picnic for tomorrow.'

'Will it work do you think, taking her?'

'It's got to, but I'm wearing three vests.'

The sun is as warm as it ever is in March, Annie thought, and for that they must be grateful. They'd certainly be the only fools out on the beach at this time of year but that was the idea wasn't it, to beard the beach alone, just the three of them, so that Sarah would not say any more that she wouldn't go to the sea because it was too childish. Annie saw Sarah's face in the mirror, so tense, so angry and knew that it had nothing to do with childishness, but with embarrassment and the fear of seeing her father without his leg, and of others seeing it too.

'One step at a time,' she thought, hoping that Bernie and his family would not be late.

Annie drove along the coast road, down the track, seeing the white-capped waves rolling, fragmenting, sucking the sand back into their depths.

They struggled against the wind as they walked down to the beach, sheltering in the dunes, seeing the sand whipping, dusting, along the beach.

'Are you sure, Annie? This early season bathing seems a bit stoic for me. We can come again.' Georgie's voice was low and Annie heard uncertainty as well as cold, but it was no surprise, she had known that he too needed today.

She nodded. 'I'm coming in too, darling. Just think of that – that no woman, in the field of human . . .'

He groaned. 'I thought you might just say that,' then

raised his voice, looking across at Sarah. 'This dune is as good as any, gives us a bit more shelter than the last. Come on, let's get 'em off.'

He eased his trousers down over his bathing costume. Sarah watched as he unhitched his leg. She'd never seen his stump before. She'd never seen him stand like this, balancing on crutches not his stick, with that great gap there, where his leg should have been. She turned and Annie watched her do so, as did Georgie.

He nodded to her. 'Come on then, Annie, get your clothes off, I'm getting cold hanging about for the pair of you. I'll meet you down there.'

Tom had put a base to each of his crutches to stop them sinking into the sand and he swung himself along, feeling the cold, feeling Sarah's eyes on his body and knew she would be feeling the same revulsion that he had felt, but knowing that she must face it, come to terms with it in all its forms. He looked either way. No others thank God, or perhaps he couldn't have gone through with it.

Sarah watched him, swinging across the great expanse of beach, all alone. So alone. She looked either way, remembering how he'd chased them last year, how he'd played cricket, how he'd swung her up in the air on Bell's Farm Hill.

Swing, swing, swing his leg was going now and he was so alone down there.

She turned. 'Come on, Mum.'

'You go on, darling.' Annie was doing up a strap, watching Georgie nearing the sea. He couldn't go into the water on crutches, he might fall.

'Quickly, someone needs to be with him,' she gasped, wrenching at her strap, the cold drawing her skin up into goose bumps, knowing she must stand and fiddle for a while longer.

Sarah looked either way again and saw another family coming down from the dunes, the children running on, then seeing Georgie, stopping. Annie saw them too. Well done, Bernie, hope the grandchildren are wrapped up well. 'He's too near the sea and he's alone,' she called to Sarah. 'Don't worry about the other people. There are these accidents so often in the pit. Remember Gracie's da?'

Sarah watched the children stare, then turn, call to the adults and point at Georgie. 'But you never saw him without his leg, like this, did you?' she shouted at her mother. 'Those kids haven't either.'

'It's another world now. Men like your father have a right to paddle without fear, without embarrassment.'

Sarah was still standing. Georgie was nearing the sea. He'd fall if the waves caught him. Annie ran as fast as she could, down the beach, but then Sarah passed her, her breath heaving in her chest, the sand squeezing up between her toes, slowing her, but then she reached him, held his arm, looked up into his face.

'Don't let the sea knock you over,' she shouted above the noise of the surf and the wind, though what she wanted to tell him was how much she loved him, how proud she was of him, because he was about to paddle in the sea and that other man, with two legs, had a damn great coat on and two silly kids with wellingtons.

They came back to Wassingham, their skin stinging from the wind, the sand and the sea spray, their hair thick with it and Sarah was laughing and saying that they should bring the gang in the summer, then Georgie could get out really deep with them all around him, that people would scream and think he'd been bitten by a shark when he came out.

They lugged the empty picnic box through into the yard and there was a man there, in a dark suit and briefcase, measuring the pigeon loft. He turned.

Georgie said, 'Just what's going on? What're you doing?'

Annie put down the picnic and stood with her hand on Sarah's shoulder, listening as the man told them he was John Evans, from the planning office. They'd received a complaint about the height of the pigeon loft from a prospective purchaser of the property next door.

'They claim it takes their light,' he said. 'It is higher than usual.'

Annie looked from Evans to the house, to the pigeon loft, then started to laugh. 'You've got to be joking. This is ridiculous.'

'I'm most certainly not joking but I do agree, it does seem ridiculous, though we've had stranger things happen. The thing is, you're going to have to take it down, or lower the roof.'

Georgie touched the loft. 'The pigeons are about to hatch out. There's no way I'm taking this roof off. Who's buying the bloody house? I'll go and speak to them.'

Annie left the yard now, tried the door into next door's yard. 'Come here, Georgie, give me a bunk up.'

She stood by the gate, waiting, hearing him limp up to her.

'What're you doing, Annie?'

'I'm going over to open the gate so that Mr Evans can see that we're not taking anyone's light. I'm just not having it. Now give me a bump up.' Her voice was angry now because no one would tell her husband to lower a roof after he'd had a leg off.

Sarah came out, and Mr Evans too. 'Oh, Mum, you'll show your knickers.'

'Good advertisement – they're ours,' Annie grunted, putting her foot in Georgie's hands after he'd wedged himself against the wall. 'Get over here, Mr Evans, in case he falls.' It was not a request, but an order. Georgie was lifting her up.

'Well, I don't know . . .'

'Get over here. There's a man with only one leg under me.' She looked down at Georgie and winked, he grinned.

She was up then, straddling the wall, swinging herself over, unbolting the gate, pulling Mr Evans in. She pointed to the loft. 'Look, you can see for yourself, it takes no light from them at all.'

Mr Evans looked around, up at the sun, measured, then

171

smiled. 'You're right. Quite right. You're quite safe – keep the loft as it is. I'll report back.'

As he left Annie asked who it was who'd lodged the complaint. 'A Mr Jones,' he said.

She rang Bill at the estate agent's. He'd shown quite a few people round, but hadn't a Mr Jones on the list, but if he was lodging a complaint perhaps he'd used a false name – or perhaps he was a disgruntled neighbour.

'Never a dull moment,' she murmured to Georgie. 'For heaven's sake, who'd do something so petty?' They stood outside the loft with its especially wide doors, its extra height. 'Everyone knows you need it as it is, for God's sake.'

Georgie was standing quietly, looking from the loft to the back alley. All their neighbours had had plenty of time to complain. The only person who'd been recently was Don – but no, not even he would do that.

The phone was ringing and Annie answered it. It was Tom. 'Jurgen Schmidt's been in touch. He'll be over soon he says, and would prefer to visit our showroom since he can come via Newcastle to Edinburgh.'

'Our what?'

'Exactly. We'll need to set one up. Jones wants to come up too so it would be worth it. Did you have a good day at the sea, did it work?' His voice was anxious.

Annie shook her head to clear it. There was so much to think about. 'Yes, it worked,' she said. 'And yes, we'll get a showroom, somehow. When's he coming exactly?'

'Within the next three weeks. He's going to confirm.'

Annie nodded. 'Fine, we'll sort it out.' She didn't know how but they would. It was their entry into the export market, but who had tried to mess up Georgie's life?

CHAPTER 11

On the Monday of the following week, Jurgen Schmidt rang to say that he would be in Wassingham in two weeks' time, on 14 April. Annie had located an old haberdashery off Armore Terrace, just round the corner from Briggs' Warehouse.

'We don't want him coming to the machine shop,' she told Bill, the estate agent. 'There are too many designs, too many samples, too much hassle.' She sat back in the chair. 'OK, break it to me gently. Has the lease tripled on this, just because we're after it?' She was grinning but tension was pulling at her neck.

Bill shook his head. 'Don't go paranoid on me, Annie, that was just business. No, this is fine. Really cheap. It's been hanging around for ages and I've more news for you. There *was* a Mr Jones, my wife took the call. He was from Whitley Bay apparently and he hasn't been back. A rather nice elderly couple are buying it so you can relax.'

Annie told Tom and Georgie in the afternoon as they sat round her desk at the office. They looked at one another and Tom said, 'Maybe I'll buy him a cigar.'

'What d'you mean?' Annie asked, checking the small print of the lease, signing where their solicitor had marked with a cross, passing it across to Tom.

'Nothing, nothing at all,' Georgie replied, reading over Tom's shoulder, adding his signature when they had finished, passing it on to Brenda to sign as witness.

173

That evening, Georgie lifted the hen and the eggs were hatched, there was a squeaker covered with down. 'A right little beauty,' he breathed, leaning to one side so that Annie could see, and then Sarah.

There were bits of white shell in the nesting bowl.

'It must prick them,' Sarah said, trying to pick them out.

'Leave it, lass, they'll sort it out.'

'How'll it feed – should we put out some food?' Sarah whispered.

'No, it'll put its beak in her mouth and her mam will throw up into it.'

Sarah snatched away her hand, stepping back, looking up at Annie and Georgie. 'That's disgusting.'

'Mm, the things we mothers do for you,' Annie said, 'Now, get back to homework please and only then can you come with us to give Tiger a toss.'

While Sarah worked in the front room Annie and Georgie went through the designs for Schmidt at the kitchen table, hearing the kettle simmering on the range and the shouts of children in the back alley. 'I'll make up the samples myself,' Annie said. 'The girls have too much work on and Brenda's on holiday next week. Can you help Gracie and me check through the work, and we'll need to pack too, though Sarah and Davy can do some at the weekend. It boosts their pocket money.'

'Shall we put the other stock forward as well?' Georgie was looking at one. 'I don't like this.' He passed it to Annie.

She looked. 'Yes, you're right. It's a young style and the fabric's wrong. We need a really fresh design on it – cotton can be so versatile but this is dreary. We'd better talk to Tom about it.'

Georgie leaned forward, resting his chin on his hands. 'We need to design our own fabric as soon as we can – it would give us so much more flexibility and our own voice. It would boost the mail order division an' all.'

Annie laughed. 'Wouldn't hurt mine either, or are we in competition?'

Georgie reached across, took her hand, kissed it. 'Never in competition, my darling, but now that you mention it, there is a race planned for the eighth of April. Just to get the "new boys" used to the procedures.'

Annie shook her head. 'Tiger knows all about the procedures – he just has to flap his wings and tuck his legs up.'

Georgie grinned. 'No, the human "new boys". The committee's arranged a practice run. I'm taking the time clock round tonight for it to be checked. The trouble is the eighth is the Saturday before Jurgen's visit.' He looked down. 'It was set up before we knew about Schmidt and I didn't quite know how to tell you then and I don't now.'

Annie leaned back in her chair. 'I'm not surprised you didn't – that's when all the hard work needs to be done. We've got to decorate and fit out the shop.'

'I won't go of course. I'll just do the best I can in the youngster races.' Georgie was leafing through the designs again.

Annie was laughing now. 'Don't be so daft. Of course you can go. Take Sarah and Davy too, have a day out. Is Frank going to be convoyer?'

Georgie looked up, his face in a grin. 'Yes, it's his first time. He's nervous.'

'Then how could you not go and hold his hand, my love, but tell the committee from me that if they ever coincide with Schmidt again I shall personally murder the lot of them. You'd better be the one to tell Tom and duck while you do it.'

Georgie nodded at her. 'I've told him and he's OK. He wants time off in the winter to see Sunderland play.'

Annie crunched up a sheet of spare paper and threw it at him. 'Fine, just fine. So Gracie and I need a few days off too eh, and incidentally, what did you mean about a cigar today?'

Georgie told her that he had suspected Don had been 'Mr Jones', just for a moment that was all, and now she really was angry and wouldn't go with them to toss Tiger but stayed in the house, not turning the light on as darkness fell, because she knew her brother would never hurt anyone like that. But her anger was directed at herself because she too had thought it for a brief moment and she was shocked at herself.

Another bird hatched the next night and by the next weekend their Union Rings were fitted and each evening they checked to see how the nestlings were 'making up'.

Annie showed Sarah how to pinch the youngster's crop. 'This is Button's nestling, so you must look after the bairn, grandmother,' Annie said gently, watching as Sarah pinched the crop lightly, hoping that it would appear to be full. It was.

She showed her how to lift it, belly upwards, to check that the breastbone was straight and the skin wasn't blue, it was red. It was fine.

'Put it back in the nestbowl now,' Annie instructed, noticing how carefully Sarah did this – she was a gentle child as well as a handful.

She looked at Sarah's nestling again. It wasn't standing up in the bowl, it was crouching. Good. 'Now put your finger near it. Don't touch it, just near.'

Sarah looked at her. 'Why?'

'I want to make sure it rocks back, and doesn't stand up. If it's feeding properly its crop will be full of soaked grain, and it'll be too heavy to scramble to its feet.'

'Did Da say that?'

'Yes, don't worry, he showed me last night.'

'I was still up, he could have shown me too.'

Annie nodded, surprised at the anger in her daughter's voice. 'I know, we were so busy talking we forgot. I'm sorry, darling.'

'You always forget me when you're together.'

Sarah turned away, put her finger forward and the nestling rocked backwards. She grinned at Annie, who felt her tension ease, not only because the bird was 'making up' and would not have to be destroyed but because the anger was gone from Sarah. Though the child was quite right, they did forget and it was unforgivable.

The next week was busy. Sarah had to be reminded to do Miss Simpson's work and the exams were getting nearer but Gracie put her foot down with Davy too, and sent Paul home to do his work, so that made it easier.

They had a new order in from Edinburgh too, and were organising the next mail shot. Late into the night she and Georgie planned the showroom with Tom and Gracie and wished they'd their own fabrics to hang at the windows, and wallpaper to match.

'One step at a time,' Tom said. 'We haven't the capital yet. Let's see how the export order goes, if it goes at all.'

Georgie checked with Annie that he'd ordered enough fabric for the apron and gloves mail shot, and she said he had. He checked with her that there was a car available to collect Herr Schmidt. There was, Tom's.

They talked then about a converted car for him. 'You need one,' Annie said. 'For business and for pleasure.' For your dignity too, she thought and your daughter, because she had decided that he must take Sarah, not her, out with him on training tosses and races – she must never feel forgotten as Annie had done as a child.

She discussed it with Tom when Georgie was talking to the newspaper about the mail shot, coaxing them into a feature. Ringing another, telling them about the possibility of an export order, arranging to ring them the following week if it was confirmed.

'Yes, he should have one,' Tom said, sitting on the corner of her desk, smiling as she flicked a piece of gum into her mouth. 'What's it worth not to tell the kids that Auntie Annie is chewing like a Yank?' he asked.

'Anything you care to name, my lad. But if I don't chew I shall smoke right now. It's the Schmidt thing. I want it Tom. I want it because then we'll be that much nearer the textiles. It's what you and Georgie want. It means we've done what we said we'd do. But I want that car more and I can't have it without the order.'

She ran Georgie and the children to the station on Saturday morning. They had been to the club the night before and a member of the committee had set the clock by Greenwich Mean Time, it had then been sealed and handed back to Georgie. Annie had smiled at the tension of those who stood around her, but she had felt it too and was glad she'd held Tiger this morning, stroked him, wished him well, told him to beat those wings hard for Georgie and Sarah, duck the hawks, for God's sake, duck the hawks.

'Did you remove his hopper after supper last night?' she asked now.

Georgie nodded. 'Just as Frank said.'

'Is the forecast good? You won't let him out if it's too windy?'

Georgie shook his head, he was laughing. Why was he laughing?

'Fifty miles seems such a long way. He's still so young.'

'Oh, Mum, no he's not. He'll be past it in a few years, stop fussing. You always fuss, doesn't she, Da? Fuss, fuss, fuss, no one can get a word in edgeways.'

Was she fussing? It was only a bird for heaven's sake. Of course she wasn't fussing but Sarah was right, no one else had squeezed a word in.

Annie said nothing more, pulling up at the station, seeing Frank unloading the panniers from his truck, seeing the committee taking the panniers into the station, on to the train.

'It'll be so strange for him. He hasn't been on a train before,' she said.

'Oh Mum,' Sarah said, pulling at Georgie's hand. 'Come on Da, Davy, let's go. We'll miss the train.'

Georgie was looking at her. 'Will you be all right? I feel bad about leaving you.'

Annie looked down at Sarah's face, at the way she held Georgie's arm, pulling him, the eagerness with which she was talking to Davy. 'Well don't. You and Sarah should share a day out more often – this must be the first of many, Georgie, she needs you, really she does.'

She waved to them, watching Sarah talk to Georgie and hold his hand. Yes, they must get a converted car for Georgie, even if the export order came to nothing, because then he wouldn't need her to drive him everywhere and he and Sarah could spend days together as father and daughter should.

They decorated the showroom a light green with white woodwork, leaving the windows open all day and all night.

'No one will break in, there's nothing to steal,' Tom said, locking the door. 'And there's enough of a wind to clear the smell of the paint out.' He looked at the clouds scudding across the sky. 'They won't have let them fly today, will they? Your lad won't be home until tomorrow you know.'

Annie did know, she'd been monitoring the weather all day. 'Will Gracie mind about Davy? Do you?'

'No, I'm off to a debate with Rob tonight anyway – bit late now but we'll catch the end of it. See you bright and early tomorrow then?'

Annie caught his sleeve. 'Do you take Davy to these debates?'

'No, he's always with Sarah.'

'Not always, Tom, and he needs you, it isn't just Rob who does.'

They worked all Sunday and the weather was better, so Tiger would be flying. Annie hung the curtains, ironed and hung the slips, the aprons, the smocks that they thought they'd try out on Schmidt. They hung the bras and pants and pictures on the wall. They had arranged for the phone to be reconnected.

'It'll be worth it,' Annie told Bet. 'We can keep this up and running for the other buyers who might want to come. Jones is visiting in May.'

'It's getting big isn't it, Annie. What would your da have thought?'

Annie paused, then continued to put the iron in the box. 'I doubt that he'd be pleased. He wanted us both to leave Wassingham, didn't he, Bet, to make it big elsewhere and certainly not in trade.'

'But he'd have been glad you're happy and you are, aren't you?' Bet took the iron.

'I've never been happier in my life and I think he'd have been pleased about that.'

Annie closed up the ironing board and walked to the car boot with it.

'He loved you, he just couldn't show it and a father should, you know.'

Annie did know and on Monday after Schmidt had been she rang a car dealer in Newcastle about car conversions. 'I'll send you the details,' he promised.

It had been a good day, Schmidt had left leaving a large order for two sets of underwear and he would have ordered the aprons too if the fabric designs had been more appealing. As importantly, Tiger had survived the hawks and won his race. Sarah sat and told her all about it while Georgie and she listened, directing their questions at her, not one another.

'And so we learn,' she groaned that night. 'But who said it would be so difficult being a parent – running a business is so much easier.'

Throughout April and May they taught the young birds how to trap and toss and in June Georgie had his car, paid for by a loan which Annie had arranged, because it was unfair that they should draw more from the profits than Tom or the workers.

He drove out each weekend on training flights, taking Sarah and Davy with him, and sometimes Annie, but only sometimes.

In early August some late birds hatched and a further order arrived from Schmidt who was eager for aprons but still didn't care for the designs.

In mid, August Tom and Gracie took the boys to Scar-

180

borough on holiday and Annie and Georgie worked late into the night, covering for them. On their return they did the same for Annie and Georgie, who took Bet to the sea for days out, though they didn't go away, for who would look after their birds, Georgie asked.

Annie just smiled and lay on the dunes feeling the tiredness draining from her body, hearing the gulls, the shriek of laughter, the thump as Georgie swung his crutches, and then his leg, thinking of how relieved Sarah had been when Davy also passed his eleven plus, and Paul too. The gang could stay together.

'I'll make your uniform this week, shall I?' Annie said as Sarah dug into the sand and began to bury her. It was so cold. 'Not so deep, you horrible child.'

'Mum,' Sarah's voice was hesitant. 'They'll laugh if I wear home-made clothes. Teresa said you'd make them, she said everyone would make fun.'

Annie lay quite still. 'We can't have that, can we? I remember how I felt. Of course I shall buy it, darling.'

'You don't think I'll get like Terry, do you? It's just girls you know.'

Now Annie laughed and the sand fell from her shoulders.

'Mum?'

'Well, let me tell you, my dear girl, that there's no danger of you becoming like that particular child, she's a one off, and so are you.'

In September they received a postcard from Don, Maud and Teresa in Spain and nobody was rude because they all felt guilty about thinking Don was Mr Jones. The night before Sarah started school she didn't sleep and neither did Annie, but she need not have worried. She, Davy and Paul caught the same bus in and the same bus out and as long as she could do that, Sarah said that it didn't matter where she went to school.

They ran another mail shot and this time there were features in two of the dailies and mention of the export order and the response was bigger than ever, and the wholesale orders were greater too.

They worked long hours building up the new season's designs and samples, though Tom would not have to include the Jones department stores in the February tour because they had visited the showroom and placed their own order.

The people of Wassingham were also visiting it, so it was decided that Bet should open it each morning and sell direct to the public at prices slightly cheaper than the shops. It gave them a greater profit but when Bet suggested opening more retail outlets they decided against it.

'Too much capital, too much hassle with staff, and supervision. We're not big enough yet,' Tom said and the others agreed.

'Let's see how the printing works out when Tom and Gracie get back off tour.' Because they'd decided to print off some tea towels and table mats and try them on the Christmas market and only if they worked would they invest in premises, continuous printers and curing ovens.

'Retail outlets are part of the future I think, but a good idea, Bet,' Annie said.

At the end of October Tom built a silk-screen printer in Bet's kitchen because she said they could use her oven if Gracie would put her dinner in the upstairs oven.

'Better than that, you'll come and eat with us until we see if this idea works,' Gracie said, kissing her cheek.

Tom bought wood and built a frame but it wasn't sturdy enough and it flexed.

'Damn it, it'll print badly, and the colours won't register,' he said.

He tried again, laying it on the kitchen table when he'd finished. This time it rested evenly with all four corners on the surface.

Annie called Georgie in from the stable where he'd been cutting wires which they would string up in the kitchen for drying, and others which he would make into racks for the oven.

'I glued and nailed the corners together and reinforced with angle irons screwed to the top,' Tom said, showing it to them, bringing Davy forward so that he could see and Annie was pleased.

'Get me the silk, Davy,' Tom said and then unrolled it on the table, putting the frame on it. 'Check the weave's parallel, Annie.'

It was.

Tom fastened the silk to the frame with drawing pins. 'Thank God Prue sent us a load of silk. Perhaps we should cut her in if we get it off the ground,' he said.

'Not if, when,' Georgie said.

Tom looked at the silk. 'It's no good, it's uneven. I know, let's take it off. I remember what we did at college now.'

They all helped to lever out the drawing pins and he turned up one edge of the silk and pinned it to the centre of one side of the frame, putting two further pins on either side of the first, pulling towards the corners for tension.

Annie watched Davy and he looked as pleased as Sarah did when Georgie and she went off together.

'Come on Annie, fasten the centre of that side, pull the silk as you do it.' Tom was frowning with concentration. It was his face as a child, it was Davy's face.

She fastened and pulled, then Davy did the other side and Sarah the last. Tom turned it over.

'Tight as your drums,' he grinned at the kids.

They watched as he masked the inside edges to prevent the ink from seeping underneath. 'Don't want a load of duff ones. Give old Manners a real Christmas treat wouldn't it?' Tom said.

The next day, Sunday, they covered Bet's table with a blanket and waterproof sheeting, stretching out the creases while the children mixed the dyes.

Tom had converted Annie's idea of a red star on a green background edged with red berries into a simple two-colour design and Bet had prepared the fabric the previous night, boiling the heavy cotton oblongs to remove the dressing and hanging them on Georgie's wires to dry.

Tom printed the green background, passing the fabric carefully to the others. They hung them over chair backs, airers or hoisted them up on to the wires suspended across the ceiling and did the same the next night, and the next, all of them coming to Bet's kitchen, mixing, printing, drying, baking in the oven to fix the dyes. Then drinking cocoa in Gracie's kitchen upstairs – which used to be my da's dining room, Annie told Sarah, wondering what he'd think of the cottage industry downstairs.

Each day they responded to orders which were coming in from the July tour, and at the end of the week Tom repeat-printed the red star and the border. They sent samples of the tea towels to Germany, and to Jones Department Store. At the end of the week there were more and Annie took the afternoon off and drove round the market stalls, showing them the tea towels, telling them there would also be matching table mats in time for Christmas – if they were interested.

They were and phoned in their orders all the next week.

Tom phoned Bill at the estate agents and he called them in during their lunch break. He checked for them that Steadman's was still available. It had been last year, and still in the summer.

'Yes, seems OK, but there's a stirring of interest, my boss says. Just a few questions being asked.'

'Not the consortium.'

'Yes, I'm afraid so.'

They didn't work that afternoon, instead they visited the planning office and discussed with them their requirements for the printing business, asking if there were any other sites within Wassingham that would be suitable. There weren't. There was only one sewage works.

That night they decided to have plans drawn up and submitted, even though they were not in a position to move on it and each of them tried to keep the panic at bay.

'If the bloody consortium's getting interested we'll have to be sharp or it'll cost us a fortune,' Tom said.

There was no word back from Germany, that week, or the next. Neither did they hear from Jones but they continued to print in the kitchen, refusing to believe that Schmidt would not like the towels, but prepared to believe that perhaps they were too primitive for Jones.

The pigeons were in moult and each morning and evening Georgie checked them, fed them, cleaned them out and by the middle of October they had shed their primaries and some of their secondaries and so there were no long training flights, just local flights and a mess about from the loft.

'Couldn't have timed it better, pet,' Georgie said as they mixed more paint, because the children were scavenging for Wassingham's bonfire that weekend. 'But I wish to God we'd heard back.'

At the end of October Schmidt placed an order, and Jones too but they wouldn't commit themselves to further goods until they saw how the Christmas take-up went on the existing stock.

It was a long two months and as Christmas came they were tired because the stalls had re-ordered three times and Jones had sold out and come back for more for their post January sale period. 'But not Christmas designs of course.'

On Christmas Eve Jurgen Schmidt rang, ordering two thousand aprons, to be delivered by Easter in a two-colour design, the rough sketch of which he would send.

They drank champagne with Don and Maud on Christmas Eve, and all the children drank too, though Maud said it was foolish and could lead to trouble in later life. No one took any notice, they were too excited, too happy, too tense.

Immediately after Christmas they heard that they had received planning permission. They also heard that the consortium had finally bought Steadman's, though the lease was still available, Bill said, his voice tired and defensive.

'Don't tell me,' Annie said, gripping the receiver. 'At triple the cost.'

'I'm afraid so, Annie, and a landlord inspection clause too.'

'Tell me,' she said this time, listening as Bill said that there would be an inspection each year and any repairs deemed necessary must be undertaken.

'Well, this is a wonderful start to 1959 isn't it?' she said.

They talked that evening as they worked in Bet's, wondering if they had ever smelt roast beef where now there were only chemicals. They talked and raged and could have wept.

'But there's nowhere else,' Georgie said finally. 'That's it in a nutshell, we'll have to take Steadman's or move out of Wassingham.'

'Which we promised ourselves we'd never do,' Annie said as Tom nodded.

'It's as though . . .' Georgie said, and then trailed off.

'Could it be personal?' Bet asked.

'Don't say that, we'll be thinking it's Don next and that's not fair. They're a London-based consortium, nothing to do with us,' Gracie snapped.

Annie listened, making herself think back to the yard, his jokes at Christmas, the kiss he had given her. No, it couldn't be Don. Yes, he'd run that loan business with Uncle Albert, yes, he'd been tight and mean but no, he wouldn't hurt his own family. He couldn't, and losing their money had been a mistake which she had instigated. For God's sake, Gracie was right, look at Mr Jones – how wrong they'd been then. Her head began to ache.

'It can't be Don,' she said, her voice firm because she could see that Georgie was filled with doubt. 'Look at the loft – that was a real Mr Jones. Look at the showroom – if we hadn't rented that we'd probably not have landed the export order.'

Georgie said, 'There were other shops we could have gone to for the showroom, but look, we needed Briggs, and we need Steadman's and it's wiping out our profits again, we're always back at square one.'

'There weren't other shops, not then.'

Bet spoke up then. 'Don was difficult, but never wicked, not as you are saying. You've asked Bill and he says it's a consortium, he's said it's being done all the time. I think you've got to stop wondering who it is and sort out what you're going to do. It wouldn't be the lad. No one would be that devious.'

Annie clasped Bet's hand. 'I know it's not him and so do you all. He's a right little bugger, we all know that but Bet's right. This is just business.'

Tom looked at Georgie, then at Annie, 'I didn't want to tell anyone but I've got to now. I've checked the names of the consortium. I'm sorry, I shouldn't have done because he's our brother but he isn't named. There's Samual Davis, James Merriott, Albert Sims, oh, and others. It isn't Don. I'm sorry, but it just gets on top of me when we make all this effort and then we're clobbered.'

That night Georgie held Annie and said, 'It gets on top of us all, my love, but you're right – it's just business and a collection of people out there that're bloody shrewd. Just wish we had them on our side.'

They paid the price and Georgie sold his car to help towards the cost of the ovens and the continuous printer. Annie hocked her walnut table to try and get it back, but it had been sold and by the time there was another there was no money left, it had all been sucked up by the printer, the shelving, repairing the heating, the ovens, and they were unable to sub-let the Briggs Warehouse at the price that they were paying for it.

Annie said to Tom, 'If I hear those politicians saying once more that we've never had it so good, I'll scream.'

CHAPTER 12

Sarah sat at her desk, leaning back against the radiator, feeling the heat in strips, waiting for Miss Bates to call her name, watching as first one girl and then another walked down the row of desks. It was the first day of the new school year and she had just been appointed window monitor, together with Hannah.

'Do we open or close them for fire practice?' Hannah whispered, her long hair hanging down her face as she drew pictures of Elvis Presley on her rough book.

'They'll tell us,' Sarah said. 'They always *tell* us everything but perhaps we'll change that this morning.'

Deborah was walking past them now, on her way to Bates's desk. Deborah always won the posture prize. Sarah sat up, put her shoulders back, then saw her breasts and hunched them again. They were a nuisance, they made her feel different, made her feel more of a girl beside Paul and Davy but they hadn't noticed, nothing had changed.

She drew guitars on the cover of her rough book. They were rehearsing tonight for the show at the Youth Club – Geoff was bringing his guitar, Paul was playing the bass they had made from a tea chest, a broom handle and a piece of string. Her fingers were sore from the washboard and Davy's looked the same but they'd have to practise or they'd never get it right and the families had said they were coming. What if they waved? No, they wouldn't, she'd tell her mum and she'd tell everyone else.

Hannah was called up to Miss Bates now and Sarah

watched her friend walk to the desk and sit down, her face hidden by her hair. She had spots. Why did people get them? Sarah felt her own skin – so far so good. Paul had spots but then he didn't want to kiss anyone, he'd said, so it didn't matter.

Hannah was walking back now. 'Piano,' she mouthed, then louder, 'Your turn, Sarah. Good luck.'

Sarah nodded, picking up her slip of paper with guitar written down. She handed this to Miss Bates who looked at it, then at her. 'Another one. As I said to the others, it is out of the question. You have a choice of violin, recorder or piano.'

'But I want to play the guitar.'

'The guitar is not a proper instrument, it's just something that's used to make a noise, these days anyway.'

Sarah nodded. That's just what her da had said. 'But I want to learn to play it properly. I'm fed up with the washboard and anyway, skiffle's gone out really. Did you know, Miss Bates, that rock 'n' roll is our present-day folk music.'

'Nonsense.'

Sarah smiled, she'd hoped Miss Bates would say this. 'It's not nonsense, skiffle was a strain of American country blues, played by blacks and rock 'n' roll's the same really. It's like our folk music and we listen to that in musical appreciation, don't we? I mean, if we could all learn the three basic chords around which the music is geared all of us could play it and write pieces, instead of plonking along learning piano chords and taking exams.'

Sarah knew the whole class would be listening. They had talked about it this morning, decided that each of them would ask for guitar and one of them would have to try to talk Miss Bates round – no one else had volunteered.

Miss Bates sighed, fingering her hair which was grey at the temples, but only sometimes. Davy said she dyed it, but Bet said only fast women dyed their hair. Sarah looked at Miss Bates. No, she wasn't fast, never had been, never would be. Had Bet been a fast woman – she'd had Tom when she wasn't married. But Sarah didn't want to think of that, didn't want to think of old people being fast – it was revolting.

'I'm putting you down for piano,' Miss Bates said. 'It will give you a musical sense and in due course you can pursue your guitar playing on your own, if you must.'

So that was that, Sarah thought, walking back to her desk, hearing the whispered 'Bad luck' 'Never mind' 'Good try'. At break they huddled around by the milk crates and wondered why adults were so stupid, so set in their ways. Why did they have to be so narrow minded? Why did they always know best? Why did they never listen? Their parents were the same – nag, nag, nag.

On the way back to Wassingham she told Davy that it hadn't worked – that they'd just have to keep on with the book. She dragged the beginner's guide out of her satchel and as the bus jerked and rattled from village to village they played imaginary chords and talked of Elvis and Haley and Buddy Holly, who had died in February, and they still couldn't believe that.

They practised that evening at the Youth Club hall, working on *Rock Island Line* until their fingers were too sore and their throats too dry to sing another note.

Roger, the Youth Leader, was sitting on a chair at the front of the stage, calling instructions to the ballet girls who were going to dance to *Swan Lake* on the gramophone.

He shouted to Davy over his shoulder. 'Much better, but still needs work. Remember that when you take the world by storm, no good without practice.'

Sarah told Annie and Georgie that when she arrived home half an hour late but it didn't help and she was packed off to bed without cocoa, but who cared, she thought, lying in her bed, hearing the cat yowling next door and the pigeons fluttering. She pulled her radio into the bed and listened to Radio Luxemburg beneath the covers, trying to cut out the interference, wishing it was her group playing, promising herself that one day it would be.

At the end of September 1959 Annie set on another worker, this time a mother with a child. They partitioned a room, brought in sand and camp beds and Gracie and Bet shared the running of the creche whilst Annie, Georgie and Tom shared the printing between them as well as their normal work. Brenda took on the supervision of the staff completely but there were still not enough hours in the day and while Sarah practised, or did her homework, Annie and Georgie worked in the kitchen and they knew that Tom and Gracie were doing the same.

Mrs Anders from next door came in each morning to clean the house and peel the vegetables and each afternoon she popped in to put a casserole in the oven.

'Better than Mr Jones,' Georgie would say to Annie each week.

As October turned to November the weather grew colder, snow fell and Annie was glad that the birds were in moult because they didn't have time for long journeys any more and besides, there was still no car for Georgie.

He fell twice the day of the snow, and twice the next day, and so Annie lugged down the wheelchair from the attic, heaving it down the stairs, dragging it into the kitchen, dusting it down as he ate bacon and eggs and Sarah played drums on her lunch-box.

'There you are m'lord, your carriage awaits. We'll bung it into the car and keep it at Steadman's, then you don't have to skid yourself across the car park.' She felt tense, he hadn't used this at all.

Georgie looked at it, and then at her, his eyes shadowed, then cleared. 'You ought to wear a cap, I insist on it. I like my chauffeurs properly dressed.'

'You'll get them as you find them, or I'll haul you to the top of a high hill and let you go.' Annie was laughing, pushing the chair through the yard, out and into the boot of the car. It wouldn't close but who cared, Steadman's was only round the corner.

She turned and Sarah was there, her face angry. 'He

shouldn't be in the chair, he should be in his car. Why can't we get that one converted, Mum, it's not fair.'

Annie felt the wind tear into her and pulled her cardigan round her, taking Sarah's arm, pushing her before her into the yard, seeking the shelter of the walls. 'Do you think I haven't thought of that? Really, Sarah. Brenda uses the car for deliveries, so does Gracie, and whoever happens to be on the run that day. It's just not possible. I'm saving as hard as I can, now don't worry.'

Sarah shrugged out of Annie's grasp, her face sullen. 'Well, someone's got to.'

She turned but Annie grabbed her arm again. 'Just what do you mean by that? And look at me when I'm talking to you.'

'I mean just what I said,' hissed Sarah, looking at her mother now, her cheeks red. 'You're all right, you can get about. You're like everyone else, rushing around looking after yourself, never listening, never seeing what people need or want.'

Annie felt anger flare. She shook her daughter. 'How dare you talk to me like that? You know I've done all I can for your father and I'm still doing all I can. I just don't know what's the matter with you these days, Sarah, you're so difficult. I think you're spending too much time up there in your bedroom listening to that damn music, you need to sit with us in the evening, or something.'

'I like that damn music, and I like my damn bedroom.'

'Don't swear.'

'Why not, you do. But then adults can do anything they like, it's just us who can't, even though we're not kids any more. We just have to do as we're told – play the piano, not the guitar.'

Annie threw up her hands, and wanted to put this child over her knee. 'So, that's what all this is about, is it? I really cannot believe I'm hearing this from you. Go in, put your sandwiches into your lunch-box, fill your flask because I'm not doing it any more if you're so very grown up, and hurry up, you'll miss your bus.'

She watched as Sarah stalked into the kitchen. She listened to the bangs and crashes. She waited until her daughter came out again, walking past her, and Annie itched to slap her. Sarah stopped by the gate. 'Anyway, it wasn't about me, not really. It's about you and poor Da.'

Annie said. 'Just go to school.' Her voice was quiet with rage.

She went into the warmth of the kitchen and stood in front of the range, gripping the guard. Kids, bloody kids, she thought to herself – and I thought the nappy stage was difficult.

That day Annie called a meeting and discussed the possibility of using their own textiles on a mail order shot. It wasn't scheduled until spring 1960 but demand from wholesalers was increasing. 'I know it'll go,' she said because they had to improve their profits. Sarah was right, it wasn't fair that he should not have a car and somehow that had been forgotten.

The workers agreed and so did the family. Georgie rescheduled and Tom suggested that they took on Bernie to help with the printing. 'He's retired from the pit, but he's bored out of his mind. We can't do everything you know, bonny lass,' he said.

'I know,' Annie snapped.

'You had a row with someone?'

'No.'

She rang the bank that afternoon and explained about the mail shot, that Georgie would need to be mobile – it was just too much for the rest of them. 'Too inefficient,' she said. 'I just need to extend the overdraft.'

The bank manager agreed. That was the easy part. The difficult one was to convince Georgie.

She sat on his desk after lunch, playing with the papers she'd brought in, knowing that she looked tired, knowing that they all looked tired. 'Now, with this mail shot, we're going to be under even more pressure so you'll need to do your own running about. I've arranged a bank loan. Tom's agreed, so will you do the same please?'

Georgie put down his pen, laid his hands flat on the table. 'We can't afford it.'

'We need to spend money to make money sometimes. We can afford it. We will afford it.'

Brenda interrupted her. 'Sorry Annie, call from Jones. They want a further supply of aprons. Interested in some children's dungarees too.'

Annie nodded. 'I'm coming. Now, just give me a break will you Georgie, take some of the load.'

He picked up his pen again, bent his head, began to write.

'Georgie, are you listening?'

He looked up. 'Sometimes I feel I want to punch my fist through a brick wall. It's so bloody difficult being like this.' He tapped his leg. 'It's so bloody difficult for everyone connected with me, and today it aches, the cold's got into it.'

Annie smiled at him. 'You have no idea how easy it is to be connected with you.'

Sarah walked from the bus to the back yard, pushing the door open, calling to Mrs Anders that she was home, hearing her reply from the kitchen.

She opened the door. The range was burning, the kettle was on and the kitchen smelt of macaroni cheese. She slumped into the chair, dropped her satchel on the floor, then stood up and walked down the road, through Steadman's car park, into the machine shop, then into her mother's office. She was on the phone.

Sarah sat down and listened to the strain in her mother's voice, saw the lines running deeply to her mouth. She looked so tired and Sarah hadn't noticed. She felt the raffia beneath her legs. It was warm and she could hear the sewing machines all around, music from the radio – Alma Cogan, Frank Sinatra, no rock 'n' roll. Sarah looked at her hands, sore from the washboard and covered in ink from her leaking pen. Her stomach tightened again as it had been doing all day. She felt the tears close again, though they hadn't fallen yet, and they mustn't. Girls of twelve didn't cry.

'Sarah, how nice. Shall I get you a cup of tea?' Annie put down the phone, started to rise.

'I'm sorry, Mum. I'm sorry. I shouldn't have said it, I know I shouldn't. I don't know why I say these things.'

She was crying now but her mother's arms were round her, holding her, smoothing her hair. 'I deserved it,' Annie said. 'I had sort of forgotten, other things to think about, other priorities but he'll have it within the next two weeks. It's all been sorted out.'

Sarah let herself lean into her mother, let her stroke back the hair from her face but the tears were still coming. 'In PE today Miss Smithers said I needed a bra and the other girls laughed.'

Annie held her more tightly. 'Growing up is very difficult, my darling. I'll bring some home tonight.' She looked over her daughter's head at the machine shop, the design office, the printing shop and wondered where all the years had gone, and knew that the coming ones were going to see more of this and the best she could do was to keep the lines of communication open. It would need a light hand.

That night she sewed yards of petticoats for Sarah's skiffle costume, then the skirt, the wide belt, the top, and then sat on her daughter's bed and talked about growing up, all the uncertainties, the conflicts, boyfriends, kissing, petting and Sarah was glad that the lights were out and wished that her mother would stop, because they'd talked all about sex at school, and then on the bus going home with Davy and Paul and it hadn't been embarrassing like this.

Her mother bent forward and kissed her, 'Don't listen to Radio Luxemburg for too long,' she said. She smelt of lavender and now Sarah hugged her, holding her tight, not wanting to grow up, but impatient for it too. 'I love you, Mum.'

Annie remembered this as she and Georgie sat in the

audience with Gracie, Don, Maud and Teresa on Saturday evening and winced at the ballet, tapping to the African drums, swaying to the English madrigals played by the organist and his friends.

'It's music through the ages and from many lands,' she told Don, pleased that he had come.

'How quaint,' said Maud, looking round. 'But no Tom, no Rob?'

No, there was no Tom, he was at a debating competition, supporting Rob. 'We had to split up,' Gracie said, 'So each of the boys had someone there.'

Annie drank her tea and wished that just for once it had been Tom who had listened to Davy.

They talked of the new mail shot, the clauses in the lease, Don's business and Teresa looked at the programme and asked if there was any piano playing. There was not, Annie said, taking Bet's cup, moving away as Teresa told them all in a loud voice about her success at her own school concert.

After the interval there was jazz dancing and then Davy and Sarah, with Paul and Geoff, rasped out *Rock Island Line* and now Annie's feet were tapping, and her hands clapped out the rhythm with the rest of the audience, though Don, Maud, and Teresa kept silent. They were good, really good and Sarah's voice was confident, powerful, brilliant, and Annie felt such pride that suddenly she couldn't clap, she could only grip her hands together because her throat was tightening and her eyes blurring and at the end she wanted to stand on her chair and whistle and shout like the kids in the audience were doing.

That Christmas Gracie and Annie took Davy and Sarah into Newcastle, gave them tea at the department store, wafted into Lingerie and said 'Good afternoon,' to Mrs Wilvercombe, who preened and asked them to stay for more tea and told them how well their garments were selling. 'Such a pleasure to do business with you.'

Annie wanted to say that she wished she could say the same, but didn't.

They refused tea. 'So sorry, no time. We have guitars to buy.'

She and Gracie smiled as they heard the children gasp and then took them out to the music shop that Roger, the Youth Leader, had suggested and stood while the kids looked, then fingered, then tried, watched them blush because no sound came from one. It was electric.

Annie shook her head, pointing down to the far end. 'Oh no, a cheap one first, just to see if you really like it.'

They each left with an American six-string National with a metal body and groaned when their mothers took it from them, saying that they must wait until Father Christmas dropped it down the chimney.

All Christmas Day, while the parents and Bet drank champagne and wine to celebrate the success of their first textile mail shot they fingered the strings, moving up and down the frets, until they were banished to the upstairs sitting room, taking their *Learn the Guitar the Easy Way*. Georgie said, 'Why aren't there any good tunes any more, that's what I'd like to know.'

In spring 1960 the consortium's inspector insisted that they update the lavatories and it did them no good to insist that it came within the landlord's province because the small print stated clearly that it didn't.

In the summer Tiger won the Club cup and Buttons took second place and Frank's grin was almost as wide as Georgie's. Sarah told Miss Bates at school, and also told her that she had learnt to play the guitar, and would teach the others if she liked.

Miss Bates said no, but she could write her project on pigeon keeping if she liked. Sarah did like and worked hard, charting the daily routine, the trapping of the youngsters, the tossing, the destruction of those who didn't 'make up', calm and analytical now, leaving out of the project her tears, her pleadings with Georgie to let them remain. But he was right, they'd never have thrived, she could see that now.

In the autumn the children were banished out to Black

Beauty's stable to practise because they had been joined by Geoff on guitar and Paul on drums. 'It's too much for an old man's eardrums,' Tom said, though he drifted out from time to time because Annie had said that he should pay more attention to Davy. Sarah still sat in her room for half an hour before sleeping, picking out the tunes that were played on Radio Luxembourg, wanting an hour, but being refused.

In the early spring of 1961 Tom and Gracie toured the European Trade Fairs and brought back so many orders that they took on three more workers and there were now four children in the creche. Annie loved to walk in and hear the sound of their laughter, their singing, because these were the simple sounds of childhood and a relief from the minefield of the teenage world.

In June the inspector called again and this time insisted on redecoration and replacing of the external doors, which had been damaged by the comings and goings of the textile workers, or so he said. They had to overhaul the heating system because the flue was dangerous. It took too much from their profits and Tom said that the creche was a drain on the business. He showed them the books when Georgie and Sarah returned from a training race but as they sat back drinking tea they knew that they couldn't close it.

'This business is not just for us, it's for Wassingham,' Annie said and the others agreed.

'It's just that our overheads are so high we're never in profit as we should be. Christ, I wish we had an alternative to Steadman's.'

'Perhaps we should build our own premises?' Georgie said, as Sarah made herself cheese on toast.

Annie felt hungry just smelling it. 'Would you put some on for me, darling. Anyone else?' Everyone else. Sarah sighed and Annie grinned.

'Tough being the cook, isn't it?' she said.

'Oh, Mum, I've got practice for the fête.'

'Be quiet, Sarah, this is important.' Georgie was leaning forward.

'So's my fête.'

'I said be quiet.'

Annie intervened. 'Leave the cheese, take yours and Davy's, half an hour's practice only and then homework, then clean the pigeons.'

'Oh Mum.'

Annie stood up. 'Go on, there's been a compromise, don't push it.'

Sarah paused, then smiled. 'Thanks Mum.' Annie grinned wryly, then grated the cheese, whipped the egg, mixed it, listening as Georgie and Tom thrashed out the possibility of building, but there was no possibility, they all knew that. They were trapped.

'Don't worry,' she said. 'In spite of everything we're still in profit, we're growing – we have domestic and export markets, and pretty soon we'll have rebuilt that damn building so they can't cream any more off us. Now eat this up.'

In August the children played at the fête and Annie heard them before she saw them, driving up to the grassed wasteland beneath the slag, laughing at Georgie's face as he heard his daughter's voice, his daughter's guitar playing, heard her growling out from the tannoy, beating across the air.

'Why aren't there any proper tunes any more? Why do I feel so old?' he said, heaving himself from the car, walking with Annie to the tombola, buying tickets.

'They're good you know.'

Georgie nodded, moving on to the coconut stall, throwing and missing, thank God, Annie thought. She hated coconut. 'Yes,' he said, tossing the last ball up. 'But where's it all going to end?' He threw and hit one and Annie's heart sank.

She carried the coconut towards the roped off area where the kids were playing. Teenagers were jiving all around them, their skirts whirling up, their arms flailing, their hair back combed and bouncing.

'I mean, Annie, they ruin their hair. She was scrunching it all up this morning.'

'Back combing.'

199

Georgie walked on. 'They throw themselves around. Look at that.'

Annie looked at a girl being thrown over her partner's shoulder, then back down again between his legs. She wanted to join in.

'I mean, we didn't have time for this,' Georgie said. 'I mean, what are they going to get up to? There's this music, all these strange fashions. I liked those pretty skirts with lots of petticoats.'

'Mm, but the children are deciding what *they* like, not following what we like and perhaps it's not before time. It's a different world, my love – careful.' The grass was tufted, uneven and the smell of it was in the air. 'They've more money, people are catering for them. We've got to forget what it was like for us, and try and understand what it's like for them, much as it goes against the grain, and go on being patient.'

Annie said that again to Georgie in December when Miss Bates told them at the parents' evening that Sarah was not working to her full potential, that she had too many interests in her life, that her guitar playing should stop, and that she should put the group to one side until her 'O' levels were over, and perhaps her 'A's.

Annie spoke to Sarah in her bedroom that night. She sat on the edge of her bed, feeling the ridges of the patchwork that Bet's mother had sewn so many years ago, looking at the ivory paper knife that had been her father's and wishing she felt old enough to be this child's mother.

'Now look, Miss Bates feels you have too much to do now that you are starting to work for your 'O' levels. Something has got to give. She would like it to be your music.'

Sarah hugged her knees and nodded. 'Yes, piano's a waste of time.'

Annie knew she would say this. She spoke quietly but firmly. 'No, not the piano, the group.'

Sarah straightened, flicking her hair back from her face. 'That's not fair. I won't give it up. I just won't.'

'There's no need to shout.'

'Mum, I won't.'

Annie took her hand and Sarah snatched it back. Annie said, 'Listen, let's leave that for now, let's talk about what you want to do in life, we never seem to discuss this sort of thing, everyone's too busy. It's our fault as well, don't worry, I'm not blaming you. Now, what do you want to do?'

Annie walked to the window, leaning against the frame, looking out across the town that she loved, hearing Mrs Anders' cat, and the pigeons in the loft outside, wishing she'd done a degree in diplomacy.

'I want to go to Newcastle to learn fashion design.' Sarah's voice was muffled.

Annie turned. Her daughter was leaning on her knees, her mouth against the quilt. 'Are you sure? I remember you saying that years ago but I don't want you to feel you have to do it just because of the business.'

Sarah shook her head. 'No, it's not because of the business. Anyway, you can't call it fashion can you – a few dungarees, aprons, smocks and underwear – but I do want to work with you.'

Annie raised her eyebrows, well pardon me for living, she thought, but merely said, 'So, if you want to do fashion design you will need your 'O' and 'A' levels. You will need to do more work.'

Sarah looked up at her. 'Mum, it's not the music I want to give up.'

Annie looked out again at the pigeon loft and nodded. She had thought as much.

'I don't know how to tell Da.'

Annie smiled gently at Sarah, walked back to the bed, straightened the quilt. 'Don't worry, I'll do a deal with you, I'll tell him – you may keep your music going, but only if your homework is done. I'm not sure what Tom will say to

Davy, because he's in trouble too. You might find yourself going solo.'

She bent and kissed her daughter.

'I'll never go solo, it'd be no fun without Davy, no fun at all.'

Annie was quiet for a moment then left the room, thinking as she walked down the stairs that her daughter's love for Davy was very deep, but was it the love of a sister for a brother as her love for Tom was, or was it something quite different? Only time would tell. That night Annie barely slept because all she could think of was how Sarah would cope with the loneliness of college without her friend, whichever love it was. But thank God it was only as far as Newcastle.

CHAPTER 13

On the Saturday after she had spoken to Sarah Annie and Georgie drove ten miles north of Wassingham, through wind-flattened moors and huddled villages. She could hear the wind screaming in from the north and soon she'd feel it. She drew her scarf round her neck, turned up her collar. Would it be a white Christmas?

'You shouldn't have come, pet, it's too cold for you. Sarah'll be here next week. I could have come by myself.'

Annie looked at his strong hands on the steering wheel. Oh no, he couldn't come by himself because what if he fell, damaged his false leg, damaged his stump? He could die in this cold, but to tell him that was to admit his limitations and that she must never do.

'The thing is, my darling, she can't bear to give up music and she has to give up something.'

They were turning into Rowen's Track and she felt Georgie turn to her, then to the front again, wrestling with the wheel as the car lurched on the rutted ice-cracked tracks.

'Oh I see.'

She could tell from his voice that he did.

'These few years have given her so much Georgie, not just success with Buttons but time with you. She'll have shared memories.'

They were approaching the farm gate, Georgie stopped the car whilst she leapt out, the force of the wind stopping her, taking her breath. She bent her head into it, her nose already numb, her lips too. She slipped the wire, pushed back the gate, stumbling over the frozen hummocks, but the sun was already coming out as Georgie drove in past her. She shoved the gate shut and ran for the shelter of the car, pushing her hands between her thighs as they lurched and bounced across the field.

'I'll miss her, she's sliding through our fingers isn't she?' Georgie said quietly.

Annie nodded. 'Just as we did. Everyone does.'

Georgie steered the car towards the north-east corner, to the lee of the hawthorn hedge and already the air was warmer.

'The wind should drop,' Georgie said, making no effort to leave the car, just sitting back. 'Let's wait and see, don't want them battling too much, it makes me stump ache and God knows what it does to their wings.' He paused. 'I love her, I worry about her, I'm glad I had all those days with her. You're a generous woman, Annie.'

He kissed her now, held her close and she remembered Bet saying to her as they stood and watched Georgie and Sarah leave one day. 'Aren't you jealous?'

Yes, she had been jealous – of Georgie's time with Sarah, of Sarah's time with Georgie but it had been necessary for them both. His lips were on hers now, kissing softly, gently and then with passion. 'I shall just have to do put up with you now,' he said at last, drawing back from her, pushing her hair off her face. 'Cold nose and all.'

They carried the basket across to the usual place and now the sun was warm as she dropped the lid back and watched Button's and Tiger's youngsters wheel, dip, then fly for home.

They drank coffee out of the thermos, cupping their hands around the mugs, moving their feet. 'I can still feel my toes, after all this time,' Georgie said. 'Come over here and let me feel your nose.'

She laughed and leant against him as he pressed his cheek to her face. She kissed him, heard him tip his coffee away, felt him take hers and toss the mug to the ground, felt his arms around her, his lips on her eyes, her nose, her lips, his hands undoing the buttons of her coat, stroking her breasts, her body, then holding her tightly to him, so tight she could hardly breathe.

'There's a time for them to grow up, isn't there, if only to give us time together,' Georgie said, his mouth on hers. 'I'm glad you're back, I've missed you.'

Both domestic and export sales rose steadily in the spring of 1962 and Annie redeemed her walnut table. Throughout the Easter holidays they agreed to take on Sarah, Davy, Geoff and Paul as temporary packers and cleaners. The tennis courts were finished – they had managed to build two – and now they wanted decent tennis rackets, shoes, and the group needed amplifiers.

'We're screwing on pick-ups beneath the strings, Mum,' Sarah said, 'and wiring them into amplifiers. All groups need them.'

Annie shuddered. 'Not in our house they don't – your father would flip and I'd die.'

'Oh Mum, it's not for the house, it's for our gigs.'

'Your what?'

Sarah flicked her hair back from her face. 'Our gigs, we're going to try and earn some money, get around, let people hear us, it's the only way to improve you know, to work for something, otherwise we just mess about – just like Da said the birds did if they didn't have competition.'

Annie looked at Davy, shaking her head, that child would take the ground right from under Georgie's feet with that particular argument as she well knew. 'So, whose idea was this?'

Davy grinned. 'Guess.'

Annie shook her head. 'You should stand up to her Davy, don't let her push you around – and there's the small matter of your work.'

Davy laughed. 'She's all right, she just knows what she wants and it's a good idea isn't it, Aunt Annie? It'll get us out of earshot of you and me parents and that way we can buy ourselves better guitars.'

That evening Annie talked Georgie into employing the kids, telling him that he was always going on about being in the pit at their ages, so they could do a bit of slave labour 'at mill' instead.

'But homework must be done. You're fifteen and working towards those exams,' she warned.

As summer came the sales were still increasing and the inspector found only that the outside needed redecorating and they felt like sticking out their tongues and blowing raspberries as he left.

In May the graph in Annie's office showed just a steady rise since December, no dips as there had been the year before. They were selling to France now and had stabilised the size ratios at last, accommodating slimmer French figures, whilst judging Holland and Germany on the British shape. Georgie's mail order division was expanding, bringing in further orders for the wholesalers.

'You were right, it's a good shop window, my love,' Georgie said as they worked out the bonus for the workers, the increase in salary for them which this year would be larger, though their overheads were rising along with their sales.

'It's not enough just to divide the profits, we need to do something together this year, to celebrate, all of us – everyone in the firm. We're so busy we never have time to talk, even at the meetings we just discuss business,' Annie said one evening as she dished out new potatoes from Bet's allotment since they had been too late with their own this year, again.

Sarah watched the butter melt on the potatoes, darkening the mint. She remembered how her mother used to scrape parsley off her food at Sarah Beeston's, not knowing that it was to be eaten. Parents were embarrassing.

Georgie reached for the salad cream. 'Good idea – how about a trip to the sea.'

'No, not the sea – if it rains we'll have Bernie grizzling

and everyone sitting on the coach steaming up the windows wishing they hadn't come.' Annie cut into her tomato. 'Bet's had a really good year with these. I like the small ones.'

Sarah looked up. 'How about Spanish City at Whitley Bay? There's lots to do.'

Georgie nodded. 'Not a bad idea. I haven't been for years and they're bringing their families aren't they Annie? The kids would love a fair.'

Annie nodded. 'Oh yes, I've been through the books, we can afford it and never mind the kids, we'd love it.'

Sarah smiled. 'Can the Easter packers come too?'

'If you want to but I'd have thought it was a bit square for you. We'll probably be wearing Kiss Me Quick hats and eating candy floss – can The Founders' image take it?'

Sarah just nodded and smiled. Some of the best American rock 'n' roll music was played there, or so Geoff had said but there was no need to tell them about that.

In June Gracie, Bet and Annie took Friday off and cooked chickens, sausages and sausage rolls, wrapping them in greaseproof paper and stacking them in the fridge until the morning. When Sarah came in from school she sliced and buttered seven loaves of bread, then helped Annie boil eggs for fifteen minutes. They filled containers with squash but when they arrived at the coach the next day they saw Georgie and Tom loading bottles of beer into the luggage hold.

'Too hot for squash, or tea,' Georgie grinned, nodding as Bet handed him the thermos flasks which the women had brought.

'Well, you just keep your eye on Bernie,' Annie warned, laughing as Tom rolled his eyes. 'And yourselves.'

They sang all the old favourites as they travelled – *Knees up Mother Brown, The White Cliffs of Dover*. Davy and Sarah sat staring out of the window, mortified by their parents who were standing up at the front conducting.

The coach driver took them via the scenic route as he had promised and they stopped for half an hour on moorland where the heather was lush and the gorse spiked dark green and yellow. There were peewits, and hawks, and the sound of insects as Annie lay down and looked up at the sky, hearing the laughter, the voices of people she employed, children the creche looked after. She heard Sarah giggling as Geoff pounced on Davy, then her, rolling her over and over down the slope, her flared jeans picking up dirt but what did it matter, they were going to the fair, weren't they?

She smiled up at Bet. 'It's a good day isn't it, Bet?'

'Aye, bonny lass, and you've done a good thing, all of you, for Wassingham. Your Sarah Beeston would be proud of you, and your da.'

When the coach finally pulled up at the fairground they could hear the music. Annie caught Sarah's eye, grinning at her, then at Davy. 'Well, well,' she said. 'Just as well your da's had a few beers and the sun's shone on me. This could lead to a severe sense of humour failure.'

The rock 'n' roll was pounding as they all arranged to meet in an hour's time for the picnic. Annie shrugged off thanks as she handed out spending money to each family.

'It's yours, it's part of the profits and you deserve it,' she said. 'We've all worked hard, just don't fall off, we want you coming back in one piece.'

She felt Georgie stiffen at her side and wondered why there were so many sayings that involved the body and why she was so stupid. She turned, touching his arm as he smiled at Meg and her husband Geoff, waiting until they had gone, then said, 'I'm sorry.'

He looked at her. 'Don't be – it's just that every so often it still gets to me. I still wish it had never happened. I wish I could grab you and run off as they're doing.' He nodded at Sarah, Davy and the other two boys, racing one another to the dodgems.

Annie held his hand, slotting her fingers between his, holding him tightly. 'There aren't many people of our age running anywhere right now,' she said, but she understood, and from his kiss she knew he realised that she did.

'She's a little devil though, isn't she? Just listen to all this,' Georgie said, but he was laughing. 'Davy's just told me he wants to do textile design so that'll please her majesty – I'll bet any money you like they'll be going to the same college, so they'll keep one another company and we can easily get to Newcastle to see them, make sure she's not getting out of hand.'

'*Getting* out of hand, I just hope she's not already there,' Annie said walking towards the music, seeing the candy floss stall and feeling the relief spreading through her at the thought that Davy and Sarah would stay together, and close to home.

'We must do this more often,' she murmured, 'it brings us luck.' Because she had feared they would disappear to London and it seemed so far away, especially in today's world.

Sarah and Davy ran with Geoff and Paul through the crowds, feeling the heat on their faces, hearing the music blasting out from the huge speakers, almost drowning the chugging of the generators, smelling the diesel, candy floss, hot dogs. They stood on the steps, watching the cars crash and thump, the drivers grimace and jerk, waiting until the music slowed, then running for a car. Sarah and Davy in the yellow one, Geoff and Paul in the green, chasing one another as the power came on, screaming, screeching, groaning, jolting.

They ran off to the Big Wheel and flew through the air, and Sarah felt the wind rush through her, like it did when she tumbled over the bar at the allotment and she gripped Davy's arm. 'Isn't life wonderful, just so wonderful and you're right, we should go to your da's college. It'll get us away from here, give us a change. This is what London will be like – the two of us and music like this, and people who understand op art, and like it too. Oh Davy, I can't wait.' She turned and looked out across the flashing lights to the sea.

On the coach back Sarah and Davy conducted the singers in *Hound Dog* and *Living Doll*, then organised them into groups using their voices to create rhythms, singing Platters songs, and Coasters numbers while Rob sat next to Annie and talked about Ban the Bomb marches and the escalation in the United States military aid to Vietnam until his father reached over and said, 'Shut up and sing.'

Annie saw Davy turn towards them, he had heard and the love in his face was for Tom. She smiled gently. Everything was going to be all right. It wasn't until the next morning that Sarah told her about London, about Davy's need to go to his father's college, about their need for a change.

Annie merely straightened her daughter's collar, gave her a kiss and said that of course she understood, they would all understand. She walked to the allotment and wouldn't allow the ache to take hold, she just hoed and dug and watered, and thought of the places she had been, and how Sarah Beeston had let her go with never a murmur – how Georgie had travelled far further and his mother had allowed him – how Tom and Gracie had spent three years in London.

By the time the evening came her back ached and her hands were blistered but she was comforted, because London wasn't so far away, Sarah would be practically an adult and she must learn to let go, it was as simple as that and this is what she told Georgie as they made love. 'I know,' he said. 'It's what I've been thinking. I'm quite looking forward to life on our own while we watch her grow. It'll be a new stage for them and us.'

His lips were as soft as his voice and she held him close to her because she knew that he was right.

Throughout the summer the kids worked as packers again, standing alongside the machinists who had voted to take turns in the packing room to ring the changes during the day.

In the autumn the kids bought second-hand amplifiers and fixed them to plywood, taking them to the Youth Club for the Christmas gig which was the only one they had secured.

They had new guitars for Christmas, ones with good solid wide bodies and black inlaid trim. They had cutaway necks for easier manoeuvrability on the lower frets of the finger board, or so the man in the shop had told Gracie and Annie.

They sat round the table, fingering them, playing desultory chords, talking of the geometric patterns of op art, the visual effect they created, and Annie asked Tom if they could be incorporated into the soft furnishings they were considering for the summer if they found they could afford new printers.

He shook his head. 'Too adventurous.'

'Oh Da,' groaned Davy.

'Oh Da nothing, just think what it would be like to live with. Interesting to create, a problem to sell, just you remember that, both of you, when you're down there in that big city.'

'And just remember too,' said Annie, pouring the last of the beer, 'that nobody's going anywhere unless these exams are passed, so rehearsals are restricted until July.'

The kids didn't groan, just nodded because they had their guitars, they had their amplifiers and after their 'O' levels they would have two years to penetrate the clubs of Newcastle before they left for London, then they'd have everything.

In the spring of 1963 Annie took on a cutter because there was too much work for just one. They took on two machinists, a bookkeeper and a clerk and at last her office was tidy, Georgie's and Tom's too.

'I feel like a real boss now,' Georgie said that night. 'I really must get myself a cigar.'

'Over my dead body,' Annie replied.

In the summer there was no maintenance for the inspector to throw at them, just profits, and so the bonus was higher, but not too high because they'd decided at the monthly meeting to invest in new printers, pad mangles, and a boiler so that they could respond to the upholstery requests which were pouring in.

'Next year,' Annie said, 'our turnover should be so much higher that the bonus, and the salary increases, should be much bigger. Hang in with us, everyone, we've nearly cracked it.'

At the end of June, Don rang and she told him of their expansion, of their increased bonus for the workers, the escalating graph, the lack of repairs on the inspector's list.

'So the consortium can go and take a jump,' she said and he was pleased for them, really pleased, she could tell from his voice.

'Come over,' she said. 'We haven't seen you for ages.'

'Can't, we're going to the Canary Isles tomorrow.'

Sarah said, 'Tweet, tweet,' when Annie told her and Annie asked Georgie that night whether London knew quite what was going to hit it.

In July, they reorganised the factory, reshuffling, making room for the two flat-bed printers, one Buser printer, two pad mangles, a step and repeat machine and the boiler. They could now print eight colours, not just two. It took a month to set up and start producing and they took on three extra print workers and a machinist called Pat who was a new-comer to Wassingham but who needed a break, Brenda said. They also took on a van and driver for distribution.

'Should we try our own retail outlets?' Bet asked.

No, they said, they couldn't cope. Not yet.

'Should we try wallpaper?'

No, they said, not yet, next year perhaps because they must recoup their outlay first and then they would reconsider. Now they should start building up their reserves because the new machinery had taken their capital, though there was no loan involved and that in itself was a victory. 'It's going to be good, just up and up from now on,' Annie told everyone.

On 1 August Sarah showed Annie details of a talent competition in Newcastle in three weeks' time. 'We want to enter. We want to get as far as we can while we're here. It'll improve us so much, hold us in good stead for London.

They're more sophisticated there, sharper. We'll need much more experience.'

That night in bed, Annie and Georgie lay and worried and the next day as she cooked breakfast Annie said, 'Where is this music taking you – will it push aside your art? Do think carefully, you need qualifications to fall back on, and we hear such stories of the music world.'

She turned the bacon, hearing it spit, watching the fat cook, the rind warp, waiting for her daughter to reply.

Sarah was reading the paper, turning the pages, speaking with toast in her mouth. 'Oh, we're only going to use it to earn a bit of extra money. It's just a hobby, Mum, like Da's birds, then we'd like to come back here and help in the business, if that's all right, because the north's our home and besides you'll need us when you start the retail outlets and the wallpaper.'

The bacon was burning. Annie flicked it on to the plates. 'That's all right then,' she said quite calmly, though she wanted to leap in the air and cheer.

The kids practised in Annie's front room because Tom's neighbours had complained about the noise coming from the stable. Mrs Anders complained about the noise coming from the front room, but no more loudly than Georgie did, stamping into the kitchen on Friday night, storming out into the yard, talking to his pigeons, complaining to Annie that the whole thing was ridiculous.

Annie laughed gently. 'It would be ridiculous if it was serious, just remember that, but they're being sensible, so count your blessings.'

Georgie slumped down on the step. 'I'm tired, you're tired. We can do without this bloody racket. There's so much to do at work, there's the pigeons to race . . .'

'There are the children to nurture,' Annie interrupted. 'And that's the most important thing of all, Georgie Armstrong.'

She joined him on the step, putting her hand on his false leg as he leant back against the door frame. 'And what about that dress she's made for the show, Annie? It's above the knee, for goodness' sake. It's a disgrace. She'll get herself into all sorts of trouble, and imagine that in London. I suppose you made it for her.' He was leaning forward now, holding her arm.

'No, I didn't make it for her, I just showed *her* how to do it, so stop being so stuffy. All the girls are dressing like that now.'

'But she's only – '

'Sixteen,' Annie interrupted again. 'Not a child, so stop panicking and treating her like one. Give her some freedom and she'll . . . oh, come back and perch, just like your youngsters do. Lock her up and she'll break out. They might not want to come back to Wassingham if you start all this, just think on that.'

Georgie rubbed his forehead, then rested his back against the frame again, looking up at the sky. It was so clear, the stars so close.

'What can we do then? I can't stand this noise, and neither can the Anders.'

Annie stood up, brushing the back of her jeans. 'I know and I've been thinking about it for a while. We've got space in the packaging area. Let them use that. There's no one there.'

Georgie moved his head slightly, looking at her, and she bent down and kissed his mouth. 'Give them a hand, we've only got them for two more years,' she said.

He nodded, putting his hand behind her neck, holding her mouth against his. 'You look very lovely in those jeans, very, very lovely, and I adore you.'

'Then get up, go in there, give them the good news and then we can have some peace.'

She handed him his stick and went to the pigeons, put her fingers in the wire. 'Poor little birds, I'm surprised you came back to this mad-house each day,' she crooned, laughing as she heard the whoop of joy from Davy and then, 'Oh, Dad,

214

you're brilliant,' from Sarah and wished that she had been able to say that just once to her father.

After work that day Annie waited in the office, looking out across the car park, seeing them struggling along with their guitars, their amplifiers. She showed them the packaging room, reminded them of the no smoking rule, gave them the keys and drove Georgie mad at home, until Sarah came in and said everything was as Annie had left it. In the morning, she found that it was.

They practised there each evening for the next two weeks and sometimes Annie would stay late at work to listen to them. They were good. Sarah explained that they were practising the descending introduction to *Move It*, a Cliff Richard song.

'We're trying to get the question and answer lead breaks right at the end of each line.'

Annie nodded, though she didn't understand a word.

'We're trying to broaden our appeal, Aunt Annie,' Davy said. 'We're covering *Living Doll* as well as rock 'n' roll. We don't know what we really want you see, which way we want to go.'

'One doesn't,' Annie murmured, 'but you seem to be doing better than most.'

As she walked away she recognised *Blue Suede Shoes* and felt very proud of these children – only they weren't children were they, not any more, but neither were they quite grown up. Was anyone every really grown up? Annie wondered, as she sat at her desk, drawing doodles, filling them in. Did anyone ever feel fully wise and in control, because she didn't, not when she looked at her daughter and knew that one day she would leave.

Three days before the talent show Georgie came into her office with Brenda. He held slips, pants and bras. 'We've got a problem,' he said, passing them to her. 'And I've got a meeting in Newcastle in two hours. We can't have this, darling. I think you should sack her, whoever she is.'

215

Annie looked at the burn marks on the garments, touched them with her fingers, looked up at Brenda. 'For God's sake, what's been happening?'

Brenda shook her head. 'I can't understand it. There's your check mark on those . . .'

There was a knock at the door and Tom came in, with tea towels in his hands, showing her the holes, sticking his finger through them, shouting at her, 'What the hell are we going to do? I've had Jones on the phone. These are his returns. He's furious – says can't we run a proper business.'

Annie stood up, taking the tea cloths. 'Keep your voice down, Tom, for goodness' sake. I'll sort it out, go and soft talk Jones, tell him it won't happen again.'

She hurried out into the machine shop with Brenda, walking round slowly now, calmly, both of them looking for cigarette ends, trying to smell smoke. It couldn't have happened here, they were sure, the workroom was under constant supervision. Annie reached the end of the room. No, nothing. It had to have happened where people worked alone, which only left the packing room.

Annie felt sweat start on her hands. That was where the children practised but they wouldn't, they didn't smoke. Surely they didn't. She'd told them, again and again. She'd told them. She walked ahead of Brenda, down the machine shop, down the corridor into the room. What would she say to Georgie? What would he do? What would she do?

They were at the door now, opening it. Pat was in there, packing clothes, her forefinger nicotine-stained against the white of the cotton. Her clothes smelt of smoke. Brenda touched Annie's arm and Annie nodded, feeling relief swamp her, walking round, checking the boxes, moving to the corners of the room, seeing Brenda doing the same and Pat packing all the time with those fingers.

Brenda stooped, picked up a cigarette butt and brought it to Annie. It was still warm.

'When did you come on packing duty, Pat?' Annie asked,

standing with the cigarette butt in her hand, hating the smell of it, glad that she'd given up.

'Few minutes ago,' Pat replied, not looking up, just packing.

Brenda checked the duty roster on the wall. 'Half an hour ago, according to this.'

'So, it might have been.'

'Pat, what do you know about these?' Annie said, standing quietly in front of the woman, whose roots were dark against her bleached hair.

Annie held out the damaged goods, showing the holes, the burn marks. 'You do know don't you that there is a no smoking rule? We explained – I can remember both Brenda and I telling you.'

'Course I know. That's not me, and I don't know whose that is either. All I know is that it isn't me.'

'Feel it, Pat.'

She watched the fingers touch it. 'It's cold.'

Brenda touched it and nodded. 'Yes, it's cold now, but it wasn't.'

'I can't have smoking. It's not just the damage to the goods, it's the fire hazard. There's so much cloth in here and chemicals that it would be a disaster if anything happened.'

Pat turned from her.

Annie put the butt in her pocket, watching as Brenda brought over other butt ends from beneath the shelves. They were a different brand, Kensitas.

'See, it's not just me. I smoke Players, not those. Those are someone else's, probably your kids. I didn't burn anything, anything at all. OK, so I had one but that's all. You know yourself they're all stacked up when you've checked them. It's them who've done the damage.'

Annie looked at Brenda. There was doubt in her eyes, and in Annie's too, she knew. She took the butts, looked at them, then at Pat. 'OK then, Pat. You'll have a warning. If I ever find you smoking, you'll go. I shall speak to the children tonight.'

Annie said nothing when Sarah arrived home, and would not allow Georgie to either. She said nothing as they washed the dishes and Sarah did her homework, just smiled and said she'd be spending the evening at home tonight, they'd have to practise on their own, without the benefit of her wisdom and experience.

Sarah laughed and left them.

One hour later with Tom and Georgie, she entered the machine shop quietly, stood outside the door of the packing room, listening to the chords, to the singing, the coughing, and Annie felt her shoulders tighten with tension as Georgie opened the door.

The kids were moving, right foot forward, backwards, sideways, trying to keep their steps in time with the music and with one another. Davy's hair was too long, she thought. But then Geoff's and Paul's was also and she was smiling because there was no smoke, no thickening of the atmosphere, their throats were just dry from too much singing.

'Just thought we'd drop in, see how you're getting on.'

Tom took a packet of cigarettes out of his pocket. 'I found these, anyone want one?'

No one did.

'We don't smoke thanks, Mr Ryan,' Geoff said, straining to get his fingers on the right strings, frowning with concentration.

They left, closing the door, checking the machine room again, then the cloakroom where the overalls were hung. And it was there that they found the Kensitas in Pat's overall pocket.

Annie showed the packet to Brenda in the morning and then called Pat into her office and dismissed her on the spot. At the end of the next day she saw her again, stopping the machinists at the entrance to the car park, stopping the printers, even Bernie and Brenda, showing them the papers she had in her hands.

Tom said it was probably a petition which no one would sign and besides she was gone when they left, hurrying to get home, packing both cars with speakers, guitars and people driving to Newcastle, telling the kids to do their homework while they were waiting to go on – it was school in the morning as usual.

They sat round the tables which were wedged into the club with Geoff's and Paul's parents and thought that no one was as good as The Founders, who kept in step and in tune and who played their question and answer breaks perfectly at the end of each line.

Annie applauded along with everyone else, while Rob and Tom whistled with approval. She looked round and people were smiling and laughing but some youngsters were just sitting, smoking sweet-smelling cigarettes and from their glazed eyes she knew that it was pot and hoped that Georgie hadn't seen.

He had and was quiet all the way home whilst the others talked of the thrill of coming second and how next time they would be first. He said nothing to Sarah but held Annie when they finally fell into bed. 'If it's like this here, what's it like in London?' he said quietly.

'They'll be together and just think, the vast majority of the kids there were just smoking cigarettes and ours don't even do that.'

But even so, she wished that Sarah had chosen the pigeons over music and she knew that Georgie felt the same. She knew though that they must trust their children, it was all they could do, but it didn't stop them worrying.

It was a relief to arrive at the office in the morning at eight, to sit behind her desk, sorting through her schedule, drinking coffee, calling across the partition to Georgie, calling along the shop to Tom. She would talk to Brenda about Pat's severance pay when she arrived, she'd laugh with Bernie about his racing tips, check on the children in the creche when they came.

But by eight forty-five no one had arrived, there was just a note from Brenda, telling Annie that they were out on strike

219

and perhaps would never return to work, because employers who were so basically unfair and dishonest didn't deserve loyalty. Annie held the paper, saw the words, but understood none of it.

CHAPTER 14

Annie heard the phones ringing, Tom and Georgie answering them. She would never have heard their voices usually, there would have been too much noise – why hadn't she noticed the silence earlier?

She walked into Georgie's office, showed him the letter while he was still on the phone.

'I'll ring you back,' he said, putting the phone down, looking up at her, his jaw slackening with shock.

She took it from him, called Tom, heard him come, his heels ringing on the floor. Hadn't he realised that there was no one here either? What was the matter with them all for God's sake?

She handed it to him as he walked in, saying, 'Christ, is that the time? Where is everyone?'

She told them then, word for word, what had happened with Pat and they agreed that there had been nothing else she could have done.

'But they must all think it's the kids, that we're protecting them, making Pat take the blame,' Georgie said. There were phones ringing in all the offices now, insistent, noisy. She'd never noticed before.

She grabbed her jacket. 'I'm going to see Brenda, this is absurd. You two man the phones until I've sorted it out, try and keep the lid on it, say nothing. I'll get Gracie in from the creche, she won't realise because Moira and Pam come in later with the kids. Georgie, you ring Bet, tell her to shut up the showroom and get on down. If you each take an office we can try to keep things as normal as possible.'

The morning air was fresh as she walked from the car park, down street after street – the slag was churning up the heaps, as it had done for years, there was smoke coming from the chimneys as it had done for years, there were women sweeping their steps and she dug her hands deep into her pockets. This was Wassingham, this was her home – all this could be sorted out but why did things have to keep being sorted out, for God's sake? Why did everything keep going wrong? She bunched her fists in her pockets, thinking of the idle machines, the printers, the ovens, the orders, their name for reliability. Good God, all over a stupid woman who smoked cigarettes – what was wrong with everyone?

She turned into Stanley Street, her heels clicking. She nodded to Mrs Arthern who was polishing her letterbox. The woman turned away, hostility in her eyes, and Annie slowed, faltered, put out her hand, then walked on. She would speak to Brenda, she would clear this up – she had to. These people were her friends.

The postman passed and she called, 'Good morning.'

He said nothing but at the sound of her voice his face set just as she remembered other faces when the bosses passed by after a strike had been called and she felt lonely and wished that Georgie was with her, because she had never thought of herself as being on the other side.

She went down the back alley, hearing a dog barking, pigeons fluttering in the yards. What would they say at the club when they heard about this? But it would all be over this morning. She'd talk to Brenda, explain, though she thought she already had, and then the machine shop would hum again, and the radio would drive her mad as it always did.

She pushed open the gate, ducked in under the washing and knocked at the back door. She did not go in as she would have done yesterday, or the day before. She waited, hearing Brenda's footsteps, her voice hushing the dog, saw the door

222

opening and there was no smile on Brenda's face, just the same look that had been on Mrs Arthern's and the postman's.

'So, Annie,' she said.

Annie stood in the yard knowing she would not be invited in, knowing that others were listening in the yards on either side.

'Brenda why? Is it the smoking? It wasn't the kids. You know and I know the cigarettes were found in her pocket. Tom and Georgie were there.'

Brenda folded her arms. 'But no one else was and how can we believe anything any of you say?' Her hair was pulled back into a bun, her eyes heavy-lidded, tired, as though she'd not slept and Annie put out her hand to touch her arm, but Brenda moved away.

'I don't understand what you mean. How can you say you can't believe us, what are you talking about, Brenda?' Annie stepped back. 'Look, what's changed since yesterday?'

Everything, her mind replied but I don't know why.

'Listen to me, Brenda, you were the one who picked up the cigarette end, it was warm, Pat *had* been smoking. I know you weren't there when we found the Kensitas but we did find them in her pocket. Our kids don't smoke, their friends don't smoke. We actually went along to check up on them in the evening.' Annie dug her hands into her pockets again, seeing the hostility still there in Brenda's eyes and not understanding why. 'Even though we trusted them, we still checked.'

'That's what we should have done years ago, checked on you, but we trusted you. Next year, you kept saying. Next year the bonus will be bigger. Stick with us, grow with us, work harder and it will be all right. It's not the money, it's the lies you see, Annie. You can't get away with that in Wassingham, you're just like your brother, Annie Manon. Just like that thieving brother of yours.'

Annie jerked back at the anger in Brenda's eyes, at the thin mouth, the words which leapt out at her.

'Yes, just like Don. He was taught very well by that uncle

223

of yours, only he didn't pretend to be doing good. He acted a bastard, we knew he was and just had to accept it and pay his bloody interest rates on the loans. But at least he was honest about being a bastard. I just don't understand why you promised bonuses you never had any intention of paying. Why did you bloody well bother? You've made fools of us by cheating us and we don't forgive that.'

Annie couldn't grasp the words, only the tone, which was one of contempt.

'I don't understand, Brenda. I just don't understand what you're talking about.'

Brenda stepped back into the kitchen, holding the door. 'Well, let me spell it out to you. I know you've cheated us, lied to us about your profits. We all know now because we've seen the proof and so we'd rather do without your grand Wassingham Textiles. We've had enough of your sort of boss to last a lifetime Annie.'

'What proof?' Annie said, stepping forward as Brenda began to shut the door, leaning on it, trying to stop her, shouting, 'What proof?'

'Go away Annie, I don't want to talk to you ever again,' Brenda shouted back and the door closed. Annie tried the handle and heard the key turning in the lock. She beat on the door, shouting, calling, but Brenda wouldn't answer and so she walked back through the streets which seemed cold, empty, full of people who set their faces against her and turned their heads – and still she couldn't understand.

Neither could Georgie and Tom, who rang Brenda but the phone was off the hook. They made coffee and Bet walked through the streets to see Brenda and Meg, but neither would open the doors, though people weren't rude to her, just embarrassed, just sorry for her, she said when she returned, her voice distressed, her hands trembling.

All morning they answered phones, checked and packed what clothes were completed, though Tom refused to help.

'I can't break the strike, Annie. I can't be a scab, not after all these years.'

'Then go home,' she snapped. 'We've got to give them a business to come back to because they will come back.'

'When and how?' Tom asked, putting on his coat.

'You try and think of a way,' she shouted, sitting at a machine and beginning to sew. 'While we get on with all this.'

Gracie made sandwiches at lunchtime but no one could eat, all they could do was talk but still they couldn't understand and didn't know what to do. In the afternoon Tom came back.

'No one will talk to me. They don't trust us any more and I don't know why.' He took off his coat, threw it over a chair and started the rotary cutter, looking at them as they sat in silence watching him. 'You're right, we need to make sure there's something for them to come back to. I'm a boss now.' And there was such sadness in his eyes that Annie could have wept.

All afternoon Annie and Gracie sewed to complete the orders which should leave today, but there was no way they could do it all and by four o'clock only half of Jones's order was complete. At least the traders would receive theirs because nobody could forget their earlier loyalty.

They filled the van and Tom and Gracie drove it out through the gates, through the pickets who jeered and cat-called, and Annie's breath steamed the window as she watched. She wanted to run out, grab them, shake them, make them tell her what the hell was going on, because this dream of theirs, not just hers, was going down the drain and nobody would tell them why.

She drank tea with Bet and Georgie, then sewed more slips, her fingers sore, her neck aching, her mind leaping and jumping. She stretched and looked at the clock. Four-thirty. The kids would be coming home soon. She stood, looked out. They were still there, milling, talking, leaning up against the gate post. Bernie, Meg, Geoff her husband. Did they remember the fair, the dodgems, the candy floss? Did they? Did they?

She looked at the clock again and now panic surged within her and she ran to the door, calling to Bet, 'The kids, they don't know. I must go, there might be trouble. Tell Georgie.'

She ran through the car park, past Meg and Bernie, shouting at them, 'Get out of my way, I'm sick of the lot of you.' On down the street, to the right down Sylvester Alley, left, then left again, feeling the wind cold through her cardigan but not caring, feeling her shoes rubbing. Left again. She looked at her watch. The bus would have dropped them, for Christ's sake. She ran faster still.

Sarah stood at the bus stop, gripping her satchel, seeing the angry faces of the boys who usually lounged outside the pub, whistling and cat-calling at the girls. She heard the voices which clamoured, jostling, closing in, felt Davy's arm around her.

'What the hell's going on?' he said, his voice tight. 'What the hell's going on?' he shouted now, putting his arm up, pushing John from Ardmore Street back, struggling to keep his feet.

What were they doing here, these roughs from the back streets, what the hell were they doing here, they should be at school? No, don't be daft, school was over, that's why she was here. Sarah felt herself being grabbed from behind, her hair was pulled, it brought tears to her eyes. She hit out, grabbing Simon, pushing back.

'What're you doing? What're you all doing?' Not understanding what was happening, for God's sake. They'd been sitting in the bus, they'd jumped off, they'd walked to the corner and then this. Her satchel was grabbed and now she heard the chants of 'Scabs, bloody scabs.'

'Bloody crooks.'

'Rooking me mam, that's what you've been doing, all you bloody Manons.'

Sarah snatched at her satchel, held it, but it was torn from her grip again.

'That's ours, it's our money that's paid for that.' Pat's boy

226

threw the satchel over her head towards the arms raised at the back. 'Go on, let's share it about, like her mam said they'd do. Only they didn't.'

Davy lunged at him, battling to reach the satchel. He was pushed back, she couldn't move, she couldn't hear, all she could feel was fear, deep wild fear, and then the stone was thrown and there was blood on Davy's forehead and he was falling, crumpling and now she heard again, quite clearly, 'Milk the profits will you.'

'Go back to Gosforn, you grammar school pigs.'

And Sarah saw, quite clearly, the blood, so red against Davy's shirt, and she hurled herself at Simon, beating at him with her fists, hearing the growls and shouts, feeling them pulling at her clothes, her hair, and then there were no more voices, no hands pulling at her, no voices raging, just the sound of her mother's voice.

Sarah fell back, turned and there was her mother gripping one boy by the collar, shaking him, dragging another by the hair, shouting at the boys, 'Go home, you silly little children. Go home and stay out of things you don't understand. Don't you ever lay one finger on my family again or I'll tear the hair out of the lot of you, like I'll do to this one.' She jerked and the boy yowled.

She shook the other one, then let them go, no longer shouting but her face was white with rage. 'You yobs, how dare you come here and start all this? But of course you dare, there are – what – twelve of you and two of them? Of course you dare – they're just about the right odds for you, aren't they, John?' Annie pointed to one boy. 'Oh yes, I know you and I know your father, and you too, Simon. I grew up with your mum, Nellie.'

The boys were muttering, dodging back behind their mates, leaving. 'Yes, that's right, disappear but I'll remember you, and you too, Steve, Jack.' Annie was pointing to others. 'Your da used to give me jelly babies, Bob. Go on home and ask him what I do to little boys who push me around, or my family. Get him to tell you about Old Mooney's rag and

bone mare. Your mother will know too, Simon.' But Annie
was only talking to their backs as they stuck their hands in
their pockets and melted away into the shadows and alleys.

Sarah held Davy in her arms, there was grit digging into
her knees. 'Get up. Please get up.' She felt her mother's arms
around her, holding her, wiping tears that she didn't even
know were falling and she felt safe and didn't know why she
was shaking, because it was all right, Mum was here. It
would all be all right.

They supported Davy back to the house, passing women
on their doorsteps who looked away, though not in hostility
any longer but in shame, and now the rain was falling, and
the blood on Davy's forehead ran more quickly. Mrs Arthern
brought the satchels back to the house, leaving them on the
doorstep, saying that the boys were stupid, angry. 'I'm sorry
for what happened, though not for the strike,' she said.

Annie shut the door because she didn't want to speak to
any of them.

Georgie wheeled his chair towards Brenda's yard. He had
no coat deliberately, just as he had the wheelchair, quite
deliberately. He was not averse to evoking pity on this
occasion. In fact he was banking on it and welcomed the rain
which soaked him, and the shivering that had begun.

He knocked with his stick on the door. 'Brenda. It's
Georgie. I'm wet, I can't walk because it's too slippery and
me stump's too chafed so I'm in me chair and I'm staying
here until you open this door.'

He waited for five minutes then banged again. He waited
another five and the cold was seeping through and his stump
was aching, as it always did in the wet, and Brenda knew
that. He waited for another five minutes, then banged again
as he saw her face at the window. The door opened.

'You fool,' she said. 'You'll be ill.'

'Then let me in,' Georgie said, putting the brake on more
firmly, putting out his hand to her. 'Pull me up and let me
in.'

Brenda stared at him and he felt the drips from his hair running down his face and knew that his trousers were soaking and dripping on to her yard. He took the hand that she offered.

They talked in the kitchen and Brenda handed him the accounts which Pat had shown to all the workers. They showed a vast profit and were false.

Georgie nodded, said nothing and left, wheeling himself to Pat's house, knocking on her door, not wanting pity now, but trying to control his rage, heaving himself up from the chair, ignoring the shivering which had begun again.

He stuck his stick in the door when she tried to slam it, pushed it open and heaved himself into the kitchen which smelt of unboiled tea towels, standing with his back to the range, watching her as she sucked deeply on her cigarette, her shoulders hunched. She was too thin and her face was nervous.

'Who gave you the accounts, Pat?'

'Someone who knew what he was talking about.'

'Who Pat? Describe him to me.'

'Why should I?'

'Because if you don't I'll report you to the police too.'

Pat ground out her cigarette. 'What for? I've done nothing.'

'The paper's a fraud. You'll be in it too so just tell me who gave it to you.'

'I can't, he made me promise and he let me have this house cheap. He's helped me a lot and I promised.'

Georgie felt the heat on his back, on his leg and the shivering slowed.

'So where did you meet him, Pat, in Newcastle was it, where you worked before?'

'What's that got to do with anything?'

'Just answer me.' Georgie's voice was quiet, firm, cold. 'Did you meet him where you worked before? Where did you work, Pat?'

229

Georgie knew before she told him, somehow he knew. 'I worked at Manners. He sacked me.'

Georgie touched her Kensitas packet with his stick. 'Same old problem, eh? You need a job where you can smoke Pat, didn't you ever think of that?'

Pat took another cigarette, her fingers were almost brown with nicotine. 'Yes, I did. I went for one in an office but the boss said he could fix me up with a house and a job, if I moved. I wanted to move. Me old man knocked me about see. That boss was good to me. He gave me the accounts. He knew what you were up to, see.'

Georgie nodded. 'Just tell me who he is, Pat.'

She wouldn't, she drew deeply on her cigarette, once, twice, and still she wouldn't, so Georgie described him to her, in minute detail because, in a way, he had known all along.

'Give me your rent book, Pat,' he demanded when she nodded at his description, his voice still cold, firm, quiet. She did and he put it in his pocket, heaved himself back out into the rain and wheeled himself home, because Annie must be told and it was she who must deal with it, not any of them, because he knew that that was what she would want.

Annie drove to Newcastle the next day, through cold and rain and there was only the swish of the wipers to keep her company, but she was glad she was alone because this must be between the two of them.

She parked, climbed the stairs, walked straight past the receptionist, past his secretary and into his office.

'Good morning, Mr Jones,' she said, standing in front of the desk looking at Don's hands, tanned against the pristine white of the blotter.

She held out the accounts and a copy of the rent book, saying nothing, just watching as he glanced at them, then threw them on the desk, rotating his chair, taking out a cigar.

'If you smoke that, I'll ram it down your throat,' Annie said, her voice quite calm.

He put the cigar down on the mahogany desk, steepled his hands and looked at her, and now she could see the hate that had been there all along.

'Why, Don?' she asked, still standing.

He didn't answer and so she handed him another sheet of paper. This time it was the copy of a statement written by Pat in the presence of their solicitor. It contained everything she had told Georgie.

'If you don't tell me why, and how, this will be sent either to the newspapers or to the police, who will, of course, be aided by us in all their investigations.'

He sat looking first at her then out of the window.

'You shouldn't have come back and taken the house,' he said finally. 'Sarah Beeston gave you everything and me virtually nothing.'

Annie just looked, then said, 'You had so much from Uncle Albert and all I had were clips round the ear and his lavatory to clean day in and day out. He loved you, he gave you everything.'

Don shrugged. 'He had no class. Sarah had and she gave it to you and how dare you move ahead of me, and how dare you come back and move into my territory and take the house from me?'

'Was that enough reason to try to destroy my life?'

Don steepled his hands again. 'Yes, I rather feel it was. I wanted you back down where I had been, I wanted you all down there, with your college degrees, your nursing experience, your officer's pips – your neat little gang, all closed up together again, leaving me outside. You never gave me a hand up, you never asked me to share your life in Gosforn. She was my relative too, you know.'

Annie watched the man and remembered the boy who had jeered at Gracie's plumpness, who had jeered at their father, at Bet, at her, at Sarah Beeston. The young man who had sided with Albert, run his business, inherited it, sneered at Gosforn. She hadn't known what he really wanted and he'd never said. If he had done so, Sarah would have helped him to achieve that, not just given him money for his partnership with Uncle Albert which was what he had said he wanted. Was it just a warped justification? She didn't care, finally she didn't care, because now she knew that this was the man who had arranged for Pat's brother to view the house next door, and then to complain about the pigeon loft using the name of Mr Jones.

'So, you fixed for Tommy Mallet to do a runner. Did you share Sarah's money with him? Val's too?'

He shrugged. 'He was going to leave anyway, got a nice little place abroad.'

'And I never did sign a form, did I, there was no letter?'

Don laughed. 'You're so bloody thick I knew you wouldn't remember whether you had or not.'

Annie felt no anger, there was nothing.

'And Manners, that was you too?'

'He was a good friend in the old days and put a number of loans my way. That little bit of business suited us both, but you're so bloody difficult, Annie. You won't give up but you'll have to now.'

Annie said, 'The consortium, that was you too, but under a different name?'

Don pursed his lips, his voice interested, objective as he replied. 'More or less but I didn't get the showroom in time though – you didn't tell me about that before you did it. As I said, you're so thick, Annie, you never twigged did you, none of you?'

Almost, thought Annie, but we just couldn't believe it. Could anyone, of their own brother?

'So what did you promise Pat to burn the clothes; she wouldn't say.'

There was silence.

She looked out of the window, through the venetian blinds, to the tall buildings and the heavy rain-sodden skies, then back at him, his thin face, his hands so carefully manicured and without any blue-stained scars.

'Come on, Don, might as well or I shall just have to show

232

this little paper to people who matter.' Annie reached for Pat's statement, waving it backwards and forwards.

'Well, I offered her an office job, but only if it was successful. She can go to hell now.'

Annie shook her head, looking at him as he pushed his chair back, watched him cross his legs, picking imaginary fluff off his dark suit.

'No, I rather think she will come to you.' She waved the paper again, even more slowly now, still watching his legs – his two legs.

'Is that quite clear? She works for you from now on.'

She was still waving the paper, and now she felt its draught on her face. 'Is that quite clear, Don Manon?'

He looked up at her, his lips thin with rage, his eyes narrow, but she just waited, waited. Finally he nodded.

'Good.' She looked out of the window again, the clouds were still heavy, grey. There would be more rain today.

'Is that all then?' His voice was tight.

Annie didn't look at him. 'More or less but I shall never forgive you as long as I live for hurting our family, for soiling Sarah's house with your presence and her money with your dishonesty. Most of all I shall never forgive you for trying to deprive Georgie of his pigeon loft, when you had already taken his leg.'

Don frowned at this, putting up his hand. 'No, you can't blame me for that. I wasn't to know.'

'You played the game Don, you were responsible for the consequences but that doesn't matter now. It's happened, it's over. You and I are over, all finished, Tom and Bet too, but I'm going to stay in this office until you write a letter to our workforce, telling them exactly how you falsified the accounts. You will write another to us explaining in detail your other activities. This will not be used against you unless anything further happens to disturb the smooth running of our business. As a family we will maintain a civilised demeanour because of the children, who need know nothing of this, but that is all.'

She held out her pen, took paper from the pile on his desk, walked to the door, called in his secretary and made her wait while Don wrote, his face red with rage.

'Please witness this, Miss Archer,' Annie said.

Miss Archer did, her hair falling across her face as Sarah's had done when she had held Davy – was it only yesterday?

'Thank you, that will be all.' Annie watched as Miss Archer left, then picked up the pen Don had thrown on the desk. She threw it in the waste-paper basket.

'Now, Sarah's money you "invested". Keep it. We don't want it now it's been through your hands.' Annie saw the glint of satisfaction in his eyes but wait for it, Don, just wait, she thought. I'm not going to take money because that won't hurt you, you have so much. You see, you need to feel pain, you need to be taught never to do this again.

Annie waited, and then said, 'But the house is a different matter. You're to get out – now. I shall sell it and set up a trust fund for the children. None of us wants to live there now, it's spoiled for us. You'll have to think up something to tell Maud, won't you?'

Annie saw shock take the place of satisfaction, then the shock became hatred and anger and she was glad, because now her own rage and hate were stirring for this man who had dared to harm those she loved. 'One more thing, Don. I will ruin you if you ever try anything again – and then where will you be? Not with Maud, I can assure you, she'll move her little painted fingernails somewhere else.'

She picked up the papers, all of them, including the copy of the rent book and the accounts, and walked to the door across the deep pile carpet, wanting to be away from this man who had once been her brother.

He called out to her then. 'What makes you think your workers will believe any of this? When people think someone's been lying they'll never trust them again.'

Annie didn't turn, didn't stop, she just opened the door and left but she knew that Don was right. There was no guarantee that their workers would believe them, or the evidence, but at least she and her family knew the truth, at last.

CHAPTER 15

Annie sat in the kitchen on Saturday morning, hearing the kettle simmering on the range, tasting the hot strong tea which she sipped from the mug Sarah had given her before she left for London – was it only a week ago? It seemed so much longer. So, she thought – 1965 and my daughter's first letter home. She reread Sarah's account of their first days at college, the enrolling, the queueing for stationery, for the meals in the refectory.

She smiled at Sarah's description of the lecturer who had explained how to use the sewing machines step by step and Sarah felt unable to tell her that she'd been using one for as long as she could remember.

She's not a bit like Brenda, Mum, tell her she'd cope with all of us with her arm tied behind her back. How's she getting on with the new machinist?

A man showed us how to cut patterns, so when we come back, if you haven't got a second cutter, I can help out. Next week we learn how to design. Davy is loving his foundation course, keeps telling me about dyes and fabrics. He's keen on African dyeing or something. It's great, Mum, really great but we're missing you all, so much.

Annie put down the letter, smoothing it, glancing again, touching the writing, imagining Sarah in the bedsit they had chosen in July. God, she'd forgotten how huge London was, how small her daughter and her nephew were in comparison.

'London nowadays is very different to pre-war London,' Tom had said as they waved them off last week. 'I hope to God they can cope.'

Annie had echoed that again and again as they drove back from Newcastle to the factory. She smiled now, clasping the mug between both her hands. Were Sarah's as sore as hers had been after her first experience of cutting, poor girl?

She rose, restless, lost, wishing it were a working day. She washed her mug, dried it, watched Georgie cleaning out the loft. He was restless too, missing his daughter, but at least they'd managed to find a second cutter. She leant against the sink watching Georgie turn and smile. He looked younger somehow and she knew that she did too.

She smiled at him, then checked through the minutes of the monthly meeting again. Yes, no wonder they were both looking better, they'd gone from strength to strength since she had shown the workers Don's letter and the bonus this summer had been as good as she had promised it would be. Georgie opened the door and called through, 'How many times have you read it now?'

'Almost as many as you, bonny lad, but I can't sit here any more. Let's go and pick Bet up and take her for a run.' Annie pushed the minutes away but tucked the letter into her pocket, grabbing her coat, throwing Georgie his and the car keys. 'Come on or I shall get maudlin but do you really think it's great for them, Georgie? God I hope it is.'

Sarah sat in the bedsit, looking at the books she had bought in the student shop, opening them, then shutting them again, sketching out a design, screwing it up, throwing it in the bin. She buttoned up her coat, rubbed her hands and then moved to the window, leaning her head on the pane, seeing her breath misting up the glass. It was so cold, so different, so big, so busy and she wanted to go home.

She looked across the roofs, at the lit sky. It was always

bright in London and she longed for the dark of home. It was noisy, too many cars, too many people, too many strange faces and she wanted Wassingham, its neighbours, its shops, its slag heaps. She turned to pick up a book but the tears were falling now, and she sank on to the bed. 'Only two months, then I can go home – we can go home,' because Davy was as lost as she.

He knocked on her door now, 'Sarah, can I come in?'

'In a minute, wait a minute, I'm changing.' She rushed to the sink, splashing water on her face, drying it, looking in the mirror. Yes, it was all right. 'Come in then.'

She sat on the cane chair and it wobbled as Davy opened the door and she said, 'Toss us that piece of paper then, Davy, I'll bung it under the leg, there's one shorter than the other and it's driving me mad.' She strove to keep her voice strong, because he mustn't know that she had been crying.

Davy brought it to her. She dug her fingers into the palms of her hand, smiling as he squatted before her, handing her the paper. She folded it, then leaned back in the chair, handing it back to him. 'It's better if you do it and I sit here getting at it at the right angle. OK, now stuff it under the one that's up in the air.'

She watched as he shoved it beneath the leg, then stood, looking down at her. 'Strange how you always get the sitting down jobs,' he said smiling but it didn't reach his eyes. 'It'll get better, bonny lass.'

He moved to the bed and sat down. Tell me that and mean it, Davy Ryan, she thought because she knew it wouldn't get any better, how could it? They'd been here a week and no one had spoken to them properly, no one had smiled in the refectory, or called them over to sit with them. Everyone seemed to have someone else to talk to, so many friends. She looked around the room and wanted to be back in her mother's kitchen, in own bedroom, she wanted to hear her parents' voices, their radio, the pigeons. She wanted to go home and now she felt her throat thicken, and knew that she would cry again and so she said, 'Oh come on, let's get out of here.'

She hurried to the door, pressed the timed light switch and rushed down the stairs, hearing Davy following her, not wanting him to see her face, not wanting to speak because then the tears would come. She squeezed past the bikes in the hall. The light went off, she knocked her shins on a pedal, and heard Davy doing the same. She banged the light switch by the door. 'Damn bloody thing, can't even have enough light to get out in one piece.'

She wrenched open the door, hearing Davy begin to laugh. She waited for him on the steps, leaning back against the railings, hearing the laughter growing louder as he came down the hall, out of the door, slamming it behind him, and now she was laughing too, holding on to the railings and on to his arm. 'Damn bloody light,' she gasped, knowing it wasn't funny, wondering where the laughter was coming from, unable to stop it.

They clung to one another and he said, 'We could always jump out of the window you know and save our shins.'

Sarah could barely speak, just nodded, clutching her sides then pointed at the railings. 'That's right, we'd break our necks but we'd have lovely shins.'

They sat on the steps, laughing, winding their scarves round their necks, then moved to one side as Tim from the end room came down the street and bounded up through the middle of them. He'd never spoken, just nodded as he did now, opening the door, going into the still lit hall, which plunged into darkness as he squeezed past the bikes. They heard 'Christ all-bloody-mighty,' and the laughter burst from them again.

Sarah ran up the steps and banged the light switch, her sides heaving, and Tim called from the end of the hall, 'I owe you a drink for that, I'll be down in a minute, we can curse Ma Tucker's bloody light together.'

Sarah looked back at Davy, and now they grinned. 'Maybe it's getting better,' he called.

It was getting better. Tim took them to Soho, strap-hanging on the tube which lurched and swung, then they walked along Wardour Street, Frith Street and Dean Street, and Tim told them that he had to repeat his last year because he'd spent too much time hanging out here. 'Got into a group,' he said, 'all play and no work got Tim the big stick. Lesson one, kids, you've got to do a bit or you get slung out.'

Sarah felt the pain in her thumb and fingers from the cutter. 'Trouble is,' she said, 'all work and no play makes you wretched, makes you want to go home.'

Tim stopped in the street, swung her round, arched his eyebrows, grabbed Davy's arm. 'Oh, we thought that's what you wanted. Always together, always serious. Didn't know you wanted to play too, that's why we left you alone. Can't have you going home, come along, see what London can tempt you with.'

He dragged them past French, Italian and Greek bars, restaurants, snack bars and delicatessens, and the smells mixed, the languages too. They heard the sounds of laughter, of conversation, of singing, of living and Sarah turned to Davy. 'I've never seen anything like it.'

'I bet your mam would laugh at that.' Davy nodded to a strip club. 'Probably try to sell them her knickers.'

They laughed, told Tim why, and he grinned, pointing out the prostitutes in dingy doorways, the teachers of French in the second-storey bedsits and Sarah felt that her world was being cracked wide open.

'Don't bother to write to your mam about them,' Tim warned, 'The last thing they need is knickers.'

He led them into a coffee bar which oozed steamy warmth. The hiss and spurt of an espresso coffee machine was drowned again and again by laughter and talk. They sank into chairs which nudged others, slipping off their coats, their scarves, while Tim bought the coffees.

'Not bad, bonny lad,' Sarah murmured, looking round at the garlic and onion strings which hung around the room, at the students who crammed round the tables. One of them looked up and smiled. She was on Sarah's foundation course and had never acknowledged her before. Sarah smiled back, blushing, pleased, and she held Davy's arm. 'I didn't know any of this was here.'

He nodded. 'Makes you feel better, doesn't it?'

They spooned sugar on to the top of the froth, watching it sink through to the coffee, drinking it, wiping away moustaches, talking of their courses, their homes and Tim nodded when they spoke of Wassingham.

'Knew you were from the north east. My uncle worked there for a while. Long way to come, long way to run away home too.'

Sarah looked down, scraping the froth from the inside of the cup with her spoon. 'Where's your home then?' she said, because she didn't want to talk of running away. It wouldn't be running away, it would just be not returning after Christmas, that was all.

Tim came from Guildford and told them of the cobbled North Street, the second-hand bookshop run by the Thorpes, one younger, one older, the younger being as old as Methuselah.

Davy said, 'What group do you play with?'

'I don't, not any more. They eh, got sent down, shall we say. Got too heavily into drugs so it's just me and my guitar now, looking for a home.'

Davy bought more coffees and more people came in, squeezed past, slapping Tim on the shoulder, telling Davy and Sarah that this man had to do some work this year or he'd never cast himself upon the world.

'We play,' Sarah said. 'We had a group at home.'

Tim looked at them both, his face serious now. 'What d'you play?'

'Most things, we've been trying to broaden our scope, covering the Beatles, the Stones, Cliff Richard, the ballads but now we're trying to write our own too.' Sarah stopped because they hadn't tried, not for the last week, everything had stopped, sucked into the long dark tunnel of loneliness.

'Fine, let's get together. We'll need a fourth but Arnie's free,' Tim shouted across the room, waving Sarah's scarf in the air. 'Arnie, over here a minute.'

Arnie shambled across, dressed in a long sweater with holes in the elbows, his hair long and unkempt and Sarah knew that her da would love to get his hands on it, cut it, slick it down with Brylcreem.

He sat with them, playing the drums on the table, listening. 'Great idea, we can audition for the Christmas gig, where'll we practise?' He spoke with a drawl.

'Mid-Atlantic,' Tim said, grinning. 'The furthest this man's been is Watford.'

But where would they practise? It could only be back at the digs and then only when Ma Tucker was out and she was always out on a Monday, Wednesday and Friday but returned at varying times. They drank more coffee and devised a system whereby they would take it in turns to keep watch at the window while still playing.

'But what about the room next to Sarah's? Doesn't anyone rent that – will they complain?'

Tim shook his head. 'Someone called Carl has taken that. Arnie knows him, he was in his house last year. Didn't say he was going to move, but here he is. He drifted in and out of Arnie's place – didn't turn up until halfway through last term. He's at the LSE but isn't there much, he's got his fingers in the pop pie and God knows what else. He was in Morocco this summer so he's probably still there – bet he brings back some good pot. Anyway, don't worry about him, we can square it if he turns up. *If* being the operative word.'

'Mm, sounds great,' Arnie said, rising. 'We can fix up some gigs for next term, still a few clubs who'll give groups a chance and we can try and talk Carl into helping.' He shambled away again and Sarah finished her coffee.

Next term was another matter, she thought as she lay in bed that night, because now that the lights and the warmth of the coffee bar were gone, the room seemed darker, colder, and Wassingham even further away.

In November she read her mother's letter and laughed gently when Annie told her that her father had nearly had apoplexy at the Beatles' MBE.

He wanted to take my scissors to their hair, and plaster it with Brylcreem. He still aches for Vera Lynn and the *White Cliffs of Dover* you know but he'll make do with Alma Cogan or Donald Peers! I'm glad to hear that you are practising again and just hope your system of signals works. I'm sure the packing room misses its nightly vibrations, I know we do.

Business is good, and getting better. It's all a great relief and Bet spends more and more time in the creche – I'm sure it's because all you birds have fled the nest. We're so looking forward to Christmas, my darling. Incidentally, Prue sent you over this sandalwood box, thought it might bring some sun into your bedsit. Are you happy? I do so hope so.

Sarah held the box, smelt it, ran her fingers in the carved grooves and wanted to write back that the lavatory was horrid, a bath possible only once a week, the gas fire gobbled shillings, that she was sick of baked beans and wanted to come home.

She put the box on the table near to the designs she had been drawing and passed the letter to Davy. She washed the dishes. Tomorrow Davy would cook – and it would be beans – and she wanted to be a child again, leaning into Bet's arms, into her mother's, her da's.

'It's better now, isn't it?' Davy said, pulling the table to one side, stacking up her designs. 'It's better now we've got the music, now we know Tim.'

Sarah nodded. Yes, it was better but only while Tim and Arnie were here, the rest of the time they were still too far away from home, from friends and family.

That evening they played the music that they would perform at the audition, playing the riffs again and again, drinking instant coffee and then beer which Arnie had brought, taking turns to stand at the window peering left and right. Taking a break, talking themselves through the score, picking out the chords.

'We're getting better. Sarah's got a good voice,' Arnie said, drawing on his cigarette.

Tim tossed him his cigarettes back. 'Yes, and we're getting better as a group, what d'you two think?'

Sarah and Davy nodded. They were getting better but they weren't as good as they had been with Paul and Geoff, there wasn't the understanding, the years behind them. They played again, practising the vocals, the breaks, the repeats, the riffs until her throat and fingers were sore.

She sipped water and they played again practising the descending introduction over and over. 'Louder,' Davy said. 'Louder.'

The air was thick with smoke, their fingers strained on the strings, Sarah's voice cracked, she cleared her throat, caught up with them, sang again, and then there was a knocking on the door and they fell silent – utterly silent.

Then Tim whispered, 'Oh God, Ma Tucker.'

They'd forgotten to watch for her. They looked at one another, then the knocking started again.

'Somebody died in there?' It was a man's voice, cultured, creamy.

Tim laughed, dumping his guitar, opening the door.

'Nearly, Carl, thank you very much.'

He was tall with blond, sun-streaked hair and his skin was tanned against his cuff as he shook Sarah's hand. 'We're neighbours I believe. I hope I won't disturb you when I turn over in the night.'

Sarah could think of nothing to say. He moved along to Arnie, slapping his arm. 'Got a new group then, you old reprobate.'

Arnie just nodded, fingering his guitar and smiling, the smoke from his cigarette drifting up, mingling with the hazy

244

cloud which hung above them. Davy grinned. 'Good to meet you. We thought it was Ma Tucker.'

'So, a little northern laddie – and how d'you like the big city?'

Carl was bringing out two bottles of wine from the bag he carried. 'Thought we'd have a welcome home party for Carl.'

Sarah said, 'We were practising.' And her voice was hard and more Geordie than usual because this man had made Davy flush.

Carl looked at her, smiling slowly. 'A little northern lassie. Good. The Animals are quite something and so are you. I was talking to them just the other day. Have you a corkscrew?'

'Of course,' Sarah took it from the drawer, blessing her mother for giving her one, 'just in case'. Her voice was cold.

Davy was smiling now, because what had seemed to be an insult now seemed to have been a compliment and Sarah felt confused. Tim brought glasses from his room, Davy one from his and they drank to the new group, to Carl's return, and his eyes met Sarah's, deep brown, almost black and his eyelashes cast shadows on his cheeks. 'Cheers,' he said, raising his glass to them all, and again to her. 'Cheers.'

They drank and he put another shilling in the gas fire, it spluttered, hissed and then burnt steadily as he told them of the heat of Morocco, the yacht his mother had bought for the holiday and then sold at a profit, the flight he had taken to India with friends, the boat they had taken down the Ganges.

'You'd have been interested in the designs, Tim,' Carl said, blowing smoke into the air.

'These two as well,' Tim said, pouring more wine for them all.

Carl smiled at Sarah. 'Textile designer too?'

She shook her head. 'No, dress design, and I agree with you about the designs of India.'

Carl looked at her more closely. 'Oh you've been?'

'No, I'm just a wee Geordie lassie, aren't I? My parents have lived there and have told me all they know about

245

the place.' Sarah heard the anger in her voice and didn't care. How dare this man come into their room and flash his tan, his accent, his wine at them like this?

Davy was grinning at her, Tim too and now Carl nodded. 'Touché, I feel.' He sipped his wine, looked away at Arnie. 'So how's it going? You licking them into shape?'

Arnie sucked on his cigarette. 'More like these two licking us into shape. They're good.'

Carl looked at Sarah again, surprise in his face. She looked not at him, but Davy. 'We'd better practise harder on Friday, we've lost an hour tonight.' Her voice was cold.

Carl smiled at her. 'Please, do go on. I shall be the audience.'

'We're not ready for an audience,' Sarah snapped, covering her glass as he moved the bottle towards her.

Tim asked Carl, 'So, who've you been mixing with then, apart from The Animals?' He was lounging back on the bed, whilst Davy and Arnie sat on the floor, their glasses between their legs. Sarah sat on the chair and thanked God that the legs were balanced or she'd be wobbling about and my God, wouldn't this prat enjoy that? She looked at him as he answered Tim, sitting across from her, facing sideways, his face thin, his lips so perfectly formed, his shirt so clean, his neck as tanned as his hands.

'Talking to a guy at a party the other night. The Stones were there of course.'

Of course, Sarah thought.

'A couple of new female singers too, but I don't know, their managers just seem set on pushing them towards Blandsville, they're just copying and magnifying the fifties ballad singers. I mean, just look at Kathy Kirby and Pet Clark, Sandy Shaw – we've seen them all before. They're just jumping on a bandwagon that's gone before.'

Arnie murmured now, lighting up another cigarette. 'Bob Dylan's just done that too. Gone electric, for God's sake, what's the matter with the guy?'

Carl laughed, scratching his neck. His nails were short,

246

clean, his fingers long and thin, an artist's fingers, Sarah thought, hiding her own which were swollen and scored from cutting and sewing.

'Got a good head on him, that's what's the matter. He's going for the money and what's wrong with that? He could get a new sound, who knows.'

Davy said quietly, his words slurred, glass at his mouth, 'It's a betrayal.'

'No way – I'm telling you, these guys are in it for the money, nothing else. That's the bottom line, for you lot too.'

Sarah spoke now, her voice cool. 'These "guys" are where they are courtesy of the kids and they couldn't produce the music they do if it was only for the money. It's got to come out of the core of the group. They're got to have a commitment.'

Tim and Davy nodded and she looked only at them, not at this man whose blond hair was too long and rested well below his collar.

'So, Sarah. Perhaps you're right, who knows. Perhaps you are.' Carl's voice was soft now, serious and he nodded at her as she turned to look at him, at those brown eyes which caught and held hers.

Arnie drawled. 'So, what's the demo about this week at the LSE, still the Vietnam war?' He held out his glass for more wine but Carl turned from Sarah and shook the empty bottle, putting it down, taking out a silver cigarette case.

Davy said loudly, 'For God's sake, not politics. I thought I'd got away from that.'

Sarah looked at him then said quickly, 'What music do you prefer then, Carl?'

He passed the cigarette case to her. She looked at the three large joints. 'No thanks.'

He smiled. 'What's up, hasn't pot reached Newcastle? Is it still just beer and pigeons?'

She stiffened, turned from him again. 'Of course it's reached us but I don't want one, not tonight.'

She watched as he offered them to Arnie, Tim and Davy,

all of whom took one, Davy avoiding her eyes because he had never smoked before.

Arnie lit the joints and Sarah watched Davy draw in too deeply, cough, choke, his eyes watering, the others laughing, but not unkindly. Carl was bringing out a pouch and papers, laying them on the table, saying over his shoulder to Arnie, 'Open the window or Ma Tucker will have hysterics.'

As he pulled out the pot and laid it on the paper she smelt the heavy sweet scent of the marijuana – Davy was coughing no longer, but taking more shallow draughts, his lids heavy, his smile relaxed. He looked happy, he looked as he had done in Wassingham. Sarah looked around the room at the people they played music with but didn't know. Strangers. So many strangers.

Carl held out the reefer to her. She shook her head again. He shrugged, lit it, sucked deeply, leaning back in his chair, watching her with kind, brown eyes and there was silence in the room. Sarah looked at her hands, so tense in her lap. She looked at Davy, sprawled and happy, at Tim and Arnie, who were strumming imaginary guitars, beating imaginary drums, and felt alone.

Carl leant forward, tapped her arm. She looked at the reefer he held out to her, damp from his mouth. 'Sure?' he said. 'Alcohol does your throat far more harm and you should look after your voice, it's good, I heard it through the door. Trust me, I wouldn't hurt you.'

She hesitated, then put out her hand but he placed the reefer in her mouth, his fingers brushing her lips.

'Just draw lightly,' he said gently.

She did, and felt the heat, the taste enter her. He took the reefer from her mouth and she breathed smoke on to his hands. The tension left her body, her shoulders dropped, she leaned back in her chair.

'I came in because I wanted to see if the body was as lovely as the voice. It is.' She watched him reach forward and pull the velvet band out of her hair, she felt him touch her cheek, her neck, pull her hair forward over her shoulder

248

so that it fell on her breast. He brushed it away, touching her. She felt a flare of heat shafting down, taking her breath from her, the strength from her fingers, and now her hands lay limp on her lap.

'Play for me,' he said but how could she, her lips felt too full, her fingers too weak. All she wanted to do was to lay her head in the hand which still held her hair.

'Come on then,' Tim said, heaving himself to his feet. 'Check for Ma Tucker then, Sarah.'

Sarah turned. Everything seemed so slow, so easy. She checked the window. 'All clear,' she said and her voice seemed distant.

She held her guitar, easing the strap over her head, tapping her foot. 'One, two, three.'

Then they played their own songs for him and she sang, and all she could think of were his fingers brushing her lips, her breasts, and all she could see were his eyes watching her, then Davy, then the others, but always back to her. Her shoulders felt loose, warm, and for the first time since leaving Wassingham she felt secure.

They stopped and there was silence. 'Very good. Very, very good, but you need more muscle, the songs are anaemic. Let me know if I can ever help you. Good luck with the audition – see you at your Christmas gig.'

He was standing, moving to the door, leaving them. The door closed but the others were talking, laughing, joking, they hadn't really heard, they were too drunk on wine, on pot and he was gone, he hadn't even looked back. She looked at the ashtrays, full of ash. She sat down, so tired, so empty and then so full of anger. How dare he say their songs were anaemic, how dare he say they needed more muscle? And now she felt cold again and slammed the window shut.

Carl was gone again the following morning and his room remained empty. She was glad she wouldn't have to see his blond hair, his thin face, his bloody tan. She was glad.

They practised three evenings a week, remembering to look for Ma Tucker each time and she also looked for Carl, but it was only so that she could stop singing at his approach, wasn't it?

She worked hard during the day, cutting, sewing, pressing seams, remembering Brenda's instructions, remembering her throaty laugh, her mother's grin and though she still wrote home saying that everything was great she crossed off the days on her calendar. Davy, though, was relaxing, enjoying the music, the fabrics he was working with, enjoying the pot which Arnie bought from 'a friend' and sometimes Sarah smoked as well, but not often, and then only with a sense of guilt.

They failed the audition. 'Your songs are too weak,' the Student Union Entertainment Committee told them and that night Sarah lay in bed, watching the lights from the passing cars on her ceiling, remembering Carl's words, his touch, his tan and she reached for one of the joints she kept in Prue's sandalwood box, drawing deep, leaning back on her pillows, two cardigans around her shoulders until at last her lids felt heavy, her body limp. She stubbed it out, replaced it in the box and slept, dreaming of pigeons, of her mother's kitchen, Bet's voice, and she knew when she awoke that she would not return to London after Christmas.

They went to the gig, packing before they did so, stuffing things into cases, cleaning the rooms. 'We'll catch the early train,' she said and Davy nodded.

'I like your skirt,' he said. 'But your da'll have a fit.'

Sarah smiled. 'I'll wear them good and long up there.'

Tim and Arnie were there, Deb and Sally too, and the girls from her year. They bought drinks at the bar, chatted, talked as they'd never done before and Davy brought his year over and there was laughter, dancing, fun. Sarah twisted with Tim, with Davy, laughing as they dragged in Sally too, listening to the group which was playing and knew that they were good, better than she and Davy had been, but it didn't matter now. None of it mattered because she was going home.

Arnie draped her in tinsel, and Sally too and Sarah picked

pieces off and hung them over Davy's ears. 'Now, just what do you think *your* da would think of that, bonny lad,' she giggled, passing him her beer to drink from, sipping it herself, then smelling pot close by. She turned, Carl was dancing close, so close to a blonde girl, who clung to him, and he to her, his joint wafting sweet smoke.

Sarah turned away, back to Davy who still had tinsel behind his ears, and tried to laugh again, but all the fun had fled and she couldn't understand herself. The music was too loud now, far too loud and her head ached and her throat as she strained to speak, strained to listen to Arnie's drawl, Tim's Jokes. She looked at her watch – nearly midnight, thank God – this time tomorrow she'd be far away from London.

She eased her way through entwined couples who moved with the music, through balloons which floated and were tapped back up into the air, feeling the streamers which caught at her, but never held. She sat at their table, drawing dress designs in the spilt beer, thinking of the train which would carry her home.

'So, Geordie lass, come and dance with me.' It was Carl, his breath heavy with wine and pot, his eyes soft, but his hands firm as they pulled her to her feet. She danced with him, felt his knee pushing again and again between her legs, his hands on her arms, gently holding, stroking.

'Forgive me for saying your songs were anaemic,' he said bending his head to speak into her hair. 'I shouldn't have done, but let me help you. There's a need for a good strong girl singer. I could make you big.'

Sarah smiled because she was going home. 'No thanks. Davy and I stay together. He's family and besides, we're going into my mother's business.'

He was still so close. 'Trust me, I'll help you both while you're down here, and then you can go back to your mother.'

Sarah just smiled again, remembering the suddenness of his departure, the rudeness of his words, knowing she would never see him again after tonight, knowing that she was going into the business now, not in three years' time. His arms tightened around her and she pushed away, looking into his face, his deep brown eyes, seeing only kindness when she had expected derision, feeling his kiss light on her forehead, when she had expected coldness. 'Have a good Christmas, Sarah. I'll see you when I return from skiing.'

Then he was ducking and weaving between the dancers, waving, smiling as people stopped him, took him aside, until he was gone from her sight.

'No, you won't see me,' she said quietly. 'I'm going home.' But she could still feel his kiss on her forehead, and his hands on her arms.

CHAPTER 16

The journey had been long. They had changed trains at Newcastle and now they were approaching Wassingham, they were coming home. Sarah stood at the window looking out at the slag heap being lowered because of Aberfan, at the houses, the pitheads and it seemed so small, so very small.

The train stopped, and there was Annie, and behind her Georgie, Tom, and Gracie. Sarah ran now, throwing her arms round her parents, dropping her duffle bag with her presents, promising herself that she wouldn't cry, proud that she didn't.

They drove her back and Davy called, 'See you tomorrow,' his face as settled and happy as she knew hers was.

The kitchen was warm, the kettle simmering. Bet had cooked a casserole and hugged her, kissed her, her plump cheeks warm and her arms strong, pushing her into a chair while Annie stroked her hair, then they made a cup of tea and Georgie brought Button's grandson in to see her. She laughed and stroked the bird, wanting to sink into the warmth of her home, of her family, not able to understand how small the room seemed, how old Bet looked, how grey Annie's hair was, how different it all seemed, how different they all seemed.

That night she stood by her window, looking out over the town, hearing the birds fluttering and cooing in the loft, seeing next door's cat prowling in the yard, remembering the new dinner plates, the plants that had not been there when she left, the new fireguard, and none of it was as she had remembered, even the loft. It all seemed so small.

The next day, she and Davy went into the factory where new machinists had been taken on, where schoolkids were doing the jobs that they had done in the packaging department and there was no room for Sarah and Davy this Christmas.

The next night they went to the pub for a drink and people said hello and told them the news – the Post Office's new counter, Meg's daughter's baby, the new Mine Manager, and they smiled when Davy talked about African dyeing, or Sarah of the new line in design, but they didn't listen, because what had this to do with them?

On Christmas Eve Sarah and Davy walked to the beck and talked together of Arnie, Tim, Ma Tucker, the lights, the bikes, Soho, and they laughed, smoking their last joint, chewing gum to take the smell from their breath, shaking their hair, running back through the frost-filled mist and that night Sarah couldn't sleep because she didn't know where she belonged any more.

On Christmas Day she and Davy were given guitars with pearl inlaid trim and a wonderful resonance, and a sewing machine. 'For you to make yourself more clothes in London. You'll need it – their fashions move so quickly.'

Sarah smiled and knew that she must tell her parents that she would not be going back but not now, it wasn't fair, it would upset their day. But when would Davy tell Tom and Gracie, because he had said he would not return if she did not?

He hadn't told them, he said as they walked to the football pitch and kicked the ball around. 'But just tell me when you do,' he said.

The pitch was frosted white and the hummocks ricked their ankles, tripped them, the ball slid from her hands, hurt her leg when it slapped into her and there was no laughter as there was with Rob, her parents and Uncle Tom, just irritation, and she could see it in Davy too.

She kicked the ball towards Tom, then stood with her arms folded, not running when Gracie kicked it towards her, just watching as it sped past. Her mother moved closer to her. 'At least pretend you're enjoying yourself, Sarah, for heaven's sake.' Her voice was low, angry.

Sarah shrugged. 'I'm cold.'

'Then go back, don't spoil this for everyone, and for God's sake, grow up.'

'But this is so childish, Mum. It's not me that needs to grow up.'

That night Sarah sat by the range, rubbing wintergreen on her feet, smelling her knees, wondering what was wrong with her and why she was such a bitch, and now she was crying, holding her knees, feeling the tears running down her face until her mother came into the room, holding her, rocking her. 'Sh, it's all right. It's all right.'

Sarah said against her shoulder, 'It's not all right. I didn't want to go back because I don't belong there but I don't belong here any more and I hate myself for it.'

Annie held her tightly. 'I know, and it is all right. I should have guessed, I'm sorry. We should know how you feel, after all, we've been through it too. Be kind to yourself, give it all a bit more time. But Sarah, you really must remember that you do not spoil things for other people, no matter how fed up you feel. Is that clear?'

In the New Year they met up with Geoff and Paul, and Annie let them use the packaging department and they played but they were out of synch. Geoff was too slow, or perhaps Sarah and Davy were too fast? They tried again and again, but it had gone and they were all embarrassed as they drank beer afterwards, struggling to find things to talk about, grasping at old school stories, old gigs but it wasn't enough and as they walked home together, Sarah said to Davy, 'How can things change so quickly?'

'It's not things, it's us,' Davy replied.

Lying in bed that night Sarah knew that it was true, that

they had changed, moved on, and that she would return to London.

'Will it work if we come back when we're qualified?' she asked her mother as she saw her off at the station. 'Will it all be too difficult – will we have changed too much?'

Annie shook her head. 'That's up to you. We'd love to have you and you will remake your old friends and make new ones if you do come back, but just live each day, Sarah, my love. Don't try to answer all the questions now, just go with it for a bit – stretch your frontiers, enjoy yourself.'

The train was coming in, screeching, doors were slamming and Sarah hugged her, held her tight, wondering at how small she seemed, kissed her father, her aunt, her uncle, then told her mother again. 'I'll be back in the spring.' The words gave them both comfort.

Snow was falling as the train drew out, thickening, cocooning them, and she just wanted to stay here, in amongst the white silence, not arriving anywhere, just sitting with Davy, feeling safe.

The windows of their bedsits were crusted with ice. There was a deep chill in the blankets, the mattress and the gas fire ate her shillings all night. In the morning they bought paraffin heaters and lugged them up the stairs, and then paraffin from the corner shop, trimming the wicks, lighting them, watching the blue flame waver, leaving it as they went into college on the first day, cycling with Tim, careering round corners, their scarves flying, their breath visible.

Sarah walked into the sewing room and Deborah turned and smiled. 'Come on over here, Sarah.'

Sally joined them and they talked of how strange Christmas had been, how different, how sad they were to leave, then they walked to the refectory together, ate lunch, cut, designed, laughed together. Sarah cycled back to the bedsit, ringing her bell for no reason, wanting to sing, wanting to shout because it was all right, the darkness had gone, she had friends, they felt as she did. She wasn't alone, her confusion was gone.

She propped up her bike, smiled at Ma Tucker, ran up the stairs, listened at Carl's door. Nothing – but she couldn't remember what he looked like, sounded like, felt like and tonight they were practising because Arnie said they could get some gigs this term, and so they bloody well would.

They played in her room, putting more muscle into the songs but keeping the fragility of Davy's melodies, running the riffs again and again, looking for Ma Tucker, drinking the beer that Tim had bought with money from the joint kitty, then drinking cocoa which she made on the Belling, sipping it, talking gently, singing through the numbers quietly until midnight struck. Nodding to one another as they left because they all had work to do.

Sarah sat at her desk, writing up her notes, writing to her mother, looking up at the condensation running down the windows and at two o'clock she fell into bed and slept as she had not done since she had come down in October.

On Sunday she cooked a stew with dumplings for Davy and Tim because they were beginning to look and feel like a can of baked beans. Davy had cooked rice in his oven and carried it into the room when the stew was finished, dumping it on the table and they drew straws over who should have the skin, which was dark and crisp.

Tim had brought beer. 'Because I'm not safe around food,' he said.

'You seem to be doing quite well,' Sarah murmured, looking at his empty plate. 'And don't you worry, my lad – I shall teach you and then you can do your share.'

'You lot must be gluttons for punishment.'

Davy leaned back, reaching for the sugar from the draining board. 'No, just gluttons.'

They walked in the park in the afternoon, calling in on Arnie for tea, then wishing they hadn't because he and some friends had bought take-away curry the night before and it was still in cartons on tables, on the floor. 'Have some,' Arnie nodded at the food.

They laughed, shook their heads. 'Another time.'

'What would Bet say?' Davy said, flinging his arms round Sarah's and Tim's shoulders as they left.

'A great deal I expect,' Sarah replied, looking up at the crisp blue sky, 'A very great deal.' She was happy, for the first time since October she was happy. She looked at Davy and nodded as he smiled. He was too. 'Race you,' he said, starting to run, jumping up to reach the lower branches of the trees that lined the street. 'Race you back,' he shouted.

She and Tim ran, leaping, whooping, their scarves flying – down street after street, then up the steps, through the hall and into her room. They sat on the floor and drank tea, still laughing, groaning when curry was mentioned, writing a song when they should have been working. They called it *Curry Afternoons*, and spent the rest of the day picking out rhythms on their guitars, singing the words, testing how they hung together.

By the end of the second week Sarah had taught Tim how to cook liver and bacon. He cooked it again for Sunday lunch and they groaned. 'Not again.'

'Then teach me something else,' he said, grinning at them, his hair lank from the rain which had poured down on the way back from the off-licence.

The following week she taught him how to cook smoked haddock. 'But I'm doing Sunday lunch and we'll have Arnie round – we don't want to see smoked haddock or liver and bacon until February!'

Arnie forgot lunch next Sunday, but they were not surprised, the only thing he was ever on time for was rehearsals and so they ate his lamb, drank his beer and looked out at the rain, shaking their heads at the thought of the park, and ran through their numbers again, very quietly because Ma Tucker was downstairs. There was an audition on the first of February at a new club which was giving spots to new-

258

comers. 'I want to get it,' Davy said. 'I want to be able to stuff that under Carl's nose when he finally does come back.'

Sarah looked at him and at Tim. She'd almost forgotten about Carl. They played at the audition and were taken on for a spot every two weeks and that night they drank too much in the pub, and stumbled back along the road, arm in arm, then up the steps, banging the light switch, giggling, squeezing past the bikes, yelping as the pedals caught their shins, creeping up the stairs, along the landing, into Sarah's room. She fumbled for the light and basked in the damp heat of the paraffin stove. They boiled the kettle for coffee and sniggered as Tim tiptoed across to her bed, with Davy following, his finger to his mouth, giggling as they collapsed and made more noise than a herd of elephants.

There was a knock at the door. Carl stood there, more tanned than before, his face relaxed, smiling. 'So, what time d'you call this then?'

Sarah felt her hands shake as she put coffee into the mugs, her face had flushed at the sound of his voice. How could she have forgotten what he looked like, sounded like? How could she when he was so beautiful? She turned away, back to the kettle.

'We're celebrating,' she said, her voice tight. 'We've been taken on by Max's – he liked Davy's new song – *Curry Afternoons*.'

She looked across at Davy and winked. He grinned and Tim slapped his back.

'I heard,' Carl said. 'Well done. Is there a coffee for me, Sarah?'

He was moving towards her and when she turned back to reach for another mug he was there, next to her. 'I've missed you,' he said quietly, taking the spoon from her shaking hand, heaping it with coffee, pouring the water into the two remaining mugs.

She didn't turn, couldn't because he was so close. She just stood there looking at the cracked tiles, the grouting which was covered in mould.

'I skied down the moguls and all I thought of was you. Am I forgiven yet?'

Sarah wiped down the drainer, rinsing out the cloth, wringing it again and again. 'There's nothing to forgive – you were right.' Because, damn it, he was.

'Oh yes, I think there is. I was unkind, tactless, I didn't say how good you all were too, not really.' He moved away and now when she turned she could still smell him. She leant back against the drainer, clutching it, feeling the heat in her face, in her body and wondered if this was love.

He stood there, talking to the boys, his stance easy, his voice level, calm, his fingers sure as he flipped them cigarettes, offering her one, looking at her with those eyes, smiling as she shook her head, turning from her to speak to Davy.

'Come to a party with me tomorrow to celebrate. Seven o'clock, here.'

'Arnie too?' Tim asked.

'As if we could go without him – you lot are like the four musketeers. But make sure he's on time and clean. It's in Chelsea.' Carl looked at the ash on his cigarette, then at Sarah, his eyebrows raised. She brought him a saucer and his fingers stroked her hand as he took it from her. She felt his touch in her belly and wanted to feel his hands on her face, wanted just to be near him for every minute, every second of each day, and she couldn't understand how she had not thought of him, not longed for him every minute since she had last seen him.

That night she lay in bed and heard him turn. She reached out and touched the wall, then kissed her hand where he had touched her, running her tongue over her skin, wanting the scent of him inside her. She turned, brought the blankets up round her neck, then turned again, hearing the cars in the street outside, seeing the lights across the ceiling, because she never drew her curtains.

She turned again, counted the hours, thought of him dancing with her, his shirt so fine and soft, his legs so long and then she stiffened, leapt from the bed to the wardrobe, searching through her clothes. Chelsea, he had said. Chelsea, for God's sake.

In the morning she dragged Davy from his room and they cycled to Carnaby Street, where they rushed in and out of shops, looking at shirts, trousers, ties.

'I can make the shirt but I can't do the trousers,' she panted as they hurried to the next boutique, hearing the music thumping out, sorting through the racks, smelling the cotton, the joss sticks. They found a shirt Davy liked with a large collar and pockets.

'It'd look nice in pale green, bring out the auburn in your hair,' she said.

Davy nodded. 'I'll get that tie.'

They bought the trousers from a boutique which was painted dark green and had lights that flashed on and off. 'God, like a bloody party already,' Davy said, shouting above the music. 'It's going to be great – I was wrong about him. I thought he was a bastard but he's nice, Sarah, he likes you too.'

Sarah said, 'He likes us all.'

Davy just grinned.

They bought an offcut of green cotton from the market stall. It was darker than they had intended but better, Davy thought, holding it up against the tie. Smoother.

Sarah smiled. 'Oh, creating an image, are we?'

Davy nodded, blushing. 'That's what Carl said last night – image is all important. There'll be music people there tonight and he wants us to be seen. I told you he was nice – he's trying to help us, bonny lass.'

They cycled on to the Kings Road and locked their bikes up again, dashing from one boutique to another, looking for ideas. It was hot in the shops and Sarah flung off her coat, handing it to Davy, trying dresses up against her, pressing them to her, swinging left and right in front of the mirrors.

'I think the one you've got on is better than any of this,' Davy said in the third shop. 'You got some real good ideas, Sarah, a real eye for fashion.'

Sarah hung the dresses back on the rack, and flicked through the rest. 'But I can't wear the one I've got on, he's seen it, it's not posh. It's Chelsea we're going to, Davy.'

They rushed on to the next one, then Davy made them stop for coffee and a Chelsea bun.

'To give us inspiration,' he said, 'and me a bit of stamina.'

They tried the next, and then the next and now they saw something that caught her eye – a simple shift with cut-away shoulders and another with a huge leather belt.

'You could do that easily enough,' Davy said. 'I'd like to have a go at creating a waxed batik design for something like that, it would be stunning.'

Sarah held it up against her, turning, twisting, liking it. She turned it inside out to look at the darts, the seams, and stretched it while Davy held it.

'Can I help you at all?' a woman's voice said and Sarah snatched her sketch to her side, then fingered the material. 'Not quite what I was looking for,' she replied, smiling at the woman whose lipstick had run into the lines dug deep along her upper lip.

The woman looked at her, then at the dress. 'Do you make clothes?'

Sarah paused, then shrugged, bringing up her sketchbook. 'Yes, I'm sorry, I was just looking for ideas.'

'Did you make that?' The woman pointed to the shift Sarah was wearing with its scalloped neckline, its thick deep purple belt which she had made of Indian cotton that Prue had sent at Christmas.

Sarah nodded, looking back at the dress that Davy still held, trying to hold it in her mind.

'Can you make me some?'

The music was flashing in time with the lights and Sarah could feel the vibrations through her feet.

'How many?' Davy asked.

'One dozen in a dark colour, one in a light, one muted, one vivid. Four dozen altogether and I want this sort of

262

textile design.' She whipped a dress off the rack. It was a simple two-colour design.

'How much?' Sarah asked.

The woman told them.

'By when?' Davy asked.

'One week.'

They looked at one another, then nodded.

'Yes, we'll be here, in one week's time.'

They left then, running to their bikes, talking as they did so, stopping at the market for an offcut for a remake of her own dress, buying an Indian scarf to pick up the colour.

'I'll make your shirt and run up another shift for tonight, then a sample for Mum because it's too big a job for us. We'll have to talk them into it somehow – we'll ring them tonight. It's cheaper.' The traffic lights were red but they kept going, sliding round to the left, ignoring the hoots, pedalling into the wind, turning right, then left. 'Oh God, Davy,' Sarah called over her shoulder, 'Deborah's friend was asked to do this by a boutique and she made a mint. These shops are just following along after the kids now, the designers aren't dictating the fashion any more. It's just . . . oh I don't know.'

'Grand's the word you're looking for.' Davy was leaning forward, pedalling hard. 'What lectures are you missing?'

'Only pattern design. Debs will cover for me, I'll get the notes off her. What about you?'

'The history of dyeing.'

'Who needs it?'

Davy laughed. 'Not many, but I hope they bloody well need our dresses.'

They worked all afternoon and as she cut and sewed Sarah thought of Carl, then of the clothes, then of Carl again. They brewed one another coffee and worked until five. Then Sarah sneaked into the bathroom to run a cold bath because Ma Tucker would only heat the water once a week, leapt in and out quickly, then opened the door a crack, her hair wet and dripping. Was Carl home? He mustn't see her. She listened, waited, then ran for her room.

She dried her hair, wondering whether to have it cut short like Mary Quant and the women in boutiques. She brought out the iron, folded a towel on the floor, knelt to lay her head on the towel and ironed her hair, wanting it straight, wanting the kinks out of the side just for once. 'Come out, come out, just this once,' she begged, rushing to the mirror. No, they were still there.

She pressed the samples, Davy's shirt, her dress and checked her watch. Oh God, it was twenty to seven. 'Davy,' she yelled, banging on the wall. 'Come on, get your shirt. We've got to phone.'

She threw it to him as he came in, his hair still wet, sticking up. 'Get your hair dry. I'll go down and ring.'

Sarah hauled on her tights, rammed her feet into shoes that she had bought from the market. They were too tight, but never mind, they looked good. Bet had always said you could tell a person's class from their shoes, she thought as she rushed down the stairs to the pay phone behind the bikes, shoving them along, squeezing in behind them, putting the money in, dialling. 'I should be a bloody princess from the looks of these, but the bikes spoil it,' she murmured, listening to the ringing tone. 'Be in, be in.'

Annie answered, Sarah pushed the button. 'Mum, it's Sarah.'

'Oh darling.' There was pleasure in Annie's voice, then anxiety. 'What's wrong?'

Sarah laughed. 'Nothing, Mum, or there won't be if you think we've done the right thing.'

She told her then about the dresses, the money, the quantity, the delivery date.

Annie laughed. 'You don't give us a lot of time, but why not? Perhaps it's time we kicked off into fashion. All right, darling, put the sample on the train tomorrow. I'll get someone to pick it up. Make sure you've put all the details down. The sizes and so on.'

264

'Oh God, I didn't get them.'

'Never mind. Give them a ring in the morning, and me a ring in the evening with those. Well done, darling. Tell Davy well done too. Hang on, your da's here.'

Sarah leant against the wall, then heard Carl calling down to her. 'What are you doing, it's nearly seven. Come on, Sarah, get off the phone, we've got to go and you haven't put your make-up on.'

Georgie was speaking then, telling her how Geoff had called in to see them today, with copies of the photographs he had taken when they were up at Christmas. 'I'll send them down to you.'

'Good, Dad, that's great but I've – '

'Come on, Sarah, we'll be late. Get yourself ready.' Carl was hanging over the banister, nodding to Arnie as he squeezed past the bikes and ambled up the stairs.

'Buttons' great-granddaughter is thriving, her squeaker's coming on nicely.'

'Come on, Sarah.'

Sarah nodded at Carl. 'Da I've got to go, I'm just off out. Mum will tell you all about the clothes. It could be good. Bye, love you.'

She hung up, her hands wet with tension.

'For God's sake, Sarah, get your make-up on.' Carl was running down the stairs.

'I don't wear make-up,' she said, catching the coat Davy dropped down from the landing.

'Will you lot be quiet?' Ma Tucker shouted from her room.

She followed Carl out of the house and stood behind him as he hailed taxi after taxi but none had their lights up. She ran her hands down her hair, felt her skin. They were going to Chelsea, she should have worn make-up. She'd show him up. Oh God.

'We could take our bikes,' Davy said.

Carl spun round. 'Give us a break – that'd show a lot of class wouldn't it, arriving on our bikes?'

Davy and Sarah looked at one another, then at Tim and

the laughter came, stupid silly wonderful laughter. 'Me grandma always said your class shows in your shoes,' Davy said.

'And try not to sound so bloody Geordie, will you?' Carl said, flagging another which swung towards them and stopped, just as their laughter had stopped.

They sat in the taxi silently. 'Can you hurry please?' Carl said, sliding the glass partition open. The cab lurched round the next corner and the next and Arnie slid from the dicky seat and now laughter came again, from Carl too, but Sarah could still not forget.

Carl put his arm around her. 'So why did you have to ring then, what was it all about?'

Davy told him.

'But why ring when we're going out?'

'Because it's cheaper after six,' Sarah said, her voice crisp. 'We're not all like you with money to burn and besides, they're not home from work until then, and we don't want to disturb them at the factory.'

She felt the pressure of Carl's arm, his hand as he stroked her shoulder. 'I didn't realise they actually worked in the factory, I thought they just owned it. It's tough on you though, little Sarah, having a mother who works, they say it harms the kids.' His voice was soft, whispering into her ear. 'Poor little girl, I shall look after you.'

They turned another corner and Arnie slid off again and again they laughed, then Sarah turned to Carl. 'It didn't harm me, I'm fine.'

'Hardly, darling.'

They were drawing up at a house which had steps as Ma Tucker's had, but they were white, and the pillars were white too. The number was in brass and Davy raised his eyebrows at Sarah, as Carl rang the bell, then opened the door.

'Shouldn't we wait?' Sarah said, clutching at his sleeve.

'Oh no, I'm almost one of the family.' A blast of light and music hit them, the scent of perfume and pot as they walked into a hall filled with people holding wine glasses, smoking

266

cigarettes or joints. Carl turned and grabbed her hand, pulling her after him, up the stairs past family portraits on her left and a hung chandelier on her right which hung over the people below.

On the landing he stopped to take wine from a waiter, handing one to her. She looked behind. Tim and Davy had stopped and were leaning over, pointing to Arnie who was accepting a joint from an older man.

'What did you mean, it has done me harm? What's wrong with me, apart from my voice and my make-up?' Her voice shook with anger, with hurt.

'Oh darling, don't be cross. It's just that you're so clingy, look at you, looking round for poor Davy. You should let him live his own life – and you ring your mother or write every week. I mean, isn't it time we cut those apron strings? This is London sweetie, the sixties, not the forties.' He kissed her cheek with his soft lips and waved to a blonde girl who lounged pouting against a mahogany table, her pan-stick make-up pale, her eye-liner dark. 'See you in a minute, darling,' he said to Sarah, kissing her lips this time, and even though the hurt and anger were harsh in her, so was the surge of passion at the touch of his lips.

She stood in the doorway, watching him leave her and thread his way through groups of people, seeing them brightening at the sight of him, slapping his back, and then he was gone. She watched the crowds, daring herself not to look for Davy, trying to smile, sipping her wine, gripping her glass with both hands until an old man with hair below his collar came up, smiled, shook her hand. 'We were just discussing how the Vietnam war has fostered a solidarity among the youth, bound you together against authority, against parental power as you watch your brothers being felled. Do you agree?'

His breath was sweet with pot and wine, his eyes unfocused. He didn't wait for an answer but ambled away.

She looked for Carl and saw him kissing the cheeks of the women, his briefcase with him as always. He was patting it now, mouthing 'Later,' to the young man in the flowered shirt. So, he could do business night and day, but not her mother during working hours?

She drank her wine, plonked it on a passing tray and took another, drinking faster this time, joining the drifting crowds, smiling when a girl came and gripped her arm. 'Dr Timothy Leary is right, this nirvana is the surest means to tune in to the higher consciousness, to break with the traditions of one's parents – we need to break free, to explore everything, after this decade, nothing will ever be the same again.'

Sarah wanted the girl to stay so that she was no longer alone, so that when Carl saw her he would see that she was mixing, holding her own, damn him. 'Who's Timothy Leary?' she asked, speaking as she had done so many years ago, before they came to Wassingham, her mouth rounded, her words clear.

'He's God,' the girl said, leaving her.

Sarah took another drink, moved closer to a group to the left of her, smiling as though she was one of them, then becoming one of them as they widened their circle to let her in, asking if she had seen Thomas Henson's surrealist art exhibition, telling her she simply must when she said no, shaking her head at the joint which was offered, looking round casually for Carl, feeling the pain when he saw him dancing with another girl. What am I doing here? She saw a man come, put his arm round Carl and speak quietly, then lead him to a table where a champagne bottle stood in ice.

'So that's her is it, Carl?' Sam Davis nodded towards Sarah.

'My backer's right, she's got the looks if she uses them properly, it's all image, Carl – come on, get going on her – and it is just the girl they want, not the group, those are the backer's instructions, and I agree, having seen her. It's a solo artist I'm after.'

Carl brought out his cigarette case and offered Sam a joint. 'I know it, but I've got it all in hand.'

Sam sucked on the joint. 'Nice stuff,' he nodded approvingly. 'So you'll ditch the group, and make sure she ditches the degree? We're not fiddling around so someone can have a fling for a couple of years and then walk away from it, it's got to be a long-term thing. Mark you, you'll have to get her trained, take her on the circuit, we'll try a recording in sixty-seven probably.' Sam leant forward. 'I had a scout there at the college audition, just to check that my backer was right and my boy said she was good. There's nothing wrong with the boys, they just don't fit with the plan, so get rid of them, especially the Ryan boy and the family. Apparently she's close to them, and that always leads to trouble. We want kids we can nurture, mould, you know what I mean? We don't want any clever sods in on it and I gather they're business people. It won't do, so sort it or you'll have no one to help you with your big break, and no more contacts, ever – got it.'

Carl nodded. 'You worry too much, far too much.'

Sam poured more champagne. 'I got where I am by worrying, my boy. You're only twenty-two, still wet behind the ears where this business is concerned. Got your gear have you? I'll give you your due, you've got that side of your life sorted out.'

Carl smiled. 'It's in the safe – I'll be in the library in half an hour. See you then.' He downed his champagne and stood looking for Sarah, waving at her, languidly passing through the crowded room. She watched him come, his walk, his hands, his face and turned to listen to the man next to her, then felt his hand on her arm, pulling her towards him, his arms sliding round her, his body moving in time to the music and she moved with him, sinking closer as his fingers slid beneath her shoulder straps, warm against her back.

'Little Sarah, come and sing for my friends.'

Carl's breath puffed her hair and she pulled away, looking for the others. Davy was drunk and so was Tim, leaning up against the wall, talking to two girls who were also drunk.

'No, we can't, not tonight. They're past it.'

Carl looked at her, kissed her mouth gently, softly, his

269

tongue stroking her lip, and her limbs felt weak. 'Then sing to us yourself,' he murmured, his mouth still on hers.

She drew back. 'I told you I can't. We're a team.'

'For God's sake, Sarah, I'm not asking you to divorce him, just sing without him, and don't shout, people will hear.'

Sarah looked around her now and saw a girl blowing a kiss at Carl, saw his answering smile. She said, 'I should have come with a brown paper bag stuck over me head and a cork stuffed in me mouth, having dropped Davy off down a bloody drain, shouldn't I, and I don't care if people stare, bonny bloody lad.'

She wrenched herself from him. 'And I don't cling.'

She stormed to the door, looking for Davy, Tim or Arnie but they were all drinking, laughing, enjoying the night, and so she hailed a taxi, and used the money that she was saving for another gallon of paraffin to pay for it.

'Damn you, damn you all,' she cursed as she lay in bed, not knowing what to think or feel, not knowing what to do with the anger inside her, but then she leapt from bed and tore up the music she'd been writing. That was all over, she'd stick to what she knew, she'd just work, and work and work.

She left the house early, took the samples to the station, rang the shop about sizes, and went back to lectures, her head aching, her hand aching from the notes she wrote because she must not think, she must not remember the feel of his hands, the unkindness of his words. She couldn't eat her sandwiches at lunch and there were no lectures that afternoon so she cycled home, lugging her bike up the steps, seeing the headless chrysanthemums in the garden, shaking her head at the kids who had done this.

The stairs seemed steep, her legs tired and then she stopped at the sight of Carl sitting on the top step, holding a bunch of chrysanthemums, Ma Tucker's chrysanthemums, his face contrite.

'I'm doing everything wrong, Sarah, but it's just because you're special to me. I get tense, the words come out back to front and I don't mean them. I love your group, and I love Davy and I love your mother. Please forgive me.'

He held out the flowers and their scent was heavy as she held them to her face, feeling the coldness of their petals, the dampness of their stems.

'Will you come and walk in the park with me, please?' he asked, holding out his hand.

They walked all afternoon and he told her of his mother's yacht, his mother's life and how he had brought himself up, how she had been away, or busy, or both and how he longed for someone to love him, just him.

'That's why I feel so strongly that mothers should be with their children. That's what I would want for my child.' He squeezed her hand. 'I've been waiting for someone special, Sarah, for the whole of my life.'

She told him then about her parents, their life in the Army, the building of the business which was her mother's dream, her father's accident, the problems which seemed to have stopped two years ago, though she didn't know why. She told him about Bet and Davy who was like a brother to her, as Uncle Tom had been to her mother.

'So he's no threat to any love I have,' she said gently, feeling so sorry for this young man who had so much, but also had nothing.

He kissed her then, holding her close, his mouth opening, his tongue seeking hers, his arms holding her up as her legs became weak and she wanted to stay like this for ever – in a park, with his mouth on hers and no space between them.

Annie received the samples and called Tom and Georgie in, showing them Davy's designs and Sarah's pattern design and sample.

Tom nodded. 'Good for them. Yes, the design department can do that in two days, what about your side, Annie?'

Annie ran her fingers through her hair. 'Even if I have to sew them myself we'll get it done. They're keen and I think it's important that we encourage them because things seem

271

to be improving down there, they're sounding so much more lively, so much keener about everything. I think we should try their designs in the showroom too, see how they do. Then cut them in on all profits.'

Georgie laughed. 'They'll be buying electric guitars and hiring the Albert Hall for a gig next.'

'Yes, you're right, Annie, cut them in.'

'You write and tell them, Georgie,' Annie said, knowing that he had been hurt when Sarah had put the phone down on him and this would be an opportunity for her daughter to write back to him.

Sarah opened the letter, read it, called out to Davy to come in. Carl came too, standing in the doorway.

'Da says we're to have a cut of the profits, that Mum's really pleased and so's your da.' She handed him the letter, feeling Carl's kiss on her forehead, his hand on her back.

Later he murmured that his mother had never had time to write either.

Sarah said, 'It's not like that.'

That evening he brought them pizza and strawberry ice cream to celebrate. She ate it, even though she hated it and as she did so she remembered how her mother had shouted at her father in the hospital, forcing him to eat the ice cream. Sarah put her hand to her forehead, rubbing her skin, forcing herself to eat. She remembered that the nurse had said that her mother was absolutely right, but why hadn't she nursed in the first place, she remembered asking, then her da wouldn't have been hurt?

She finished the ice cream and accepted a joint, sucking deeply, welcoming the haze, the relaxation, the numbing of the senses, the deadening of an anger which had come. She drew more deeply, to blot out the memory.

CHAPTER 17

Annie and George decided that the take-up on the clothes had been enthusiastic enough for them to extend into the retail trade.

'Just in Newcastle to see how it goes, and later in the local towns,' Annie suggested and Tom agreed.

Bill, the estate agent, scouted for premises and at the end of February, in good time for the spring season, they took on Jessica, a middle-aged woman who had been a shop manager in Surrey. Annie wrote to Sarah.

> So keep on sending up samples, darling and let's see how it goes. Your dad has organised a few local advertisements but we're hoping that word of mouth will do the trick. Tom's decorated it in green and white and all of them will be the same. I say 'all' but it depends on how it goes. Brenda and the girls are right behind us. I hope you and Davy are pleased too.

She handed the letter to Georgie to finish and took a cup of tea from Bet, stirring it because the milk was yesterday's and cream floated on the top. She hated that, it was like the skin of custard – it stuck in her throat.

'Have you heard from them this week?' Bet asked, undoing the top button of her blouse and wiping her neck with her handkerchief. 'Oh dear, I don't know, I get so hot these days, must get some more pills from the doctor.'

Annie smiled. 'Well, it can't be a hot flush, Bet, I'm getting

273

all of those. Yes, you must go back, your blood pressure might be up again.'

Bet nodded. 'So have you heard?'

'Yes, they're back into the music again and want to go up to Scotland on what they call a chewing-gum tour. I gather this friend Carl has fixed up a lot of gigs, so they're going there in early December, by coach, stopping off along the way.'

Georgie was still writing, his head bent over the table. Bet poured more tea. 'Are you letting her?'

'How can I stop her? It's always been so important to them – it just shows that they're enjoying life, getting the most out of it. It's better than them wanting to run away home.'

Bet pursed her lips. 'I don't like it, you know, it's not healthy the way kids today live, eating vegetables, all this s – e – x.' Bet spelt out the letters. 'There's this pill now and all these other drugs, it's in all the papers.'

Georgie looked up. 'I know, but you don't want to believe all you read, that's just a few of them. Ours are good kids, sensible and they're together – and they eat meat, so perhaps the other is all right too.' He smiled. 'Oh, they'll be all right, it's like I said to Annie – look at my birds, give them a safe warm home and they'll come back after they've felt the wind beneath their wings.'

Annie walked to the sink and looked out of the window, wanting to shout at him to be quiet about his bloody birds, this was her daughter and she was growing up, growing away. Was it as wild as the papers said? And who the hell was this Carl that Davy had mentioned, but Sarah hadn't?

She added a postscript to the letter, asking Sarah to let them know their itinerary and they would come to support her if there was a show nearby.

Sarah read the letter, passed to to Davy, not wanting Carl to see it but he did, and smiled at her. 'So, the apron strings are being drawn a little tighter, are they?'

She didn't send her mother the itinerary and boarded the coach with the boys and Carl, sitting with the other acts as they drove through pouring rain to Northampton, unpacking their luggage, sleeping in a boarding house that Carl had arranged, playing that night to a half-empty drill hall, moving on the next morning to Newcastle.

It was still raining but much colder and Carl helped her drag her case from the luggage hold, saying that they'd have to go straight to the club, they were late.

They played and Davy caught her eye. 'We should have told them,' he said, as they eased back for Arnie's break, listening, moving in time.

'I know, but it just seemed easier for them, they'll be so busy with the spring season coming up and the shop's doing well. They've got more than enough to do without traipsing through the rain to sit in amongst all this smoke and these drop-outs.' She nodded at the audience who were drinking and talking, doing anything but listening.

'Yes, you're right, bonny lass.' His smile was gentle, but became a grin as Arnie wiggled his hips and the waitresses screamed, but momentarily Sarah lost her rhythm because she had felt such a wave of guilt. She listened, skipped a few bars, came in again concentrating on the music because Carl was right, they must grow up. Tim's mother hadn't asked for an itinerary, or Arnie's, just hers and Davy's and it was no excuse that they were touring the north, not the south where the others came from. It was ridiculous.

They drove on up to Scotland and now they knew the others well, and had jam sessions on the coach, leaping off at garages to use their lavatories since there were none on the coach. Sarah was the only girl but she was with Carl and so no one pinched her bum, or spoke sweet nothings and she was proud of him as he extolled the Beatles and their experimentation, their anticipation of future tastes, their originality, their foresight in putting in the sixth chords into their numbers.

'So simple,' he said, 'and it's the simple things that work.'

Her mother said that too, but she didn't tell him that, just watched his lips, his hands as they touched her knee, his mouth as he laughed.

He left them in Glasgow, flying down to London to meet some business friends who were taking a skiing lodge, waving to her, grinning. 'See you after Easter, my sweet little Sarah. Look after her, Davy. I'll talk to them about you all.'

The gigs in Chester and Wales were dull, the hours dragged, the music seemed flat and slow, like the train which took them from London to Newcastle at the end of term.

They worked hard during the day, catching up on the notes which Deborah's and Davy's friend had copied for them, and played together in the evening in the packaging room, and Annie stood and listened.

'The tour was a good idea,' she said on Good Friday as she took Sarah hot chocolate in bed. 'You're sounding more solid, more substantial, you're looking well too, my darling. Was it better this term?'

Sarah held the cocoa between her hands, feeling the steam on her face. 'Yes, much better. The sun seems to be out, if you know what I mean. There's so much to do, it's all so interesting.'

She didn't mention Carl, somehow she couldn't and she didn't know why. She looked at her mother's hands on the quilt, her nails were dirty. Carl never had dirty nails. Annie saw her looking and shrugged her shoulders. 'Bet and I have been putting the potatoes in.'

Sarah nodded. Yes, that's what they always did on Good Friday, it was all so predictable.

Annie lay awake that night, knowing that her daughter was growing away from her as she had done from Sarah. She eased herself against Georgie, wanting the warmth of his body, the comfort of his familiar shape, wishing she had asked Sarah why she had not told them that the group were appearing in Newcastle, why she had to read it in the newspaper. But she knew she mustn't ask, that she must let

276

go. In the morning she checked that the cutting was safely hidden from Georgie, because he must not know.

In the summer term life was wonderful, Sarah felt the sun warming her, the wine in the evenings loosening her. She bought pan-stick, eye liner and mascara and talked at parties about the extension of consciousness and the limitlessness of life as it now was, and heard Davy do likewise though they failed to understand their own words.

They went to a Rolling Stones concert and found themselves twenty feet from Mick Jagger and Keith Richards, blown away by the music, blinded by the lights, surrounded by hot jostling bodies.

They played at a Young Farmers gig and here there were no jostling bodies but restrained dancing until too much beer had been drunk and then raucous choruses and jiving shook up the whole room.

She and Davy bought their own pot now, because Carl could not keep supplying them out of his own pocket, he said, his face red with embarrassment, neither could he pay for all their taxis to and from the parties, so they worked harder to design and sell clothes to their friends at college and to local market stalls.

They auditioned for a college gig and were accepted. They also had more commissions from the students for shirts, dresses, skirts specifically for the gig and by June were working each morning, evening and lunchtime, copying notes when they could, eating when they could, remembering also to send up new samples to Annie from the shops they had gathered into the circle, until Sarah's head was splitting and Davy looked drawn and pale.

Carl took them to another party that week and they were too tired to smile and talk of Dr Timothy Leary, or the duty of the young to explore and push back the frontiers of the mind, or the brilliance of Bob Dylan. 'I can't understand his songs,' Sarah said to the man who had spattered canapés in her wine and now had some on his beard. 'I think he's a pseudo-intellectual.'

She felt Carl's hand on her arm, saw Davy mouthing 'ouch', and didn't care, she was too tired. She didn't care that Carl pushed her out before him, that his voice was sharp in the taxi. 'For God's sake, you can't afford to be tired, nobody can. If you do that once you've made it, it'll be splashed all over the bloody newspapers and that'll be that. And when did you last rehearse?'

She laid her head back on the seat, her hands sore from cutting and sewing, knowing that Davy's were too.

'We haven't time, for God's sake. We're running a business here and trying to get through college, then we did your tour, all the tour, not skiving off for a bit of skiing like some of us here.'

'There's no need to run a business.'

'There's every need if we're to afford our lives, especially all this.' She waved at the taxi, banged his cigarette case, shouting now. She leapt from the cab when it arrived at Ma Tucker's, storming from him, slamming her bedroom door, locking it, just needing to sleep but she couldn't and then she heard a scratching at the door.

She opened it a crack. He pushed in a joint and whispered, 'I'm sorry, I know you're tired, have this to help you sleep.' She rested her head on the door and wept for his kindness.

The next day she was up early sewing, cutting, pressing, then cycling to college, returning early and sewing again while Davy sat with her, checking, cutting, designing. Arnie and Tim came round to practise but there was no time tonight, Sarah said, jerking her head at the coffee. 'But you can make us all a drink.'

She lifted the mug with hands swollen from the scissors, refusing a joint because she couldn't relax yet, shaking her head at Davy as he took one. He grimaced and put it back.

'I'll just breathe in deeply,' he said, chasing Tim's smoke across the room, making them all laugh. They worked again when the boys left, necks aching, heads pounding, not looking up when Carl knocked, just calling, 'Come in.'

Carl stood there. 'Where're the others, it's rehearsal night, for God's sake, not your mother's bloody factory. This is no good, you've got to dump this and get on with the music.'

Sarah pushed harder on the pedal, heard the machine whirr, listened to that as Davy said, 'For God's sake, Carl, it's OK for you to work, I see you've got your briefcase as always, but it's not OK for us – and that's ridiculous because we need to do it. Anyway, we've nearly finished for tonight, we've just got the samples for Auntie Annie now.'

Sarah looked up now, seeing Carl stare at the floor, then at her as he spoke slowly. 'Oh yes, of course, the gig can go to hell, all my efforts too – but we must make sure Auntie Annie gets her pound of bloody flesh.'

Sarah lifted her foot from the pedal. 'Leave my mother out of this, we learn from it as well, don't we? Davy's right, you're bloody well working, you always work, wherever we go. I'm sick to death of that case, of your friends, and of you.'

Her head was pounding, nausea rose in her throat and she didn't care as he stormed out, slamming the door. She just worked and then smoked with Davy, too tired to talk, too tired to ache at the thought of Carl's anger, almost too tired to sleep when Davy stumbled from her room.

Carl's room was empty in the morning, his door locked and in lectures Sarah couldn't concentrate, all she could think of was his beautiful face, his hands, his tan, his lips. Had he kissed another girl, had he slept with her? Had he? Had he?

Would he come back? Would he?

That evening she smoked the joints that Davy had brought, one, two, three, and the room faded until there was nothing but warmth, looseness, peace and she smiled as Davy left, smiled as Carl came in, held her in his arms, cradled her on the bed.

'I'm sorry, my darling girl. I just felt worried about you, so worried. Please stop sewing this weekend, stop working, stop rehearsing and come with me. Sam Davis is having a party at Bracklesham Bay in a house he owns.' He was stroking her arms, undoing her blouse, running his fingers beneath her bra, touching her nipple, easing the strap from her shoulders, taking her in his mouth and she arched her back, wanting more, knowing that he had wanted it for weeks, but she was too frightened.

'Come away with me, my darling,' he said, against her skin.

'All of us,' she said.

'Just you.' His tongue stroked her breast, her shoulder, her lips.

'No, Davy should come too, it's not fair, he's been working too.'

His hand was on her thigh now, gently stroking. He undid her jeans, stroked her belly, her groin and then his fingers were between her legs, probing, gentle and his lips were on hers, his tongue deep.

'Davy too,' she gasped, because she was frightened of being with this man alone for a weekend – it would be so hard not to sleep with him.

Carl lifted his head. 'He needs to practise, he's not as good as the rest of you.'

Sarah felt his fingers leave her as her own anger rose. She pushed him aside, scrambling to her feet, feeling faint, falling back on to the bed, tasting the marijauna.

'He's just as good, he's better. Arnie says so.' She was wrenching at her zip.

Carl still lay on the bed, resting on his elbow. 'So, Arnie's the expert now is he – our fine electronics whiz-kid knows all about it, does he?'

Sarah was buttoning her blouse, her fingers trembling, her head swimming. 'I know he's good, and that's what's important and I'm not going without him, if I go at all. We do nothing but row, it's all so pointless, the whole damn thing.' She sat with her hands between her legs, her shoulders slumped. 'So damned pointless.'

His arms came round her then, holding her, pulling her back beside him, not kissing her, just rubbing his cheek on her hair, cupping her face in his hand. 'Fine, we'll take him then.'

It was Friday the next day and they were leaving in the evening so Sarah cycled to Marks & Spencer and bought new bras and pants, not wanting to wear her mother's any more because it wasn't only Sarah's hands that knew them now.

They took the train, then a taxi which entered a sweeping drive, gravel crunching beneath the wheels, light pouring from the latticed windows of the old redbrick house with its moss-spattered roof.

Sam Davis met them at the door, kissing Sarah with his moist lips, drawing her into the dark panelled hall, his arm about her waist, moving from one pool of soft yellow light to another, introducing her and Davy to quietly spoken men and women, handing them plates for the buffet, guiding them to the table, tempting them with lobster, crayfish, crab.

'It's a lovely evening, lovies, take it into the garden, there are tables and chairs.' He wafted away from them, his cravat matching his gold watch perfectly. They walked on to the terrace, smelling the sea in the soft wind, and ate the crab with their fingers as they found a table, sitting down to listen to muted Beatles music and it was as though everything had slowed, as though she'd stepped off the roundabout for a moment.

She felt Carl's hand on her knee, saw him wave to an auburn-haired girl who was dancing alone on the terrace to *Love's Just a Broken Heart* by Cilla Black. The girl came over and Carl pointed to Davy. 'You two match, sit down and share his lobster.' His voice was gentle, his eyes kind and Davy flushed, looked at Sarah and she nodded. 'You do make a pigeon pair, you know.'

She leant back in her chair, feeling the cushion behind her, watching couples who ate, drank or danced.

'I hope love isn't just a broken heart,' Carl said, his arm around her, pulling her towards him.

Sarah drank her crisp cool wine which she recognised as Chardonnay. He had never spoken of love before.

Carl spoke again, very quietly low. 'Let's dance, I'm not hungry, not while I can hold you.'

He laced his fingers through hers, pushing back his chair, slipping his arm round her as she joined him, pressing his body against hers as they danced and the music was *We Can Work it Out* by the Beatles.

'We can, can't we?' he murmured into her hair, running his hands down her back, holding her buttocks, pressing her to him.

She leant into him, breathing his scent through his shirt, watching Davy laughing with the girl, his arm round her, their two heads close together and she relaxed. 'We have worked it out, we're here and it's as though we're in another world. Carl, you've given me so much.' She looked at the pop singer on the next table, the photographer smoking pot and nodded to the woman he was with, smiling as she came across and talked to them of *The Secret Of The Golden Bough* which Sarah had bought from the Indica Bookshop, and of John Coltrane.

'Brilliant, of course,' Sarah said, wondering if anyone in Newcastle had ever heard of him, knowing that no one in Wassingham had.

'I'm not too keen on jazz though,' Carl said, rubbing his hand up and down her back, then whispering into her ear, 'Just on you.'

He eased her away from Marlene and walked her away from the patio across level sweet-smelling grass, kissing her, stopping, holding her close, running his hands down her sides, her bare thighs, the outside of them, the inside, easing his fingers into her pants, stroking her gently. Oh God. Then he withdrew and held her buttocks, breathing, 'Thank God you came into my life just when mini skirts arrived.' He pulled her after him, towards the trees which edged the lawn, stopping again, undoing her dress now that they were far from the noise of the music, the chatter, undoing all the buttons, letting it hang loose.

'Jesus, you're lovely,' he murmured, standing back, pushing the dress aside, running his fingers from her shoulders to her thighs and she felt as though she was swollen, exposed, raw-nerved, on fire but frightened. She pulled her dress to her again, doing up the buttons, because it didn't matter if she recognised Chardonnay and John Coltrane, she was just a girl from Wassingham who was too frightened to give herself.

Carl pulled her to him. 'Trust me, darling, here let me do them up properly.' He bent his head to see by the moonlight, then took her hand, leading her further into the wood, down a beaten path and there were lights at the end.

They approached a stone pavilion hung with lanterns and with cushions strewn about. Sarah hesitated at the foot of the steps.

'Come on, my darling,' Carl said, pulling her with him, taking her inside the one-roomed building, holding her to him, kissing her gently, so gently, licking her lips, her cheeks, his eyes looking into hers, his hands holding her face. Kissing her again and again but there was nothing else, just kisses and she relaxed again.

He moved to the table which was laid with bowls and a burning spirit stove. He took a silver spoon from a cut glass bowl, removed the lid of a porcelain jar and dug deep and she saw the hash gleaming darkly as he tipped it into the glass bowl, kissing her again as he put the spoon down, touching her mouth with his fingers.

'I love you, darling,' he murmured, looking deep into her again and she saw that he did, and knew that she loved him too.

He lifted the glass bowl, heated it and she saw the glass turn cloudy, then thick grey, watched him as he trapped the smoke, turned and held it to her, his lips glistening with moisture from her mouth.

'Breathe it,' he commanded gently, bending her head down to the glass. She looked into his eyes and again saw the love and nodded. He removed his hand and she breathed deeply, so deeply and now he did too and she gripped his shoulders, kissing his head, holding his arms, kissing his hands as he breathed in the smoke, taking the glass from him, breathing again, feeling a stroking begin inside her head, the kisses on her face.

He laid her on the cushions and took the clothes from his own body and he merged into the soft light of the lanterns, the soft sound of the music which drifted around them, in them, through them, then he came to her, kneeling over her, and she stroked him, pulled him on to her, kissed him and then he was gone but there was no sense of loss, just the floating of her body.

Then she felt his hands again and they were pulling apart her dress, ripping the buttons and she watched as they rolled across the paved floor, spun then fell, one, two, three.

She felt his hands on her breasts, tearing at her bra, ripping it from her, kissing her body, licking it and now she was floating so high, and her limbs were loose and lost.

'Please,' she begged, 'please.' But the words were so far away, the stroking in her mind so strong. 'Please,' she whispered, kissing his smile, running her hands down his body, finding him, stroking him then pressing his body on to hers. 'Please.'

He raised himself to kneel over her again and now his hands found her, easing off her pants, stroking her gently, bending, kissing her, licking her and she moaned from the pleasure that rippled from his tongue, again and again until she could hardly breathe, and the ripples grew and the pleasure surged, again and again, inside and out.

She shut her eyes, and all she could see was a golden light. There was no fear. She looked at him, so golden too in the light, his lips parted and swollen, his eyes half shut.

'Please,' she said, lifting her arms to him and he looked at her and took a condom from the pillow behind her, easing it on.

'No,' she said. 'You, just you.'

He shook his head. 'No, we don't want babies yet, my darling.'

She wanted to weep for the babies she wanted to have with him, and for his love which protected her, but the stroking was still there, the floating, the pleasure and now he was on her, pushing himself gently into her, so gently and after a moment's pain there was nothing but a surge of light, of being, and another, and another, again and again until she thought she would die.

That night they lay together on the cushions and loved again, and then he held a joint to her lips and they breathed in deeply, before walking across the dewed lawn when dawn was breaking, sinking into the bath which led from their room, his legs round her, his hand soaping her body, hers soaping his.

As the sun warmed the day they lay on the lawn with the others, smoking pot and she smiled at Davy, who lay with the auburn girl, and they tapped to the music of the Beatles together and Sarah could still feel Carl inside her and knew that she would only ever love him.

They drank coffee and she smiled at Sam as he dropped sugar lumps into all their cups.

'I don't take sugar,' she murmured, lying back in Carl's arms.

'You'll like this, my darling,' Carl said, rubbing his finger down the curve of her neck.

She drank, sipping slowly, and the music began to pound and then to slow, to thump, to pulse faster and she turned to Carl in fear. He held her.

'LSD, darling. We're getting all the treats this weekend; don't worry, I'll look after you, just remember that your mind will fly open, this will open doors to unbridled creativity, to another world. I know, believe me, I know.'

She lay back in his arms, feeling the waves of euphoria sweeping over her, gasping in wonder at the swirling colours of the sun through the trees, the flowers in the bed, the dresses of the girls, but then it was too bright, it was swirling too fast, she was breathing too fast, the music was pounding, rushing and then a flower opened up inside her and she basked in the sun which was warmer than it had ever been and the flowers brighter, the scent of Carl sharper. She didn't have to talk, to think. All she had to do was to be.

The following week, she went on the pill and to more parties with Carl. They took LSD tabs and as they cycled to college in the morning Davy told her that it was as though he had never tasted, smelled or heard anything before, that he wanted to keep that depth and clarity of perception all the time and she understood every word he said.

They played at the gig and Sarah explained to Carl that Davy fumbled because of the LSD. That was why his timing was wrong, his voice too quiet. Carl took her to bed, loved her and then heated hash for her.

She replied to Annie's letter, telling her that the gig had gone well, that she was sorry she hadn't written for three weeks but life was hectic, busy, and such fun.

She wanted to write and tell her of her love but she didn't, neither did she tell her of the drugs because how could she understand that it was not as harmful as they had always told her it was. It was just light, love, the unlocking of doors, an explosion of talent, because Davy's art had broken new boundaries and leapt into psychedelia and their rooms were festooned with his work.

'But don't send any up to them,' Sarah warned. 'They'd freak. They wouldn't understand.'

They played at a party of Sam Davis's the following week and Sam praised them, but said that Tim and Davy needed just a bit more polish, a bit more experience. In bed that night Carl said, 'Don't worry, I know how you feel about him, I'll think of a way to brush up his style.' Then they sucked hash and she sank into its arms, and Carl's, not thinking, just being, just accepting.

In July Davy went to Hamburg with Carl and another group, who took him along as lead guitar.

'To give him that edge, darling,' Carl said as he kissed her goodbye at the station.

'Write,' she called as the train pulled away. 'Please write and don't be sick on the ferry, Davy.'

Her bags were heavy as she lugged them on to the train, heaving them into the luggage rack, smoking cigarette after cigarette and stubbing them out in the ashtray, watching the countryside unfold, the blackened verges, the wheat ripening to the colour of Carl's hair and she ached for him and the glow which surrounded their lives together.

She slept, woke, tried to read her course notes. She'd passed her exams, but only just, there were no flying colours for her but who cared, life was too short. That's what Davy had said too, when he got his results.

Wassingham was as small as she remembered it, and just the same, always the same, and so were her family, the pigeons, the neighbours, the smell of coal, the grime. She lay in bed that night and ached for Carl again then walked to the beck in the morning, smoking pot as she sat by the willow, wondering if they were there yet, wondering why she couldn't have gone too.

'It's business, not a holiday,' Carl had said. 'I only just managed to swing it for Davy, couldn't get them to take Tim.'

She smoked another joint, holding her face to the sun, exhaling slowly, feeling her thoughts become submerged beneath the haze, and she preferred it that way.

That evening her mother asked why she hadn't gone with them and treated it as a holiday.

'Because it's not a holiday, it's business. You of all people ought to be able to understand that.' Sarah flung down the tea towel and slammed up to bed.

That night Annie held Georgie in bed. 'She's in love, in pain. She's not sleeping, you can tell that. She looks so drawn and pale – I'd like to meet him, just to see what he's like.'

Georgie sighed. 'She needs to keep busy – let her have this

week to settle down, she seems so jumpy – then give her some work to do in the design department, Tom's all for it.'

The next day Georgie took Sarah with him to the tossing point three miles to the north and she sat in the car, wanting to scream at the creaking of the basket, the fluttering of the birds, the boredom of it all, the rawness of her nerves. God, she must be tired.

She stood in the north-east wind, turning up her collar, thinking of the warmth of Bracklesham Bay, the touch of those hands, the feel of his lips, the feel of him inside her, the glow of the hash, the softness of a joint, the vividness of a tab.

'Let 'em go then, Sarah,' Georgie said, leaning on his stick, gauging the wind. 'Easily calm enough for them.'

She stopped, undid the straps, let the lid fall back and watched as the birds fluttered and took flight, wheeled, dipped, then soared.

'It's so good to have you home, to do this with you again, bonny lass,' Georgie said.

Sarah smiled. 'I'm so glad I'm here, Da,' but she wasn't. She wanted to be with Carl, wanted his hands to undress her at night, heat her hash, roll her joints. She wanted all that and none of this, and she hated herself for it.

A letter arrived from Davy at the end of the week and she tore it open, scanning the page, skimming over the flea-ridden digs, the smoky club, the heckling British sailors calling for the Beatles, then slowed and read again and again of Carl taking photographs of them all outside the Kaiserkeller, then walking them all down the Reeperbahn dodging the prostitutes.

Finding it tiring, the sessions are so damn long, but Carl's helped me out, he's a great guy, Sarah, he really looks after us both, doesn't he?

Sarah waited for the second post, but there was no letter from Carl. There was none the next week either, and she

288

shook her head when her mother asked her if she would help out in the local shop while they moved the manager across to supervise the opening of the new one in Gosforn.

'I've too much college work to catch up on, Mum,' she said, bending her head over her file.

Another letter came from Davy the following week and his writing was scrawling, untidy and there were psychedelic motifs beneath his signature.

Annie leant over her shoulder and picked up the envelope. 'Good lord, is he writing it on a bus or something?'

Sarah smiled. 'Yes, he's off on a trip.' Not your sort of trip though, Mum, and she went up to her room, looked out across the levelled slag heap and could have screamed with boredom and frustration and the pain of getting no letter from Carl.

At the end of August Annie cooked supper while Georgie was at the pigeon club and said, 'Would you like us all to go on holiday, it might make the time pass more quickly for you, Sarah? You still look tired.'

Sarah lit a cigarette, avoiding her mother's eye, waiting for the comment again but Annie said nothing, after all, she had smoked, how could she complain about her daughter?

'No thanks, Mum, I'm too old to go with you and Dad, if you know what I mean.'

'Then go and give Betsy a hand tomorrow in the creche. I'm not asking you this time, I'm telling you. We're all working very hard and you are not.'

Annie put down the pork chop, passed the apple sauce. Sarah looked at it, stubbed out her cigarette.

'We have lobster quite often you know, I find it suits me more than meat.'

Annie put down her knife and fork. 'Well hard bloody luck, you'll just have to put up with this.'

The next day Sarah helped Betsy in the creche and she wiped noses and read stories to the children, sitting them on her knees, but hating it. She wanted to be in the world she knew, not here, with all these people and kids who never looked beyond the bloody slag heaps.

That evening she arrived home and there was a postcard from Carl.

Should be having a lovely time, but am not. Miss you, miss you, miss you. Carl.

She made tea for her mother and cooked steak because Betsy was coming then sat with them all, talking and laughing, feeling the card in her pocket, touching it, smiling to herself. That night her mother made cocoa and brought it into her, sitting on her bed, sipping.

'So, you've heard from him.' Annie's face was kind.

Sarah nodded.

'A long one I hope.'

'Yes, sort of.'

'Oh?' Annie said quietly.

'A postcard if you must know.' Sarah's voice was hard, defensive because what right had her mother to ask? She had no right, for God's sake.

'He cares for me, he's there for me, always there.'

Annie said dryly, 'Not this minute though, business comes first eh, even before letters?'

Sarah flushed and put her cocoa on the bedside table, it was revolting, thick, horrible. She wanted a joint, speed, anything but this woman sitting on her bed criticising Carl.

'You should know about business coming first,' she hissed. 'And why are you still in this stupid little house – you own a factory, we could be in Gosforn, somewhere smart.'

Annie just sat there, gripping her cup, then she said slowly, 'We're here because it's our home, and besides we can't afford anything else because we plough the profits back into the business and then split what's left over. You know that.'

'But it's so boring, so small. There's a world out there, Mum, a world that left this place behind ages ago.'

Annie stood up, looking into her cocoa. 'I know there's a

world out there and that it's exciting, stimulating. I felt I had to leave once too, Sarah, and I did, and then I came back because I wanted what it had to offer. I do understand how you feel.'

She stopped and kissed her daughter but there was no warm arm flung around her neck as before, just the heat of her daughter's damp skin and the confusion in her eyes.

Annie walked from the room. Dear God, why weren't there any lessons in being a parent?

Sarah left for London early, she couldn't stand being suffocated by her family any longer, she would rather be alone.

CHAPTER 18

Carl and Davy arrived back in October, just before the start of term when the leaves were falling from the trees and there was mist morning and evening and a crispness in the air. They burned their paraffin heaters and Sarah put Davy's pale drawn looks down to sleeping in dank rooms and too many hours playing in smoky bars.

Carl agreed. 'Oh yes, it was tough, but it's done him good.'

They rehearsed on Wednesday and there was a hard edge to Davy's playing, and his fragile melodies were gone. In bed Carl said they were the best he had heard in a long while and flipped her a tab, and they made love as she had remembered, though better, deeper, surer, sharper.

Carl planned more gigs for them, including a week's tour in November in the Midlands so they all played sick at college and laughed and sang in the van as Carl drove up to Leicester where it was cold, and the audience uninterested. They slept in the van too, eating in a fish and chip bar, using public conveniences which were cold and smelly. Carl made a phone call the next day, before they should have left for Northampton.

'I have to go back, bit of business has come up. Tim's got the itinerary, I'll see you in London on Sunday. Just be good, all of you.'

They drove to Northampton and Sarah cursed his business, his college work, his contacts, because she wanted to be the whole of his life and if they had to sleep in a van she wanted to be next to him. They played Davy's music that night and the audience roared and clapped to it, dancing round the tables, calling for more.

That night Sarah couldn't sleep because the adrenalin was pumping in her body and the van was cold, the floor hard, the whole bloody thing was impossible, she thought, turning over and over. The next day she felt sick with tiredness, and her voice was flat when she sang. Davy handed her water during the break and she saw that his hands were trembling.

'For God's sake, you're tired too. why are we doing this?'

He grinned, his thin face creasing. 'I'm not tired, Carl sees to that. Here, take one of these tonight.' He handed her an orange and blue pill. 'It's Tuinal, it'll help.'

She looked at it. 'Mm, I always did like the orange smarties.'

She sang and played but Davy started to make errors and she was glad Carl wasn't there. In spite of what Davy said, she knew it was only tiredness. She used the public lavatories that night then crawled into her sleeping bag, taking the pill, feeling her mouth becoming sticky, then dry and she slept as though she'd never wake, and couldn't wake when Davy shook her, beating him off, feeling her head pounding, her mouth dry.

'Go away, let me sleep.'

He laughed. 'Come on, let's have the Prellies, they help, I promise you, it makes it all possible.'

She took his flask from him and swallowed the upper, hanging her head on her knees, watching as Arnie took one too, Tim refused. 'I'd sleep through an earthquake.'

They drove hard the next day, making for North Wales, sweeping along the rugged coast where the waves broke on to the shore, and she wanted to run along the beach and dance and shout and so they sang all day instead because their hearts were pounding so fast, their energy bubbling as it had never done before.

They played and it didn't matter that they made mistakes, because they were leaping on the stage, repeating riffs, bending towards one another, eyes glistening, voices shouting, lapping up the applause, the whistles, the screams.

They took downers in the van, uppers the next morning and there was no ache for Carl, no guilt about Wassingham, just success, exhilaration, excitement and again the next day, and the next and it was all so easy. They bought more pills from a guy at the last club, refusing cocaine and heroin. 'We're not into that,' Sarah said. 'We're not druggies.'

They worked hard the next week to catch up on college work and used the Tuinal and Prellies to keep them going for that too. On Saturday Sam Davis asked them into a studio to do a practice demo tape. Sarah's hands were trembling too now but all she had to do was sing, not play, and she rasped out the hard edged music.

It was a one-track studio and when they made a mistake they had to repeat the whole number again, and again and again.

'For Christ's sake,' Carl shouted at Davy, 'get it right.'

Sarah looked at Davy's trembling fingers, at her own. 'Leave him alone, for God's sake. He can't help it, can't you see he's tired?'

They tried once more but even after three hours the engineer was not satisfied with their performance and Carl threw his coat over his shoulders and talked to Sam, shaking his head, looking across at them, while Sarah stood with Davy. 'It's OK, we're just tired.'

Sam walked them to the taxi. 'You should think of going solo, you know. Davy's a better composer. He could write your stuff for you, he knows you so well.'

Sarah nodded, kissing the old man's cheek, smelling the gin on his breath and she smiled. 'We're a group,' she said, then slid across the seat. They drove back in silence with Carl sitting stiffly beside her. He left them at the bottom of the steps. 'Bit of business,' he said, not turning, leaving them there.

Tim and Arnie left. 'Get some rest, Davy, it's not the end

of the world,' Tim said, walking with Arnie back to his pad for a curry.

Sarah put her arm through Davy's. 'Come on, let's get on. We've those designs to finish for Mum and you've your course work, remember.'

That night Carl returned and dropped some hash on to Davy's lap. 'Try this, it's new. Arnie told me where I could get some.'

Sarah paid him from the tin, watching as Davy heated it, wanting it, wanting Carl, glad that his anger was over, that he said nothing more about Davy. She did not need Tuinal tonight, and neither did Davy. They didn't have any uppers left for the morning but they woke in time, cycling to college, feeling the cold sweat beneath their macs, the pounding of their heads.

'We'd better be careful of those smarties, bonny lad, hash is safer and the tabs. Let's stick to those.'

Carl held her in bed that night, having spent the evening with her and Davy, listening to the Beach Boys, to Dusty Springfield, to the Rolling Stones and it was better than any party, it was heaven, just the three of them, Sarah thought.

'You do understand now why I won't leave the group?' she breathed in his ear that night as she floated into sleep.

'Yes, I understand, my darling, never doubt that.'

There was a letter from Annie in the morning, asking if they had managed to sort out any more samples as they hadn't received any for three weeks.

But not to worry at all, if you haven't time. We are getting the hang of it here now, so can just carry on.

Sarah swore and knocked on Davy's door, entering, looking at the design he was drawing, the swirling, swooping shapes, the vortex of colour. 'Brilliant, but not for Wassingham, lad. And our masters call. We're very late with the samples. I'd forgotten.'

They sewed all week, their hands steadier now, their seams

straighter, but Davy couldn't get the textile design right, and so they left it for a few days then went back and rechecked the students' dresses which were far from perfect. They unpicked seams, working far into the night, drinking too much coffee, and Carl slept in his own room because he was trying to catch up on lectures and seminars – when he wasn't out, doing business.

'What business?' Davy asked, as he unpicked the last of the mini skirts.

'He never says,' Sarah replied, her voice muffled with pins, and they laughed together. 'I'll swallow one in a minute and probably end up top of the hit parade.'

Davy looked up at her. 'D'you want to go solo, Sarah? I don't mind. I love me art you know.'

Sarah put down the shirt she was working on. 'I know you love your art but it's fun isn't, this music business? I mean, it's opened so many doors, we've met so many people, so why should I want to go solo? Anyway, Carl's forgotten about that particular bee in his bonnet.'

Davy grinned. 'Rob's still in the debating society at Leicester, you know. Wonder if he ever lifts his head out of his books, or opens his mouth to sing.'

'Don't ask for miracles, Davy. Anyone who stays on to do an MA is seriously deranged. I mean, he even works when he gets home.'

'Or goes debating with me da,' Davy said, picking up the shirt again, finishing off the seam, throwing it on to the pile. 'That's about it.' He smiled but there was an edge to his voice.

Sarah switched on the iron. 'Don't forget you're named after your da's cousin and me mum says he loves you very much.'

Davy just nodded.

They completed the designs on Saturday afternoon, but Sarah still had her own clothes to make for the party they were going to that night with Carl. As she lined up the seam beneath the needle, she suddenly remembered that she should have met him for lunch at the Bistro. It was the second time she had forgotten that week and she closed her eyes, enraged at herself, running to his door, knocking to apologise but he wasn't back.

She packed up the samples, boxed and addressed them, then pressed her own dress and heard him come up the stairs, heard him stop outside her door and she turned, holding the last sample as he came in.

'I'm so sorry, darling,' she said. 'I was so busy, I just forgot.'

He walked over to her, snatching the dress from her, ripping it, throwing it in her face, punching the boxes to the floor, kicking them, then turned on her, his face furious, red, thin-lipped and she flinched as he raised his hand, then dropped it.

'For God's sake, now I know how your father felt,' he raged. 'You're just like her, working working. You "forgot" on Wednesday, you "forgot" today. And what about the parties you missed on Thursday, and on Tuesday. It's important to me that you're there, you help me, you help *my* business but it's only you that matters, isn't it? You're just like your mother. If I lost my ruddy leg you'd leave me in the hospital too wouldn't you, and rush back here and get *your* business on the road and bugger anyone else. You use everyone, like she does, look at her making you and Davy work like this. Just like you make me work for you, fixing up gigs, tours, God knows what . . .'

He slumped on to the cushions. 'And what about your rehearsals? Those go to the wall too, damn the group.'

Sarah picked the ripped dress from the floor. There were threads all over the table, all over her tights, her skirt. She went to him but he brushed her off, striding from the room.

'The address of the party is in my room, come and find me if you've got bloody time.'

She bathed in cold water, smoked a joint, collected Davy and took a taxi to Fulham, hearing the sitar music as she climbed the stairs, and thinking, always thinking.

She looked for him. He wasn't there. Would he come or would he think she was like his mother, leaving him alone? Would he still think she was like her own mother, using h'm? There was a deadness inside her, a vacuum of darkness and she smiled at Davy and took the wine he brought.

'It's my fault you rowed, isn't it?' he asked, his pale face thin and worried.

She kissed his cheek. 'No, bonny lad, it's not your fault, nothing to do with you, just with me.'

They sat with the others on cushions covered in Indian cotton, listening to the eerie twang of the sitar music, drowning in its resonance, sinking into its dreams and all the time she thought but felt nothing, gripping the cushion, wanting to jump off the roundabout again, stand and sort her mind out, in peace.

The musicians stopped and drank wine, and she leaned back on cushions watching as the men rose, stretching their limbs, easing their fingers and she was surprised that they did anything so mundane in this darkened room, full of incense and India.

There were drawings of Hindu gods on the walls between the hanging carpets, and she looked around, sipping the wine which was not Chardonnay but just plonk. There was one drawing beside the window which looked familiar and she moved closer, peering at it.

'Do you like it?' a sing-song voice asked behind her.

Sarah nodded. 'I have a paper knife at home with that design on it.'

'So, that is Tara, one of the Hindu goddesses, or you would say Star but whether you use Hindi or English, it is still a beautiful name. Shall we call you that. Aren't you to be Carl's star?'

She turned now, slopping her wine, dusting off her dress as she looked at the Indian who had been playing the sitar.

He smiled. 'Forgive me, I have the advantage of you. Your Carl rang earlier to say he had been held up and asking me to take care of you, if you arrived. He described you rather well. I am Ravi.'

Sarah smiled, the vacuum filling now because Carl had thought of her, had forgiven her.

'I think Tara is a little previous, don't you? I'm a student and my name is Sarah Armstrong. My father was in India, you know.'

Ravi led her back to the cushions. 'No, I didn't know. Where?'

Sarah told him, asking him if the plains were really as hot as her parents had said.

'They certainly are much hotter than your English summers.'

She asked him then where he lived. 'North of Delhi. My father runs a clinic which is open to all castes, all faiths, but run by Christians, many of them converted. I am finished here now, a truly fledged doctor and soon to return to add my help.'

Annie nodded. 'And you also play music rather well. We like music too but there isn't time for everything, is there?'

Ravi leant back, waving to the saffron-robed shaven-headed monk who was now leaving, having tapped out mantras on his prayer beads since Sarah arrived.

'It's kind of you to say I play well. I'm not sure how well but I was taught by an old man who was one of the Maharajah's musicians. The poor old thing is living in splendid solitude near my father's compound but that is what he wishes and it is to our benefit because he has told us many stories of those glittering times.'

Sarah listened to tales of splendour, of indulgence within the fort and longed for a joint, feeling restless, feeling the trembling in her hands, longing for Carl. She looked for Davy, he was taking a tab and she tried to catch his eye, but he wouldn't look.

She looked down at her hands, gripping them tightly, seeing the red weals that the scissors had made. Carl was right, she was doing what her mother had done, forgetting everything for her own ends. She no longer heard Ravi, just thought of her mother who had rushed from hospital to start her dream business, who had shouted at her da, forced strawberry ice cream down him. He wouldn't have lost his leg, but for her bloody business. She should have nursed, even Terry and Aunt Maud said that.

Ravi was taking the glass from her hand. 'Let me get you some more.' He rose easily and she looked towards the door. Carl still hadn't come, but he had rung, he had cared.

Did her mother care about anyone, or did she just use them?

She watched Davy staggering over by the far wall, hanging on to the picture frames. Just like she was, hanging on to the past, hanging on to her mother. She took out a joint then, lit it, inhaled deeply, holding it, longer, longer, and then exhaling, sucking in again, feeling the world slowing, her head floating. She arched her neck. But no, her mother loved her, she'd come to them when the strike had flared. Of course she loved her, she didn't use her.

Ravi said, 'Do you use a great deal?' He was nodding towards Davy who had sunk on to the floor.

Sarah smiled. 'No more than anyone else, we need it to break into another dimension, to experience and explore just as everyone else is doing.'

Ravi handed her the glass. 'By no means everyone, Sarah, and there are other, slower ways.'

Sarah shrugged. 'There's no point in taking life slowly if you don't have to is there?'

The door opened and Carl came in, looking around, but she was already on her feet, moving away from Ravi, as he said, 'But it leads to other things. Be careful, I beg you.'

She didn't look round, but went to Carl and held him. 'I'm so sorry, my darling, there will always be room in my life for you, just as there is room in my mother's life for me, there is no need to feel insecure. But I promise there will be less sewing, and that way I can help Davy practise too. We must make room for everything.'

300

The next week she and Davy bought posters of benevolent gods, from Buddha to Brahma, from a shop near the British Museum and asked Annie and Tom for money from their account to buy sitars. For some weeks the music gave them no time to suck hash or trip. Ravi came on Fridays to teach them, sitting, smiling as he showed them, plucking the strings, telling them they needed to go into their own temple once a day for the benefit of the soul, that there was no haste, no need for short cuts.

He took his hands from the sitar and tapped his head. 'It is better than the chemicals you take. You should try to chant the mantra like our friend the monk did. Perhaps I should send you some *japa mala*, to finger while you chant. Perhaps you should come to visit me, return to the land your father once knew, my Sarah.'

He guided Davy's hands on the strings. 'Perhaps,' she said, looking from Davy to Carl. 'Perhaps we could all go.'

Ravi nodded. 'You land at Delhi and you travel the whole country, staying at Gurdwaras, Sikh temples open to those of all faiths, that way you will sleep and eat with the people of my country, and we are very diverse – and then you come to us.'

Sarah grinned at Carl's face. 'Bit different to Sam Davis's pad?'

Carl grimaced. 'Too right.' He paused. 'Maybe one day Ravi, but not yet.'

Sarah listened as Ravi played, then Davy repeated the sound and it was as gentle as his melodies. It was right for him. She said. 'I think we should go, one day, when we've finished. We can get all sorts of design ideas, Davy, and there's all that Indian cotton.' She turned. 'You've really got to get more work done, Carl, or you'll end up without a degree. You just spend your time wheeling and dealing like Uncle Don.'

Davy laughed. 'Oh, Carl's nothing like Uncle Don, don't insult him.'

301

They practised with Tim and Arnie and at the next college gig they played a number of Davy's using a sitar, an Indian drum and two guitars and a hush fell on the dancers as they stopped and listened to the fragile melody easing out across the smoke-filled hall. There was silence when they finished and then applause and Sarah kissed her cousin, seeing the joy in his eyes, feeling the fullness in her own throat.

She told Carl that night but he laughed and said, 'That gig's just amateur night. Trust me, and keep that stuff for yourselves, might save you having to go into your own temples too often.'

Ravi left for India at the start of December and Carl brewed them all hash that night and the next he took Davy out for a drink and Sarah was grateful to him because Davy was fond of Ravi. 'I'll miss him, he understood what I was trying to say,' he told her as they climbed the stairs after seeing him off.

'I understand,' Sarah said, 'really I do,' but Davy had just squeezed her arm.

Each night now, Carl took Davy out, sometimes with her, sometimes not and they came home too late for love. She missed Carl in her bed but at least she had written up Davy's notes for him, and sorted out his project into some sort of order and sucked hash to help her sleep.

She and Davy travelled to Wassingham for Christmas, and as the train rumbled and rocked towards the north she closed her eyes and thought of the passion of Carl's lovemaking last night and wondered how she would last for a month without him.

There was the same smell of coal in the air, the same bitter wind, the same small kitchen in which she and Davy worked, bringing their projects up to date, sketching new ideas for next term, hoping to run them up on Annie's machine.

'It'll give us more time for music if we do it now, Davy. She needn't know, I'll put them in my case and send them up every two weeks or so.'

On Christmas Eve she cleaned out the pigeons for Georgie and cursed at the smell, the echoes of a childhood which seemed miles away now and so dull.

She watched as they had their afternoon flight, trying to pick out Buttons' great-grandson, unable to, though she pretended to Georgie that she could.

On Christmas Day they opened presents in Betsy's kitchen, drinking sherry and wanting a joint, Christ, she wanted a joint. She picked up Teresa's present to her, and peeled off the paper, to find slippers, the same as Bet's.

She looked at Annie and grimaced, then laughed as she did. It was the first time she had laughed since she had come home. She put them on, then stood by Betsy. 'I reckon you and I should start a chorus line then, Grandma, how about it?'

She felt Bet's arm come round her, hold her tightly. 'If I were a few years younger I'd take you up on that, my love.'

They shuffled their feet, lifted their left leg, their right leg, and shuffled it all about.

'Steady, Mam,' Tom called. 'Remember what the doc said, not too much excitement until we've got that blood pressure down.' He grinned as he picked up Teresa's psychedelic wrapping paper. 'So I'd better put this away or you'll end up blowing the top of your head off. Blimey, if you two ever send me up anything like this I'll be down like a shot to see what's going on in that den of vice.'

Sarah laughed and helped Bet back to her chair. 'If only it were a den of vice. It's just like here, but bigger.'

They had turkey, plum pudding, and mince pies, but Davy left most of his.

'I'm just tired,' he said to his mother, picking at his napkin, his fingers restless, his eyes active and Sarah felt the same. She wanted a joint.

They sat on over brandies. 'Bad for the voice,' Sarah told her father, leaning forward, listening as Annie talked of the wallpaper they were thinking of introducing into their shops, and the wholesalers.

'We thought we'd reproduce the design of the curtains so that there is a matching effect,' she told Sarah.

Davy put down his brandy goblet, turning it round and round, saying slowly, 'Wouldn't it be better to invert the design, have the curtains the reverse of the paper. I think the same would all be a bit too much.'

Annie thought for a moment, then nodded, calling out to Tom. 'Tom, will you and Rob stop talking about the Americans in Vietnam or whatever it is, and listen to your son for a moment. He's come up with a brilliant idea.' She was smiling but her voice was sharp. 'Say that again, Davy.'

He did so and Tom turned in his chair, putting his arm on the back of Davy's chair. 'That is so simple, but so good. Yes, we'll do that. Now tell us more about your term.'

Davy told them how much he liked silk painting because the light could shine through the silk and create brilliant transparent effects.

'You see, you can achieve subtle nuances of colour with colour blending, it gives a feeling of other-worldliness, or of something quite unique. I feel it could be incorporated into the business, though I'm not too sure in what way.'

Tom was looking at his son, at his tired face, his hollow cheeks. He'd been working too hard, he'd immersed himself in the world of design, just as Tom had done as a student, and he felt immeasurably relieved because they had all been so worried at the look of him, and Sarah too.

After lunch they didn't go to the football field, but into the stables where Tom kept the old silk-screen he had made and they stood around Davy as he blended paints while Tom cut a length of silk. He placed it on the table, running inside to bring water for dampening the silk, as Davy laid two intermediate colours next to each other, standing back while his father rubbed the silk under more water, looking at Davy.

'Go on, a bit more, the shading's not quite right.'

Sarah saw him blend more blues, saw the look of concentration on his face, the expertise with which he added more colour. She had never seen him at work like this before.

304

He brushed on more colours, one above the other, working with Tom, their faces both with the same expression, the same intensity, the same love of the medium.

By five it was finished, a landscape in tones of blue, in which the lines and contours had been created simply by colour displacement. It reminded Sarah of his sitar compositions and she knew that her cousin had the soul of an artist.

They talked all evening about its application. 'It'll just have to wait until you have time to set up a branch line to handle it,' Tom said finally. 'It's your interest, it should be you that develops it. We'll talk about it more tomorrow.'

Annie sat up in bed with Georgie, her glasses slipping down her nose as she read her letter from Prue.

> Thanks for the biscuits – wonderful to have good old
> England tucked away in a tin. Are you any less worried
> about Sarah? Do remember ourselves at her age and
> today life's so much more exciting, demanding. They'll
> make mistakes, but we've all had to do that. Just help
> them pick up the pieces afterwards. This Carl may not
> be such a bad lot, you know, just because he didn't write
> to your daughter. And remember, she and Davy have
> one another.

Annie took off her glasses, passing the letter to Georgie, reassured not so much from the letter as from this evening.

The next day Tom didn't talk to Davy about painting or design, because he and Rob were off before the others rose to plan a demonstration about the American build-up in Vietnam.

'On Boxing Day, for God's sake,' Davy said to Sarah as they walked by themselves to the beck.

'I'll do some silk-screen painting with you,' she panted as they walked quickly beneath the frosted branches of the lane. 'Slow down a bit.'

Davy shook his head. 'No, I don't want to, it's boring, it's all boring.' His head was down, his hands in his pockets, his breath cloudy in the sharp air. There were traces of snow on the ground, frost hardened in the ruts. There was snow in the meadow and ice at the edge of the beck and the willow hung lifeless and still.

'So damned boring,' he repeated as they stood there watching the water pass beneath the ice. 'You know, I'd be all right if I drew silk paintings of Trotsky.'

Sarah took his arm. 'Remember he loves you.'

'I know,' Davy said, his face as white as the snow on the rocks near the willow. 'So everyone says. I'd have gone with them, but they never asked. They never do. They never even said they were going. If they had, I could have butted in and invited myself.'

He looked at her and his eyes were dark, then he smiled. 'Life's too short, Sarah, it's too damned short to be feeling sad. Come here, this is my Christmas present to you, something a very good friend introduced me to.' He took her arm, led her across to the rock, took out a polythene packet and laid a line of cocaine near snow which lay in rivulets.

He handed her a straw and together they snorted the coke and she felt the euphoric delights immediately, sitting with him on the ground, not feeling the cold, only hearing Davy as he said, 'The road to excess leads to the palace of wisdom. Do you think they know that Balke said that, bonny lass?'

She didn't know and she didn't care because it was the first time she'd tried coke and it was wonderful.

They played and sang for Annie that night, sitting in front of the fire, smelling wintergreen, still floating, still dreaming, playing *Afternoon Curry* with the new hard edge.

'I don't like it as much, it seems so hard, almost like the Rolling Stones. Davy's songs were always so fragile, so delicate, like his silk painting.'

Sarah looked at her mother as Davy fingered the strings, his eyes heavy-lidded. 'Don't be absurd, Mother. This is what the punters want. You're always saying that we shouldn't allow our personal preferences to come between us and the market.'

'This is different, isn't it? This is Davy's soul. Who's altered you so much?'

Sarah sat back. 'You don't know anything about it. Music isn't a roll of bloody wallpaper or a pair of pants.' Sarah took out a cigarette, tapped it on the pack, lit it, inhaled.

'But that's my point, you're treating it as though it is, or is it someone else who's treating it like that?'

'Why don't you just come out and say it's Carl? You don't like him, do you?'

Annie reached forward, held her hand. 'Darling, I'm not saying that, I don't even know the boy.'

'He's not a boy, he's a man, I'm a woman, Davy's a bloody man and music's our world. We know it, we understand it, you don't.'

Annie said nothing for a moment, just looked at her daughter who looked almost as pale and thin as Davy. It was nearly 1967 and Sarah was nineteen – did that make her a woman? Dear God, she was fifty-two and she still felt like a child in the face of this changing world.

'You're right of course, I don't understand it, but I do love you and I'm proud of you, you've achieved so much but don't get too tired, you both look so exhausted.'

Sarah and Davy left on 29 December when Carl phoned with news of a New Year's gig. Tom and Annie took them to Newcastle and asked if they would like to send up some up-to-the-minute wallpaper designs. 'As you say, darling,' Annie said as she held Sarah on the station, 'I don't understand your world so you must lead us, but only if you have time. We don't want you getting tired.'

They fell into their bedsits, laughing and calling out to Carl, heating the hash, lying on cushions on the floor, hearing of his skiing, groaning at his falls, laughing as they told him of the beck, of the white of the coke alongside the snow. That night she and Carl made love for hours, drifting in and out of the night, heating more hash, snorting coke in the morning, playing at the gig in the evening, just the two of them, without Tim and Arnie and it didn't matter that Davy's errors left them little applause, nothing mattered in the world they were swimming in.

They drifted from party to party and it was so much better than Wassingham, than pigeons, than slippers and chorus lines. In the second week of January Annie rang, asking if they would like to send up any designs. Sarah left a note for Davy as she left with Carl for a party at Sam Davis's London pad.

In the morning she crawled from bed, shrugged into her dressing gown, pulling it round her as she slapped to the bathroom, seeing the ice on the windows, feeling the cold water on her body, rushing back to her room, a room without Carl who had stayed on with Sam to work out more business.

She lit the paraffin stove, made tea, sat at the table drinking it, feeling the pounding in her head from the LSD of the night before, lighting a cigarette with trembling hands, watching a match fall, still alight on to the papers on the table.

She doused it with the palm of her hand and brushed it to the floor, seeing Davy's designs for the first time, holding them, not believing that he could have done this off-the-page psychedelic design for their parents, the fool.

She dropped it, ran to his room, banging on the door, opening it knowing it wouldn't be locked. He was sitting on the bed, tripping. She shook him. 'For God's sake, what have you done? They'll be down, you fool. Oh Davy. What the hell are we going to do? They'll take us back.'

Davy watched her leave the room, still feeling her hands on him, her lovely warm hands and then he wept, because at last his father would come and take them back.

CHAPTER 19

Annie took Tom's phone call two days later and rushed straight round, in through the yard and into the kitchen, snatching the designs from Tom.

She looked at him and Gracie. 'It could mean nothing.'

Tom nodded. 'I know but then on the other hand . . .'

Annie let the designs fall on to the table. 'I've left a message at the club for Georgie, he'll be round any minute. Oh God, I just don't know. They seemed so different, so thin, so difficult when they came up, or Sarah was.'

Gracie took the tea that Bet put on the table before easing herself into her carver chair. 'Davy wasn't difficult, he was just too quiet, so different.'

Bet took out her handkerchief and patted her top lip. 'I don't know what to think about the bairns. I don't understand this world any more.' Her lips were trembling and Annie patted her hand. 'It'll be all right. I mean, these designs are all the rage, it doesn't mean they're into drugs and things, we'd know, surely we'd know. Look at all the work they brought back, all the parties they go to, I mean the kids of today never rest, it's no wonder they get frayed. I mean, I've never seen them with anything, well, any drugs, have you?'

No one had and now Bet said, 'You and Tom looked tired and pale after your time in London, you know, Gracie.'

Annie nodded. 'I certainly felt it when I was nursing. I remember being so tired I couldn't write, my hands shook so much.'

Georgie came in through the door. 'What's happened?'

Tom slung across the designs, telling Georgie what they'd been saying, looking at Annie. 'We must go down. We have to see what's going on – but they wouldn't be so stupid, surely?'

Georgie shrugged, his face anxious. 'We mustn't let them think we're checking up though. We must think of a good reason for going down.'

Tom was looking at the designs again, then he pushed them from him. 'I'm disappointed in him either way. These are a load of rubbish.'

Annie sat forward. 'Tom, that's completely unfair, nothing your son does is a load of rubbish. He's so talented, why can't you see that? Whatever else we do, you will not tell him you think of them in that way. You must not reject him. Anyway, I don't know about anyone else but I'm worried sick about them and I want them back here where I can look after them and make sure they eat properly, sleep properly. I hate that bloody city and I want them back for good.'

She walked to the sink, washing out her mug, wanting to rush down, bring them back, look after them, wipe the differences from them.

Gracie said, 'I want them back too.'

'Oh, for God's sake,' Tom snapped. 'It's 1967, we can't just go and bring them back here because some silly little sod's drawn a mindless doodle.'

'Tom,' Gracie and Annie shouted together.

Georgie spoke now, his voice measured, his hand beckoning to Annie, pulling her close to him, leaning his head against her body. 'Now look, we can't bring them back, it's just not on. We were allowed to fly, weren't we, make our own mistakes? This design is just a mistake. What is there here for them until they're qualified, until they've got the excitement out of their systems? Let them finish their courses then let them decide what to do. Remember, it's a different world down there, we're so out of step, I can see it when they come up.'

'But I just feel there's something wrong,' Annie said.

Georgie squeezed her. 'Women always feel there's something wrong. It's only a young man and woman putting their heads together and coming up with a modern design – exactly as we asked.'

Tom shook his head. 'I still feel we need to go down, we just need a good excuse.'

Annie suggested that they went down to discuss the design. 'Because Tom, it really would be quite good if it was changed to black and white.'

Gracie objected. 'But there's no need to go down to tell them that, we could do it over the phone and they'd know.'

Bet spoke now, still patting her lips. 'Well, why not take some stuff down there for their friends to try out? Tell them it's a bit of market research – weren't you thinking of running up some of those PVC blown-up armchairs, Annie, and some Indian cushions? They'd believe that.'

There was silence and then Annie grinned, left Georgie's side and hugged Bet. 'You are a bloody marvel, woman. You're wasted here, you should be Prime Minister.'

Sarah brushed the carpet, wiped the paintwork, put the magazines into a neat pile, straightened the bed and checked that there was nothing of Carl's still here. She checked Davy's room too, piling up his records, standing the sitar and guitar in the corner, taking down the psychedelic swirls as she had done in her room.

'You've got to shave, boil the kettle. Come on, they'll be here soon.'

She looked at him sitting on his bed smiling at her, his eyes sunken, his stubble as auburn as his hair, his shoulders sharp beneath his shirt and something caught in her chest. She went and sat with him. 'Look, we've got to cut down on the stuff we're taking. I know we hardly ever take coke but maybe we shouldn't take any at all and cut down on the hash. I just don't want to eat any more and we've got so thin. It's so expensive as well, especially the tabs. We don't

311

need to trip so much, look where it's got us. Anyway, I've been pulled up at college for non-attendance and poor effort. What about you?'

'You could say that. OK, we'll cut down.' His voice was tired from too much hash. 'What time are Auntie Annie and Da due?'

Sarah looked at her watch. 'In half an hour. Oh God, I hope I haven't missed anything.'

'You've missed nothing, it's as clean as a whistle. They'll think nothing's wrong.' His voice was flat and she looked at him again and now she took his hand. 'Davy, you're not on anything else are you? You're so thin.'

Sarah gently pushed up his sleeve but there were no needle marks as there had been on Sam's friend Lou before he overdosed at a party over Christmas, and she felt a flood of relief.

'Yes, we'll cut down,' she said. 'You can do more of your silk painting, think about the future.'

Davy watched her as she walked to the door, seeing his dream of returning fading because she wanted to stay so much, and he would die for her.

Sarah boiled the rice, then put it into an enamel dish, adding sardines and tomatoes, grating cheese on top. Carl liked her rice hash. She checked the table, tidied the napkins she had sewn to match the tablecloth, stood back and adjusted the mats. She looked at her watch again, glad that they were coming, that they cared enough to be worried and take the train to London to check on them, because that was why they were coming, there could be no other reason. They would meet Carl and see him as he truly was, not as they feared.

Davy came in, washed, shaved, a sweater on that hid his thinness. 'I'm just going to get some beer, can I borrow your scarf?' He unhooked it from the back of the door.

'But Carl's bringing back wine from Sam's.'

Davy smiled gently. 'Me da's a pitman, he likes beer.'

She heard him walking down the stairs, past the bikes. Oh God, the bikes.

She rushed down, pushing them against the wall, standing back, seeing one wobble, adjusting it until they were all stable and there was more room to pass. She ran back up the stairs and opened a tin of peaches and another of pears. She tipped the cream into a jug, the milk too. She put on the kettle, then heard them ringing the bell, pushing open the door and she leaned over the banister, calling, 'Come on up.'

She saw them inching past the bike, lifting large cartons high above the handlebars, knocking the phone and laughing as Annie propped hers on Tom's back whilst she put back the receiver.

They struggled up the stairs and into her room, dumping the cardboard boxes, hugging her, looking round. 'It's so lovely, so fresh,' Annie said, taking off her gloves and coat, looking at her daughter keenly. 'You look well but still tired.'

Sarah laughed. 'I am tired, there's a lot to do, but what're those?' She pointed to the boxes.

Tom laughed. 'We'll tell you later.'

Sarah nodded, puzzled, but now she could hear Carl coming up the stairs, along the landing and she was nervous as he knocked before opening the door. Thank God, he'd remembered not just to barge in.

He stood there so beautiful, so golden and she took his arm, leading him to her mother. 'This is my mother, Annie Armstrong, and my uncle, Tom Ryan.'

She watched as they shook hands, as Annie smiled and Tom too, though there was reserve in their voices, in the shortness of the handshake.

'I brought wine,' Carl said. 'Where's your opener Sarah?'

Thank God he'd remembered that he shouldn't know where it was.

Tom started to shake his head at the glass Carl offered him, then smiled as Annie pressed his foot. He took the wine.

Sarah felt tension tighten her shoulders because Davy had

313

gone for beer for his pitman father. 'I thought you liked beer, Uncle Tom?'

Tom stood awkwardly sipping. 'No, no, I like wine, just don't have it much somehow. When in Rome, you know.' He laughed and Annie talked then of the crowds, how it seemed to have become so busy since her day. 'But these bedsits are lovely. Is Davy all right? I thought he'd be here?'

'He's just slipped out,' Sarah said, as she checked the rice, stepping back as the heat billowed up into her face, wishing she had stopped him, wishing Tom had refused. Oh God, it was all going wrong.

Davy ran up the stairs as they sat talking of Carl's skiing holiday and burst in, his scarf flying, his arms full of beer. His smile faded as he saw the wine in his father's hand. Annie stood up, glancing at Sarah, concern in both their faces.

'How lovely to see you Davy. The designs were very interesting. We were fascinated.' Annie was taking the beer from him, kissing his cheek as Tom came across.

'Yes, lad, we couldn't wait to see you so that we could discuss them but we were wondering if they could be in black and white? Didn't like to do it before we had spoken to you but it would give a greater feeling of perspective – what d'you think?'

Sarah smiled at Carl, whispering, 'You see, they do care, they don't use us, they've come all this way to check, using the design discussion as an excuse. I knew you were wrong, my darling.'

She watched as she saw Davy's slow smile, his brief nod as he unscrewed the beer bottle, pouring it for himself, lifting it towards his father, who looked at Annie, then grinned and said, 'Well, I'm not a Roman, am I?'

Sarah laughed with her mother, though Carl stood there silent. She squeezed his arm, knowing that the warmth of her family had taken him by surprise, that there was regret in him at all he had said, at all he had not experienced with his own mother.

They sat down at the table, listened as Davy talked to his father about the salt method he was using to obtain different effects with his silk painting.

'You see, Da, the salt absorbs water which has paint dissolved in it, and this leaves traces behind on the fabric. They can form all sorts of different outlines, some clumsy, some delicate. I've some in my room.'

Tom laughed, his hand restraining Davy, his elbow nudging Annie who sensed his delight in the enthusiasm, the lack of any signs of drug abuse. She toyed with her rice, putting small amounts in her mouth, forcing herself to swallow because Sarah wasn't to know that after the camps she had never been able to face it again.

Davy went to his room when he had finished eating. Annie forced down more rice, but with it half eaten she put her fork down. 'It's the excitement of London getting to me. I can't eat but it was lovely, my darling.'

Sarah cleared away, bringing the tinned fruit and the cream as Davy showed Tom and Annie the salt effects on twill, satin taffeta and chiffon, and Sarah was pleased that his hands trembled only a little.

Annie held them up, comparing them. 'I wonder if this could be used for evening dresses – it's so beautiful, each one's different.'

'That's it exactly, Auntie Annie – it is unique and the punters like that.'

Tom finished his beer. 'Mm, but it would still need to be run as a department on its own. Let's think about it some more when you next come home.'

Annie washed the dishes, understanding now how they had become so thin in London – there was so much to do, so much self-exploration. Just look at Davy's salt effects, his enthusiasm. Of course the nights were a waste of time when there was all this to discover.

Sarah called her for coffee and they laughed at Davy's story of the art lecturer who was so vague he not only forgot which lecture he should be taking, but at which college. Carl

315

passed Annie the sugar. 'What are those boxes?' he asked quietly, nodding to the cartons.

Tom looked at Annie. 'Well, it's the reason we're here really. You see we thought we'd try out this new fad for PVC and we've run up some inflatable chairs that we thought we'd bring down for you to try for us, and ask your friends. It's a bit of market research. There are some cushions too, which we gather people like to sit on − like that one over there.' Tom nodded towards the one Sarah had bought from the market.

Sarah felt something die in her. 'Fine, I'll ask.' Somehow she didn't cry. Somehow she laughed and talked until they'd gone, somehow she kissed her mother and nodded when Annie said, 'If you ever need me, ring me.'

Now, as the door closed she looked at Davy and knew that they were both feeling the same. She put her arm through her cousin's and leant her head on his shoulder but then Carl called her back into the room. He stood by the boxes, pushing at one with his foot. 'So, they came because they were concerned, did they?' he said, his voice tight with anger. 'Did they hell. They came so that they could use you again, and me this time. When's it going to bloody stop?'

They heard Davy slam the front door and she ran to the window, shouting 'Davy, come back, let's talk about it, all of us.' But he didn't turn, just waved his hand and kept on walking.

Carl pulled her back. 'Leave him, he's the one who nearly blew it, he's the one who always nearly blows it while you pick up the pieces.'

'That's not − ' but his mouth was on hers, hard, savage, his arms about her, holding her. 'They're all a dead loss,' he said at last, heating up hash for them both which she drew in deeply, wanting to ease the pain because at last she saw he had been speaking truth for all these months.

That evening she and Carl blew up one of the armchairs, taking turns, feeling their sides aching, their heads bursting

316

as they did so, and then they shared a joint, and kissed, hard, deep but all the time she listened for Davy.

Carl undid her buttons, and she his. Their naked bodies were against one another. She clutched at him, holding him close and still there was no Davy and anger rose in her from the dead coldness there had been since her mother left. She gripped Carl's head between her hands, kissing him. He pulled back and kissed her breasts her belly, her thighs, her mouth again, then pulled her down on top of him, on top of the chair.

She pressed her body against him, then she was easing him inside her, moving with him, cursing the bloody chair. Then she eased herself away from him, pulling him to the bed, and lighting a joint. They smoked, and as her head began to float she crawled to the chair and pressed the butt into it, watching it shrivel and deflate beside her and now she laughed again until the laughter turned to tears.

That night she didn't sleep but lay with Carl and thought of her mother who hadn't eaten the meal she had cooked, who hadn't come because she cared but because she'd wanted to use them. She thought of her shouting at her da, forcing him into the mine, who lived for her life for the factory and had been too busy to come pigeon-racing with her daughter and husband. Carl had been right all along and it was time she grew up and let them go.

Tom and Annie sat on the train, their feet throbbing, their heads aching.

'What did you think, bonny lass?' Tom asked.

Annie rubbed her eyes, pressing her fingers into her forehead. 'If I lived in London I'd look pale and interesting too – I think they're all right. They say you can smell pot. I didn't smell anything.'

'You didn't eat much either, but you did well to get through as much as you did. Yes, I think they're fine too. It was great, Annie, seeing that enthusiasm in their eyes. I mean, that salt technique is very interesting and I'd forgotten. I'd also forgotten how hard I worked when Gracie and I were down. I painted murals to make extra money, d'you remember?'

She did. She remembered the Mickey Mouse gasmasks too, when Tom told her of his journey back up. 'One little horror kept blowing raspberries with his, blimey I pity the family that got him.'

'Did you like Carl?' Annie asked Tom, looking at her hands, at the broken Ruby Red.

'No, he reminded me of Don.'

Annie nodded, rubbing her finger. 'I thought so too – so why does she love him, because she does you know?'

Tom shook his head. 'Because he's handsome, blond and she hasn't been through everything we have. We might be wrong. We were wrong to panic over those designs – Georgie was right. Anyway, didn't you ever make mistakes with your men?'

Annie blushed and looked at him. Oh no, Tom Ryan, you're not going to hear about my mistakes. She laughed and shook her finger at him. 'Just you make sure that you keep in touch with young Davy, not just Rob. You didn't tell him you were going away to the conference with Rob, did you?'

Tom blushed. 'I had to, he asked me to come down for an exhibition he was interested in seeing. I had to tell the truth.'

Sarah and Davy didn't go home for Easter, but pleaded pressure of work, telling Tom and Annie that the cushions had a market but there were too many down here doing it already and the armchairs hadn't taken off at all. She and Davy still sent samples because they were smoking as much pot and hash, taking LSD, and needed the money. But no coke, they promised one another.

Sarah had started driving lessons in February, and never smoked before them, though she often smoked afterwards as she made the others laugh about her kangaroo jumps, her back to front hand signals, her terror, but she did well and loved the freedom of it all. Davy wouldn't learn. 'It's too much hassle,' he groaned. 'And one lunatic on the road is enough.'

Sarah's letters home were short, but she did write or they would be down again, taking them back, hauling them from this life they loved. There was no anger in her, just nothing and she didn't bother to answer her mother's query about the turmoil at the LSE. What did they understand about students up in Wassingham?

In May she took her test and passed and they celebrated with champagne and LSD. In June they played at even more gigs and she and Davy bought a Mini to share which they painted purple and decorated with sunflowers. Increasingly Davy could barely stand, let alone play at the gigs.

'I'm fine, bonny lass,' he said when they played at the club behind their digs as heat beat down on the city at the end of June. His arms hung limp on stage, his eyes were glazed, the smell of beer was on his breath, the smell of pot on his clothes.

Tim hissed. 'Get him off, Sarah.'

She called into the microphone, 'Time for a break, kids,' and guided Davy down the stairs, feeling the thinness of his arms, the brittleness of his ribs as she put her arm round him to steady him.

'You mustn't drink so much with the pot, Davy. Come and sit down,' she said, shrugging at Carl.

She sat with them, watching Tim and Arnie threading their way through the tables, sweat dripping off them, staining their shirts. The air was thick with smoke and dark beneath the shaded lights.

She took Carl's hand in hers, asked whether he'd caught up with his work yet and seen Sam's phone message. 'Have you rung him back?'

Carl nodded. 'Just business, I'm seeing to it tomorrow. Could you write up the economic notes I've borrowed from Charles? I've a seminar on Monday.'

She smiled and nodded. Oh yes, she'd type up his notes,

wash his back, give him the time that her mother didn't give, that she herself had been in danger of not giving. 'Buy me another tonic and I'll walk barefoot to India for you.'

Carl laughed. 'That's not likely to be necessary, thanks madam.' He beckoned to the waiter and ordered.

'We should go to India in the summer, Davy, and see Ravi. We could all go.'

Carl laughed, passing the tonic to her, beers to Tim and Arnie, and a lemonade to Davy. 'I think he's had more than enough booze tonight,' he murmured, then raising his voice he said, 'Summer's a bit too hot for India, even if you head for Kathmandu like the rest of the weirdos.'

Sarah punched his arm lightly. 'Well, thanks for that, it's nice to think my boyfriend thinks I'm weird.'

Carl leant across and kissed her. 'You'll be an unemployed weirdo if you don't get back on that stage, but leave Davy with me.'

They played well into the early hours of the morning and she waved as Carl took Davy back to their digs at midnight. He was so wonderful, so kind.

She worked on his notes the next day, then sorted out the designs for the wallpaper, sifting through Davy's ideas while he slept, then their joint ones which were better, infinitely better. Sarah sat back, chewing her pencil, looking at the lines of Davy's sketches. They were uncertain, and there was no core to the design, no theme, no skill or talent, no soul.

She brewed herself coffee, drinking it as morning turned to afternoon and still Davy didn't get up, but then he seldom did now she realised and she wondered why she had not noticed before. She completed her notes, putting together the last of her end of term collection. She pressed the seams, wanting to show someone, wanting to send them to her mother, but there was no point, because they were not for the business. Annie wouldn't be interested, and besides, there was no love in her for her mother any more, and no need either.

She looked again at Davy's designs, walked to the window,

leaning her head on the pane, looking out at the plane trees in full leaf, the dusty road, and thought of the beck, so clean and clear, the black-eyed daisies, the meadow grass. She thought of the coke lines on the boulder. They had promised there would be no more coke.

She looked at her watch. It was six o'clock and still Davy slept and she walked quietly from her room into his, stepping over the sitar which lay on the floor, picking up his mug which he had dropped, seeing the coffee stains on the floor. It was so hot in here with no windows open, no curtains drawn. She pulled them back and opened the window. Davy lay sprawled on the bed and Sarah remembered how Tim had said he would be in trouble if he didn't appear at lectures more often. She hadn't registered.

The bed sank as she sat on the edge. He smelt of stale sweat and dirt. She hadn't registered that either. Now he opened his eyes, so blue, so gentle, and he smiled and put up his hand to touch her long hair.

'We promised to use no more coke. Have you, Davy? Have you used anything else?' Sarah said softly.

'I'm fine, bonny lass,' he said, smiling at her, his eyes no longer seeing her, closing.

'Roll up your sleeves, Davy,' she said but he no longer heard her.

She took his arm, unbuttoned his sleeve, rolled it up and saw the needle marks she'd known would be there. She rolled down the sleeve again, buttoned it, stroked his hair and couldn't see him any more for the tears were falling down her cheeks, staining his shirt. She bent and held him, and wondered how she could not have known before that this boy was now a heroin addict.

She rang her mother that night and told her that she and Davy would not be coming home that holiday, they were going camping in Cornwall.

'Just the two of you?' her mother asked.

'Yes, Mother, just the two of us, you're quite safe, Carl is not coming with us.'

'I didn't mean that, Sarah, really I didn't.'

But she did, Annie told Georgie that night. 'I'm just so glad they're going away together, getting some fresh air in their lungs, spending time with one another as they used to. Perhaps the relationship with Carl is weakening.'

Georgie looked at her as he put Buttons' great-grandson in his basket. 'If that's the truth, perhaps it is.'

'Oh, Georgie, that's so unlike you. Of course it's the truth, she's never lied to us, ever.'

Sarah sat in the dark that evening and when Carl came in she told him that she was taking Davy away because he was main-lining.

She watched the shock on his face.

'I don't know where he got it from or how he can afford it, and I don't know why, that's the worst thing. Why? Why? But I'll make him stop. Deborah's old schoolfriend was taken to a Scottish island by her parents and they cured her. She was new to it and he must be. He was clean at Christmas. Will you come?'

Carl squatted in front of her, taking her hands. 'How can I, I'm going to Morocco with my mother but anyway he needs proper treatment – you don't know enough. He needs to go home.'

Sarah shook her head. 'No, he won't want to go home. He'll want to stay with me. I do know enough, I talked to Deborah about it tonight, I know what those other people did. I wish you were coming.'

Carl kissed her hands. 'Poor little bugger, what was he thinking of? Where did he get it? Has there been any talk?'

'No, there's nothing. Tim doesn't know and I can't find Arnie but none of that matters, it's just Davy that's important.'

Carl kissed her and held her gently and she needed the

322

strength of his love at that moment more than she had ever needed it from anyone.

CHAPTER 20

Sarah drove through Somerset and Devon, then over the Tamar Bridge into Cornwall, heading always onwards, wanting to put as much space behind them as possible.

'We need to be as far from London as we can. Deborah said we need a different environment,' she told Davy, who sat with beads of sweat on his forehead, his nose running, his eyes too, his mouth opening and shutting in prolonged yawns. They stopped on the moor and she looked away as he rolled up his sleeve, tightened the fixing belt round his upper arm to pop his veins, and inserted the needle. He pushed the plunger, withdrew the needle and passed it to her.

She bleached it and put it in the box he kept at his feet, seeing the blood trickling down his arm, the haze coming into his eyes. She looked at her watch, five o'clock, they'd be at Polperro in an hour. Deborah had rung her farmer friend and he expected them by six. The sun was still hot and the shadows were long. Please God make it stay fine, if only to put the tent up.

'Don't tell him why you're there, for God's sake,' Deborah had said. 'Just remember, weaker and weaker doses, and then cold turkey. God help you. It'll take weeks before he's ready to come back.'

They drove on but she stopped at a pub for lemonade and pasties, bringing it outside to one of the tables, wanting Davy to eat. 'Not hungry,' he murmured, leaning back on the bench, his head loose, his limbs too.

'You must eat,' she insisted, breaking his pasty in half, holding out a piece on her napkin. 'Please, for me.'

'For you?' he queried and then opened his mouth.

She pushed it in and saw the family at the next table looking at them. 'Come on, Davy, do it yourself.'

She broke off another piece and put it in his hand which lay limp on his lap. The pasty fell to the floor and she wanted to shout at him. She didn't. She broke off another piece and fed him herself – what did it matter what people thought? She stared back until they looked away.

They drank their lemonade and she walked with him to the lavatory. 'You must go in there, Davy. We're camping, let's have our last taste of luxury.'

He looked at her. 'A pub lavatory – we've come a long way, bonny lass.' His grin was the old grin, his eyes sparkled. She laughed and left him.

He was waiting by the car, leaning against it, his hands in his pockets, his shoulders so thin under his shirt. The sun was being overtaken by clouds, there was a chill in the air and he was shivering.

She unlocked the car, leant in and brought out his pullover, put her own on. 'Rain is all we need,' she groaned.

She looked at him but the sparkle had gone, there was just the haze. 'Come on, in you get. We've still half an hour to go.'

She checked the map, then drove on, missing the turning, reversing, driving down the track, bumping over the ruts, seeing honeysuckle in the high banks, smelling it through the open window.

'It's so beautiful, Davy. I'll get you better, I promise.'

She stopped at the farmhouse. The farmer pointed out the field they could use.

'You can stay in the house if you like, we've spare rooms.'

Sarah shook her head. 'No, that's fine, we love camping, we're all-weather idiots but I'd like to buy some milk, please, and eggs and butter perhaps some tomatoes.'

The farmer's wife bustled out smelling of newly baked bread. 'You sure you don't want a room?'

How could a drug addict take a room, how could he slump and sleep, and moan when the drug wore off, when there was no more and the cramps began? Sarah shook her head but bought the provisions, waving to them, glad that the far corner of the field was out of sight. That's where they would pitch the tent, overlooking the sea but sheltered by hedges.

Davy sat in the car while she took the tent from the roof rack, put the aluminium frame together, banging in the pegs, tightening the guy ropes, cursing as the rain began, feeling it soaking into her back, dripping down her hair.

'Blimey,' she said to Davy as she urged him from the car to the tent. 'Tim didn't tell me it was the Ritz. Look, you can stand up. Here's the cooker, and there's the bedroom. Sorry you'll have to share it with the staff.'

Davy said nothing, just sat cross-legged on the floor of the tent. She ran to the car, carrying back sleeping bags, loose sheets, boxes of plates, cups and food because soon, when the doses had decreased to nothing, they would not be leaving the tent for days on end.

The rain was pattering on the roof. She blew up the lilos and laid out the sleeping bags side by side. 'Sorry, you'll have to put up with me next to you,' she said, setting up the camping stools, taking his arm, pulling him up, sitting him on the chair. 'I don't snore.'

She lit the petrol stove and heated milk in an old aluminium pan of Tim's. She looked around. Everything was Tim's and she had kissed him when he brought them round but he had said, 'He should go home. You need more help.'

'No we don't,' she'd replied. 'He doesn't want to go home because they won't let him back but I'll get him well, then keep an eye on him.'

She poured the milk on to the cocoa, stirring it, watching the blobs of cocoa rise to break on the surface.

'One or two?' she called above the rain.

Davy didn't answer so she put in one and carried it to

him, watching as he took it in two hands. 'Hold it tight.'
There was no ground sheet and she could smell the grass.

She cupped her own and sat next to him. 'D'you remember putting the sheet over two sticks at the beck, there was the same smell.'

Davy said nothing, the mug was tipping over in his hand. She took it from him, emptied both drinks on to the grass. She poured water into the bowl.

'Wash,' she said.

He did.

She peeled his clothes from him and couldn't bear the thinness of his body, the scarred veins of his arms, the scabs.

'Into the sleeping bag,' she murmured, standing at the opening to the inner tent until he was comfortable.

She washed, undressed and lay beside him, sleeping lightly, hearing the rain, Davy gasping beside her, turning, and with dawn there came the moans, the sweat on his forehead. She handed him a syringe with a decreased dose.

She cooked breakfast, bacon, eggs, tomatoes. He ate little. The rain was still strumming lightly on the tent.

'More like a sitar than a guitar, sort of fragile, like your music. Would you like to play, shall I bring it in from the car?'

Davy shook his head, sitting in his sleeping bag, his plate on his lap, the bacon congealed.

'Get dressed, Davy.'

He did.

The rain stopped and she tied back the tent opening, stepped barefoot into the wet grass. 'Come out here, Davy.'

He came.

The sea was grey, the sky too and there were white tops, rolling and rolling to the shore. She looked towards the small bay to the left. 'We'll swim when you're better.' Polperro was to the right but too deep in the valley to be seen. She felt the wind lift her hair, tasted the salt on her lips, took Davy's hand and held it tight. 'Yes, we'll swim.'

They wrote cards which she had bought at the pub – to Gracie and Tom, Georgie and Annie.

'Write three, Davy.' Deborah had said that while withdrawing all life stopped except survival. She'd post them when she could.

She lit a joint, counting the number she had in the sandalwood box. They would need them for withdrawal.

There were seagulls circling, screeching, blackberry flowers in the hedge. 'Draw this, Davy.'

He couldn't. He just sat in the sun until the stomach ache came again and sweat beaded his forehead and this time she wouldn't let him have another fix immediately.

'Not yet.'

'I want it,' he moaned.

'Not yet, we've got to do it like this.'

He stood up and grabbed her arms. 'I want it.'

'No.'

He turned from her, his hands to his eyes. 'I need it, my eyes hurt, my belly hurts. Give me some.'

He was stumbling from her into the tent, lying down on the sleeping bag.

'Soon,' she said, sitting in the entrance, knowing that he watched her every breath, her every move. She looked at her watch. Another hour – just another hour. This is how the girl's parents had done it, but there'd been two of them. She put her face in her hands. Carl, couldn't you have told your mother to go alone?

Davy was quiet, lying with his face to the tent wall, his hair deep copper against the lilo, his sweat staining dark beneath his head. He turned. 'Please, give it to me.'

His eyes were dark, desperate, in pain, his skin sunk blue. 'For Christ's sake, you bitch, give it to me.'

She rose and said, 'Another half an hour.' He stood, then fell as the lilo shifted beneath him. He crawled towards her, on the ground, grabbing for her leg. 'Give it to me.'

She shook her head, prising his fingers from her. He

grabbed her hair then, pulling it, his lips thin, twisting his fingers in it, pulling again and again. 'Give it to me.'

She pushed him back and he fell and didn't rise, just lay there with his legs pulled up. Deborah had said this would happen too but the tears were falling because of the pain in her scalp and the sight of her cousin in ruins at her feet.

Annie read their card the next week, sitting in the kitchen with the door open on to the yard.

'It looks so lovely,' she called to Georgie, turning it over, looking at the fishing village, the crowded cottages, the small harbour. 'They say they're having a lovely time – mixed weather, lots of swimming when the sun comes out, lots of pasties.'

'Just what they need,' Georgie called back. 'Any chance of a beer, it's hot out here with me head stuck up a pigeon loft.'

Annie laughed, made herself a coffee and poured Georgie a beer, carrying them out, handing him the card as well.

He said, 'You're right, it's a canny place. Makes me wish we were there.'

Annie sat on the back step as Georgie perched on the old stool. 'Could we, do you think? I mean we could take a week off, drive down, surprise them.'

Georgie was looking at the froth on his beer, holding it up to the sun. 'Bye, you've got a head on this, Annie, what'd you do, give the bottle a good shake before you poured it?'

'That's the problem isn't it, my love, you can't get the staff these days, can you? You'll just have to sack me.'

He was laughing, scooping the froth off with his fingers and shaking it on to the ground, then drinking, lifting his face to the sun. 'It's an idea though. We could drive down in two days, find Polperro and then try and locate them.'

Annie reached for the card. 'They don't say where they're staying. How big is Cornwall?'

'Big, when you're trying to find two kids.'

Annie stretched out her legs, kicked off her shoes. 'I wonder whether they'd want us, they sound so happy, so well – perhaps we'd be interfering – perhaps we'd better leave them to it.' She wanted to go, to spend time with her daughter to laze in the sun, swim, eat pasties in pubs and talk of nothing very much, just be there, but it was crazy. Two cousins had just taken off, dusting the city from their heels, they didn't want parents popping up at every available opportunity. 'Yes, we'd better leave them but if they can be by the sea so can we. Come on, I'm packing a picnic. Finish the birds and we'll take Bet to the coast.'

Tom and Gracie came too and they parked behind the dunes, walked across sand which was hot beneath their bare feet, spreading rugs, propping up thermos flasks, beer.

Gracie and Annie walked with Bet to the sea, standing in it, cold against their hot skin, their words fighting against the breeze which swept their hair from their faces, laughing as children ran past, splashing them, taking the breath from them as it hit their bellies.

'Little devils,' Annie said, thinking of Sarah at that age, always with Davy, back with Davy now.

'They seem happier,' Gracie said. 'Their letters have been so short, they've been busy but if they're having a breeze like this it'll blow a thousand cobwebs away, do them so much good. I remember feeling as though I could never get a good lungful of air in London.'

Annie held Bet's arm and they walked a little deeper, feeling the waves slowly breaking against their legs, the sand running away beneath their toes.

Bet growled. 'They needed to get away, relax, paint, talk. Perhaps it'll see that Carl off.'

Gracie laughed. 'You've never even met him.'

'I heard what Tom and Annie said and that's enough for me. I think he's on the way out, or they would all have gone together.'

Annie was silent, looking out to the horizon. God, she hoped so.

They joined the men for lunch, cracking and peeling hard

boiled eggs and talked of the holiday they would have next year.

'Wonder who's doing the cooking in Polperro?' Gracie said.

Annie laughed. 'No one, they'll be having sandwiches and eating at the pub, makes me wish I was young and carefree.'

It was the end of the second week and today there had been no more heroin, just a boy who cried out to her, swore at her, hit her or who lay still while she bathed his body free of cold sweat and wiped his chin of the saliva he dribbled, and the mucus which ran from his nose and eyes.

That night the stomach cramps clawed at his guts, his limbs jerked and kicked and she was bruised, but never felt the pain, just sat and watched and waited, and longed to do more, but there was nothing more she could do.

She bathed him in the morning but he pushed her from him. 'It hurts. It hurts,' he gasped. 'Please give me some. Please.'

'No, I'm going to get you well.'

He lay back and she lit him a joint, which he sucked, again and again, and another, and then he slept but it was so hot, for God's sake, Sarah thought, as she fanned his naked body, kissed his forehead, touched his hand.

She threw back the tent flaps, and undid the windows. At last there was a breeze. She took the basin out into the sun, pouring water over the flannels, washing, wringing, but they still smelt. She dragged the cooker from the tent and pumped up the petrol stove, putting them on to boil.

She tore off her shirt, feeling the sun on her back, pouring water over her body, dragging on a T-shirt, shorts, hurrying to the farmhouse for more water, asking if they would post the cards for them as they were shopping, feeling her shoulders straining as she lugged the water back, rushing to check on Davy. He was still there, lying motionless but the flannels had burned, for God's sake. She'd forgotten and they'd burned. She dragged her fingers through her hair, knocked the pan off the stove, kicked it across the grass. She wanted her mother, wanted Bet, anyone.

'Sarah,' Davy called. 'Sarah, help me, please.'

She looked across the field, to the sea, to the birds which wheeled above her. Oh God.

By night time the tent was fetid from his vomit and she sat outside under the awning, watching him in the moonlight because he could bear no light, not even the glimmer from the hurricane lamp. She rested her head on her knees, her sleeping bag unzipped and wrapped around her for comfort, there was no need of warmth on a night such as this.

All night she sat, or bathed him with towels she had ripped apart, took his slaps, his despair, his rage, his calm and knew that she must have slept because time had passed for which she could not account.

The next day was the same but this time she didn't burn the cloths, but boiled them properly, wrung them out, hung them on the guy ropes, drank coffee, but she didn't smoke a joint, because she mustn't sleep, she must only doze. She must eat. She cut bread, opened a tin of corned beef. He called her. She went.

'No,' she said. 'Hang on Davy, just a while longer. Hang on.' She lit a joint for him, stayed while he smoked it, left when he was asleep. There were flies in the corned beef. She just ate the bread and was surprised at the tears which ran into her mouth.

The next day she gave him a book on silk-screen painting to read.

'They're jumping,' he said. 'The words are ants scrambling, jumping.' He threw it at her. 'You bitch.'

She took the book and sat outside in the sun, reading it, listening to him rage, watching him crawl to the entrance, then curl into a ball as the cramps came again.

She sketched the honeysuckle the next day and the birds which called and wheeled, and wondered how she could survive for another seven days.

On the sixth day she talked to him of the beck, of the

cool water, the soft willow fronds, of the honeysuckle which surrounded them here, in this field, of her sketches which were not as fine as his.

'We'll sketch soon, both of us. Not long now Davy.'

He rolled over and looked at her then. 'I want to die. I need it or I shall die.'

She shook her head and looked into those violet eyes which were not the eyes of Davy, but of someone she didn't know. 'You'll die if you do take it.'

His abuse followed her but she just turned her face to the sun as she left the tent, picked up her pencil and drew the headland with its wind-whipped gorse, and then picked a sprig of honeysuckle and sketched each leaf, petal, stamen, listening all the time to his foul mouth, and then his pleadings, and then his sobs.

She took him water as the sun went down and he told her that when his eyes were closed they stayed open and looked into the back of his head and all he needed to be better was a fix, just one.

By the eighth day his skin was yellowing, his hands shaking, his body shivering and Sarah wondered how all this had happened. 'Why?' she asked. 'Why?'

'Because it takes me to a better world.'

She looked at him and thought of the boy he'd been and walked into the sun. She drew the blackberry flowers meticulously, carefully, again and again, because she didn't want to think any more.

By the ninth day the vomiting had ceased.

'I hurt with a deep, deep ache,' he said, reaching for her hand.

'So do I, Davy,' Sarah whispered.

The next day he sat up and took the flannel from her and wiped down his own body, hiding his nakedness beneath the sheet, accepting the tea she gave him, drinking it without vomiting, then he slept for hours, coming to her as she sat at the entrance, the moon soft in the sky.

'Will I ever stop needing a fix, Sarah?' he said, standing there, looking out across the sea.

'Deborah's friend has, but you have to really want to stop, bonny lad.'

She looked up at him.

'Have I been very . . . difficult?' he asked, still looking at the sea.

'No, you've been grand.' Sarah laid her head on her knees, feeling her shoulders relax for the first time since they'd been here.

The next day she posted another card, washed her hair, plaited it, feeling its weight between her shoulders, cooked bacon and eggs. Davy ate a little, sitting under the awning, out of the sun because it still hurt his eyes, his skin.

'Would you like to swim?' she asked. 'There's a track down the cliff?'

He shook his head. His muscles felt as though they'd been hammered, his bones as though they had been cracked, his skin as though it had been peeled.

She handed him his sketch pad and pencil, brought him honeysuckle but instead he drew the tent, the stove, the Mini, her. The next week the weather was cloudy and he drew the sky, the sea and Sarah in her flares lugging water back from the farmhouse.

'Soon, my lad, you'll be fit enough to carry these, not just that little bitty pencil,' she said, smiling gently as she dumped them by the stove. She poured water into a bowl, rinsed out a flannel and wiped his forehead. But not fit enough for a long while she thought.

At night he was restless, still needing heroin but no longer cursing her, no longer needing to be watched every minute of every day, and so she slept and in the day they talked of the beck and he drew it. They talked of India and he drew Ravi at his clinic, or as he imagined it.

'We'll go one day, when we've finished our degrees. It would be interesting. Think of all the designs, the colours,

334

the cotton,' she said. 'It'll give us time to think about what we really want to do.'

They walked around the field slowly and sketched the valerian, the lichen on the boulders.

'Ravi said the landscape as you fly into Delhi is like lichen on a stone. He said the colours of the land are muted, a perfect backdrop to the richness of the cottons.' Davy picked at the lichen. 'You're right, perhaps one day we should go.'

The days passed and there was time to talk of the art of Andy Warhol, of the new wave architecture.

'One day I shall go and see the Sydney Opera House, it will be wonderful when it's finished,' Davy said.

There was time to do nothing, say nothing, just be together as they had been long ago. At the end of July they walked down the cliff path to the beach, easing themselves into the water alongside children who splashed and screamed. She stayed with him as they swam because he was still so weak, but stronger, definitely stronger.

He turned on to his back, kicking his feet, moving his hands and she did the same, feeling the water lapping at her face, over her breasts. Where was Carl now? She turned and trod water. It was the first time she had thought of him for so long.

They ate hard-boiled eggs on the beach and then climbed slowly back up the cliff path, their skins tight from the salt, their shoulders sore from the sun. She rubbed lotion on him and he on her and they sat cross-legged on the grass as day became night and talked of the beach above Wassingham, the seaweed they had chased one another with, the dreams they had had.

She looked at him. 'They've come true. We're at college, in London and it will be all right now. We'll play in the group, you'll do your silk painting. But not in Wassingham. We can't go back can we, not after the "market research", not after everything.'

She pulled at the grass. 'That's what made you take drugs, wasn't it?'

Davy looked at her, saying nothing for minutes and then he shrugged. 'Who knows what makes people do anything – perhaps it's the thought of being suffocated.'

She nodded. She knew what he meant, Wassingham and their families took the breath from around them.

He continued. 'And perhaps it's always failing. I wish I was like Rob, political, brave, standing in the front line, just like Da. I don't know how they do it, all those police, standing there. Those fascists with Da, I couldn't have done it. I froze at the bus stop that day in Wassingham, so I know. I'm so proud of him. I'd love him to be proud of me.'

'He is, he really is. He loves your art.'

The next week his skin was tanned and there was flesh on his bones and laughter burst from him as he chased her around the cove with seaweed, draping it around her neck when he caught her, dragging her back into the sea, ducking her, being ducked by her. It was as though he'd never been ill, Sarah thought, or almost, because he still shivered, still craved the drug in idle minutes.

By mid-August they were swimming each day and there was laughter in both of them as they basked on the sand and ate pasties from the wooden café at the rear of the beach, or played their guitars outside the tent deep into the night, feeling the wind on their backs, hearing their voices in harmony.

In the last week of August they packed the car, paid the farmer and drove to the 'Festival of the Flower Children' at Woburn Abbey.

'We need to go somewhere like this, Davy,' she said. 'Just to see how you cope. I don't want us going straight back to London, in amongst the old scene, without you feeling confident. I'll be with you here, I can help if you need it.'

She touched his hand and he held it. 'It's been like old times,' he murmured.

Sarah nodded, changing gear. Yes, it had and she remembered the sound of his laugh on the beach, the feel of the seaweed and felt a deep ache and didn't know why.

They slept on the ground with the rest of the hippies, smelling the joints all around, smoking a little, but not much because Davy now relished the taste of food, the smell of the grass – all of which had been lost to him since heroin.

They listened to the music, joined in the dancing, wove flowers in their hair, painted their faces, but didn't trip. They didn't need to, not today, not in the sun as they danced and talked of peace and all the love that there was in the world.

She walked to the lavatory tent with him. 'If you're long, I'm coming in, so it's your fault if all the men have to run out screaming,' she said, laughing, but she meant it.

'I'm fine now. I want to be better. I want to stay like this for ever,' he said as they walked through the dancing bodies, or stepped over bodies loving on the grass.

She asked him again that night where he had bought the heroin. 'Just a mate,' he said.

'What will you do when you see him again?'

'Nothing, I've told you, I don't need it any more. I'm me now. I'm happy. I don't need it.'

They looked at the fashions, the bells, the beads, the multi-coloured clothing.

'If we go to India we can bring back some of their cottons. Look at these colours, it's really catching on in a big way,' Sarah said, drawing an overskirt of muted blue over an underskirt of vibrant purple.

'You've just got a thing about purple,' Davy said, quickly sketching the detail of a silk-painted design. 'That'd look better.'

'Cost a bit too.'

'There's money around, and I still think we could adjust the technique to work well on cottons. Think of that sari Prue sent you, it's wonderful.'

They played fragile melodies on their guitars and the other kids danced around them, singing with them long after the light had died as they picked out the tunes of *San Francisco, (Flowers in your hair), Strawberry Fields Forever, Mellow Yellow.*

They left on the third day, along with everyone else,

winding in a long trail from the Abbey, with flowers still in their hair and beads which a girl had given them.

They approached London and she looked at him, gripped his hand. 'Ready?' she asked.

'Ready.'

They sent off for visas for India on their return and she sewed long shirts for him, and skirts for her, cutting up Prue's sari, using it as an overskirt, preferring the floating drifting length to the minis she'd been wearing.

They worked all day on their projects and notes. They ate in pubs, drawing out money from their joint account.

'There's plenty left,' she said, as they finished their lagers, and twisted spaghetti round their forks, splashing the bolognese on their chins.

They sent up Indian designs to Annie who loved them.

. . . and yes, I think it would be a wonderful idea to travel to see your friend Ravi, you and Davy will get so many ideas from that country. It's so very different. I know we've talked about it but you need to see for yourself.

Carl returned at the beginning of October, knocking on her door, coming in, scooping her from the chair, his lips and tongue hungry on her mouth. She pushed away from him. 'He's fine. It worked, Davy's better.'

His arms came round her again and his mouth was on hers and she pulled back because there was so much she wanted to tell him but he was pulling at her clothes, and so she held him to her although she would have preferred to talk, not love, but there was such eagerness in his eyes. His hands found her breasts and his fingers her crotch, and finally, his body found hers.

She talked then, telling him of the tent, the flannels that had boiled dry, Davy's courage, his thinness, his swimming.

Carl put a joint in her hand.

'No, I'm all right thanks.'

338

He took it from her and lit it, sucking it, putting it in her mouth. 'A welcome home present,' he insisted. 'And this.' He held up a bracelet. 'And this.' It was hash.

She smiled. 'I love the bracelet but we're trying not to take drugs. I don't want Davy getting back to anything.'

Carl laughed. 'This is safe, darling. This will just relax us all, nothing to worry about.'

She was relaxing and her voice was quiet as she told him of Woburn Abbey, the increase in Davy's confidence. 'It shows in everything, his art, his music, his bearing. Deborah said we had to get his confidence back and then he'd be all right.' She inhaled again. 'They loved his music at Woburn, so you see there is a place for his sort of touch.'

He passed her another joint, going next door to fetch Davy, handing him one. 'But only one,' Sarah insisted.

'I'll look after him now, you've done so much,' Carl said. 'I'm here to help.'

They played at the club behind their digs when Tim and Arnie returned to college and the audience fell silent at the skill of Davy's playing and the close harmony of their voices.

'You see,' she said to Carl as they walked home. 'There's no need for me to go solo any more, we can stay together.'

In November Arnie shambled into her room on a Wednesday evening telling them that he couldn't practise on Saturday morning as they'd intended because there was to be an anti-Vietnam demonstration at his college.

'We'll all go,' Carl said.

'No, we won't,' Sarah said, looking at Davy. 'There's no need for us to go – it's not our college, it's Arnie's.'

'For God's sake, don't be so wet. What were you talking about at that festival? Peace and love – only talk then is it?'

Sarah felt the anger rise because she had told Carl about Davy and his father.

He apologised that night. 'I'd forgotten. We won't go, I'll say we're too busy.'

On Saturday they put on scarves and coats and went with

Arnie, because Davy insisted that they should. 'Never let it be said that we're wet, eh, bonny lass.'

She put her arm through his, following the others to the meeting place, slowing their pace so they could be at the back though there had never been any trouble, Arnie had told them. But Davy was still too fresh from drugs for any of this, God damn it.

'Come on,' Arnie called, beckoning them forward.

'There's no need to be at the front,' she said, holding him back.

'Yes, there is,' Davy replied, his eyes dark.

The march began and they were in the fifth row, pressed between too many people. They walked slowly, chanting, holding up fingers in the peace sign, looking out for hecklers, seeing only support from the passers-by.

They sat on the ground in the road while a sociology lecturer talked of the obscenity of war, the hopelessness of the US involvement, this bullying by a superpower. The ground grew colder and harder and the police just stood in front of them, waiting until the cold soaked into their veins, smiling at them, joking with them.

'Load of bloody rubbish,' Tim said. 'I'm getting nothing from this but piles.'

He stood up as others were doing and Davy grinned at Sarah. 'So this is what Rob spends his weekends doing, is it? We could do a few more of these. I'll write to Da tonight.'

They ambled away with the crowd, seeing the banners held high, hearing the chanting, feeling hungry. They peeled off with others down a side street of small shops, following a banner, which suddenly dipped and disappeared. There was a scream and now they were piling up one on top of the other, and those in front were turning, pushing through them, rushing, knocking into them. Sarah looked at Carl.

'For Christ's sake, what's happening?'

He was standing on tiptoe, trying to see. 'Wait here, we'll go and find out.' He grabbed Davy's arm, pulling him through those who were trying to escape.

'No, leave him here,' Sarah yelled, rushing after them, forcing her way through, seeing a crush of black leather jackets, the bicycle chains that were being swung round the air, the punches. A gang had attacked the marchers.

'Bloody flower people,' she heard.

'Don't like war? Take a bit of this.'

A stone was hurled and there was Davy, still being held by Carl, still being dragged forward. 'Let him go, come back.'

Carl turned and saw her, let Davy go. She saw him turn to look at her, and there was blood on his forehead so red against his white face.

She moved towards him, looking for Carl. 'Get out, get away,' she screamed then looked for Davy again, but he was pushing through the scrum, running away, running. 'Wait for me,' she called, turning to follow him, seeing his face as he swung round. She tried to shake off the hands which held her.

'Leave him, let him go.' It was Carl holding her arm, but she still struggled to be free because she had seen the look in Davy's eyes.

Arnie came running from the front, his clothes dishevelled, one eye swollen. 'Come on, let's get out of here too.' They ran, with Tim catching them up, his shirt torn, Arnie shouting out, 'I can't understand it, there's never been any trouble before. Why pick us?'

Davy came back late that night and went straight to his room. She went to him. He was sitting in the dark, plucking the sitar.

'Don't turn on the light,' he said, his voice flat, slurred.

She knelt next to him, smelling the beer on his breath. 'I ran too, we were so frightened.'

'You ran towards me, I ran away,' he said, his voice calm. 'Now I want to be alone.'

She kissed his cheek, unable to forget the look of self-disgust in his eyes as he had run that afternoon.

'Your da would have been proud you were on the march at all,' she said, but he didn't reply.

CHAPTER 21

Annie looked up at the sky on 5 November, seeing the rockets explode in the air, hearing Betsy's soft laugh as she stood by Black Beauty's stable. 'I wonder if the kids have fireworks in London.'

Betsy shook her head, her breath coming quickly. 'Too busy playing their Indian guitars, what did you call them, sitals?'

Annie smiled. 'Nearly there – sitars. Gracie and I have been back to the shop in Newcastle where we bought their first guitars. They're getting us new sitars for them in time for Christmas. Tom's going to tell them about his decision to start a one-off silk printing division the year after next. Then it's there if they want to get involved. They might not of course but they're so talented and Tom can't wait to work alongside his son.'

'Took some time for him to wake up, didn't it?'

Annie smiled. 'I know but we all make mistakes. I know I have, but I never thought being a parent would be so difficult. How did you cope, Bet?'

Bet shook her head, moving slowly over to Annie. 'I didn't, lass.'

Annie put her arm round her. 'Oh yes you did. I remember you covering for us with Da when we hammered out those lead coins in the allotment for the fair. I remember you coming and holding me after I heard Mrs Maby and Francy talking about Mam taking poison. Oh yes, you did cope, Betsy, and don't let anyone tell you different. Now, inside

342

and get your feet up – do as the doctor said or he'll be round with a big whip. We've got to get this blood pressure down so no more chocolates.'

She squeezed Bet's arm, helping her into the warmth of the kitchen, loving her.

Sarah did enjoy fireworks on Guy Fawkes Night, laughing with Carl as the catherine wheel whizzed off its nail in Sam's London garden.

'Bit of a damp squib,' Carl shouted and everyone groaned.

'Davy would have enjoyed that,' Sarah said, taking a glass of wine from Sam.

'How is he, still off the hard stuff?' Sam ducked as a rocket exploded well above him. 'Damn things, don't know why I have them.'

'Oh yes, either Carl or I or one of the boys stays with him when he's out. He's with Tim tonight, but you'd have been proud of him at Woburn, Sam. He played so beautifully, the hippies loved him.'

Sam sucked his cigar and the smell reminded her of Uncle Don. 'Hippies don't buy records,' he said. 'We need what the market wants.'

Sarah shrugged. It didn't matter, she wasn't fussed about music any more. All that mattered was that Davy was well.

'You just wait until you hear him,' she repeated.

They ate caviar and smoked salmon and she refused LSD because she had work to do when she returned home, and she must check on Davy.

She smoked pot, enjoying the taste, the drifting, and nodded as Carl kissed her and patted his briefcase. She murmured against his cheek, 'Fine, go and do your business, I'll just stand here and wish I had a sparkler,' she smiled at him, caught his hand and kissed it.

Sam walked into the study, shutting the door behind him. 'My backer wants her in a proper recording studio by the New Year, what the hell's going on, Carl? The bum recording didn't work, heroin didn't. He's still there for God's sake, larger than life.'

Carl lit a cigarette, picking a piece of tobacco off with his finger. 'Not for much longer – trust me, we're almost there. I organised a nice little diversion at a demo the other day, should just flip him over. The rest of the family's out of the picture so she'll be ripe for the picking soon, then we'll all get our money.'

Sarah found Davy in his room, drunk, lying in a stupor on the bed. 'Must have been one hell of a party, bonny lad,' she said quietly as she eased his shoes from his feet. He struggled up, kicking her from him. 'Leave me alone.'

She laughed. 'OK, but you're going to have a head like a punch bag and a mouth like the bottom of a budgie's cage in the morning.'

She kissed his forehead and he gripped her arm and whispered, 'Better than a pigeon loft though.'

She was still laughing as she eased into bed beside Carl, feeling his arm around her. 'He's going to be all right,' she said. 'I thought the demo might push him over but he's going to be fine.'

Carl took Davy out the next night while she wrote up her notes, and then finished the long skirts that the girls from Arnie's college had ordered. Davy didn't get up the next day.

'Delayed hangover,' Carl told her as she cycled away in the morning.

In the evening he told her that there was a gig the next week. 'So Sam can hear the *new* sound, he'll tell us how he thinks it will go.'

Davy was too tired to practise much in the week, and when he played at the gig he was clumsy and the hard edge was back in the music. That night she checked his arms for needle marks but there were none.

Carl shook his head. 'He's just lost his touch, that's all.'

'He'll never lose his touch, he's too good. He's just tired, too much booze. He's not on heroin again, I know, I've just checked. I'm getting paranoid about this, it's ridiculous. I'll be ripping everyone's sleeve up the moment they have a runny nose, or feel knocked out.'

She couldn't settle, thinking of the change in Davy, in his music, what could she do? She smoked the joint that Carl gave her and sucked the hash, it made her sleep.

Carl took him out the next night, and the next and she was grateful, kissing him with passion, moving with him into the small hours of the morning, smoking the present he had brought her back, drifting because it was easier than thinking, than being paranoid.

On Saturday morning Carl talked to her of going solo but she shook her head. 'No, I told you, we do everything together and we *do* make a good sound – if only you could have heard us. But I'd rather not bother at all if it makes him this tired.'

Carl's voice was angry as he replied, 'It's not music making him tired. He's just weak, you know, physically, emotionally, look at the way he broke and ran at the demo. God, the booze he's put away since then – it's all too much for him, you'd be doing him a kindness you know. Tell you what, I'll bring it up when we go out tonight.'

Sarah laughed. 'Again, that's every night, no wonder he's so tired in the day. He's got work to catch up on at college, he was late in this morning, Tim told me. Don't be too late tonight, darling, we mustn't get him run down again.'

Carl put his hand on her arm. 'You're right. I just thought I'd take him for a light meal, take him out of himself. Come with us if you want to, but I was hoping you'd run up a shirt for Sam. I'm getting him interested in your gear – could be another opening for you and Davy.'

Sarah stayed in and worked, wishing that her parents could see Carl and the way he cared for them both. She smoked the joints that Carl left her.

On the Wednesday of the first week in December the phone rang.

Sarah ran down the stairs when Ma Tucker called up.

'It's a Teresa Manon for you, Sarah.'

'Terry, what are you doing in London – are you in London?'

'It's Teresa actually, and yes I am in London. Doing a Cordon Bleu course, you know. Mummy's idea.'

'Of course,' Sarah said.

'Thought I'd pop round Friday, catch up with the cousins.'

Sarah smiled with relief.

'Sorry, no can do. We're playing at Smokey Joe's, what a shame.'

'Lovely, I'll meet you there.'

'Wonderful,' Sarah said.

She told Carl that night, and he laughed. 'God, not another one of you.'

'Oh she's different. Our Terry's a one-off, but Teresa please. Must make sure Davy knows, he's none too keen on that particular little item.' She started to move towards the door and he grabbed her. 'Give the lad a break, he's having a rest – Tim's taking him out later.'

Sarah gripped his hand. 'Tim said he thought he must be taking too much hash, he thinks he's too . . . oh I don't know.'

'For God's sake, you're like a dog with a bone. You've got to learn to trust the lad, though he's so well chaperoned he must doubt that anyone does. Or don't you trust us either?' His voice was cold and Sarah hugged him. 'I just get worried.'

'He'll be all right. We'll put on a good show for the cousin and have a look at how he's coming along at the same time. I mean, Sarah, if he's not interested and is slacking off we ought to let him take a back seat. It's not fair to drag him to rehearsals if he's bored.' Sarah felt his arms tighten around her.

'He's not bored, I'll never forget his face at Woburn, he looked so happy. It'll come back, you wait and see.'

Davy went with Tim and Arnie to Smokey Joe's and was

346

sitting with Teresa at a table when Sarah and Carl arrived, listening to her talk nineteen to the dozen, smiling gently and, dear God, he looked as he had done when he was on heroin, but how could he be? He played as though he was. Sarah felt the coldness in her as they sat at the table in the interval, drinking tonics and she looked again at Davy's arm, but he wore his sleeves rolled up, and there were just old scars. Nothing.

She turned to Carl whispering, 'I don't understand, I know there's something wrong. Has he been doing coke?'

Carl shook his head, taking her hand, whispering back, 'I told you, I've been looking after him. He's just tired, bored. He doesn't want to play any more and he's had a bit of hash.'

Perhaps then, they should stop these gigs, all of them, though she didn't say that, not yet. She would tell him tomorrow because she didn't want to play without Davy, but neither did she want to drag him down as it was doing.

Teresa was telling Tim about the profiteroles they had made today, and how Daddy loved them.

'How did you get my phone number, Teresa? I keep meaning to ask you.'

'Daddy gave it to me. I suppose he got it from your mother – how is your mother? Still nicking people's houses from under them?'

Teresa was smoking a joint which Carl had given her, her lips were glistening and her breath smelt of gin. Sarah said, 'My mother doesn't nick houses. She owned it in the first place, you always seem to forget that.'

Her voice was tight with rage and she wanted to slap this stupid drunken girl.

Carl pressed her shoulder. 'Joe wants you back on.'

She shrugged him off, then felt sorry. She looked at Davy lolling next to Teresa.

'Take him home,' she begged Carl. 'We'll talk about it in the morning. I'm due to finish at two.'

She, Tim and Arnie played, and Sarah's voice was rough

with anger at her cousin but why? She didn't like her mother, did she? She looked for Davy, not knowing what the hell was going on, but they were going, Teresa too, and now there was more rage and fear because Carl was smiling, his hand was on Teresa's back.

They played until midnight only and by then her throat was raw and her feet swollen but the applause was loud.

'I'll pay you until two. You were good but we've got this Blues group who want to do a couple of hours. You'd do even better on your own,' Joe said, paying her.

'I don't like being on my own,' she snapped, walking out of the club, her eyes stinging from the smoke, looking for a taxi. Where the hell were they all?

'Coming on to a club?' Tim called to her. She shook her head.

She started walking, looking over her shoulder, hailing one. It stopped. 'Hurry please,' she said, telling him her address.

Davy's door was ajar, she pushed it open, turned on the light and saw him lying on the bed, a syringe dangling from his ankle vein. She moved so slowly towards him, her arms like lead as she touched him. 'Who gave this to you Davy? Who?'

He turned to her, his eyes opening slowly, his mouth in a gentle smile. 'He's so kind to us, always so kind.'

'Who, Davy?'

'Why, Carl, of course, he helped me. He's got it in his case. It's always in his case.'

She touched his cheek and let him lie quietly now, but took out the syringe, bleached it, put it away in his box, cleaned up his ankle and only then went to Carl's room.

She tried the door quietly. It was locked. She inserted the key that he'd given her so long ago, turned it, then the handle and entered.

Teresa was in his arms, both were naked, groaning, heaving, their skins sheened with sweat in the lamplight. She threw the key on the bed. It glinted.

348

Carl saw it, saw her, started up. 'I thought you were staying until two?'

He pushed Teresa away, throwing her clothes at her. She stared at Sarah, then laughed. 'I rather like your golden boy.'

'Get your bloody clothes, Terry, and get your stupid little backside out of here, or do you want to end up a junkie too?'

She stopped and threw the girl's shoes at her, not looking at her now, only at Carl who was scrabbling for his pants, and trousers. 'Get out, I said.' Sarah shrieked now. 'Or I'll tell your bloody father.'

Teresa stopped dead at this, then scrambled into the rest of her clothes. 'Don't tell him, Sarah. Please don't. I'm sorry,' the girl was edging past her.

'Get out you little fool and stay away from filth like this, you'll save yourself a lot of grief.'

Carl stopped, his trousers almost on. Sarah heard the door slam behind her. She moved towards him. 'Why have you tried to destroy him? Why?'

Carl brushed back his hair with his hand. 'Come on, darling. I'd had too much to drink, Terry was coming on strong, I'm sorry, I only love you, you know that.' He moved towards her. She pushed him away.

'Why did you give him drugs?'

Carl looked amazed. 'Me, drugs. He's not on drugs, is he? We took such good care of him.'

She looked around the room, looking for the briefcase. There, by the window. She dived for it, clicked it open. There were the packets, the syringes, the fixing belts, the pills, the uppers and downers. He was moving in on her. 'Put the case down, Sarah. Don't do anything stupid.'

She stood with it poised at the lower pane. 'One shove and it goes through, Carl. Why?'

He shrugged. 'Because I wanted you, loved you and you wouldn't leave him alone so we could get on with our lives.'

She said again, bringing the case back, ready to smash the pane. 'Why?'

His face was ugly with anger now. 'OK, you silly bitch.

Because I had a contract to get you as a solo artist and would you listen? Oh no, "we must stay together," ' he mimicked. 'So I gave him back the habit which you thought you'd cured, the big I am, eh? He was grateful the first time, more grateful the second. You only cured him so that you could still cling to him – never able to stand on your own two feet, were you?'

She lowered the case now, walking past him, feeling him grab her. She slapped him hard across the face and his hand came up and hit her, jerking her head back. She was glad of the pain, it unleashed her thoughts. She moved quickly now, along the landing, down the stairs.

'Going to phone, Mummy, are we? She won't come. When did she ever come? Only when she can use you. Just as you used that poor little sod in there.'

She dialled her mother's number, resting her head on the wall. She heard Annie's voice.

'Mum,' Sarah whispered.

Annie said, 'Thank God you've rung, when are you coming, we need you, it's – '

'Mum,' Sarah cut across her. 'I need you here. You said you'd come if I ever needed you.'

'But darling, we can't come, we left a – '

Sarah put down the phone, feeling the anger surge again. Carl called over the banister. 'Didn't think she'd come, did you? Has she ever come? She rang earlier you see, some crisis with a strike. Can't leave dear old Tom on his own. Wanted you to ring her.'

Sarah ran up the stairs now, pushing past him, dragging out her rucksack, shoving in her clothes, pass book, passport, papers, money, address book. She rushed into Davy's room, and packed his things, shaking him awake, slapping him, feeling the blood from her own swollen lip.

She pushed him before her down the stairs, dragging the rucksacks, stopping, saying to Carl, 'What'll you do now you've got no solo singer, now you've messed up the life of

350

a lovely boy?' She was no longer quiet, she was shouting with rage, spittle spraying on to his shirt.

Carl shrugged. 'Doesn't matter – I've made enough contacts through all this, and had a nice bit of sex.'

She looked at him, her golden boy, and followed Davy who stood on the steps, arms hanging at his sides. She unlocked the car and pushed him into the front seat, the rucksacks into the back, and drove to the nearest phone box. She rang the police, giving them Carl's name and address, but not giving her own.

She started the car and left their area, her hands shaking. She stopped again, looked in her address book for the Dutch clinic that Deborah had told her about because she couldn't do it alone again.

'Davy, we're going away. We've got to get far away. No one here can help us, no one cares enough. Mum wouldn't come. Do you understand me? Mum wouldn't come.' She was shouting now, shaking his arm.

'I'm fine, just fine,' Davy said smiling at her. She put her head in her hands. I must think. The ferry. A map. Money. Customs. He'd need some heroin to last the journey but not enough to carry.

'Davy, how much stuff have you got left?'

He was lolling against the car door. 'Davy,' she shouted. 'Where's your fix?'

He shook his head. 'Carl's got it, he's very kind.'

She gripped the steering wheel, letting the engine idle. 'Look, we've got to get some more stuff, we're going on a journey. Have you any money?'

He had and so had she. 'Where can I get some heroin?' She kept her voice very calm.

He smiled again, his eyes unfocused. 'Davy,' she shouted. 'By the bridges, just by the bridges.'

'Which bridges?' she shouted again.

'The workshop bridges. Carl showed me.'

She knew now and put the car into gear, driving carefully, not wanting to be stopped, down to the bridges where the road was unmade with deep holes. She steered in between them to the end where the squatters had taken over the empty terraces.

'Where, Davy?'

He pointed to the one with shutters and she took him with her, knocking quietly on the door, smelling urine in the hall when it opened, buying one fix of heroin, a syringe, and one snort of cocaine. It was all they could afford.

She drove through the night to Harwich, stopping once for petrol, once so that Davy could snort cocaine, and she saw traces on his jumper, as though he'd been baking bread, and she remembered the farmer's wife, the sunshine, the hope. It was on his lip too but he didn't care, did he, because it was taking him away and she brushed him gently, kissed his cheek. 'We're on our own Davy, but I'll look after you. I always have, always will.'

She made the bank in Harwich phone their London bank and she withdrew all their money. She got a berth on the ferry, but before they drove on she pulled into a side street, looked both ways and handed him the syringe. 'It's got to do until we get there.'

He nodded, his nose running, his eyes too. She squeezed his arm to fix his vein, unable to look as he inserted the needle, depressing the plunger, withdrawing. She wrapped the syringe in newspaper then put it in the box, wrapped the box in old newspaper and put it into a wastebin.

Then they drove on to the ferry, and up the steps to the deck, leaning on the rail as they left harbour, and she wanted to see her mother running towards the quay, wanted her to see the boat leaving with her daughter on it, because she had left her alone in London for a strike.

Annie sat in Sarah's bedroom, watching Betsy's shallow breathing, knowing that she would die before the night was out. She held her old friend's hand. Ring again, Sarah, she begged inside. Ring again.

She called softly to Georgie. 'I should have told her it was

Betsy straight away. I just didn't want her to drive up here distraught. I should have told her. I tried but she put the phone down. Oh God what's wrong with her?'

Georgie stood in the doorway. 'Nothing much. I've just rung Carl, they've had a tiff, he says, and she and Davy have gone off to a club, would you believe. Selfish little buggers.'

Betsy died at dawn.

CHAPTER 22

The ferry rode the winter waves, rising and dipping, and they stood at the rail, their hair whipping their faces and Sarah was too cold for anger, for pain, too tired for thought.

They drove off the ferry at The Hague and now there was no time for speech because she had to drive to the clinic, looking at the map on her knee, keeping to the left. She went the wrong way round a roundabout. Oh Christ. Took the right road, driving fast as the daylight faded.

'The countryside's so flat,' she said, her voice tired.

Davy said nothing as the sweat beaded his forehead. She gave him three joints. 'Smoke these. Just two more miles.'

'Are we nearly home?' he murmured.

The clinic was white-tiled, clean, with ochre chrysanthemums in a bowl at reception.

Davy sat shivering on a grey leather chair.

Sarah said she must see a doctor. She would not leave until she had. She knew Vanessa Morgan who had been treated here.

A doctor came, his broad face tired, his smile calm. He took them into his office where a stove burned and delf tiles were set in the fireplace.

'You know Vanessa?' He spoke good English.

Sarah shook her head. 'I know of her. It's Davy. He's on heroin. I've tried to get him off, it seemed to work but it hasn't. You've got to take him. He's so important and I can't bear it.'

She looked at her hands on her lap, wet from the tears that were streaming down her face. 'Please, help us.'

He told her how much it would be and she nodded. She would sell the car.

He called in Davy, and sat him in the chair next to Sarah whilst he propped himself on the edge of the desk.

'So, Davy, you want to be rid of this addiction?' The doctor's hands were clasped, his voice was casual, his eyes serious and fixed on Davy.

Davy looked at him, at Sarah and then at the doctor. 'Yes.' That was all, but it was enough.

'Please wait out in reception. You may wish for a coffee?'

Sarah sat on the grey chair and drank the coffee and another, stirring in sugar this time, round and round, hearing the click of the spoon against cup, watching the spiralling bubbles, not thinking of anything, not feeling anything, not yet. There was no time.

The doctor called her in again after an hour. Davy wasn't there and now the doctor waved her to a settee in the bay window. He sat opposite.

'He's been taken to his room. You may go later. Now I have to tell you some of the things that I have told him. The first is that his addiction is recent, months not years. He is the same as many others. That I have also told him and it comes as a shock to the ego to learn that one is not unique.'

He crossed his legs, his white coat falling open. 'There is a way to get off drugs, and stay off. That I have also told him but there must be a great need within that person to rid themselves. You see, heroin is stronger than anything. It takes so much of your life, so much time. You come off and then what do you do with that time? You need help to come off. You need help to stay off.'

Sarah pulled out her cigarettes. He shook his head.

'That is also an addiction. It is very hard to come off those for some people.'

She put them away again. Her mother had come off, but then she had wanted to, because of the business. Always the

355

business and now there was some feeling, but she shoved it away, deep inside. Not yet.

The doctor smiled at her. 'As long as an addict believes he has any control at all over drugs he will never come off. Davy has come to that knowledge, but you knew that, of course?'

No, she didn't know that and now she looked down at her lap. Somehow they hadn't talked since Cornwall, somehow the days and weeks had passed and there had only been Carl, standing between them. But she couldn't think of him. Not yet.

The doctor spoke again. 'Working together, Davy and I will get rid of this drug. We will take it from him, but what will we put in its place?'

'I'll help. I've always helped. I always will.'

The doctor didn't look at her. 'You should speak to him, I think. He has been given methadone. He is coherent, able to make decisions. Do you understand me, Miss Armstrong?' He was looking at her carefully.

'Yes, your English is very good,' she replied.

He smiled gently.

He led the way to a room which was carpeted, clean, bright, but the lights were low now and Davy smiled at her as she stood by the bed and held his hand. 'We'll kick it, together,' she said.

The doctor looked at Davy. 'Shall I inform your parents?'

Sarah shook her head. 'No, there's no need, we'll handle this together.'

The doctor just stood there and looked at Davy.

He took his hand from Sarah and the smile was gone. 'Yes, please. I want them here, and then I want to go home.'

He looked at Sarah as she shook her head and clutched his hand. 'But we can't go home, I told you what she did. How can we go home? I'm here. I'll look after you, I always have. You need me. We can do this together.'

He withdrew his hand and leant back on the pillows. 'I want to go home. I, Sarah, me. This is my mouth, not yours.

356

You keep talking for me and I've let you, but I need to breathe, to think. It's you that suffocates me, no one else until I don't know anything any more and I've got to know my own mind, if I'm going to live. I've got to be free of you. Please, just go away.'

She looked at the doctor whose face was grave but kind. 'Now do you understand me?' he asked again.

Sarah nodded and turned to Davy. 'I'll go.'

She left the room and didn't look back. She slept that night in the Mini, then sold it the next day, taking the money back to the clinic, keeping half for herself.

'Will you go home?' the doctor asked as he walked with her to the door.

'I have no home.'

Tom had received the phone call at seven that morning. He couldn't speak as he listened to the calm kind voice of the Dutch doctor. Then Gracie came and took the phone and it was she who spoke, taking down the details, thanking the doctor, telling him they would be there as soon as possible.

It was Gracie who walked to Annie's because Tom was hunched over Betsy's table, wanting his mother's arms around him as they had been when his cousin Davy had died.

Gracie told Annie that the kids were at a drug rehabilitation unit in Holland, that Davy had been a heroin addict for some months, that Sarah was with him and now she couldn't speak either but crumpled against Annie, who held her, holding her tightly against the horror of it all.

Georgie stayed to arrange Bet's funeral whilst they flew to Holland, then hired a car to take them to the clinic. The doctor ushered them into his room and told them that the treatment had begun, the methadone would be decreased, the withdrawal would begin but not before they had spoken to their child.

Annie waited with the doctor as Tom and Gracie went into Davy's room.

357

'Where is Sarah?' she asked, understanding now why her daughter had needed her, hating herself for denying her.

'She's gone, I'm afraid.'

Annie looked at him, not understanding. 'Gone where?'

The doctor shook his head. 'I don't know. You must talk to Davy.'

Tom called her in some time later and she sat with her nephew, her brother and his wife and listened to Davy tell them of Carl and the drugs, of the psychedelic pictures he had painted and the cover-up they had carried out, of Cornwall, of the phone call, how Carl had said that Annie wouldn't come because there was another strike. How she and Tom had only come down after the pictures because they wanted them to carry out market research. How Teresa had slept with Carl and Sarah had found them.

Tom raged at Carl, standing at the window, banging his fist on the sill while Gracie held her son's hand and Annie sat silent, thinking of their trip down, the inflatable chairs.

'Where is she now?'

Davy ran his fingers through his hair. 'I sent her away. I wanted to go home, I wanted me family here. I wanted time to think. I just wanted her away from me. I didn't mean her to go for ever.'

Annie said, 'Do you believe we didn't care?'

'I did for a while, but then I didn't know what to think, or feel. And there was Carl, you see, always talking. We didn't know anything by the end. She doesn't even now. She's on her own out there and she's frightened of being on her own. I sent her away because I had to be alone. I'm sorry, Auntie Annie. I'm just so sorry.'

Annie walked in the garden of the clinic, looking up at the windows which were yellow in the low light of winter. The trees were leafless. Sarah, how could you use this boy as you did? she raged, anger tearing at her, you selfish little brat. How could you keep him down in London, in Cornwall when we could have helped? Davy's right, he needs to be on his own without you. She turned from the sun and looked out across the miles of marsh, her arms folded tight, until the anger died and then she wept, the sound harsh and loud because her daughter was out there, all alone and neither of those kids from Wassingham had stood a chance against Carl. And finally she wept because over all the years she must have failed her daughter.

Sarah walked along the busy road, her rucksack rubbing on her shoulders. She didn't know where she was going, she was just putting one foot in front of the other, walking away from them all, hating them all for the love she had given them, when they had given her none.

She walked until dusk and then a red van with huge marigolds painted on its sides stopped.

'D'you want a lift?' the young man drawled. He wore a band on his forehead, his hair was long, his smile lazy.

Why not?

The rear doors opened and hands pulled her in.

Tom stayed on at the clinic when Gracie and Annie returned for the funeral. He wouldn't leave his son, and it was right that he shouldn't, Annie thought. Betsy would have approved.

The days were dark and Christmas came and went. Sarah's sitar stood in her bedroom, waiting for her return. Annie and Georgie alerted all their export contacts, sending photographs of their daughter, telling police who said there was very little they could do, but what could be done, would be.

It didn't help, nothing helped their anguish, the sense of loss, the sense of self-blame, and so they worked. What else was there, Georgie said. 'Do we drive all over Europe, looking?'

'Yes,' Annie said, hunched by the fire.

'No, she could come here and find us gone.'

'Gracie would tell us.'

They took the ferry and spent a month driving round

looking, thinking they had found her, stopping girls who were not her, ringing home to see if she had phoned.

In February Gracie said, 'There's a card here from her.' She read it out to them. "I'm alive. Don't look for me, I'm with friends." '

They drove home, read the card, Italy. They alerted their contacts but Gracie was needed in Holland and so they stayed, installing an answering machine in the house, and one at the office for when they were not there. They hired detectives in Italy and then they waited but there was no lifting of the darkness.

Tom brought Davy home in the second week of February. Annie held him in her arms, smiling, hating him for being home, for being safe, but only for a moment, knowing that she loved this boy as if he were her own son.

They set up a silk printing division in the factory and it was this that filled Davy's hours, the hours that were empty now that heroin had left him. And Davy knew, as he lay at night in his room, or talked to others at Narcotics Anonymous in Newcastle that he loved Sarah, always had, always would, but that he had needed the time without her to understand that. But could he ever forgive himself for sending her away? Would she ever come back?

Sarah sat in the front seat with Fred, the US draft dodger, as they drove into Venice, smoking the joint the others had made up in the back.

'So, where're we staying then – is it somewhere your mother fixed up?'

Fred nodded, edging the van in through an archway, his headlights reflecting back in the mist. 'The things mothers do for their kids.'

Sarah shrugged. 'Don't knock it, she's taken good care of you, at least you're not being blown to pieces in that little bit of "trouble".' She blew her smoke up into the air, running her hands through her short hair, cut by Sally last night.

'Short, really short,' Sarah had commanded.

She felt it now, two inches left. They left the van, took a water bus, then walked down alleyways until they entered a courtyard. Ahead of them were double doors standing ajar. They heaved their stuff into the building. There was a smell of damp, and the plaster was crumbling on the walls.

'Not a palace but who cares? Good old Mom.' Fred led the way into a room on the right. 'Marco,' he called. 'Marco.'

Sarah followed him. 'Who's Marco?'

'He's the guy who looks after it for Mom.'

Sarah looked round at the heavy furniture, the carpets on the walls. Ravi's flat had carpets on the walls. Did his clinic? She shrugged, not caring. She was happy with her friends – why want anything else?

'You own it?'

'Sure, lots of Italians in America. We're some.' He bent and kissed her mouth, she kissed him back, liking the taste of him, that was all.

They slept on an unaired bed that night and he kept her warm.

They painted the next day, sitting in coats in San Marco Square and the glowing gold and white, the gold and grey of the façade took her breath away and her fingers moved, her mind worked.

'Kinda good,' Fred said, 'But like I said, you've got to have some soul there too.'

Sarah shrugged. She had no soul any more.

They drank wine that night which they bought in Venice, and spaghetti cooked by Marco. They sucked at the strands and the bolognese stained their shirts, their chins, and she wouldn't think of how it had once stained Davy's. He had sent her away.

They all took LSD and spun in the colours and the extension of consciousness and then lay in bed in the morning, all of them, and later played their guitars in the afternoon sunlight which was thin and cold, but what did it matter?

Tom left Wassingham for Newcastle a month after he had

returned with Davy. There was a chill wind and snow lay on the ground. Would the winter ever be over, would the waiting ever end? He parked his car and walked up the steps into reception.

'I have an appointment with my brother,' he said, shrugging out of his coat.

She spoke into the intercom. Don came to the door of his office, his hair sleeker, greyer, his smile cold. 'Come in, this is an unusual pleasure.'

Tom shook the hand that was offered, holding it for a moment. It was soft and flabby. Davy's was still so thin.

Don returned to his desk, gesturing towards the chair Tom stood by.

'Such a sad day when we said goodbye to Betsy. We were all most affected.'

Tom nodded, sitting quite still. He wanted to smash his fist into that face again and again.

'Yes, it was a great loss, especially at that time, with Davy as he was, and Sarah gone.'

Don nodded gravely, his hands steepled, his fingers against his lips. 'Yes, it's been a very bad time for you all.'

Tom nodded. 'It has been the worst time of our lives and it's far from over. You see, we don't know where Sarah is, we don't know what condition she's in. It's not fair, Don. Annie's had more than enough in her life.' His voice was level.

Don nodded. 'Ah yes, indeed, but life isn't fair – these things happen, especially with children who . . . well you know, headstrong children.'

Again Tom looked at that face, so empty, so cold. 'Sometimes things are helped though, aren't they, Don?' His voice was still level, his eyes steady as he held his brother's gaze. 'I know who Sam Davis's backer was.'

Don's eyes weren't empty now, they were scared and his arms had slipped from the chair. He said nothing.

'You see, Don,' Tom's voice was still quiet, level. 'You see, I talked to my son as he groaned and wept and pleaded in

362

the clinic for the drug Carl gave him. I listened to him in the weeks leading up to his discharge. I came home and looked up the names of the consortium because I knew that I'd heard the name of Sam Davis before.'

Tom sat quite still, watching as Don wiped his mouth with his handkerchief. His hands were trembling. 'I went to see Sam.' Tom's voice was conversational as he rose and walked round the desk and stood close to Don. 'He told me that you had found out from Annie where the kids were staying. Sam moved Carl in. You gave your orders – that on the pretext of creating Sarah as a solo artist he was to break up the family by any means possible. Sam knew Carl was a drug dealer. You knew too.'

Tom put his hand on Don's shoulder. 'I want to kill you, Don.' His voice was still level. 'I want to tear you limb from limb so that you suffer all the pain that can be suffered. I can't though, can I, Don?'

Don looked up at him, leaning back into the chair. 'You see,' Tom continued, 'we live in a civilised society where people don't ruin other peoples lives, or do they? What would you say, bonny lad?'

Tom shook Don's shoulder. 'What would you say, I said?' His voice was no longer level but full of hatred.

'I didn't know he'd get them on drugs. I was never told what was happening.' Don was rearing back, his head arched away, waiting for the force of Tom's blow.

Tom removed his hand, wiped it with his handkerchief, which he dropped in the bin.

'I remember others saying that – was it in 1946?' he said, standing with his back to the window. 'The thing is, Don, I don't know what to do with you because I can hardly believe it, even of you. You did know he'd get them on drugs, didn't you – now it's important that you answer me properly.'

The phone on the desk rang. Tom moved quickly, put his hand on it. 'Tell your secretary on that thing,' he waved to the intercom, 'to hold all calls until further notice.'

He waited while Don did so, his voice cracked and dry.

'So tell me now, Don, you did know, didn't you?'

Don patted his mouth again, looking round the room, then back at Tom. 'All right, I knew it was a possibility I suppose.'

'Just for the hell of it, was it, Don? Or to get back at us finally, since you hadn't killed the business. Kill the kids, kill the hearts of the parents? Hatred is a terrible thing. I should know. I feel it now.'

Tom sat down again, leaning forward. 'Did you know Teresa was with Sarah and Davy on their last night in England? She rang them, went to the club with them, went back with Davy and Carl. Did you know that Sarah found them having sex together?'

He stared at his brother as the handkerchief fell from Don's hand. 'She was high on pot. Where is she now Don? Still in London?'

Don gripped the table. 'It's not true, she's a good girl.'

'Oh it is true. I can get you the written statement if you like. Carl's in prison now. He wrote it for me. I thought I'd show it to Maud.'

Tom stood and walked to the door. 'Don't you come near us again. Don't you come near any of us again and see to your own family, Don, not ours.'

'The statement,' Don gasped. 'Maud.'

'I don't know what I'll do yet, Don. I really don't know.'

He drove to Wassingham and walked into Annie's kitchen where she sat by the range, her eyes sunken. She smiled when she saw him. 'You look like Rudolph,' she said. 'You could lead an army to safety in the dark with that nose.'

He stooped and kissed her. You could lead an army anywhere with your courage, he thought.

He handed her Carl's statement, watching as she pushed her hair back from her face, put on her glasses and read, waiting until she had finished before saying, 'I've been to see him.'

He told her all that had been said. 'I don't know what to do,' he ended.

'Nothing. Too much damage has already been done. But I hate him with all my heart because our children didn't stand a chance and we couldn't protect them, Tom, or we didn't, I don't know which it is.'

Sarah and Fred took the public boat to Torcello at the end of March, feeling the sun on their backs, their sketch pads and lunch in the bags they carried. They skirted the long brick wall of the island of San Michele, the white chapel and the blue-grey cypresses and she took out her crayons and matched up the colours, merging them, overlapping them.

They passed Murano, saw the Grand Canal, then shingle, then glass factories and she sketched the shape of those, matching the colours again, falling and rising with the boat, taking no notice of the passengers, of Fred.

The boat increased speed along the open avenue and Sarah sketched the *pali*, three, four, five to a bunch. She noted the electric lantern on one, the seagulls on another. They skirted the islet of San Giacomo in Palude and she sketched the trees choked with ivy.

They slackened speed and chugged down the wide canal of Mazzorbo, past ugly little modern houses with their varnished and glazed front doors, their varnished and glazed little families. She turned away.

They accelerated into Torcello.

Fred led the way, walking ahead of her along a towpath beside the stagnant green canal which smelt of drains and fish. She stopped and sketched the marshland either side, and some vineyards. It was flat like Holland. How was he?

She walked on, looking only to left and right, not thinking.

'There's honeysuckle and hawthorn in the summer,' Fred called.

There had been honeysuckle in Cornwall.

They arrived at the cathedral. She sketched its plain brick façade, its six blind arches. They moved inside and Sarah sketched the simple, rich interior and the light which came through small circular panes on the south wall.

'The wind's too icy from the north,' Fred said, looking over her shoulder. 'There are some peacocks over there, on the inner *plutei*. They symbolise the Resurrection and the new life given by baptism.'

She moved along, drawing their long, stretched necks as they pecked at the grapes in a bowl. Did she have a new life? She ate, drank, breathed, talked, slept, loved. She looked at Fred. No, she didn't make love, she just kept warm. No, this wasn't life – but what was life? She didn't know any more.

They ate lunch outside back to back, not talking, just eating, drinking. Afterwards Fred pointed to the campanile which stood a few yards from the east end of the cathedral. 'We should climb that at twilight but now will do.'

They climbed it and she sketched the island spread out all around, and the sea, and she noted the colours with her crayons.

'At twilight the Adriatic seems pale, to the south the lagoon can be purple or green, depending on the sky. It's kinda nice.'

She looked at Fred, his beard, his loose shirt, his hands which drew competently, but not like Davy. She shut her mind, sketching Fred as he stood there. Was he nice? She supposed so.

They walked back along the towpath, caught the boat and now the wind was fresh and cool and the light was fading. Another day had passed, thank God.

They disembarked and walked silently from the boat, through a Venice sunk in shadow, the light behind the buildings turning them azure, lilac, violet, their shutters hard-edged and black. They turned into the courtyard, past the marble well-head, the empty flower urns standing on the moss-covered paving slabs, into the house where the sound of guitars and singing drifted from above.

Marco came, his apron greasy, his face worried. 'There are men at the trattoria asking about a girl called Sarah Armstrong.'

366

That evening Fred took her to the station and put her on a train for Rome. 'Let me stay,' she said.

'Look, Sarah, it's been fun but I can't have cops checking up on me. They'll kick me out and I'll be in Nam before I know what's hit me. You'll have to go. Use the money for a plane ticket. Just get the hell away from here.'

'Please let me stay.' She grabbed his arm.

'Look, don't cling, you're a big girl, time you made it on your own. Don't always need someone else, for Christ's sake.'

Sarah stood at the window as the train drew out, waving, but Fred had turned and was walking away. He didn't look back. She was alone, quite alone, and his words echoed round her mind.

Rome was like London, crowded, chaotic, noisy. She stayed in a small hotel that had bed bugs. She walked the streets, looking up at the Spanish Steps, at the stalls in the markets, at the artists, the students. She looked into the cafés but hadn't the courage to go in alone and always Fred's words echoed and that night she dreamt at last, of Carl, of Davy, and woke in the morning bathed in sweat.

She ate breakfast alone. She bought a map and toured the Colosseum, looking up as a pimp sidled up to her.

'All alone? Come with me.'

She turned and walked away quickly, frightened, checking the map, going back to the hotel, lying on the bed. Don't cling. Don't cling. She didn't eat that evening. She just lay on her bed, thinking. She lay awake all night, all the next day, hearing Fred's voice, hearing Carl's. 'You only cured him so that you could cling to him.' She heard her mother say years ago, 'Let him decide. He might not want to go into art.' Again and again she heard their voices until her head ached with the echoes of them all and in the morning she had travelled many miles and many years. She went out again to the Colosseum waiting as a pimp came up. 'All alone? Come with me.'

'Piss off,' she said, staring at him. 'It's time I was alone.'

He moved away and Sarah finished looking at the Colosseum, before eating at a café. She rang the Dutch clinic from the café. The doctor said Davy had gone home. So far, there had been no relapse.

She walked to the river and stood there, knowing she would never be the same again because she acknowledged now the fact that *she* had decided that they must cover up after Davy's psychedelic pictures. She hadn't asked him. It was *she* who had taken him to Cornwall. It was *she* who had changed from Newcastle to London to be with him. It was *she* who had not listened to Ravi as he warned her of the drugs. She hadn't wanted to listen.

She had never asked Davy what he wanted. It was what she wanted that had mattered to her. He had wanted to go home and she hadn't seen it, or if she had she had ignored it because she wanted to stay, and now she knew that he had once loved her, and that she had seen it, and used it. She was as much a user as her mother and the knowledge broke her heart because all along it was Davy that she had loved, she knew that now. It had never been Carl.

She stood until the sun went down and it was dark and there was just the sound of the city around her. She walked back to the hotel and packed her rucksack, heaving it on her back, and took a taxi to the airport, knowing at last where she was going.

Annie listened to the Italian, straining to understand his broken English, her heart sinking as she did. Sarah had left before the private detectives reached her. Her friends had no idea of her destination.

CHAPTER 23

Sarah lay in the dormitory wondering how she could bear such heat for another moment. She rolled over and checked her watch. Midnight.

'Lie still,' the old woman in the next bed called out. 'If you lie still the heat is not so bad.'

Sarah eased on to her back, feeling the sweat running off her, smelling India all around her, hearing its music, seeing the shadows the street lamps cast through the curtainless windows. Ravi had been right, the landscape as she had flown into Delhi looked like lichen on a stone but nothing had prepared her for the smell, the noise of the streets, the number of people, the bikes, rickshaws, tongas.

In the morning the old woman brushed her hair, twisted it up into a bun, her arms scrawny, her fleshless skin hanging, shaking.

'I should have mine cut like yours. Have you had a broken love affair – my mother always said that those with broken hearts need to despoil themselves.'

Sarah looked out of the window at the people who were buying from hawkers, eating chapattis in the street, others were scrabbling for scraps in the gutters. Some were still sleeping in corners.

'I need to get to this clinic,' she said, digging Ravi's address out of her bag, handing it to the woman.

'Take a bus, number nine. It'll get you there. I'm going the other way. Every year I come – it beats Worthing.'

Sarah stuffed her clothes into her rucksack.

'So, you're working at a clinic – atonement, is it?' the woman asked.

Sarah heaved the rucksack on to her back.

'Something like that.' She left the room.

'Boil your water, don't eat food from the street stalls for the first week, then you'll be immune,' the old woman called. 'Remember, broken hearts can mend.'

She walked out into the heat and the dust and the noise, joining the stream which ebbed and flowed, bright-coloured. Men hawked, spat betel juice. Street vendors called, children begged, pulling at her long cotton skirt, she kept walking. Past silk wallahs squatting cross-legged on the ground, past the derzie sitting on an old durrie sewing on a hand machine. She stopped to look but she had a bus to catch and sewing was of no interest to her now.

'Carry your bag, missy?'

She shook her head.

An old Sikh in a white tunic and turban was weighing rice, lentils, flour, from baskets that stood on wooden planks. Their colours were good together. She should draw them but that was of no interest to her now either.

On past the betel leaf shop, the toddy shop, stalls where ghee and cooking oil were sold, on and on through the hot bodies, with the heat on her head, the heat beneath her feet, in her lungs – and everywhere there was the ordure of India.

Bikes were piled high on the roof of the bus, the seats were crowded, people stared but she turned from them as the driver lurched forward and eased into the sea of bikes, rickshaws, lorries. She looked out at the suburbs, peeling, shabby, dirty, the blacksmiths by their wagons, the VD clinic, the rickshaws which had died together like a farmer's yard full of rusted equipment.

She sat still because the heat was too much and it was only nine in the morning. They were out now amongst short scrub grass and there were flat-roofed houses squatting beneath the sun. She closed her eyes, feeling the sweat bead her forehead, then run into her eyes, her mouth. She felt the flies on her lips, everywhere, hearing them all around.

They drove and drove, stopping at midday for fuel at a broken-down shack. She shook her head at the food hawkers and just drank warm water from her bottle, standing beneath the shade of the awning, looking out across the plain which shimmered and danced and she could hardly breathe. It was only April.

They drove all afternoon and the woman who sat next to her, her body pressed too close, smelt of curry. They passed scrub, and the horizon danced as villagers squatted beside cow-pats kneading them.

'To cook,' the woman beside her said.

Sarah turned, surprised. 'You speak English.'

'Many do. I am having a little.' She smiled, slight against Sarah's European build. Ravi had made her feel coarse, huge. Would he remember her? Would he let her stay?

They drove past a fair. The bus stopped and everyone clambered off, buying food from the fly-specked stalls, and music blared from a loudspeaker tied to a tree. She ate nothing but thought of the fair in Whitley Bay, the cool east wind – Davy. Did broken hearts mend? She thought not and wanted to die, but that would be too easy.

They drove on until well after dark, when the driver stopped at the crossroads of a town.

'Missy,' he shouted above the chatter, standing up, pointing at Sarah.

She struggled through the people, murmuring, 'So sorry, I'm sorry.'

They smiled or shrugged – all stared.

She took her rucksack from the driver and walked towards the bazaar where old natives were smoking pipes, fruit and vegetables were being sold and derzies were sewing. Did nothing alter? She hired a tonga and now it was cooler but the mosquitoes were biting. The horse was thin, his hooves kicked up dust, it was in her mouth, her nose. The moon was bright and she could see to the horizon. They turned off the road, on to a track between fields until they came to the gates of a compound, the shapes of the buildings flat black against the moon.

She paid the tonga wallah, heaved her rucksack on to her back and walked through the gates, towards light which came from behind a building. She reached the entrance to the courtyard and stood looking at the women who sat on charpoys around a fire of cow-pats.

'Ravi,' she said into the silence that fell. 'Is Ravi here?' Did her voice sound as desperate as she felt? Did it sound raw with pain and despair?

He came to her, hurrying across the compound from a long low building. She stood, letting her rucksack fall to the ground, wanting to run to this man from her past but she didn't need to because he was here, holding her, leading her away out of the circle of light, away from the silence and the stars, holding her hands in the soft light from the moon. 'You came,' he said. 'I hoped you would. But you have come alone?'

'Yes.' That was all.

He looked at her and nodded. 'You are tired, but you are also different. We will talk tomorrow.'

She held his arm. 'No, I don't want to talk, I want to work. I want you to use me, please.' There was the sound of cattle moving, lowing, the soft voices of the women, and Ravi's eyes were gentle.

'You need sleep, come with me. I will use you, but – forgive me – perhaps not yet in the clinic.'

'I will do anything.'

Ravi nodded. 'Come with me, you need sleep, my dear Sarah.'

She followed him to a room beyond the courtyard. She sat on the charpoy.

'Wait here, I will be back.' Ravi left her and Sarah lay back in the coolness of the windowless room. Tomorrow she would work in the heat, the dust, the dirt, with the flies, until she dropped and at last there was a sort of peace within her and she closed her eyes and slept.

Ravi returned carrying chapattis and water. He stood over Sarah, seeing the exhaustion in her face, the shortness of her hair, hearing again the pain in her voice. Where was Davy, whom she had loved?

Davy stood in Annie's office, waiting until she had finished the phone call. She was so drawn, so grey and though she smiled at him, at everyone, there was always agony in her eyes.

Annie put down the receiver. 'Hi, how's it going? Did the design work as well in practice as in theory?'

'I think it did, Da's looking at it now. May I sit down?'

Annie nodded, leaning back in her chair. There were daffodils on her desk.

'I want to go and find her, Auntie Annie.' Davy said. 'I love her so much and it's my fault. I'm better, fitter, I feel like I did before I went to London.'

Annie smiled at him. He was fit, he was the boy they'd known, gentle and strong. She shook her head. 'No, don't go. Where would you look?'

'I've been getting all the names and addresses of friends abroad. I wrote to them all last night, telling them I was coming. I'll just comb the streets until I find her.'

'The trouble is, my dear, she just doesn't want to be found.' Annie's voice was quiet. 'We've had private detectives trying to trace her. They've found nothing. They've checked the airports in and out of Venice, Rome, everywhere. They've checked the airports into and out of India, America, everywhere, the seaports too.'

Annie touched the daffodils, the yellow was so brilliant. 'Wait until you hear from your friends. If they've heard anything, then do go. Please don't rush off, Davy, just stay until you hear, or we might lose you too.'

Sarah woke at first light, and heard the animals moving in

the byre. She lifted the mosquito net, eased her feet on to the dirt floor, searching for and finding the Indian sandals she had bought at the fair. There was a broken cane chair at the end of the bed. Her rucksack had been unpacked, her money, passports and address book were on the small table by the bed. Had Ravi noticed the second, false, passport and visa that the pimp in the Colosseum had provided?

She stood in the doorway looking out across the land which seemed huge, the sky which seemed even bigger. In the distance was a derelict fort, at her feet was dust and in her face was heat.

Ravi waved to her from the entrance of the courtyard.

'Come, Sarah, you must be hungry, but first you will need the more basic things of life. Maji will help you.' He smiled and beckoned to her.

Maji took her to the thunder box which her da had told her about. She shut her mind to her past and washed in bowls of water, standing behind the wall by the pump, stripping, throwing it over her body, letting the heat dry her.

She ate chapattis, drank water with the women around the fire, squatting as they did, her skirt in the dust.

'Ravi?' she said, feeling the panic in her. She must work, couldn't he see that? There was not time to eat or talk or feel.

They smiled and pointed towards the clinic.

'He will be here,' Maji said.

He came, his feet kicking up the dust, telling her that he had to go to the outlying villages for three days. His father was away and so a male nurse was in charge of the clinic.

'Do you wish to rest or to work?' he said.

'To work.'

That morning she took the four beasts out into the fields to graze, eating their dust, tapping them with her stick, looking across at the yellowed wheat, sparse and limp, the same colour as the huts. Within minutes the sky grew pale with heat and she walked on widening cracks. Did the cracks go

374

down to Australia? Was that how Annie's Aunt Sophie had gone? How absurd and who cared anyway?

She moved slowly in the heat and Maji gave her lime juice and salt to drink and said she must stop in the heat of midday, everyone did. She didn't want to but her head was bursting, her tongue swollen and Maji was calling her, so she came in from the fields and lay on the charpoy, her hands and arms and feet burned and blistered by the sun. Sleep wouldn't come, there was only Davy's voice, her mother's. There were only memories.

She brought in the beasts when the sun went down, carrying fodder on their backs, she carrying it on her head, as Maji did. The dust was no longer wheat yellow but deep ochre from the low tired sun – it cloaked her and Maji. She watered the beasts and cared nothing about her blisters as she sat around the fire with Maji, with Ritu, feeling her head aching, her feet burning, wanting total exhaustion, wanting more discomfort. Sleep didn't come that night, only echoes, and for God's sake she didn't want those, she ground out into the darkness of her mind.

The next day she took the beasts to the fields again and then squatted and kneaded the cow dung for fuel, carrying it in, dropping it in the courtyard.

'This is not for you to do,' Maji protested, shaking her head.

'Yes, it is for me to do,' Sarah said.

Maji gave her a basket then, but said, 'It is too hot, it is too dirty for you.'

Sarah said, 'I like the heat.'

She drank lime juice and salt and when the sun went down she ate chapattis with dal and sat with the women again, still smelling the stench of cow dung, and that night she slept a little but not enough. She did the same the next day and this time worked through the midday heat, ignoring Maji's pleas to rest. That night the ache in her head was too bad for echoes, for feelings, for anything and so the next day she worked in this way again.

375

Ravi came back as night fell, easing himself down from the old Morris, walking towards the courtyard. She was too tired to feel pleasure at the sight of him and that was good. She watched as Maji walked towards him and spoke quietly in the darkness of the compound. She watched as he nodded and then approached Sarah, taking her hand, pulling her to her feet, easing her away from the light of the fire.

'I need you in the kitchens tomorrow,' Ravi said, his brow furrowed, his smile anxious and Sarah knew that Maji had spoken of her fieldwork.

'No, I like the fields,' she said, her voice quiet.

'Please,' Ravi said, squeezing her hands. Sarah welcomed the pain on her blisters. 'Please, no one else likes to do it.'

'Yes,' she said at that.

'And then we should talk, my little Sarah.'

'No,' she replied, looking away from him, not wanting to see or hear the gentleness that came from him, because it opened up her heart.

The next morning she helped Maji light the fire and brew the tea, then scoured last night's pots with yesterday's ash and straw. She set new milk on a slow fire to make yoghurt and churned butter in an earthenware jar. She watched the sweeper brushing the verandah of the clinic, and the sun as it crept over the roof.

They mixed chapattis before the sun rose hot and baking, rolling the dough on a circular board, chopping fresh vegetables.

'For the patients?' Sarah asked.

'No, that is cooked over in the hospital, though many of the families bring food, if they have any. This is for the staff.'

When they had eaten she washed her clothes under the hand pump, using a block of hard yellow soap, which stung her blisters. She washed other clothes, boiled up lightly soiled bandages, rolling them in the shade of the awning, watching the queues forming for the clinic, seeing the heat shimmering, knowing that she needed to be back in the fields.

That evening she flavoured the eggs and dal with ground coriander, pepper and black cardamom and they ate by the light of a paraffin lamp, slapping at the mosquitoes, and so it went on, day after day. Now there was a pattern to the days that was comforting, predictable, safe – but she didn't deserve that.

'This is like any village, like yours in England,' Ravi said one evening as they all sat together round the fire.

'I have no village,' she said and the pain was so sharp for a moment that she could hardly breathe.

She washed and cooked the next day and the next and the harvest was brought in and the heat became even more intense and now she wasn't sleeping again because the work was too easy. Instead she walked up and down the courtyard throughout the night, counting her steps, anything to stop herself thinking.

'You will work in the clinic tomorrow,' Ravi said, as he ate his dal that night. 'You are ready, I think, and Maji tells me you walk in the night, instead of sleeping. Perhaps the ward work will help. Perhaps talk would too?'

His eyes held hers and she shook her head. 'No, I just want to work, not talk.'

She walked across the square the next morning, before the heat burnt the very air she breathed.

'We have pregnant women, we have children, men. All sorts. We can operate or we can just nurse,' Ravi told her on the verandah. 'You will work with Pitaji today. He will tell you all that you need to know, all that you need to do.'

He left her then and Pitaji smiled and walked before her into the wards which were wood-lined, white-painted. Fans whirred and moved the hot air.

'Here,' Pitaji said, walking down the ward, 'we have pregnant women whose bones, especially their pelvis, are disintegrating because they do not eat enough and so their babies eat their calcium. They cannot give birth normally. We try and feed them properly, we help them give birth but still

377

seventy per cent of their babies are diseased. They will become semi-invalids.'

Sarah followed him, looking at the large-eyed women. 'Can nothing be done?'

'How can we feed the world?' Pitaji pushed open the door at the end of the ward and stepped through into an annexe where a man was putting food into a huge pan.

'Can you dole this out to them? We give them rice, vegetables and lentils. Then yoghurt.'

Sarah moved down the ward with Pitaji, ladling stew into the bowls the women held up.

They washed the bowls later, as the heat beat down on the corrugated iron annexe before moving into a ward of elderly women. They distributed stew here too.

'You come to the clinic now,' Pitaji said.

Sarah stood behind Pitaji who wrote down the details of those who had queued since before the sun rose. One by one, they filed in, filed past, into the day clinic.

'Ravi's father is away, he is very busy,' Pitaji said.

'Can't I do more? I'm doing nothing. I want to be used.'

Pitaji smiled at her. 'Go with this man, take this form and see Ravi.'

Sarah walked beside the native, holding the form which she could not understand. 'Can I help?' Sarah asked.

Ravi read the notes, then looked at her. 'Yes, I think you can. Help Bhim to remove the foreign body from this man's nose.' He handed her the card. Bhim beckoned to her, leading her to the cubicle, washing his hands, telling her to do the same, then handed her a light.

'Please hold this quite still,' he said, taking an implement from the steriliser, patting the man on the shoulder, making him lie down.

Sarah held the light as Bhim dug gently, while blood and mucus ran. He said, 'This man is a stone breaker. It is a familiar problem.'

The old man's eyes sought hers.

378

Bhim said, 'Wipe him clean please.' He withdrew the pebble.

Sarah picked up a swab and wiped the old man's face, nose, lips. She smelt disinfectant and there was blood and mucus on her fingers. She dropped the swab, looked at her fingers and felt the bile rise in her throat. She swallowed, wiped with a new swab and collected up the soiled pieces as the old man stood, salaamed and left.

Ravi called through. 'Pitaji is returning to the wards now. Perhaps you could go too, Sarah.'

She walked into the heat, feeling it beat into her face, across to Pitaji. They bathed the old women, and the stench of their illnesses brought the bile to her throat again. They moved from bed to bed drawing back the sheets, sponging them, smiling, drying, moving on, but the woman in the last bed was dying. 'Just her face,' Pitaji said, handing her the last of the clean water, leaving her.

Sarah wiped the lined brow, smiled at the woman who did not smile back but lay with her eyes wide open, and there was no breath from her nostrils, no movement of her body, and Sarah dropped the cloth and ran from the ward, vomit spewing from her, on to the parched cracked earth.

She ran then, back to her room, lying on the charpoy, vomiting again, crying because she had never seen death before, never touched it, because that is what she had done.

Ravi came to her that night as she lay unmoving on the bed. He sat on the cane chair and took her hand.

'Now we talk,' he said.

'No,' she replied, her voice dull.

He gripped her arms. 'Sarah, you are in pain, you will harm yourself. You came here to talk, not to die, for heaven's sake.'

'I came here to work, not to talk, or to die. One is too difficult, the other too easy.'

Ravi looked at her and his shoulders slumped. He touched her cheek. 'Oh Sarah,' he said. Then left.

She sat up, not looking after him but at her hands which

379

had swabbed an old man, and hated it, bathed an old woman who had died. She had hated that too. She was just like her mother. Even where nursing was concerned she was like her bloody mother.

'So, where is Davy?' Ravi said and now she looked up. He hadn't gone as she had thought. 'Tell me, Sarah, because I shall not leave until you do.'

She looked at him, then back at her hands. She didn't want to talk, she didn't want anyone to know what she had done, but the words were coming, tearing themselves from her throat. 'He's alive but I nearly killed him. I used him you see, even at the very beginning. I clung to him because I couldn't bear to be alone.'

Ravi said nothing, just stood silently.

'I even changed colleges from Newcastle to London right at the start.' Her words were stilted, abrupt. Ravi waited but she said nothing more. Her mind couldn't produce any more words. There was just a darkness.

Ravi moved towards her now. 'Of course you did,' he said. 'You loved him, it is what anyone would have done, you just did not know that you felt this for him.'

The darkness was pushed aside at the sound of his voice and the words came back, harsh and dry. 'You don't understand. I cling. Fred said I did, Carl said I did. I used him, Ravi, I nearly destroyed him.'

She told him about the drugs, about covering it up with Tom and Annie that day, about Cornwall. 'I used him.'

Ravi was silent and now he reached for her hand. She felt his warmth on her skin, but it didn't reach inside her.

'Yes, you did use him, but it wasn't you, it was the drugs, it was the madness of the times – for you both. It was Carl. You couldn't think when your mind was blurred, when someone was pulling in another direction, dripping poison as he was doing.'

Sarah dragged her hand from his. 'No, it wasn't the drugs. I'm like my mother, you see. People aren't important, it's only our own needs that are, our own ambitions.' She lay back and turned her face to the wall and wouldn't speak any more.

That night she ran a fever and for the next three days the hate raged in her, for herself, and for her mother who had always put her business before her da, before her. She hadn't come. She hadn't come.

Annie took Don's phone call at the end of April. He asked her to meet him that evening. She walked to the allotment, past the bar, to the shed. He stood there, his face pale, his eyes uncertain.

She felt nothing as she looked at him. 'Well Don, what do you want?' He reached for her and she moved back. 'Please don't touch me, Don.'

His hand dropped.

'I want to say I'm sorry. Teresa is home in Gosforn. She's going to the local secretarial college. She didn't get into heroin, or cocaine, or LSD.' His voice broke. 'I don't deserve that luck. I don't deserve your forgiveness but I'm asking for it. You see, I know now a little of what you must be feeling. I thought for a moment Teresa was in danger, and my world crashed. It just stopped. I didn't even know I loved her until then. All I knew before was rage and envy for you. I was mad. You took back the Gosforn house you see. I went crazy inside. I just wanted to say I'm so sorry and that I've told Maud and she can hardly believe what I did, and now neither can I.'

Annie looked across the allotment. She had come on Good Friday and planted potatoes as she and Bet had always done. Sarah liked them fresh from the ground – translucent, tasting of the earth.

'Thank you, Don,' she said, turning from him, walking back towards the bar because what did it matter how sorry anyone was when her child wasn't here and what did forgiveness have to do with anything?

Sarah was weak when the fever ebbed and Ravi brought her

381

a boiled egg, because he had remembered that she liked them. He brought her tea too and talked quietly as she ate and drank.

'You must rest for a few days, you know. You have worked too hard. You need time to think, my Sarah. To come to terms with all that has happened.'

'No, I don't want to think. I want to work.'

He shook his head. 'You are too weak and I repeat, you need to come to terms with your life. However, I am going to another village today and I cannot leave you here because you will not promise me to stay on your charpoy will you?'

Sarah didn't answer.

'Then you must come with me.'

Her legs were weak as she moved towards the Morris and the heat drenched her. They drove silently as the plain unfolded before them and there were no thoughts in her head, there was nothing. How could he think she wanted to come to terms with anything? She knew all there was to know about the past, about hate.

They entered the village, driving past buffaloes which grazed on parched grass and wallowed in the pool. She stepped out of the Morris, following Ravi to the mud house, where people were already queueing. She stood with him, handing him forms, whilst Bhim, who had travelled with them, swabbed, bathed, comforted. They sat with the villagers as the midday heat rose and worked again in the afternoon.

At the end of the day, Ravi walked her round the village as the heat eased. They passed black-trunked acacia trees.

'The villagers make furniture and doors, tools and charcoal from these,' Ravi said. He broke two twigs, handing one to her. 'They make good toothsticks too. Chew it until it makes a brush, Sarah.'

She did, tasting the bitterness of the twig, stopping as Ravi did, turning round to look at the village.

'Everything on this land is used by the villagers. The mud is for building and plastering, the wood for rafters, hemp

382

fibre for charpoys, and so on and so on. But the young men are leaving, going to the towns, to England. The villages are changing. Their parents are so brave to allow them to leave. It takes courage to let your children go. Come with me, over here, Sarah.'

Ravi took her hand and they walked over to one of the houses. He spoke to the woman who smiled and showed him into the grainstore. 'Look at this, Sarah.'

She peered past him into the darkness and saw a loom. Ravi was close to her. She could feel his heat and that of the mud walls.

'The village women still weave daris for the family from the cotton they grow. People need clothes, and families need to be clothed, to be fed, to be provided for, my Sarah. Had you never thought of that?'

She pushed herself away from the building, walking back to the Morris. 'I'm tired,' she said. 'I'll wait for you in the car.' She stumbled and his arm was there.

'Yes, you are tired and we will go home. Perhaps when you have thought more, we shall talk again?' Ravi said, nodding to Bhim who was loading the boot.

But there were no thoughts in her head as she travelled back, just an anger that was growing.

The next day she rolled bandages, and then followed Pitaji into the children's ward, smiling at the children, telling them stories they could not understand, giving lunch to those whose parents brought them nothing, because they had nothing. She gave Polo mints to one child, though Pitaji said she must not.

'One won't harm her,' she replied.

Pitaji fetched Ravi who took her outside, his lips thin with anger. 'That child was to have an operation this afternoon. Now she cannot, not until tomorrow. There is no goodness in spoiling, there is only stupidity, Sarah.' His voice was firm, hard. 'Now go and roll bandages and do not again enter the wards.'

She rolled bandages, feeling the panic inside her, hearing

his anger again and again. She cooked chapattis when the sun went down and sat alone, because she had been stupid, foolish, and Ravi stayed in his office.

There was no sleep that night, and as she lay on her charpoy her head wasn't empty, it was full of shame, and Ravi's voice, firm and angry as it had been this afternoon. It swamped the night sounds, and then it was joined by another voice and it was her mother, shouting at her father because he wouldn't eat.

She sat up, shaking her head, feeling the sweat running down her face and neck, but the image and the sound would not go away and now she heard the nurse who had taken her to one side and told her that there was no goodness in spoiling a patient, it was too easy. Her mother was quite right.

She thought of the loom in the grainstore, the women who wove to clothe their families, and now she pushed back the mosquito net and stood in the doorway, hearing the chatter from the courtyard, seeing the lights from the clinic. She gripped the doorway, making herself think, making herself face up to her past, opening her mind to things she had forgotten because the anger was dying, the hate was gone, replaced by doubt as she remembered her mother sewing outfits for her auditions well into the night, when her hands were already shaking with tiredness.

Sarah looked at her hands which were trembling at the memories which were seeping back. She walked across, stood at Ravi's door, knocked, opened it. He was working, his head bent over the desk.

'Please, can I talk? I have been so very wrong.'

Davy's letter reached Ravi after Sarah had left but Ravi had already written to say that Sarah was safe, and loved them, and would one day be home.

Davy took the next flight to India. Annie and Georgie let the birds out for their evening toss, watched them dip and

rise and return, and as the spring night closed in they held
one another as though they would never let go.

CHAPTER 24

The plains were hot and dry, the train rattled and clicked, Indians hung from the sides and lay on the roof. The smell of curry and India was with her day and night but the heat was made bearable by a fan which stirred the air. She shared her compartment with a middle-aged woman who smoked cigarettes in a holder and put her lipstick-covered stubs into a brown paper bag. She seldom spoke except to curse this godforsaken land.

'I love it. My parents were here after the war,' Sarah said, looking out of the window at the landscape which was no different to Georgie's and Annie's descriptions. She wanted to talk of them, to draw them nearer, to somehow make them know she loved them, because she did, so very much – she knew that now.

'To love a land like this is very strange,' the woman said, turning from Sarah. 'You must have had very little of beauty in your life.'

Sarah looked at the sweat which streaked down the woman's neck. A week ago she would have agreed but now she knew she had grown up amongst great beauty. It was there in the beck, the sea and even in the mines and the narrow streets. It was there in her home, in her parents, her aunt and uncle, in Davy, but she mustn't think of him, because that love was closed to her. She didn't speak to the woman again.

The next day it was the dust which bothered her, cloaking her skin, hair and throat, especially when a sand storm blew up and turned day into night. But none of this really mattered because she was impatient now, all doubt had gone. She had been wrong about her mother, she was sure of that and now there was so much to do, so much to discover, so many bridges to mend.

She left the train as dawn of the third day broke, pale through the cloudy sky. Would it rain? Of course not, the cloud cleared and the heat baked the ground again. She shouldered her rucksack and pushed through the throng of hawkers, beggars, stallholders, weaving through the tongas to the bus station, waiting as bicycles were heaved on to the roof, and the driver shouted and waved his arms.

She listened, watched and longed for the bus to start because she had much to do, and more to discover about her mother. She looked into the distance where the Himalayas soared. Would her mother's friend Prue Sanders still be there? Would she talk to her? She must, Sarah wouldn't go until she had.

The bus left at last and they journeyed towards the foothills. The air was clear, cooler and sweet smelling and at seven-thirty in the morning they stopped near a dhak bungalow and drank tea. Soon the driver was shouting again and they boarded the bus, driving on in increasing heat until they reached the level of the pines. They stopped and Sarah ate cold vindaloo from the rest house and then lay on pine needles as the others did, resting until four, before continuing. The Hindu girl sitting next to Sarah left the bus as they entered the next village. 'This is my home. You may stay with me,' she told Sarah. Sarah smiled but shook her head. 'No, I shall stay at the rest house, but thank you.' She didn't want to stay with anyone, she didn't want to have to talk, to smile. She just wanted to train her thoughts on Prue, on the truth.

The next day they left early again and Sarah watched the Himalayas unfolding before her, their white peaks, their shadowed foothills, the terraced and irrigated slopes. Where was Prue's village? Was she looking at it?

The road was winding endlessly through rolling heights of grassland. They crossed a long precarious bridge of logs. Sarah looked down and it was as though she was looking at her life over the past few months, a bottomless drop. Then they were climbing to the pass. Above them Sarah could see five tiers of road winding away into the distance, at times it seemed to end in space and was so narrow she wondered how the party of Indians approaching with ponies could pass but they did. Were they much bigger than her mother's pony had been? One day perhaps she could ask, if she felt she could ever go home after the grief she had caused them.

The bus stopped at the top of the pass. Sarah climbed out with everyone else, and looked at the river which formed a semicircle at the base of the mountain thousands of feet below her. Had her father seen this? Had her mother?

She sat on a boulder and breathed in the clear cool air and looked at the wild flowers and the rose bushes which were not yet in bud. Yes, Ravi was right. There must have been reasons why her mother hadn't nursed. There must have been reasons why her mother hadn't come with them to race the pigeons. There must have been reasons why she hadn't come that last night.

She lifted her face to the sun. How could she have been so stupid, how could she have remembered Carl's words above all others, when Carl had always lied?

'Have I been mad,' she had asked Ravi, 'to have been so cruel?'

He had shaken his head. 'Just young, just confused, just muddled by life, and by drugs. Go home.'

But she couldn't go home yet. How could they still love her?

'Love in a family doesn't die,' Ravi had said. 'But grief tortures. Let me tell them you are safe, but that your journey isn't finished.'

No, it wasn't finished, not nearly because, after Prue, there was still something more she had to do.

The driver hooted his horn and everyone clambered back

on board. Sarah smiled at them, talked to those who had English, marvelling at the river valley as they wound slowly downwards, then up again through silent pine forests, gazing at the massive snow-covered peaks which came into view and then were hidden by the trees again.

The bus set her down in the late afternoon near old shacks on the outskirts of Prue's hill station. She took a tonga which plodded past brambles and heather, seeing butterflies the size of sparrows, remembering the nettles by the allotment shed, the tortoise-shells. There was a church on their left and now they were coming into the town.

The tonga lurched as the wheel mounted a rock, then straightened. Sarah hung on, settled again, then looked down to the valley and over at the bazaar. Further away to the left were old buildings set amongst trees.

That must have been where Dick Sanders had worked after the war. She craned her neck round, knowing that behind the trees she would just see the clinic and there it was, as Prue's letters had described. She sat back. It was almost like coming home.

The hotel was old with a sagging verandah; so they hadn't replaced it as Prue said they had hoped. Sarah was glad. She paid the tonga wallah and heard him hawk and spit betel as she walked towards the steps. Crows were rising from the trees, there was a slight breeze. The verandah creaked and then she was into the darkness, ringing the bell at reception, booking a room for just two nights.

The dining room was on one side, the lounge on the other. She sat on a red cretonne sofa which was worn and old. Palms stood in brass pots that were smeared with finger prints. New brass spittoons gleamed. The tables were draped with dark red cotton. She drank the tea that was brought and heard sitar music as the office door opened, then silence as it was shut. Fans hung motionless above her.

'Your room is ready, Miss Armstrong,' the manager said, bowing over the key.

She smiled as a boy carried her rucksack up the stairs. She

389

bathed in the old mahogany bath. The water was cold, fresh. She changed her skirt for another, and her blouse also. She walked to Prue's, following the directions with which she had grown up. Past bungalows with compounds, keeping the valley to her right, the sounds of the bazaar to her left. Not yet, not yet because she hadn't reached the clump of pine trees which stood between the Sanders plot and all the others. Here they were.

She walked towards the verandah where crimson canna lilies grew. Oh Mum.

She climbed the steps and stood there, not knowing what to do now and frightened. What would she do if Prue wouldn't speak to her of the past? The door opened and a plump, pale-skinned, blue-eyed woman with long lashes and blonde hair stood there, dressed in pastel shades.

'Prue? It's Sarah Armstrong.' Sarah could think of nothing more to say. She just waited, wanting to grasp this woman and shout, Help me to know my mother.

The woman said nothing, her eyes widening and Sarah's hopes plummeted because this must not be Prue. Where could she now look? She must search until she found her. Sarah half turned, then turned again as the woman put up her hand.

'I'm Annie's daughter,' Sarah said, feeling the hand on her arm.

Now the woman smiled. 'Did you really think I wouldn't recognise you? You are her image. I was just too moved to speak.'

Prue's arms were round her now, holding her gently and Prue's kisses were on her cheek, her hand stroked her hair as her mother used to do. Sarah put her head on the older woman's shoulder and felt tiredness sweep over her as she cried for the first time for a long while.

Prue held the thin body and knew if she spoke she would cry too because she had shared each day of Annie's pain.

She led Sarah to a chair set back against the verandah wall and called, 'Ibrahim, tea please.'

She sat opposite and Sarah heard the creak of the cane chair under Prue's weight. Sarah took the handkerchief that was offered and smiled. 'I'm sorry. I didn't know if you'd be here and I had to talk to you.'

Prue thanked Ibrahim and poured the tea. 'Yes, I'm usually here, but Dick's in Delhi I'm afraid, on business. Never mind, you'll see him on his return.' Prue put the cup in front of Sarah, her bracelets jangling as Annie had said they always used to. 'Now look, my dear. Your mother is sick with worry. Please, may I telegraph or telephone her to say you are here?'

Prue looked across and now Sarah saw the deep lines to the corners of her mouth – they were the same as her mother's.

'She knows I'm safe, she knows I'm sorry and that I love her.' Sarah broke off because it was as though the tears would come again. She drank her tea, it was strong, good – now she could speak. 'Please don't tell her yet – tomorrow will do.'

Prue looked closely at her, then agreed. 'Now, where's your baggage?'

'At the hotel.'

Prue laughed, throwing her head back. 'No child of Annie's will stay anywhere but under my roof. Ibrahim,' Prue raised her voice. 'Please send the mali to bring Miss Armstrong's bags.'

Sarah put down her cup and leaned forward. 'Prue, I need to talk to you.'

Prue poured more tea, her finger on the silver lid. 'And I to you, my dear, but not tonight, tomorrow. Tonight we have guests for dinner – you will like them. It is a girls' night.' Prue waved at the Chinese lanterns hanging on the trees. 'You see, it will be fun. Now, in a moment I shall show you your room and then I have to go and supervise affairs in the kitchen. I have this total fascination with my stomach, as you will know already – it and I spend many happy hours together planning its next extravaganza.'

Prue led her now to the bedroom. 'Good, Ibrahim has organised towels and so on. Do please make yourself at home. You will find your clothes in the wardrobe. Please leave anything you would like washed in the bathroom. We now have flush lavatories my dear. Such a treat, one almost wants to go in there, just to admire.'

Prue smiled at her and Sarah grinned. 'There,' Prue said. 'That's the Sarah I remember from the photographs. Tomorrow we will talk.'

At half past seven Sarah was introduced to Mrs Carter, Mrs Smythe and Mrs Taylor. She sipped her gin and tonic and looked at the lanterns, the town, its lights, its noise. It was so cool, so fresh – how Ravi's patients would improve if they were here.

Mrs Carter sat next to her. 'I just love your skirt, the colours are so vibrant. Did you make it yourself? I expect you've been on an ashram somewhere, have you, exploring Hindu philosophy and religion, or some such thing? One hears that so many are doing that sort of thing these days. So many lost souls.'

Prue cut across the conversation, leaning back in her chair which was beside Sarah's. 'Oh Veronica, for heaven's sake, let the poor girl get a word in edgeways.' She patted Sarah's knee. 'This old girl has chronic verbal diarrhoea, always has had. We were at school together in Devon, you know, and she looked as though butter wouldn't melt in her mouth, but she was a devil.'

Veronica held up her glass. 'Enough, Prue, good grief, this child doesn't want to hear stories from the past.'

Sarah smiled at her. Oh yes she did, but she'd hear those tomorrow. Tonight it was enough that she was here.

Ibrahim poured more gin and they ate canapés while Prue told them how they had been 'talked to' by the biology teacher, about men's and women's 'things', which had puzzled them all greatly until they read *Lady Chatterley's Lover*. Whereupon Veronica had been sent from morning service

392

for changing the words when singing *All Things Bright and Beautiful* from 'he made their glorious plumage, he made their tiny wings', to 'things'.

Sarah laughed with the others and moved to the table where coq au vin was served. Prue winked at Sarah. 'I do so like a treat from time to time.'

Mrs Taylor asked. 'Where have you come from?'

Sarah drank her wine, it was cool, dry – a Chardonnay. Where was Sam Davis, still giving parties? Where was Carl?

'I flew into Delhi, then on to a clinic north of there.'

The chicken was good. She ate carefully, listening to the women talk of Delhi as they had known it, long ago. The parties at Government House, the silver plates, the toast to King-Emperor, the desserts.

'Oh yes, the desserts, darling,' Prue gushed. 'I mean those sugar baskets, girls.' Prue's eyes were bright. 'Sarah, they were magnificent, stuffed with fruit salad. The cooks would compete, positively compete, to create the most splendid and fragile concoction, spinning crisp brown sugar until it looked like a translucent amber dish. The trick was to serve the fruit salad and then crack the bowl and serve that. It must have broken their hearts to have seen all that work go down the gullet. But so delicious. I just can't tell you.'

Prue looked down at her chicken. 'Sorry, girls, tonight we just have fruit salad, couldn't rise to the sugar basket. Chocs after, I promise.'

'I remember sleeping under an apricot tree when I was very young,' Mrs Smythe said quietly as she finished her chicken. 'I can remember the crickets singing me to sleep and being woken by Daddy's regimental band – it all seems so long ago.'

Sarah sat back and looked at these women, lined, content, at home. 'Did you never want to go back to England?' she asked.

There was silence for a while and now there was the scent of jasmine on the breeze. Mrs Taylor spoke at last, smiling at Ibrahim as he took away their plates. 'It's not the same as it was before Independence, but something about the country gets under your skin.'

Prue poured more wine. 'There's a spiritual quality to *his land. It haunts you somehow, and the richness of its history soaks into your bones. I missed it when Dick and I came to England after the war. We couldn't stay, it wasn't home. You see, Sarah, we were born out here, we know its patterns, its rituals, its timelessness. Daddy couldn't go home either.'

Mrs Smythe said, 'I remember our parade ground on Independence Eve. We dined at the House, then sat in stands around the parade ground. The whole place was floodlit, I remember, and we watched the small British contingent march on behind all the Indian troops. The band played as all the floodlights were doused, leaving just the flagpole lit. I remember the Union Jack fluttering, there was a slight breeze, you know, quite chilly really.'

They were all silent now, not drinking, just listening.

'I remember the Union Jack being lowered as everyone stood to attention. It was so quiet. It must have been the same all over the country. I dropped my programme. As midnight struck the Indian flag was raised. We all sang the Indian national anthem. It was so strange, so dark, so different.'

No one spoke or moved until Mrs Taylor said, 'We all thought it was the end but it was a new beginning. We stayed on, lived differently, better because we weren't contained within a cantonment, having to abide by rules, by tradition. We could be ourselves.'

Prue looked at Sarah and lifted her glass. 'To new beginnings,' she said softly.

Next morning Sarah woke to see pale light spreading over the mountains and slowly filling the town, the valley. They ate *chota hazari*, little breakfast, and Prue sat in her dressing gown, buttering toast, drinking fruit juice. 'Squeezed by Ibrahim,' she said, pouring some for Sarah. 'We'll bath, then go to the bazaar for food. Then we can have bacon and eggs if you wish?'

Sarah smiled. 'No, I've had sufficient.'

'Oh how disappointing, then I may not indulge either.'

'I would like to talk to you, please Prue.'

Prue smiled. 'Then we will return for coffee and to talk.'

They walked down the road the tonga had taken and always there was the freshness of the air, the glory of the mountains, the valleys, the trees.

'Are there walnut trees here?' Sarah asked.

'Many. Your father wrote to your mother about them, didn't he? It made her feel closer to him because Sarah Beeston had a walnut table in the hall.' Prue pointed out the trees. 'And over there is an apricot.'

'Is there anything you don't know about my mother?'

Prue spoke softly. 'Very little. We had many years to talk to one another, many long years.' She wasn't smiling now and the lines were deeper around her mouth.

They were in the bazaar. Sarah stopped at a khadi stall.

Prue stood with her. 'It's the locally woven cloth, a relic of Mahatma Gandhi.'

Sarah loved the colours, felt the loosely woven cloth, talked of the designs that would suit them best, the muted colours of the landscape transferred to them, the vibrant colours also.

Prue laughed. 'You're your mother's daughter all right.'

They bought vegetables from the stall. 'It's produce our mali sells from our kitchen garden.'

'Why d'you let him?'

'Why not, it's a sensible cycle, leaves everyone with some dignity.'

They walked back past the cinema, into the garden, passed the delphiniums, stocks. There was a garden shed amongst the vegetables. Did this smell the same as the one at home? She stopped, opened the door. No.

This time they took coffee in the sitting room, leaning back on cane furniture whose cushions were covered with

Wassingham Textiles upholstery sent by Annie, and now Sarah could wait no longer.

'Please tell me why my mother couldn't nurse.'

'It wasn't a question of your mother being unable to nurse.'

'Well, why wouldn't she nurse?'

'Neither is it a question of your mother being unwilling to nurse,' Prue said quietly. 'I need to explain some things to you, so that you can understand others. It is a time of my life that I discuss with no one, just as Annie does not because its shadows could reach out and scar us all over again. But you have your own shadows, my dear Sarah, and they must be seen off.'

She told Sarah then of the camps – of the endless years of brutality, of heat, hunger, misery. 'We nursed in the hospital that we built ourselves. We had no medicine, no tools but a wonderful doctor, Dr Jones from Australia. All day, every day we nursed, scooping ulcers, calming the dying, boiling bandages, rags, burying our friends. We were beaten for many things. Have you seen your mother's finger? Yes, that was because she was late on parade. They beheaded our friend Lorna Briggs. It was raining, her blood was so very red.'

Prue wasn't looking at Sarah, she wasn't looking at anything but the past.

'They made us write postcards. Your mother was frightened to write to your father in case it tempted fate and put the mark of death on him. They found the cards at the end of the war in a box. They'd never been sent. They found medicine too, and Marmite, boxes and boxes of Marmite – we could have saved so many of our friends. Dr Jones wept, they all wept. I say they, because I was not there, not in mind, only body.'

Prue touched her lips, swallowed and then continued. 'Near the end of the war diphtheria raged. I became ill, your mother nursed me but I lost my mind. I wandered the camp and was almost shot, so she tethered me to her wrist, day and night with a piece of rope and fed me, because I wouldn't eat. She would take a spoon and make the rabbit go into the hole.'

Sarah sat quite still remembering her mother running from her father's side after she had tried to make the rabbit run into the hole. It was when she returned to the room that she had spoken to him firmly and Sarah had hated her until the nurse had told her that her mother was right.

'I ate,' Prue continued, 'though it was rice, which by then made us want to vomit because we had eaten nothing else for more than three years. I still can't eat it today, neither can your mother.'

Oh yes she can, Sarah thought. She ate it when she came down with the inflatable chairs, she forced it down through love.

'I wondered why she wouldn't nurse. I've always blamed her for it,' Sarah whispered. 'I couldn't have done what you both did. I know, I've tried in a very small way and I couldn't bear it either.'

'Let me finish,' Prue said, her hands clasped together, her bracelets still on her motionless wrists. 'Please. Your father found her camp after the war and took her back to India, where he was stationed. One night the rains came, hammering on her roof whilst he was away defusing a bomb. 'Does he want to die, is that why he does it?' she asked me before I left her that evening. Later she took too many sleeping pills – it had all been too much – her life had been too much. You see, her father killed himself and left her alone. The war had nearly killed her, now perhaps her husband wanted to die too. So she tried to leave this life, Sarah, and the only way your father and I could make her walk, make her drink in order to save her life, was to shout at her in Japanese. She obeyed out of fear.'

Prue's voice was quite calm though there were tears running down her face, like an endless stream. 'It nearly killed your father and it was he who refused to allow your mother to nurse, though she had conquered her past. He refused through fear for her and through the need for an edge to his

397

life, the same edge that defusing bombs had given him. The same edge that your mother now had to live with again. She agreed out of love, though it nearly broke her again.'

Prue rose now and still the tears were falling but it was as though she didn't know. 'Now, come with me, Sarah, and read the answers to all the questions you would like to ask me. It is better that way for both of us.' Sarah followed Prue into the study stacked with the Peak Frean tins that they had sent her every year.

Prue touched the tins. 'I sorted these out last night, while you were asleep. There is nothing in this box that is personal to me, but it might hold the answers you need. If not, come and find me. I shall be in the garden. It is where I go when I need to hold on to the present.'

Sarah sat at the desk and touched nothing for a long moment because her tears were also falling and she could not see to read. She began after Ibrahim entered and brought her lime juice with ice. All morning she read and by noon she knew the truth of her mother's love for both her and her father, her respect for their dignity and the death of her beloved Betsy.

She left at two p.m. taking the bus back down the winding road. She had borrowed money from Prue and had asked for the address of Dr Jones in Sydney.

At two-ten, Prue telephoned Annie, telling her that Sarah had been and gone, but she didn't know where or why.

'Be patient, my darling Annie,' Prue said over the crackling line. 'Be patient for just a bit longer.'

Sarah barely noticed the long journey back through the Himalayas. She stopped at the same rest house and slept on the verandah, she ate vindaloo at lunch time and mangoes at breakfast but tasted neither. All she could think of were the letters she had read in her mother's writing, the love, the pain, the hope, the steadfastness of the woman whom she loved and now respected above all others.

As the train rattled across the plain she didn't feel the heat, or the stirring of the air as the fan whirred, she just felt the love her mother had always borne her and grieved for what she had done. She grieved, too, for the life her mother had led, not just the war and after, but her lack of a mother's love. So many had come and gone. First her real mother, then Aunt Sophie, then Betsy until Sarah Beeston had taken her away. They were all dead now, except perhaps for Sophie. Sarah looked out of the window, willing the train to hurry. Except perhaps for Sophie, she echoed.

Sarah flew from Delhi to Sydney and it was strange to travel without the cacophony of hens clucking, or the sing-song of Urdu, or the smell of curry, or the beating heat. She missed India already.

Sydney was bright, smart and still warm, though the summer was nearly over. The buildings were clean and European. There were cars, but no rickshaws or tongas, no dust. There was a harbour that glistened, the clipped accent that was almost, but not quite, like home.

She stayed in a hostel with other girls. She nodded and smiled when they asked if she too was travelling round the world, filling in before or after college, breaking free from the family, seeking experience.

'Something like that,' she said, lying on the bed in the dormitory which in some ways was the same as in Delhi, but also so very different. She looked at the address that Prue had given her. Dr Jones lived in Vaucluse. She would take the bus out there tomorrow and hope that the woman her mother had worked with in the camps still had access to hospital records. After all, Aunt Sophie had borne a child, perhaps it had been delivered in a hospital. Perhaps there was an address.

The bus left at ten and this time there was no driver gesticulating, no dust, no sea of humanity into which the driver eased. In Vaucluse the houses were large, gracious, moneyed. There was so much space, so much sky, established gardens, an air of ease.

Sarah stood at Dr Jones's front door. This time the woman who answered the door would not know her, would probably think she was mad.

Dr Jones did not think she was mad. She drew her out to the back garden, sat her down with coffee and listened as Sarah spoke of her mother's wartime life and some of the years that had gone before, and all the years that had come after.

Dr Jones cupped her mug in her hands. 'I remember your mother. I remember everyone and everything about those years. How could any of us forget? Prue writes occasionally and so I knew Annie Manon had married her Georgie Armstrong. I knew, too, that you were missing. I did what I could here.'

Dr Jones frowned at Sarah, and now the lines that Sarah had thought could be no deeper on that thin, old face, were. She continued. 'But that is past. Your mother knows you are safe so why are you here and not at home with her?'

Sarah put down her mug, looking out across the clipped camellia bushes with their glossy leaves, their blooms had been and gone. 'I can't go home yet. I've hurt her too much. All along, people have hurt her too much. She's gone to them with her arms open, only to see them slip away. I want to try to bring one of them back to her.'

Sarah explained that Aunt Sophie had left for Australia when Annie's father had returned to Wassingham after the First World War.

'He took her away from Sophie and Eric, Don too, to live at the shop with him and Betsy. Don had already been staying on and off with his Uncle Albert, he didn't care about Sophie and Eric – I wonder if he cares about anyone – but Annie loved them, and they her. They sent her letters and cards and in one they told her that their own daughter had been born. She was called Annie too. Mum never replied, she thought she had been replaced. The correspondence died out after she moved to Sarah Beeston's. A few years ago she placed advertisements in the Australian newspapers trying to find them again, but there was no response.'

Sarah handed Dr Jones the details she had written down last night – the year of Sophie's daughter's birth, the date of their arrival in Australia, all that she knew of them. 'Please, can you use your contacts – perhaps the new Annie was born in hospital. Or perhaps I should trace the registration of her birth, but then I won't have an up-to-date address, though there would be something to go on.' Sarah was leaning forward, pushing the paper towards Dr Jones.

The doctor took it, read it. 'I would like to do this for Annie. I respected her, held her in great affection. But what about you, what will you be doing while all this is going on?' Dr Jones's eyes were sharp, piercing. 'I don't approve of posteriors on chairs while others are busy.' She poured more coffee.

Sarah smiled as she lifted her cup. 'I could do anything you like to help. I was going to go round the markets and retail outlets, to see what gaps there are in the markets, see what possibilities there are for Wassingham Textiles. Mum and Dad haven't an outlet and Australia's growing, isn't it? But I can do that later. I'll do anything, Dr Jones.'

The old woman stirred her coffee and smiled. 'I think you are doing quite enough my dear. Let me use my contacts, it is more efficient. You do what you know most about.'

As Sarah left Dr Jones said, 'Give me a week – I won't tell your mother you are in Sydney. But Sarah,' Dr Jones added, 'don't get your hopes too high, Sophie will be elderly, she might be dead.'

For the rest of the day Sarah walked around the shops, stopping at the small outlets, the kitchen shops, talking to the managers, making lists. She stayed on at the hostel and that evening a boy brought his guitar on to the steps where they were all sitting and they sang. He handed it to her and she played *Curry Afternoons* and then more gentle ones, for

Betsy. Now there was a calmness in her that she had never known before.

All week she toured the city making notes, thinking of the fabrics she had seen in India, telling the traders of these, writing down their comments.

In the late afternoon, she would stand and look at the incomplete Opera House. Yes, it would one day be as wonderful as Davy had said. She watched the yachts in the harbour, the bridge, the blue of the sky and wished that he were here with her, but knew that part of her life was over, there were some things that love could not survive and her behaviour had been one.

At the end of the week she talked to the market traders, then rang Dr Jones, scarcely able to breathe with tension.

'I have the address you want, my dear,' Dr Jones said and read it over the phone. 'But remember, Sophie is old, she might not have her faculties, she might be ill, oh, any number of things. Good luck.'

That afternoon Sarah wrote to Yerong Creek and took the train two days later to Wagga Wagga where she hired a taxi and drove along a straight road with red parched earth either side, and now there was dust again. In places there were gum trees that hung limp, their bark stripped and loose. The taxi turned left over railway lines into the small township with a garage on the left, a Post Office on the right. They drove on until they reached a small bungalow with rose trees in circular beds.

Prue had grown roses. Did the English abroad always do so? Her hands were trembling. Why was she thinking of roses? Sophie had to be the same, she had to remember Annie. Sarah tried not to rush. She closed the taxi door and paid the driver. She walked up the path hearing the cicadas, feeling the warmth, seeing the corrugated iron roof.

There was a fly door on the verandah. Her pace quickened but before she could reach the wooden steps the door opened. An elderly woman came down on to the path, her face tanned to leather. An older man came after her, his leg stiff.

Sarah said, 'Sophie? I wrote to you. I'm Annie's daughter, she's been trying to find you for years.'

Eric was beside Sophie now and it was he who pulled Sarah to him, holding her so tightly that she could hardly breathe. 'You're the image of your mam,' he said and his voice had all the flavour of Wassingham in every syllable and so too did Sophie's when she touched Sarah's cheek. 'I never thought this would happen,' she said, holding the girl's arm, then kissing her forehead as she had kissed Annie's when they had left for Australia so many years ago, unable to bear living without that lovely child.

She held Annie's daughter in her arms now and Sarah smelt lavender as her mother had done.

'You must come and meet our own Annie,' Sophie said. 'She's a bonny lass, with grown bairns of her own.'

Sarah returned to Sydney that night, but sent a telegram to her mother before she left Yerong Creek, telling her Sophie's and Eric's address, knowing they would come, knowing it would complete her mother's life and that was the least Sarah could do for her.

The next day, and the next, and the next, she went to see the Opera House, to stand and stare at the ferries ploughing through the water, the boats, their sails so white. Would they come? She had left a message with Sophie, telling her mother she would be here each day, if they wanted to see her. Would they?

On Saturday, six days after she had left Yerong Creek she watched the sun cast long shadows across the water. The ferries were crowded, carrying people who would one day buy clothes and furnishings made by Wassingham Textiles, and Indian cotton and silk printed as Davy would wish. Yes, one day, whether she was there or not.

She turned and walked away from the water. 'I'm sorry,' she said, moving out past the people who stood behind her, brushing the hair from her eyes.

'You have no need to be, my love,' her mother said. 'No

need at all,' and all the flavour of Wassingham was in her voice.

Sarah looked now, and there was Annie, her face older, thinner, her hair grey, but the smile was so wide, the eyes so full of love. How could she not have seen her? Then Annie's arms were round her daughter, holding the thin body as close to her as she could, never wanting to let her go, feeling Georgie put his arms round them both. 'Oh Mum,' Sarah said and that was all. There was no need for words, not any more.

Annie kissed her daughter's forehead, stroking her hair, her poor shorn hair and now they walked, their arms around one another until Annie stopped, laughing. 'Oh God, I've left my bag where we were standing.'

Sarah squeezed their arms. 'I'll go.'

They watched her run, their arms around one another, and saw her stop when she saw Davy standing where they had been, saw him walk towards her and Annie felt her breath tighten as he put out his hands, and then she breathed again as her daughter took them.

Davy said, 'I love you, Sarah, I always have. I love you, I'm in love with you. I can't stand life without you. Will you come home now and swing from the bar?'

Sarah looked at his tanned skin, his strong face, felt the pressure of his hands. She turned and looked at her parents, at the smile on her mother's face, her father's too. 'I've never wanted anything so much.'

Also available in Arrow

After the Storm

Margaret Graham

**War can end more than one life, and break
more than one heart.**

*'I am in despair too, but I want to go on living,
fighting, getting out of here to something better.'*

Born into hardship in a Northumbrian mining village, it takes all
Annie Manon's spirit to survive the bleak years following the First
World War. As her family fractures around her, she longs to make
something of her life.

Through hard work and determination she eventually leaves
the poverty and despair of her childhood behind her. But then
war breaks out once more, taking her further away from her
dreams and those she loves most. And it is all she can do to
keep hope alive.

Previously published as *Only the Wind is Free*

arrow books